ALPHA OMEGA

ALPHA OMEGA

Max Childers

Wyrick & Company

Published by Wyrick & Company
Post Office Box 89
Charleston, SC 29402

Copyright © 1993 by Max Childers.
All rights reserved.
Printed in the United States of America.

Library of Congress Cataloging-In-Publication Data

Childers, Max.
　　Alpha Omega / by Max Childers.
　　　　p.　cm.
　　ISBN 0-941711-21-8
　　I. Title.
　PS3553.H4855A79　1992
　813′.54—dc20　　　　　　　　　　　92-33676
　　　　　　　　　　　　　　　　　　　　　CIP

First edition

1

Bobby Snipes turned thirty on a Friday in early August. The next Monday, at noon, he was released from the state maximum security prison in Columbia. A guard escorted him from his cell block to the administration wing, where another guard presented him with a money order for one hundred dollars, sent by his mother, a plastic bag containing his wallet, and a bus ticket to Gastonia, North Carolina.

After he collected these items, he waited in the outer office of an assistant warden. He held himself very still and erect during the wait, his hands folded in his lap. He did not even stare at the good-looking secretary who processed his release papers, the one the men in his cell block hungrily discussed. The assistant warden motioned him into his office, read the papers that the secretary had prepared, and declared that he had served his sentence, paid his debt to the State of South Carolina, and that he was free to go. The assistant warden wished him good luck, shook his hand, and returned to the pile of papers on his desk.

The guard who had presented him with the money order led

him to the main gate and phoned for a taxi. Bobby stood beside the chain link fence next to the guard house and smoked a cigarette. He was of medium height, blonde and muscular. From a distance, he appeared to be a good deal younger than his age; like a boy, awkward and wary of the world. And he had a boy's face, as if the years in prison had not touched him. His pale blue eyes did not fit with the rest of him, though. They shifted, examining everything; old, but not yet tired. He stood as if at attention, not sweating in the heavy, gummy heat.

He smoked three cigarettes before the cab arrived, one right after the other, still stiffly posed against the backdrop of the prison. He told the cabbie to take him to the bus station. As the taxi moved through the streets of Columbia, streets he had barely glimpsed when he arrived there ten years earlier, the driver tried to make conversation. Bobby did not respond and the cabbie gave up.

Bobby watched the yards, houses and stores pass by. Once, from atop a hill, he made out the prison below him; the river at its back, the ancient, streaked stone of the cell block where he had lived, the machine shop, the school, the guard towers. All of it shimmered in the heat, and the light made him wince. The cabbie took a left and the prison disappeared from view.

At the bus station, he cashed the money order at the ticket window and folded the bills into his wallet. He then asked the clerk where he could find the closest pawn shop.

Bobby walked slowly, giddy in the space that pushed in on him as the walls once had. He often halted before store windows. Too many things, he thought, gaping at a display of female mannequins in bathing suits. I can't let all these things confuse me. Gotta remember what's important. He picked up his stride. It was best to concentrate on what he needed and to keep moving.

People came at him from all angles, out of offices, restaurants and hotels, all going in any direction they pleased. He had forgotten that such choices were possible. He came to a standstill again—in the middle of Lady Street. A car slammed on its brakes beside him and the driver yelled and jabbed a finger toward the green traffic signal. Bobby hopped back to the curb.

Hootchie-Cootchie had told him that pawnshops were good places to buy used guitars; the kind he could practice on until he had enough money for a new Telecaster or Yamaha. Palmetto Loans was cool inside, and the guitars hung from racks along the ceiling. They were laid out in cases along a wall. They burst forth from every corner of the narrow, brightly-lit shop. When he saw the guitars, he forgot about the people and the streets.

For eighty-five dollars, Bobby purchased a twenty-five year old red Harmony Rocket, a small amplifier, and a guitar case. The clerk, bored because business was slow, asked Bobby if he played much.

"Can I plug in?" Bobby asked.

The clerk hesitated. His boss, who had gone to lunch, had a rule against music on the premises. There were no other customers in the store, though. And the boss would not be back for at least half an hour.

"Yeah. No concerts. Just try it out."

Bobby tuned up. The strings were new and tight.

"What you wanna hear?"

"It's up to you. Don't play but one number though."

Bobby hit the strings once and began: A blues, one of Hootchie-Cootchie's originals. Despite the tiny amp, the music came out deep and pure, bouncing off the other guitars, the trombones, the trumpets, the display cases filled with knives, guns, handcuffs, rings, and watches. As the song ended, the clerk whistled, long and low.

"Where'd you learn that?"

"Me and a friend made it up."

"Sounds familiar. I mean not just because it's the blues. It's . . . it's distinctive, too. I guess that's the right word."

"It's mine. And my friend's."

"Maybe you'll make it big."

Bobby picked up his change from the counter.

"I'm not gonna be surprised if I do."

Bobby Snipes had learned the song, as he had learned the guitar, from his cellmate of the last nine years: Arthur "Hootchie-Cootchie" Magee—artist, master showman, dope-dealer, and murderer. Hootchie-Cootchie was forty-five when Bobby met him. He had been called Hootchie-Cootchie since he was fifteen, playing with his own band in clubs that stayed open all night, and observed no laws. He was tall and deep black, with long tapered fingers, and half-moon inlays in his front teeth. He had a powerful build, the body of a much younger man. When he moved or spoke, and especially when he had a guitar in his hands, people paid attention.

The first time Bobby saw him was in the dayroom at the cell block, where Hootchie-Cootchie worked out on an old Stratocaster while another inmate played bass. Other prisoners and two guards urged them on, nodding and smiling, rocking with the music. Bobby had never heard anything like it. He had seldom paid attention to music, except as a kind of background noise to his life. He asked Hootchie-Cootchie to show him how it was done, and he had never before asked anyone for anything. Three weeks later they were cellmates. A few days after Bobby moved in, at Hootchie-Cootchie's reasonable insistence, they became lovers.

By the end of the next year, Bobby, using a battered guitar from the prison music room, accompanied Hootchie-Cootchie in the jam sessions. The dayroom crowds grew larger, and men from other cell blocks begged to be allowed to listen in. Every six months or so they, along with a drummer named Willie, performed for the whole prison population; a deal worked out with the authorities, as it was said, "to improve institutional morale". They even got a write-up in the local newspaper, and the radio station at the University aired a tape of their songs, all Hootchie-Cootchie originals.

For nine years they lived the music.

"It made me what I am, good and bad," Hootchie-Cootchie said. "It gave me love. I've never loved nothing else. And it gave me fear. Like the people listening might eat me. All mixed up. Those feelings. You know, at one time I believed I could make music that would cause people to die and cum at once. And that they would love me and hate me for doing it to them."

Bobby did not understand all that Hootchie-Cootchie told him, or everything he did. For instance, there were the scrapbooks. Hootchie-Cootchie kept them in a cardboard box beneath his bunk, and every couple of weeks he went through them, page by page, picture by picture, while Bobby watched and listened. There were six books in all, thick, gilded volumes that Hootchie-Cootchie had carried with him for years. He never allowed Bobby to examine the books alone. Instead, he provided a guided tour of what used to be.

There was Hootchie-Cootchie in his first glossy publicity photo: sixteen, in a tuxedo, a Les Paul propped at his knee, smiling. There were the playbills announcing appearances at the Dynamite Club in Columbia, the Utopia Lounge in Charlotte, the International Hideaway in Atlanta, the Apollo in New York. Clubs and concerts and outdoor festivals in Los Angeles, Chicago, Houston, London—places that were only names to Bobby. There was Hootchie-Cootchie with Howling Wolf, B.B. King, Little Richard and Etta James. Hootchie-Cootchie stood beside his first Cadillac, a foot on the front bumper, a three hundred dollar shark-skin suit draped across his muscular shoulders. He posed with each of his four wives and, in various groupings, with his nine children. He smiled in front of the brick house that he had built in Charleston; seven bedrooms, four baths, white columns and a wide green lawn.

There were reviews of each of the ten albums from *Variety*,

Cashbox and *Rolling Stone*. There were other pictures: naked bodies in a motel room; Hootchie-Cootchie's old saxophone player, a syringe buried in his arm, a tie in his mouth, his eyes big and startled by the camera. There was Hootchie-Cootchie passed out in the back seat of his fourth Cadillac, his pants to his knees, his mouth open in a drunken snore. On the last page of the sixth book was a clipping of a newspaper account of Hootchie-Cootchie's trial and conviction.

"I did the killing," he once told Bobby as they reached that final page. "I'm sorry I did it. One of us was going to get opened up, and it wasn't me. I'll die in here. Mandatory life. It don't matter. Everybody dies somewhere."

Then Hootchie-Cootchie closed the scrapbook, and slapped it into the box.

On one of the last nights Bobby spent in prison, he lay on his back, unable to sleep. The fact that he was to be released did not keep him awake, since he regarded that event as so unreal as to be without validity. There was something else; it had taken shape over the years, and until now he had not had the words for it.

"Hootchie?" he whispered in the steel darkness of the locked-down cell block. Hootchie-Cootchie was awake, smoking into the night. For long periods, days, even a week once, Hootchie-Cootchie did not sleep at all. Bobby tried again.

"Hootchie. I gotta tell you something."

"Tell me," he finally said.

"I want . . . I want to be you."

A long exhalation of breath came from the bunk below, followed by a short, mocking laugh.

"You want to be me."

"That's right. I . . ."

"Not like me. But me. That's what you're saying?"

"That's it. You're the best . . . there ain't nobody like you."

"Don't."

"Don't? What's that mean?"

An orange cigarette butt sailed through the darkness and splashed lightly in the toilet.

"It means don't. That's all. You figure it out."

Bobby waited for Hootchie-Cootchie to explain what he meant. But he never did.

Bobby had been convicted of arson and robbery. After three days at a Myrtle Beach motel with a boy about his own age and two girls with plenty of money, and after a large, undetermined amount of pills and vodka, he had stolen fifty dollars from someone's wallet. He spent most of the fifty, on what he could never remember, and, when the last dollar was gone, he returned to the motel. There did not seem any place else to go.

The boy came at him with a lamp, and Bobby knocked him down, grabbed a lighter, and set fire to the draperies. As the room burned, as the fire trucks arrived, as the motel manager ran in circles, and as the girls dragged the boy from the room, Bobby wandered away up the beach. He was arrested in the pavilion, where he had rung up four hundred thousand points on a pinball machine named Big Daddy. It took three cops to get him into the squad car, and then only after one of them grabbed him by his flowing hair and drove his face into the sidewalk.

At his sentencing, he told the court that he was not sorry for his crimes. His lawyer tried to shut him up, tugging at Bobby's sleeve and begging the Judge to silence his client. Finally, in desperation, the lawyer asked for a recess. Instead of a recess, however, the Judge ordered the lawyer to be quiet.

The Judge had sentenced Bobby to "a term of not less than five, nor more than ten years." The Judge, a small, neat, prissy man, told Bobby to please continue with his statement. Bobby, his upper lip curled, said that there wasn't any sense in messing around with five years; that the Judge should have the balls to give him ten, or else forget about giving him any time at all.

Mildly amused, the Judge did as Bobby suggested, and added that there was to be no provision for parole. Bobby grinned as the bailiffs led him out of the courtroom. His mother, Laverne, let out a wail that caused the Judge to pound his gavel for order, and Raymond, Bobby's father, loudly proclaimed that he had raised a goddamn fool. Bobby was sure that he would never be forgotten in the Superior Court of Horry County.

He began to learn about prison soon after his arrival. He was raped in the shower by three inmates who had taunted him for a week with visions of what they were going to do to him. He had laughed at them. The idea of anybody raping him was ridiculous, and he did not believe that it could happen until they were on him. It took them a long time to subdue him, even though they took him by surprise. Bobby fought them in a pitching, cursing mass in the steam of the showers and into one of the stalls before they got what they wanted. They complained that it had not been worth the trouble since the motherfucker was about knocked out before they had a chance at him.

When it was over, Bobby stumbled back to his cell and told his cellmate, a safecracker from Rock Hill, what had occurred. The safecracker, who was on the toilet at the time, told Bobby that he was a sure enough pussy-boy now. Bobby began to kick the safecracker in the face, and was still kicking when the guards rushed in and hauled him off to isolation.

He spent two weeks in isolation. He howled and went naked for the first three days, urinated and defecated on the floor, and smeared food on his body and the walls. On the fourth day, the guards handed him a mop and bucket and made him clean the cell. When he finished, one of them jabbed a wooden club into his chest and told Bobby that he would kill him if he kept it up. Bobby ceased howling, used the toilet, and ate a little from each meal that was passed through the door to him. He figured that he would do enough to keep the guard with the club away from him. The urge to howl, to make a gesture, was still strong, however.

He made that gesture on the day he was released from isolation. He searched for, and found, one of the men who had raped him, and pushed him down a long flight of metal stairs in full view of about three dozen witnesses. The gesture cost him a month in isolation. Once inside again, he began to think. He understood, for the first time, that he was ignorant of everything except driving, snorting, drinking, fucking, smoking, fighting, and watching whatever crossed his path. He had been in prison for only a short while, yet he had difficulty seeing himself anywhere else. He had no calling, no reason for being other than satisfying immediate urges—and not taking shit from a living soul. Those things had once been enough, but they were no longer sufficient.

When he was released from isolation the second time, he went his own way, forming no alliances, ignoring the gangs and cliques that dictated life in the prison. He seldom spoke, and avoided other inmates, most of whom had decided he was crazy anyway. He enrolled in the GED classes for lack of anything better to do. The classes bored him, and he dropped out a few weeks before he would have completed requirements for a certificate. He lifted weights, worked in the laundry, and even read a few books. None of these showed him where he needed to be, and he settled into the routine of dull fear that prison imposes on all within its confines. Then he heard the music and saw Hootchie-Cootchie, his fingers caressing the guitar, his power living and true.

2

He was the last passenger off the bus, the guitar case thrust in front of him, the amplifier clutched under an arm. Laverne rushed to embrace him, and kissed him on the cheek. He had slept through most of the trip, and was still groggy as she hugged him long and hard. He struggled to keep from dropping the amplifier. When she had satisfied herself with the hug, she pulled away from him, both hands still on his shoulders, and smiled, quick and bird-like.

She led him to the parking lot and unlocked the trunk of her old Toyota. He carefully stowed the amp, and gently edged the guitar case into the back seat, which was filled with boxes of donuts and two-litre bottles of Pepsi. Laverne bought them at a discount from the Handy Pantry where she worked as a clerk. She watched him as he positioned the guitar.

"I didn't know the prison would let you bring a guitar home," she said.

He did not answer. There was still too much light and space.

"So the prison gave you a guitar? That was nice of them. I'll bet they don't do that for just anybody. Can you play it?"

He had never told her about the music, or Hootchie-Cootchie.

"They didn't give me nothing. I bought it."

He settled into the passenger seat. She started the Toyota and maneuvered it onto Franklin Boulevard. He closed his eyes, waiting for a response.

"You don't mean you used the money I sent you?"

"Sure did. Except for about fifteen bucks."

She stopped for a red light, and Bobby opened his eyes. The sun was harsh, and Gastonia did not appear to have changed in ten years. He closed them again, the light beating white and orange all around him.

"That money was for expenses. Clothes, shoes. You didn't bring any new clothes with you?"

"The guitar's an expense."

"You know that's not what I mean. You were supposed to buy things you really need."

The light changed. They passed the Courthouse, the Confederate monument, the big cemetery off Highway 321.

"I need that guitar."

Laverne sighed. She sighed often.

"I suppose we can call it a birthday present."

You can call it whatever you want, he thought.

"I'm so happy you're out. I worried and worried. Ten years. And I prayed every day. A friend made up a special prayer for mothers whose boys are in prison. It goes like this: 'Dear Lord, watch over and protect my child while he is paying his debt to society. Aid him in learning humility and forgiveness. Allow him to be reformed by those authorities who control him. Teach him love and honesty.' There's a bunch more, only I haven't memorized all of it yet. Don't you think it's beautiful?"

He nodded and kept his eyes closed.

Laverne was forty-eight, fifteen years younger than Bobby's father. Raymond died the second or third year of Bobby's sentence. He drank a quart of cheap whiskey and went to sleep on the railroad tracks in East Gastonia. A slow freight chewed him up.

Laverne's face was tiny and doll-like; and thinner than when Bobby was put away. Her hair was arranged in an elaborate, sculptured permanent, and she favored frilly dresses, excessive make-up, costume jewelry, Jesus and strong men.

Raymond had not been strong; just drunk and mean. He worked in the textile mills for most of his life, and escaped to the beer joints in Mecklenburg County every Friday and Saturday night. When he came home, he cursed and roared, and beat Laverne and Bobby when they got on his nerves. Occasionally, to Bobby's relief, he disappeared. Once he was gone for six months, and when Laverne and Bobby returned one Sunday from the Free Will Baptist Church, they found him seated at the kitchen table, consuming a large platter of bacon and eggs. He never told anyone where he had been, although Laverne cried and begged for an explanation. The last time Bobby had seen him was at his trial. He had never heard from him while he was in prison.

He opened his eyes as they passed a place called Battery City. Laverne spoke of how difficult life had been. He had heard most of it before during her twice-yearly visits to Columbia. She talked about the Handy Pantry where she had gone to work after she quit the mill. About how much things cost. About how Gastonia had turned into a regular city. As always, she talked about Jesus. In the last year or so she had begun to mention Elvis Presley, too; almost in the same breath as Christ himself. She usually asked Bobby if he was getting enough to eat and if he was trying to straighten out so that he could have a good life when he left prison. He told her that everything was fine. It was the only answer that she would have listened to.

Laverne took a left at Modena Street; frame houses fronted by small yards in the shadow of a five story, red brick, windowless mill. Laverne unlocked the front door and he followed her inside. The draperies were drawn in the dim room, and at first glance it appeared that nothing had changed. There was the same Sears living room suite, Raymond's La-Z-Boy recliner. The tinted family portrait photograph, made when Bobby was nine, hung over the mantle. Bobby placed the guitar case and amplifier beside the faded, flower patterned red couch, and scanned the room, his vision adjusting to the light. He switched on a lamp and realized that changes had been made. He turned in a circle, trying to catch all of them.

Elvis and Jesus were everywhere; velvet paintings of them separately and together; a 3-D depiction of Elvis and Jesus astride rearing white stallions; an Elvis rug beneath Bobby's feet; a lamp in the shape of Jesus' head. Slowly, he sat down in the La-Z-Boy. Opposite the chair, next to the television and the VCR, was a four-foot statue of Elvis, in glossy colors, its arms spread in a gesture of welcome.

He counted at least two dozen pictures, ash trays, tapestries and statues. Among the pictures, one puzzled him more than the others. It hung next to the family portrait over the mantle, dwarfing it in size.

The man in the picture was wide and heavy set. Whoever he was, he had tried hard to model his appearance after that of Elvis. There was the same swept-back, jet-black hair, glowing like neon. The mutton chops were there, too, along with the caped costume, the scarf, the jewelry. The face did not work; it was too broad, the lips too thin, the eyes too small. Laverne handed Bobby a glass of iced tea.

"That's Reverend Joy. From the Temple," she said.

"The Temple?"

"The Burning Love Temple. I guess I haven't told you. I've been going there for about a year. The services are . . . well, I haven't never had an experience like it. Never."

"He wants to look like . . ."

"Elvis Presley? Of course he does. But Virgil, that's his first name, what I call him when we're not at the Temple, Virgil said that he's his own man. He wants to . . . how'd he say it? Commemorate Elvis. Keep him alive."

"It's a church?"

"What else would it be?"

"I don't know. You don't go to the Free Will Baptist no more?"

Laverne had been a fervent and faithful member of the Free Will Baptist Church and, until Bobby was thirteen and refused to attend any longer, she had dragged him to church two or three times a week. She had spoken in tongues at revivals all over Gaston County, and had once broken her arm attempting to leap over a pew while in an especially exalted state.

"I give it up. You understand, I loved the Baptist Church. Only, the Temple is different. I feel young when I'm there, or with Virgil . . . Reverend Joy. And I'm so happy about it, I could bust."

He lit a cigarette and dripped the match into an ashtray shaped like a guitar.

"That's why you got all this stuff. Elvis and Jesus all over the place."

"They're reminders."

"And this Reverend that dresses up like Elvis is your preacher."

"It's not dressing up. I told you. He commemorates. I swear, Bobby, you act like there's something wrong with Virgil. The Reverend Joy, I mean. You don't even know him."

"I'm trying to figure it out. Does he sing?"

"Of course he sings! Nobody sings better. And he writes songs, too."

"Jesus and Elvis. Together."

Bobby tried to imagine how Hootchie-Cootchie would react to Laverne's new church. He could not be completely certain, although he guessed it would produce a low, bitter laugh. Laverne glanced at her watch.

"Gotta hurry. He'll be here in an hour."

"Who?"

"Why Virgil! He's having dinner with us. Your homecoming dinner. And he wants to meet you."

"Why would he want to meet me?"

She was already moving around the kitchen, opening the refrigerator, stirring a pot on the stove.

"Because you're my son," she yelled. "He takes an interest in the people of the Temple. Only last week he was with Mrs. Mayhew at the hospital. She had her gallbladder out. He stood by her bed and sang 'King Creole'. Until some nurse made him stop. She said he was causing a racket. Can you imagine? Some people don't know a thing. And he had cheered Mrs. Mayhew up so much."

Bobby looked once more at the Reverend Joy's picture. What kinda smile is that, he thought.

He took a shower; the first he had taken in ten years without asking permission. He stood under the water for a long time, and as he soaped himself, he remembered that Elvis had been dead for years, since right before he went in the slams, or else right after. He could not be sure. He had heard a few things about Elvis over the years: dope, obesity, extravagant gestures. Hootchie-Cootchie once said that Elvis had stolen the music and whored it out. Bobby agreed with Hootchie-Cootchie, as he did in all things, but especially anything relating to music. And yet, he had hypnotically watched a number of Elvis' films on television in the dayroom. The movies were invariably stupid and silly. However, there was Elvis himself, his face and hair reaching forth from the screen. The other inmates, especially the white ones, never missed an Elvis movie if they could help it. Even the guards watched, and some of the black inmates, too. All of them made the same comments as the movies ineptly meandered from song to song, from bad joke to poorly staged action sequence: Elvis was the coolest guy that ever lived, I wish I had his money, think about how much pussy he got, how many cars do you reckon he owned?

Bobby dried himself and shaved. Laverne had bought a razor and shaving cream for him at Handy Pantry employee discount prices. In prison, he had gotten to shave twice a week, and he had to ask the guards for a razor. He felt as if he was breaking a rule as he pulled the blade across his chin. He had had that feeling all day, and he wanted to hang on to it. Hootchie-Cootchie said that there were more rules, more things to block you up on the outside than on the inside. He made this observation often, laughing each time, slow and rueful.

Laverne was still in the kitchen, and the stereo was playing the soundtrack from *Viva Las Vegas*. Bobby turned it off and plugged in the Harmony Rocket and the amplifier. When Elvis stopped singing, Laverne rushed from the kitchen.

"I was listening to that. It's one of my favorites."

"I'm gonna play some."

She went back to the kitchen and slammed the pots and cabinet doors so he would understand how angry she was. He tuned up and picked out a few chords, and she hustled back into the living room.

"If that's all you're gonna do, I'm putting my record back on. I know you just got out and all, and you don't understand how to behave . . ."

He concentrated on the guitar.

". . . Virgil will be here any minute, and he loves to hear Elvis when he walks into a room . . ."

It was one of Hootchie-Cootchie songs. It did not have a title or lyrics. It needed neither. It was a hot blues, and it felt good, the heat running up through his fingers. He bent to the music, reaching for the presence of Hootchie-Cootchie, who had played with such effortless, wild, sad grace. Laverne watched and listened, but Bobby had forgotten that she was there; just as he was unaware of the other person who had entered the room and who stood behind him.

He finished the blues; Hootchie-Cootchie was in the far distance now.

"Go on. Do another one," a high, male voice said.

Bobby turned. He hated for people to sneak up on him. The Reverend Virgil Joy extended his hand. He wore about a dozen gold chains, numerous rings, a heavy watch; he was pear-shaped, his head too small for his body.

"Son," Laverne said, "I never thought . . . why, when I saw that guitar, I thought it was only a toy."

She sat on the couch as Virgil enthroned himself in the La-Z-Boy.

"Play. I didn't mean to interrupt," Virgil said.

Bobby contemplated putting the guitar away; it was wrong to play Hootchie-Cootchie's music for them. Still, they acted as if they really wanted to hear him, and not many people had ever wanted him to do anything. He worked through Hootchie-Cootchie's version of the Beatles' "Day-Tripper". He would never get it down in the same way that Hootchie-Cootchie had, but he felt he was pretty close. When Bobby hit the last notes, they applauded.

"I'm impressed," Virgil said. "You mind if I try one?"

Bobby handed him the guitar and Virgil held it in his small white hands.

"A Harmony Rocket. I haven't seen one of these in years."

Virgil pretended to tune up, making small, delicate adjustments. He don't need to do that, Bobby thought. He only wants to look like he knows what he's doing.

Virgil did "Moody Blue", singing in a high, slightly slurred imitation of Elvis' vocal style. When he was through, he handed the guitar back to Bobby.

"You do another one," Virgil said.

Bobby played "Mystery Train", one of the few Elvis songs that Hootchie-Cootchie had any regard for. Bobby added his own improvisations after the first verse, and sang in an unrestrained, semi-yodel. The song concluded with an eerie fade-out. Laverne and Virgil applauded again, more vigorously than ever.

"You're fabulous," Virgil said as he hunched over his second helping of Mrs. Smith's Apple Pie. Bobby lit a Winston and took a pull from his third can of Old Milwaukee. The beer was cold and sweet. He had lapped up the chicken, the mashed potatoes, the black-eyed peas, the cornbread, the whole meal, in five minutes, shoveling the food in as he had done in the mess hall in Columbia. When he finished, he walked three blocks to a package store and bought two six-packs and more cigarettes. Laverne tried to make him stay until the meal was over, but he had ignored her. The very existence of beer had come back to him during the meal, and he had to have one. When he returned, popping the first Old Milwaukee as he sat back down at the table, Laverne gave him a disapproving glance. He could afford to ignore that, too. And he noticed that Virgil was still eating, having slowly and methodically worked his way from first, to second, to third helpings until he got to the pie. He swallowed a big chunk of crust, syrup and apples.

"Fabulous," he repeated.

"You're into Elvis, huh?"

"Not *into*," Laverne said. "He stands for . . ."

Virgil swallowed, waved his hand, and she stopped speaking.

"I wouldn't want you to confuse me with Elvis impersonators. They live off the meaning of the King."

"They don't have ethics," Laverne said.

"You see," Virgil continues, "my role is to keep the memory of Elvis alive through our Church. Jesus is important too, of course, although we believe that Elvis also had much of the divine in him. He touched so many of us in so many ways. It's only natural that we should give him our praise. I only represent Elvis, as he once represented us when he walked on Earth."

An image from the movies came to Bobby; the serene, all-knowing Elvis before a lush tropical landscape.

"What did Elvis mean?" Bobby asked.

"What did he mean?" The question puzzled Virgil.

"Yeah. What's that word? What did he . . . represent?"

"Forgive him, Virgil," Laverne said. "He's only been out of prison a few hours."

"It's a good question," he said as he scraped the remains of the pie from the plate with the edge of his fork. "He's part of us, you and me. The best in us. Jesus was the same way. They show us about love. And grace. Elvis had grace."

"Like Graceland?" Laverne said.

"Exactly! It wasn't any accident that Elvis bought a home named Graceland! I can preach on that next Sunday. Grace. Graceland. Sure!"

No one spoke for a while, as Laverne cleared the table and Bobby drank another beer. Virgil appeared to ruminate on the connection between grace and Graceland. Suddenly Virgil lept to his feet and clapped his hands, causing Laverne to nearly drop the remains of the apple pie.

"I've got it," he announced brightly. He leveled his smile on Bobby. "How would you like to be the newest member of the Burning Love Temple Band?"

"Oh, Virgil!" Laverne squealed.

"I . . ." Bobby began.

"Don't say no. I need a guitar player like you. Elvis needs you. So does Jesus. What do you say?"

"Please, son. It'll do you a world of good."

He could not think of a reason to refuse. The guitar was all that he had.

* * *

They—mostly Virgil and Laverne—talked for another two hours, Laverne gushing with gratitude toward Virgil, who was obviously pleased with his own kindness. Bobby could only listen most of the time. Once Laverne and Virgil got started on the Burning Love Temple, they had an apparently endless number of upbeat, positive anecdotes about the place. They reminded Bobby of the evangelists he had seen on T.V., almost exploding with hysterical delight in themselves.

He discovered, as he listened and managed to get a few questions in, that Virgil was a hair stylist when he was not preaching and singing. Virgil hoped to one day run the Burning Love Temple full-time; to maybe even rent an hour on the public access cable channel to, as Virgil put it, "reach those who desperately need our message." Virgil dwelled on the generosity of the congregation; it never failed to provide all that the Temple needed, including a "non-collection gift" to meet the rent on the building. In fact, the lease was in the congregation's name.

Bobby would get seventy-five a week, the same as the other members of the band. Virgil regretted that the salary was so small; much of the money for the band came from a second "non-collection gift", and Virgil could only expect the generosity to go so far. Bobby wondered what Virgil paid for at the Temple. The money sounded fine to him, though. He had never made that much before he went to prison. Then again, he had only worked when absolutely necessary. The seventy-five would be plenty, especially since Laverne had declared that Bobby could live with her as long as he wanted.

Virgil was vague when it came to describing Bobby's musical duties. Finally, Bobby deduced that he would play back-up rhythm, since the band already had a lead guitarist who was familiar with the songs. Many of the songs were Virgil's compositions, although a healthy number of the King's hits and some good old-time hymns were part of every service. The services took place on Sunday mornings and Wednesday nights, and each lasted between two and three hours.

Laverne, who had grown more fond of pronouncements as the evening wore on, proclaimed that her son's entrance into the Burning Love Temple Band was the finest, best thing that had ever happened in her life. She poured numerous glasses of iced tea for herself and Virgil as Bobby finished one six-pack and started on another. She congratulated Virgil on giving Bobby a fresh start, and helping to put prison behind her only child. Virgil continued to exclaim over Bobby's God-given talents. Three or four times, he asked Bobby where he learned to play so beautifully. Bobby said that he had picked it up in prison. He did not want to tell them about Hootchie-Cootchie. Somehow, it did not seem right.

Without warning, Virgil turned serious.

"You believe, don't you?"

"In what?" Bobby had been thinking of the music and Hootchie-Cootchie, and he was quietly and thoughtfully drunk, ignoring Virgil and Laverne's testimonies.

"Why in Elvis, Bobby!" Laverne shouted.

"Sure. Jesus, too, if that's what it takes."

They laughed uncertainly, as if they had not quite gotten the answer they wanted.

The three of them adjourned to the living room, where Laverne put on a video tape of Elvis' 1968 comeback concert. Virgil provided an introduction, explaining how the concert had re-established Elvis, once and for all, as the greatest entertainer in history, and one of the greatest human beings ever. Some had doubted the King, Virgil noted solemnly. With his appearance on national television, however, all that negativity vanished.

Elvis, trim and handsome, covered in leather, sang about a swinging little guitar man, while the audience, composed mostly of young, attractive women clad in mini-skirts and boots, pressed against the stage, longing to consume every atom of his being.

Presley's face was slightly different from the one Bobby had seen in the movies. It was meant to be God-like, despite the frequent aw-shucks grins. Bobby's fatigue and the drunkenness dropped away a little. Elvis had an understanding that Bobby had not yet discovered; a magnificent carelessness. He could throw it all away and remain the King. The music ain't a big deal to him, Bobby thought. Not like it ought to be. What gets him off is that the whole world wants him. Elvis picked at the guitar every now and then, treating it like a prop that was no more useful than his perfect, white smile.

The only light came from the television set, but he could see that Virgil and Laverne were seated very close to each other, holding hands, their knees touching, their faces intent upon the screen.

The tape ended. Laverne switched on the Jesus-head lamp, and Virgil asked Bobby whether he enjoyed the show. Bobby nodded slowly. When he had the chance, he would watch the tape alone.

Virgil and Laverne dropped to their knees, Virgil praying before they hit the floor. Bobby saw the prayer coming and escaped into the bathroom to wait them out, leaving the door open so that he could tell when they were through. He emerged as Virgil said Amen. Virgil shook his hand and said that it was time to go. He had an early appointment for a curly perm. Laverne followed him out to his van, and Bobby stood by the screen door, out of their angle of vision, but able to see the driveway. He could hear their voices, but he could not make out the words. After a minute or two, the only sounds were the crickets and the traffic from up on Franklin Boulevard. Slowly, he edged into the doorway for a better view. They were flattened against the side of the Burning Love Temple van, partially concealed in the shadows, clutching and grinding at each other, Virgil's hands slowly and methodically kneading Laverne's ass.

3

The Burning Love Temple was a low, cinder-block building located on Highway 74, directly across from the Hospitality Motel and the Dixie Salvage Yard. It was painted in alternating bands of pink and black. According to Laverne, this had been Elvis' favorite color combination. Except for the colors, the Temple reminded Bobby of the beer joints he used to visit: flat-roofed, windowless, a couple of holes cut in the walls for air-conditioning. The kind of place where you could get your ass kicked, he thought, as Laverne dropped him off for his first rehearsal with the Burning Love Temple Band. As she pulled out of the parking lot, she reminded him that she would return soon. First, she had to pick up a five-layer coconut cake at the bakery. Virgil loved coconut cake, and she especially wanted him to have one for Bobby's first night.

The two air-conditioners labored futilely in the hot, wet air. Card tables lined the wall near the front entrance, and six rows of metal folding chairs were arranged behind a cleared area before a low wooden stage. Behind the stage, a gold cross had been painted on the white wall, curving and dipping with the contours of the cinder blocks. Flanking the cross, and extending back to the main entrance, hung tapestries of Elvis and Jesus, singing to a Las Vegas audience; walking on water; presiding at the Last Supper; strumming a guitar; shaking hands together in Heaven— a place of clouds, clean flowing streams, and golden streets.

Virgil and three younger men occupied the stage, which also contained a drum kit, guitar, mike stands, and two large amplifiers. A sound board had been set up at the right front of the stage. Next to what had once been a kitchen, there was a walk-in refrigerator, and a long, still-greasy grill. Bobby guessed that the Burning Love Temple had once been a restaurant, filled at lunch time with the hungry crews from the Dixie Salvage Yard. A tall skinny boy hunched over the sound board, connecting and reconnecting electrical cords. Virgil hopped from the stage and rushed to the board, telling the boy to be more careful with the connection on the left amp. He saw Bobby and motioned him down front.

The drummer's name was Dean, and his twin brother Doyle played lead guitar. They were nineteen or twenty, even skinnier than the sound man, whose name was Larry. Dean and Doyle were about five-four, and seemed pretty burned out; or, to Bobby, they at least wanted to make others believe that they were, with their shoulder-length hair, torn jeans and tattoos. Larry was a drunk or a doper. Bobby could tell from the disjointed, goofy way he moved around. Tommy was the bass player. He was a little older than the twins, heavy-set, running to fat. His round face was set off with thick glasses, which gave him a studious appearance.

After Virgil introduced Bobby to the rest of the band, he lowered his head in prayer. He asked God to make the service a good one, to put His power in the fingers of the band, and to let the grace of Jesus and the love of Elvis come into their hearts. When the prayer ended, Larry ran them through a sound check and the rehearsal began. Bobby had little difficulty in following Doyle's leads. The music was simple, dominated by the basic chord changes Bobby had learned in his first year with Hootchie-Cootchie. Besides the songs, the band was expected to play throughout Virgil's service, backing him with either basic gospel or rock and roll rhythm. Virgil would signal for the rhythm he needed, and told Bobby it was especially important to play "with reverence" during the collection and the sermon.

Bobby evaluated the band as Virgil directed them through rehearsal. Dean was a sound drummer, although there was not much a drummer could do with the kind of music that Virgil wanted. Doyle was a mechanic. He understood what to do on the leads, but there was not much drive in him. Tommy was the best of them. He put down strong, hard bass lines. Bobby nodded in approval to him as the band finished the run through.

Satisfied, Virgil patted Bobby on the back and told him that he would do fine, and that it was time to change clothes for the service. Bobby followed the others into the kitchen, where they began to undress. From a duffle bag, Virgil handed Bobby a red leisure suit and a white shirt, the same outfit the others were putting on. The clothes smelled musty, as if they had been worn for a long time without being cleaned. The shirt's collar was frayed, although, like the jacket, it fit well enough. The pants, however, were at least four inches too long. They bunched and billowed over the tops of Bobby's tennis shoes. Like a fucking clown, Bobby thought.

Virgil disappeared into what he referred to as his "private dressing room", one of the two rest rooms near the kitchen.

"Your suit stink?" one of the twins asked Bobby.

"A little."

"They all do. Virgil got them from a lounge band that went broke. Five bucks apiece. Says he'll get them cleaned as soon as he takes up a special collection."

"He got a good deal," the other twin said, his pants ballooning out beneath his jacket. "You like Metallica?"

"I don't know what Metallica is," Bobby said.

"Heavy metal. Me and Doyle, we're into heavy metal. You like Anthrax?"

"I don't know them neither. I ain't a heavy metal fan."

Bobby had heard of heavy metal, even listened to it before he went to prison, before he met Hootchie-Cootchie.

"What do you like?" the first twin demanded.

"The music. Rock and roll. Blues."

Neither twin spoke to him after that, and they finished dressing in silence. What the hell they doing here if they're into heavy metal, Bobby thought.

Virgil emerged from his private dressing room. He had squeezed himself into a white, gold-embroidered jumpsuit. An eagle flared across his chest and a short cape hung from his shoulders. He huffed and blew, his breath constricted by the costume. Bobby wondered how he would be able to move during the service. After a couple of minutes of blowing, Virgil's body adjusted itself, as if it was possessed of a malleable, rubber-like quality that allowed it to adapt to the taut polyester. Larry straightened out the cape and told Virgil that he looked real fine. The red, flushed color that had burned beneath Virgil's make-up disappeared.

"I'm gonna take care of business," Virgil said, composed and professional now. "That was the King's motto," he said gravely to Bobby.

"He had a motto?"

"Taking Care of Business. He abbreviated it. TCB. Those letters were painted on his private airplane."

"The *Lisa Marie*. Named after his child," Larry said.

"Yessir. Taking Care of Business. TCB. I'm gonna put it on the van."

"On account you ain't got no airplane," Bobby said.

Virgil smiled. There was a little glint behind his eyes that showed he did not care for Bobby's comments.

"Not yet, Bobby."

Bobby went out back for a cigarette. He started to light up inside, but the Temple was supposed to be a church. And he did not want to hear any more from Virgil about Taking Care of Business. He found the back door, which faced on a circular driveway that connected with the parking lot.

"You want a beer?" It was Tommy. He followed Tommy to a Chevy van. Tommy pulled two Old Milwaukees from beneath the front seat and handed one to Bobby.

"Got to get primed for the evening. Too bad I didn't bring a joint," Tommy said.

The sun was dropping behind the tree line on the far side of the driveway. They sipped the hot beer.

"You're good," Tommy said.

"Thanks."

"I bet you can push that old Rocket. Not that we get a chance to do much real playing."

"Them twins. Heavy Metal freaks. What're they doing here?"

"What're you doing here?"

"Well . . . hell. That's a good question. I guess because I ain't had no other offers."

"Me, too. Little extra money. You don't think that I like that shit do you? Elvis. He's a joke. But I can't afford to get on with a real band now. And this is weird, too. I ain't never been around nothing like it. You ain't seen a service yet, have you?"

"This is my first night."

"Oh, yeah. Well, just wait. Where'd you learn to play?"

"In prison. In South Carolina."

Tommy gazed off toward the mountain of wrecked cars in the Dixie Salvage Yard, his thick throat working with beer.

"Prison," he finally said. He finished the beer and rummaged through the van for another one.

"You want another?" he said as he climbed out of the van.

"Still working on this one. It bother you I been in prison?"

Tommy's glasses had worked their way to the end of his nose.

"No. I guess all of us could end up there."

He laughed nervously.

"Maybe. You gotta get caught first."

Tommy laughed again, less nervously. They drank in silence.

"You know Virgil long?" Tommy asked.

"Since Monday night."

"You heard him go on about Elvis?"

"Some. I got a feeling that he could get real wound up."

"He can. You stay around here long enough, you'll hear him. And you oughta see who belongs to this church, or whatever it is. Nothing but women, old women. I'd never fuck a one of them."

"My momma comes here."

"No offense," Tommy said quickly.

"That's O.K. Forget it."

Bobby remembered Virgil's hands on Laverne's ass. The sound of tires on gravel drifted to them from the parking lot.

"About time to get going. Elvis and Jesus. Jesus and Elvis," Tommy said.

They finished their beers.

"Hey," Tommy said shyly. "You wanna play together. Us. I don't mean with this fucking band."

"I'd like that."

The cars came faster, one right after another, bearing the worshipers.

About fifty women clustered around the tables, which were piled high with moist, glistening sweets. Laverne arrived, holding high the five-layer coconut cake. She placed the cake in the center of the middle table and waved to Bobby as Doyle signaled to the band members to take the stage. Bobby slung the guitar strap around his neck and scanned the congregation. Tommy was right. Most of the women were Laverne's age or older, dressed in a variety of outfits: prom gowns; double-knit pants in various unnatural colors; square dance dresses, flaring with a dozen petticoats; cut-off jeans and tube tops embossed with Harley-Davidson logos; slacks and dresses of the ordinary housewife. A large woman, at least two hundred pounds of fat and muscle, caught Bobby's eye. She winked, coy and girlish. Her hair was bright red, an ill-fitting wig too large by at least a size. Beside her, almost clinging to the big woman, was a girl in a cowgirl costume, complete with hat and blue boots. Her eyes roamed about as if she was unsure of what was to come. The big woman smiled, showing long yellow teeth. Bobby pretended to tune his guitar.

"Where's Virgil?" he asked Tommy.

"Getting ready. He's going to do his Elvis entrance."

The band ground into a heavy, strip-joint beat. The women abandoned the tables, many of them still chewing, and rushed toward the stage, swaying to the music as they came. Doyle picked up the beat and the women vibrated with it, some of them moaning and shouting.

They remained in this expectant frenzy for at least five minutes before Virgil swung into the room, leaped onto the stage and jerked a mike from its stand. The band switched from the strip-joint beat to the first number, "When Kings Meet." Virgil crooned and panted the lyrics, which described the royal welcome Jesus gave to Elvis in Heaven. He lumbered back and forth, his rear, arms and head shaking in different directions. As soon as "When Kings Meet" ended, Virgil, without a pause, began the second number, which told of Jesus' visit to Graceland on the night of Elvis' death. Dean and Tommy slammed away on the percussion and bass lines. The women broke into a kind of clog dance, hopping and hurdling, their eyes uplifted, intent on Virgil, Elvis and Jesus. Laverne stood on one spot, stomping the concrete floor. The big woman turned in a circle, her tiny feet moving so fast it was difficult for Bobby to see them. Her wig slid to one side of her head, then fell to the floor. She was bald. She never slowed down, nor seemed to notice that the wig had been kicked toward the kitchen by another dancer. The cowgirl jumped back and forth, as if she were leaping a low, invisible fence. Another woman—she could have been a grandmother—attired in a bright orange prom dress, sat down hard on the floor, gasping and laboring for breath. In a moment, she was up and dancing faster than ever.

On the last note, Virgil threw the mike toward the ceiling, caught it, and dropped to one knee. The stage shook violently and Doyle had to steady his drum kit. The big woman retrieved her wig and carefully placed it one her head. The grandmother fell into a chair and fanned herself with the hem of her dress.

"Good evening," Virgil boomed. "And welcome to the Burning Love Temple! Tonight, we're TAKING CARE OF BUSINESS!"

As Virgil spoke, Dean and Tommy reverted to a subdued, softer version of the strip-joint beat. The women resumed their swaying.

"We're here to love the Lord and honor His greatest servant through PURE HAPPINESS!"

The women clapped and yelled. Their fumes washed up to the stage and caused Bobby to wince; perfumed, warm, excited flesh mixed with the stench of his leisure suit and a massive dose of Old Spice emanating from Virgil. The hot beer churned up from his stomach into his throat.

". . . and tonight we got a new member of the Burning Love Temple Band! For the first time! Laverne Snipes' son Bobby! Let's hear it for the red guitar!"

Laverne led the applause, beaming up at the stage. Virgil signaled for the next number and Doyle and the band cranked out an extended version of "It's Now or Never". The women formed a conga line, the big woman in the lead, her arms uplifted, wet half moons spreading from the armpits of her lime-green sheath dress. The line snaked around the Temple, chairs tipping over and clattering behind it, a chocolate cream pie splattering on the floor as the big woman bumped into a table.

It was time for a pause as Virgil and the congregation recovered their energy. The women mopped their faces with napkins and paper towels and touched up their make-up. The band maintained a low, gnawing rhythm as Virgil moved about the floor, passing a red plastic bucket for contributions. The bucket was almost half full when he returned to the stage. Bobby watched as Virgil peered at the take. He made a small grimace of dissatisfaction before he removed the bucket to his private dressing room.

Virgil opened the second half of the service with "There Is a Fountain Filled with Blood" and followed with forty-five minutes of the old hymns that Bobby faintly recalled from the Free Will Baptist Church. Except that he had never heard them performed with drums and electric guitars. Virgil did not exhibit the same enthusiasm as when he did his own songs. He barely moved as he sang, and his voice cracked on the high notes. The women remained seated, a little restless, a little bored. It was as if all of them were doing their duty to Jesus.

Virgil finished the gospel set with "Keep on the Sunny Side" and the women were up again as he began his sermon, swaying gently, shouting "Amen" and "Thank You Jesus". Virgil delivered his message in whispers and bellows. He began by presenting the obvious connections between grace and Graceland. And Bobby, strumming slowly on his guitar, imagined that this pleased Laverne. Soon, however, Virgil turned away from grace and spoke mostly of himself, linking Virgil Joy with Jesus of Nazareth and Elvis Presley. Bobby had the feeling that he gave the same sermon at every service, perhaps changing a few words here and there.

Seven or eight of Virgil's songs followed the sermon, the lyrics strained, the music flat and predictable. Bobby yawned deeply and often. The songs were all the same, even the last one, which described Elvis riding a Harley 74 through outer space and into eternity.

It all ended with a medley of a half-dozen Elvis songs. The finish came with Virgil on his knees mumbling and shouting away at "All Shook Up". He remained in that posture for at least thirty seconds after the song ended, his arms extended toward the women, his head bowed. He then climbed to his feet, wobbling. He raised his head, smiled lovingly, and gave a short closing prayer.

"Now we're going to be Taking Care of Some More Business! Amen!"

On cue, the congregation rushed to the tables and began to devour the remaining sweets. The doors were flung open. There was no breeze in the hot, still night. Thunder boomed in the distance.

His flock clustered about him as Virgil fed from a plate laden with cake, pie, brownies and homemade cobbler. Compulsively, the women touched him, pressing closely, tugging at his costume. Laverne, who stood closest to Virgil, called for Bobby to join them.

"You were wonderful, son," she said as she embraced him.

Virgil swallowed a mouthful of coconut cake.

"A real talent," he gurgled.

The big woman also embraced Bobby. She held him so hard and so long, he thought that she might not let go. Her name was April. Sheri, the cowgirl, did not hug him, and when their eyes met, she looked away.

"Me and Sheri live over at the Monte Vista Mobile Home Park. Number Six. That's our number."

She wrapped a thick, muscular arm around Bobby's waist.

"This is Sheri's first time at the Temple. Ain't that right, honey?"

Sheri nodded, still refusing to meet Bobby's eye.

"I been coming here twice a week since Reverend Joy started his ministry. I'm free here. They's times when I feel like I could fly right up to the ceiling," April said.

She removed her wig and fanned herself with it. Her face, like the wig, was bright red, right to the top of her head.

"It don't matter that I ain't got no hair. I guess you noticed that back during the dancing."

She laughed, tinkling and melodious, her fingers caressing Bobby's side.

"At work, I work over at the Burger King. Mostly the drive-through. I'm fast on the register. Anyhow, I wear my wigs over there. I'm what you call self-conscious when I'm at work. Most other places, too. Even if I ain't had hair since I was six on account of a funny case of the mumps. But in the Temple, when the music start, and Elvis and Jesus come down, that's a different story."

Bobby edged out of her grip. She was quick, however, and seized his hand.

"You was sent here," she said in a whispery, feathery voice. "I know you was."

Bobby stretched out full length on his bed. He was alone. Laverne had disappeared with Virgil after the food was consumed and the Temple cleaned. April and Sheri had given him a ride home in April's '71 Chevy pick-up. Somehow he had gotten himself wedged between the two women. He had tried for the seat next to the door, but April had insisted that he sit in the middle. She told him that he was cute, even without his red suit, and grabbed his knee several times like a shopper testing a ripe piece of fruit. Sheri did not speak except to say good-bye when they reached Modena Street. April did not let go of his knee until he promised to come for a visit after the Sunday service. He started to say no, then realized that Sheri would be there, too.

He took a long pull of beer and listened to the rattling of the air-conditioner from the living room. He finished the beer and went into the kitchen for another. He paused at the living room door. The tape of Elvis' '68 concert was still in the VCR. He punched it in, opened the beer, and reclined in the La-Z-Boy.

There was Elvis again; young and glossy, his face unblemished and shining. It was no longer a human face. It had been transformed into a contour map of a distant, unexplored country. The camera moved to include his face and crotch while Elvis preened and cooed. Bobby turned the beer up. The music was distant now, half-forgotten. That Elvis was smart, he thought. He understood what people wanted, and the music was just a way to get them to want you. For Hootchie-Cootchie the music came first. And hardly anyone knew whether Hootchie-Cootchie was dead or alive any more. Elvis would live forever, and have people like Virgil recreating him over and over.

He switched the tape off and sat in the darkened living room. The beer tasted flat and metallic. Things are wrong, he thought. It's all upside down. Then an idea came to him. It was simple. He would write Hootchie-Cootchie and ask him about these doubts. He would plan the letter until he got it just right.

He pushed the tape back in and focused on Elvis like a student pouring over a text.

4

The double-wide was jammed with even more mementos of the King than Laverne's living room. It was devoid of any reminders of Jesus. There was even a copy of Laverne's statue, in living ceramic color, wedged in the space between the cabinet model stereo and the television set. Maybe all of the women got that statue, Bobby thought.

He had left quickly when the service ended. He had wanted to do a solo during "Promised Land", but Virgil said no. Solos, Virgil said, had nothing to do with Taking Care of Business, and the business of the Temple was Elvis and Jesus. Virgil had patted him on the back and reminded him that he was part of a team, and that teammates must do what was best for all. Virgil had told Bobby those things during rehearsal, and the words rolled sullenly around in his head the rest of the morning.

April was surprised and pleased when he took her arm and said that he had to get away from the Temple. He had not even bothered to change the smelly red leisure suit. He sat on the couch next to April, while Sheri perched stiffly on a metal dinette chair.

April rolled joints on the coffee table, keeping up a steady commentary about Elvis and the Temple as she expertly packed the dope into the papers. She ordered Sheri to fetch beers from the refrigerator, and she condemned those members of the congregation who were poor dancers. They only took up space on the floor, she said. And half of them were too old or too chicken-shit to really shake it up.

She asked Bobby if he had anything against pot; and when he shook his head, she lit a joint and handed it to him. He sucked the smoke inside. That goddamn Virgil, he thought. He passed the joint to Sheri. She still would not meet his eyes, although he felt her watching him.

April drew in a long, deep hit, consuming half of the first joint. She lit another as the trailer filled with smoke. The statue of Elvis swam in it; the pictures and tapestries were indistinct and distant. He could not stop thinking about Virgil. Virgil's got him a little power, he thought. He's got his act all sewed up. Suddenly, he had to have his hands on his guitar.

Outside, the heat and light blinded him, and he staggered a little as he pulled the Harmony Rocket and his amplifier from the bed of April's pick-up truck. He leaned against the rear fender. The dope was powerful and the day had slowed to a stop in the empty, burning trailer park. The whole goddamn world's empty, he thought.

"What you doing?"

It was April.

"Getting my guitar. Gotta play."

"Come on back in. You gonna get sunburned."

Her voice carried a hint of threat. She had removed the jet-black wig she had worn for the morning service. The top of her head was dead-white. Bobby had not noticed the color before. He imagined that it would be cold to the touch. He followed her back into the trailer.

"You gonna play long?" April asked, lighting another joint.
"As long as I need to."

"Do you mind if I get personal?" April asked.
Sheri shifted in the dinette chair, turning toward him. It was the first time Bobby had seen her move, except to fetch beer. April went on, without waiting for an answer from Bobby.
"You about the cutest guitar player the Reverend Joy ever had."
"Is that right?"
He inhaled more dope, floating now.
"Them other boys ain't got it. Like you do. I think you're a lot like . . ."
"Elvis!" Sheri blurted.
"Just like Elvis," April said.
Bobby was sick of Elvis, for the moment, so he tried the old blues he used to do with Hootchie-Cootchie. They made him forget and remember. While he played he was pleasantly unaware of who, and where he was. April and Sheri listened politely. Bobby finished "Crossroads" and Sheri handed him another beer.
"That's real nice," April said, "but it ain't exactly my kind of music."
"Your kind?" Bobby asked.
"I need the kind that makes you get up and dance. That makes you go wild. Like at the Temple."
Bobby propped the guitar against the Elvis statue and turned the amplifier off.
"You stopping?" Sheri asked.
"Thinking. That's all."
When he composed the letter to Hootchie-Cootchie, this would be part of it.
"Too much thinking going on," April said.
She rushed to the big cabinet stereo and put a record on. Elvis

moaned "Stuck On You". They got their Elvis, he thought. April launched into an oddly graceful version of the pony, transforming herself into an enormous go-go dancer. She bounced around the trailer, gliding deftly around the furniture and the icons of the King. "Stuck On You" was replaced by a ballad about taking a chance on love. April pulled Bobby close, wrapping him in a bear hug. He felt weak and helpless in her grip.

"Dance," she trilled, her breath hot and beery in his face, a knee thrust between his legs. April led, guiding him between the coffee table, the statue and the television.

They danced through five songs before April took a breather. She lit another joint, and Sheri took over. Bobby began to enjoy himself, and abandoned thinking for awhile. Sheri was shy and tentative, and he had to draw her to him. They stayed that way, even on the fast numbers.

April finished the joint, and declared that it was her turn again. The women alternated with him, dancing through the *Greatest Hits*, *Viva Las Vegas*, *From Memphis with Love*, and *G.I. Blues* before he dropped, gasping, to the couch. April stood over him, tugging her dress over he head. With a dramatic gesture, like she might have seen Ursula Andress make in *Fun in Acapulco*, she flung the dress away. She wore what seemed to Bobby to be a man's yoke undershirt and a pair of bright red bikini panties. Her belly terraced out below her tiny breasts, rolling into thick, columnar legs.

"April!" Sheri squealed. Bobby heard her, but could not see her. April blotted out his vision. The she was on him, all meat, smells, heat, and Elvis.

He sensed the sun was much lower than when April first loomed over him. The guitar was, magically, back in his hands, his fingers rippling out power chords. He had the power, too, standing naked and sweating, the red leisure suit in a ball at the foot of the couch. He whammed away at a song he could not name. April was passed out, spreading herself over most of the couch. She had the face of a gigantic baby. He laughed.

"What's so funny?" Sheri said. She was on her knees before him, naked too, her mouth sweet and slick.

"You ain't laughing at me are you?" she said.

He did not answer.

"Ain't no man ever *laughed* while I done this to him."

"I feel . . ."

"I won't do it no more if you keep laughing."

He did know why he had laughed. It was not April, or all that had occurred that day. He could not say what it was. He stopped playing. Sheri crouched below him, small and lost. There are things to find out, to know, he thought. He wanted to laugh again. Instead, he caressed her head.

"I ain't laughing at you."

"You sure?"

"Real sure. Don't stop. Whatever you do. I'll play 'Dixie' for you. You really think I'm a little like Elvis?"

"Yeah. Me and April both. She seen it first, just like she said."

He swung into a high tension, nightmare version of "Dixie" and she glued her face to him.

April, in a curly blonde wig and a Burger King uniform, dropped him off at Modena Street on her way to work. She was cheerful and energetic, as if she had awakened from a good night's sleep. Sheri had gone to bed as they were leaving, even though it was only four o'clock. April told him that Sheri slept a lot; that she was delicate and needed her rest on account of how hard she had to work at the American Way Dry Cleaners.

Laverne was not home and he had sobered up a little when he sat down at the kitchen table and began to compose the letter to Hootchie-Cootchie. He wrote in a spiral notebook he found on top of the refrigerator, thumbing through it until he found some blank pages, reading notes that Laverne had written to herself about errands and job duties. On one page, the name of the Reverend Virgil Joy was written two or three dozen times, the way junior high girls copy their boyfriend's names.

He had never written a letter before. He worked on it for a couple of hours, trying to get it right. He described the Burning Love Temple, especially the music and how Virgil would not let him do the solo.

He complained further about Virgil and Virgil's songs, and said that he practiced the guitar so much that when he had his chance he could make music that really mattered. He tried to explain the feeling he had as he stood naked with the guitar in his hands, but the words would not come, so he gave up. "Someday," he wrote, "I wish we could get on the stage together, going like we used to." He imagined Hootchie-Cootchie receiving the letter. He had never gotten a letter in all the years that Bobby had known him. He finished as Laverne and Virgil came home with a video tape of *Blue Hawaii*.

In late September, the heat broke. Bobby passed the test for a driver's license and put a week's salary down on a '70 Vega with bad shocks that he found at a used car lot not far from the Temple. He visited April and Sheri a few more times, and they made the double-wide rock with Elvis and their bodies. He brought the Red Harmony along on his visits, and, eventually, even April admitted that his music was good. She became jealous, however, when she saw that Bobby preferred Sheri. After Bobby had to slap her when she threatened Sheri with a steak knife, he refused to go back. He called Sheri a couple of times at the American Way Dry Cleaners to see if she would sneak off with him in the Vega. She turned him down; she was afraid of April. At the Temple, April refused to speak to him, and gave him hard, outraged glances as she danced.

Alone, he drove around the Gaston County backroads. He kept the Vega's windows down, the cool air washing over him. He had been penned up so long that any movement brought deep satisfaction; almost as much satisfaction as the guitar. After he wrote to Hootchie-Cootchie, he began to write songs, the first he had ever tried. On the third or fourth try, he had one that he thought was pretty good. It was about life in the isolation block. The music came easier than the words, but finally, the lyrics were there. Once, during rehearsals at the Temple, he played the song during a break.

> "In D Block you're lost and afraid
> In D Block you die everyday . . . "

When he finished, no one said anything; except for Tommy, who told him that the song was great. Virgil said that the song was nice, but it was time to get back to work. During another rehearsal, Bobby tried out a couple of more songs, and the band liked them so much, they joined in with him in the second number. The first was about an execution. The other concerned a woman like April who had fallen in love with a velvet painting of Elvis. Virgil solemnly stated that while Bobby's talent was God-given, he lacked a proper sense of direction.

Since it was futile to try to inject himself into the service, Bobby decided he would at least have a little fun with it. Once, when Virgil was preaching on the necessity and meaning of his costumes, Bobby abandoned the required gospel beat, and launched into "Layla". Virgil whirled and glared, but he never complained directly to Bobby. He got Laverne to do it for him. She whined for several days about how ungrateful Bobby was.

Three or four weeks passed without an answer from Hootchie-Cootchie. Bobby wrote another letter, much longer than the first. He repeated much of what Hootchie-Cootchie had taught him about the holy nature of music and asked how he could get away from the Virgils of the world; people who turned what was important into a lie. After he mailed the letter, he realized that

Hootchie-Cootchie would tell him to leave the Temple, to find his own way. Only he did not know how. Except for the drives in the Vega, or when he was writing songs, his mind whirled away at nothing; a powerful longing vibrating within him. He checked the mailbox every day for an answer.

Tommy Aycock lived in a three-room house on the edge of a slow-running, muddy creek. The house belonged to an uncle, who did not bother to ask for rent. Tommy had lived there for four months, ever since his wife had thrown him out. Bobby visited a couple of times a week. They played for hours—until they were exhausted, or until Tommy had to go to bed. He worked on the loading dock at the General Electric warehouse in Charlotte, and figured that he needed a little sleep just to get by.

Even though Tommy was younger than Bobby, he had been a musician for much longer. He started out on the drums when he was seven. By the time he was eighteen, he had toured with a lounge band. Later, he played with a band called the Slime Dogs on the punk-new wave club circuit. The Slime Dogs signed a contract for an extended play record with a small company in Raleigh. The record fell through when the lead singer was stabbed by his girlfriend. The singer lived, but gave up the band to work in his father's hardware store. The Slime Dogs died instead.

Bobby liked playing with Tommy. Tommy was good, and he would work on Bobby's songs. For Tommy, the music was serious; one of the few things worth being serious about. The Temple was a job, as the lounge band had been; a way to get a little compensation for doing the only thing that mattered to him. He disliked Elvis, and when he got on the subject of the King's music, his good humor vanished. Bobby, who had been reading through Laverne's library of Elvis books, was not sure how he felt. And when he recalled those shimmering images on the video tapes, he was sure that Tommy was wrong. Still, as Tommy pointed out, Elvis had made songs with such titles as "Do the

Clam" and "You Can't Do the Rumba in a Sport's Car". Songs that even Virgil would not perform.

Bobby parked the Vega at the top of a hill, next to a deeply rutted road that ran down to the creek and Tommy's house. It was twilight and the air was cool and rank with the breeze off the water. The house was bleak with peeling paint and a sagging roof, and Bobby had to hoist his guitar case up to the porch and climb up after it because the front steps were missing.

Tommy was in the front room smoking a joint. Besides Tommy, the room contained two big amplifiers that he had gotten cheap when the Slime Dogs disbanded, three guitars, a couch, and a large cassette player. Other than these items, Tommy owned a mattress, his van, and a pile of dirty clothes. His wife had the rest of it, including his three year old son, Sid Vicious Aycock. Tommy had insisted on the name. His wife had found Jesus when she was persuaded by her mother to attend a ten thousand member fundamentalist church in Charlotte. When she returned from church that Sunday, she informed Tommy that Jesus wanted him to give up rock and roll, and that their son's name was to be changed from Sid Vicious to Joshua Jericho. He laughed at her, but she found a lawyer and the lawyer persuaded a district court judge to sign an order that barred him from his home.

He often cursed his wife, and he was especially bitter that she refused to let him see Sid, or Joshua, or whatever the boy's name happened to be. He had thought of finding a lawyer of his own, but between his job, the Temple, beer, dope, and music, he never quite got around to it.

Loud, chaotic rock and roll filled the house as a working class English voice sang about the end of the world. Tommy offered the joint to Bobby, who shook his head.

"You ready to play?" Bobby asked.

He was impatient, ready to plunge into the music.

"Sit down. I got an idea."

Bobby settled into the other end of the broken-backed couch. He pumped his left leg up and down with nervous energy.

"You ain't too fucked up to play are you?"

Tommy's eyes were red with dope. He often had ideas when he was high.

"There's an open mike night at Buddy's Lounge. Over on Albemarle Road in Charlotte."

"What kind of place is it?"

"A club! What'd you think?"

"What kinda club?"

"Don't know. But we can find out."

"What's open mike?"

"The stage is there for anybody who wants to get up on it. All we got to do is be there, sign up, and we got us an audience."

"How long we get to play?"

"Half hour, maybe."

"That ain't long enough."

"Shit. It's what you get. Come on. I've done it before. It's fun."

"Fun."

"What's wrong with that?"

"Nothing. You're the one that's serious all the time. Putting Elvis down."

"This ain't got a thing to do with that goddamn Elvis. I'm sick of hearing about Elvis all the time. Talking about him. All that shit. It's us I'm talking about. People'll be there. We can play what we want. Your stuff. Your songs, man. Not like that shit Virgil puts us through."

They packed their equipment into the van and Bobby's doubts began to dissolve. My songs, he thought. He could see the audience, a throng, bending to him with longing.

* * *

Buddy's Lounge sat in the middle of a two-acre parking lot, far out in the butt end of Charlotte, where the whole of creation seemed to be composed of apartment complexes, strip malls, and fast-food franchises stretching out forever. The lounge was fifty thousand square feet of cinder blocks, stucco, concrete and cheap paneling. Buddy's name was illuminated in red neon letters ten feet high, rearing from a flat roof. It was dark when they arrived, but only a couple of dozen cars were in the lot, parked close to the building. Inside, beer signs provided most of the illumination in the cavernous, table-crowded main room. Pool tables and video games filled a large sub-chamber, and that was where most of Buddy's customers could be found. On the stage, a leather-faced man in a black outfit labored painfully through "Ring of Fire".

At the bar, Tommy asked for the manager and signed up to play. A country and western group replaced the leather-faced man, and struggled with the opening chords of "I'm Proud to Be an American." The manager was pale and heavy. He wore an expensive haircut and a Hawaiian shirt. He yawned as he took their names.

"Thursdays are dead around here. That's why we got this open mike thing. Tomorrow night, though, we got Ferlin Huskey. First stop on his come back tour. Big crowd. Big."

Tommy bought a couple of beers and they took a table near the stage. The cowboy band, five men in straw Stetsons with sunbursts on the front, and sporting carefully trimmed beards, were putting the finishing touches on their version of "Ghost Riders In the Sky".

"You didn't tell me that this place would be full of country shit-kickers," Bobby said.

"Hell, I didn't know. At least it ain't the Burning Love Temple. Goddamn, that band's awful. Listen to the drummer."

The head cowboy coughed as he hit the final verse, and struggled to end the song. Tommy whooped.

"Son of a bitch was bad enough without the coughing," Tommy said through his laughter.

When "Ghost Riders In the Sky" ground down, the singer glared in the direction of Tommy and Bobby's table. A knot of spectators at the far end of the stage applauded enthusiastically.

"Guess they brought their relatives with them," Tommy said.

The cowboys did four or five more songs. They were followed by a female vocalist, a woman about Laverne's age, who performed high-pitch versions of Loretta Lynn's and Tammy Wynette's greatest hits. She's even dressed like Laverne, Bobby thought. All got up like she's going to a party. Contemplating Laverne soured him, for she conjured up Virgil.

The female vocalist finished her set, smiled, and bowed to the audience. She seemed grateful for the little bit of applause she received. Another cowboy band followed her, and they were even worse than the first one. They tried to work comedy into their act, the lanky, pock-marked lead singer telling jokes about life down home in a mythical version of the south. Is this what I'm up against? Bobby thought. By the time the second cowboy band was through, he was filled with certainty.

"Let's go," he said to Tommy as the cowboys removed their instruments from the stage. "They're packing it in."

The single spotlight was brighter than he expected, and, for a moment, it blinded him, distancing him from the audience. It was almost as if they were not there.

"What're we going to start with?" Tommy asked as they finished tuning up.

"Smoke Stack Lighting."

He had often done the song with Hootchie-Cootchie, and he had worked on it with Tommy, too. They went at it hard. They finished in dead silence. Someone yelled for them to get country or get their asses out.

"They enjoyed the hell outta that one," Tommy said. "What's next?"

"The Plague."

Bobby had worked on the song for a couple of weeks, picking up the beat and rhythm from Tommy: driving, insistent, brutal. He put his mouth close to the mike and sang, his face grim, his skin tight.

> The plague came down from everywhere
> They said you couldn't cheat it
> It whispered and cried
> It flattered and denied
> All the people ran out to meet it . . .

Through seven verses the words described how the plague ate and chewed, and how much people loved it, how they longed for it. Bobby had written the verses one night after listening to talk shows on the Vega's radio. When he wrote it, he thought of himself, of April and Sheri, of Hootchie-Cootchie. Tommy had told him that it was the best he had done yet. It would have been perfect for the Slime Dogs.

"The Plague" ended. Again, there was no applause. This time, however, Bobby could feel a vague hostility from the audience. Desperately, they resumed playing. They made it through three verses of "Isolation" before the manager pulled the mike away from Bobby and announced that their set was over. Bobby said that they were going to do a couple more songs. The manager again said that the set was over. Bobby jerked the mike from the manager's hand. His mouth twisted as he screamed, "THEN GET FUCKED!"

His voice reverberated and crashed through Buddy's lounge, drowning out even the sounds from the gameroom.

"It was a bad idea," Tommy said.

Bobby did not answer. Tommy had done all of the talking since Bobby howled into the microphone back at Buddy's Lounge. He had talked them out of having to fight the combined membership of the two cowboy bands, and he had convinced the husband of the female vocalist not to shoot Bobby for cursing in front of his wife. Bobby slumped in the passenger seat and tried not to think.

"I'm sorry," Tommy said.

"Don't be. The assholes."

The lights from the interstate traffic bounced off of Tommy's glasses. He sounded relieved that Bobby could still speak.

"Hey, when I was with the Slime Dogs, a guy threatened us with a shotgun. We got hired sight unseen by this club up in Statesville. They'd never seen people like us. I wore a mohawk then. A tall blue one. They called us queers. Imagine calling me a queer. Then this guy gets a shotgun outta his trunk. I didn't think I'd get my ass outta there in one piece."

"It ain't gonna happen to me again."

"Let's play some more when we get back to my place. Go all night. I'll lay outta work tomorrow."

"No. The motherfuckers."

"Come on, man. We'll work on your songs."

Bobby did not answer. He wanted to go back to Buddy's Lounge to kick their asses. He'd start with the manager and work his way through the whole crowd. He was sorry he let Tommy lead him out. He had been too furious to speak or act.

"Look," Tommy said. "There's something you gotta understand. People wanna hear music they already know. Most people do anyway. I learned that when I was with the lounge band. Oldie goldie shit. Listen to the radio. All of them listen to the goddamn radio. Those old songs, over and over. The music don't mean much to them."

"It's not gonna be that way for me," Bobby finally said.

"Think about Virgil. He gives the ladies what they want. Can you see them if you did "The Plague" at a service? They'd be worse than those people tonight."

"There's a way to do it."

"Sure. There might be. Maybe if you played with an outfit like the Slime Dogs. Only you're not that way either. I don't know what you are."

"I'm . . ." Bobby paused. He did not yet know what he was either.

He sat at the kitchen table, drinking a coke and eating donuts. For once, Laverne was home. Her snores drifted softly into the kitchen. He finished his third donut and started the fourth. She usually brought two boxes of donuts every day from the store, and she would not care too much if Bobby ate all of them. What she cares about, he thought, is Virgil and the Temple. The Temple and Buddy's Lounge were the same; only the crowds are different. People don't want real music. Tommy had said that, and he did not even seem to mind. Like that was the way it was supposed to be. He tossed the half-eaten donut back into the box. He was no longer hungry.

He eased into the La-Z-Boy. He was tired, but could not sleep. He thought of calling Sheri and April, of patching it up with them. He gave up on this idea when he thought of April dancing. And the dancing forced him back to Virgil again. Virgil believed he was the reason the women danced. He was wrong, though. It was Elvis. It always got back to Elvis. Elvis had this attitude. Attitude was a word he remembered the shrinks using in prison.

Bobby pulled an armful of books from Laverne's Elvis library. He opened an illustrated guide to Graceland, full of brightly-colored, glossy pages revealing the interior of the King's home; Tiki-gods, ceiling-to-floor mirrors, white shag carpet. Elvis let the world see that he was rich, he thought. First, he had to be poor. Born in a shack in Tupelo. An only child after his twin died.

Bobby dropped the guide to Graceland to the floor beside the La-Z-Boy and opened a history of the films. There was Elvis in *Jailhouse Rock*, dressed up like some actor's idea of an inmate.

He had watched the film a week or two earlier with Virgil and Laverne. Virgil asked if the prison scenes brought back bad memories. Bobby had laughed long and loud. And yet, Elvis had gotten the attitude right: me against them.

Another book commemorated the Las Vegas years. Virgil had given it to Laverne for her birthday. He claimed to have seen Elvis at the Las Vegas Hilton. One of the greatest moments in his life, he said; right up there with accepting Jesus Christ as his personal savior. How come he bothers with Jesus, Bobby thought. What does Jesus have to do with it? If it was my church, it would be just me and Elvis.

My church: the phrase spun and dove around him as he examined the picture of Elvis in his ultimate manifestation, a creature from a dream of timeless power, possessed of all truth.

Bobby read occasionally, but he mostly concentrated on the pictures. When he did read, however, he focused hard on the words, sometimes whispering passages aloud. Elvis was mystical. Elvis healed the sick. Elvis had second sight. Elvis studied important metaphysical texts such as *The Late, Great Planet Earth*, and *The Holy Shroud of Turin*. Elvis had been contacted by UFOs. Many believed that he still lived; that he might appear in your home town, on your doorstep some miraculous morning; a dawn of grace that would prove the triumph of Elvis over death.

Bobby awakened to the sound of running water. Laverne was in the bathroom and he was still in the La-Z-Boy, the books scattered around him. He vaguely wondered why he had spent the night with the books. Buddy's Lounge came back to him. He cursed softly. Laverne emerged from the bathroom, perfectly groomed for her day at the store. He followed her into the kitchen, badly in need of coffee.

"What was you doing last night?" she asked as she bit into a donut and waited for the water to heat. He sat down and lit a cigarette.

"Practicing. With Tommy."

He did not feel up to describing his set at Buddy's Lounge. And Laverne would not understand if he did. She had the same opinion of his songs as Virgil and Buddy's customers.

"That boy."

She did not approve of Tommy. He lacked respect for Virgil's ministry.

"He's a bass guitar player. Plays guitar, too. About the best around here. Outside of me."

She prepared the coffee and handed him a cup. She took a sip as she quickly opened a copy of the *Gastonia Gazette*. She quickly flipped the pages to the department store advertisements.

"I've got to get me some new outfits. Sheri 'bout ruined the purple one last Sunday. She's might clumsy to be so young. Dropping a whole piece of banana cream pie on me."

She did not approve of Sheri either.

"She's not right for the Temple. There's something cheap about her. Don't you think?"

Bobby shrugged and drank the coffee. He seldom spoke to Laverne, and he wanted it to stay that way. She folded the paper and placed it on the table.

"Been reading about the King again?"

"That's right."

"Them books are almost sacred."

She made this statement in complete innocence, with complete belief. Virgil had offered the same observation more than once.

"Time to go," she said.

She gave him a quick kiss on the cheek.

"I'll be back late tonight."

"Virgil needs you, right?"

"We're going to dinner," she said with dignity.

He remained at the table, smoking and drinking coffee. In a while he would practice his songs. He practiced for hours, every day. What good is it, he thought. Nobody's gonna listen.

He opened the *Gastonia Gazette*. He rarely read newspapers.

The paper was the closest alternative to thinking about Buddy's Lounge, or Virgil, or his mother, however. Former President Reagan beamed up from the front page. He had visited Florida to dedicate a new Disney World. He declared that life was good in America. Reagan's smile reminded Bobby of Virgil's and he quickly opened the first section and scanned the stories: planes hijacked, AIDS, foreigners slaying each other, Americans arming themselves and proclaiming the sanctity of spermatozoa. He threw the section on the floor and grabbed up the local and regional news. The county commission debated a tax proposal. A pit bull bit a retired textile worker. A man was found beaten to death in a motel room off I-85. He was about to give up on the newspaper when a small headline on the third page caught his eye.

FORMER RHYTHM AND BLUES STAR'S DEATH RULED SUICIDE.

The story was from Columbia and described the death of Arthur "Hootchie-Cootchie" Magee, who had been found hanging in his cell at the Central Correctional Institution. The story briefly summed up Hootchie-Cootchie's career and noted that he was serving a life sentence for the slaying of alleged drug dealer Horace "Cat Man" Burch in 1973. Magee left no note, the story said, and his funeral would take place in Charleston, his home town.

Bobby read the story three times before he wadded the paper into a ball and hurled it toward the sink. After that, he remained motionless for a long time. The only sounds in the world were his own deep, rattling breaths, and the ticking of the clock on the knick-knack shelf above the stove.

5

One Sunday, after the services, Virgil and Laverne invited Bobby to lunch. He met them at Shoney's in the mall off I-85. Laverne said that Shoney's was their—hers and Virgil's—favorite restaurant. A line stretched from the front door, the after-church crowd lined up for Sunday dinner. It was not hard to find Virgil and Laverne, however. Virgil still wore his jumpsuit and cape. Children pointed. A teenaged girl giggled. Heads turned. Virgil nodded and smiled to all, as if he were receiving the tribute of vassals. Laverne held his arm and pressed herself against him.

They plowed through the meal: soup, salad bar, char-broiled chicken and french fries, cooing to each other, chewing and swallowing. Bobby quickly finished his cheeseburger, shoved the plate away, and lit a cigarette. Virgil and Laverne had enough food to keep them busy for another half hour at least.

He wondered why he had accepted the invitation. Laverne kept saying, "We don't do enough together," and kept begging him to come along. And they were pressing and rubbing each other more than usual. He tried not to think about them, but that meant that he would probably end up thinking about Hootchie-Cootchie. More than a month had passed since he read the story, and it was still as if he held the newspaper in his hands and felt the words boring into him. He could not rid himself of the feeling. The cigarette tasted hot and bitter and he stubbed it out.

It don't make sense, he thought. Hootchie-Cootchie was the only person he had ever known who could make people believe what he wanted them to. To kill himself was to cancel out his music, his power. It musta been prison, he thought. Prison was death. Only Hootchie-Cootchie had seemed beyond death. And he never answered the letters. Like I wasn't even there. Like all we done was nothing.

This fact had enraged him from the moment he saw the headlines. For Hootchie-Cootchie to refuse him was too much to bear. He had told no one, not even Tommy, who would have been the only person capable of appreciating what Hootchie-Cootchie meant. He stopped writing songs, and the evening sessions with Tommy turned into tight, manic, often frustrating workouts. Tommy seemed puzzled, but never asked what was wrong. At the Temple, Bobby no longer tried to disrupt Virgil's performance. He did only what was expected of him. This pleased Virgil, and he took to slapping Bobby on the back and telling him what a fine guitar player he was. Laverne said that he was beginning to fit into society.

When he studied the Elvis books, he could forget Hootchie-Cootchie and the Temple for awhile. And when he tired of the books, he picked up copies of the tabloids like *The Weekly World News* when they carried stories about the King: how the ghost of Elvis haunted Graceland; how Elvis had been cloned before his death and that dozens of his replicas were spreading across America and the world; how a statue of Elvis on Mars had been photographed by an unmanned Soviet space vehicle in 1985. Grimly, he studied and read.

Virgil and Laverne ordered strawberry pie for desert. They made happy, sucking noises as they consumed it. Bobby smoked, and drank iced tea. They finished the pie, and Virgil, swallowing the last bite, smiled at Bobby.

"You enjoy your lunch?"

"Sure." He did not feel much like talking, but there was not much choice.

Virgil's smile hung in the air, his teeth pink from the pie. Then he hunched across the table toward Bobby, who drew back, exhaling smoke.

"Me and your mother got something important to tell you."

Virgil slid his arm around Laverne and she leaned forward, too.

"Should I tell him, or should you?" Virgil asked.

"Bobby, son, we wanted you to be the first to know that . . ."

". . . that you're gonna get married," Bobby said.

That fits, he thought. Fits fucking perfect.

"How . . . how did you guess?" Laverne asked.

He wanted to laugh, but held back. He could laugh later.

"It was easy to tell."

Laverne and Virgil turned to each other, surprised. They don't know shit, Bobby thought.

"Easy?" Virgil said.

"You two been heading for this for a long time. Congratulations."

There's signs again, Bobby thought. He extended his hand to Virgil and they shook. Laverne came around the table and embraced him. She smelled of char-broiled chicken and strawberry pie.

Virgil revealed that they would be married on Tuesday at the Courthouse in York County, across the state line. That would be the legal wedding. The real wedding would be on Wednesday night, at the Temple, when the congregation gathered. Actually, Virgil went on, there would not be a wedding as such. Instead, there would be a celebration, a party, catered by Carolina Country Barbecue. And Virgil was not even going to take up a special collection to pay for it. He would foot the bill himself. The band would meet an hour early on Wednesday to practice a special wedding song that Virgil had composed. The highlight of the celebration, Virgil said.

"And don't tell anybody. I don't even want the boys in the band to find out until the rehearsal."

"A big surprise," Bobby said.

"The biggest."

"It's gonna be real special, huh?"

Laverne took Bobby's hands and held them tightly.

"I know how hard things have been for you, son. Prison and all. We can be happy now. And even if you are thirty years old, I understand about how you missed having a real daddy, how things was with you and Ray . . ."

Hootchie-Cootchie came to him again, hanging in his cell, sightless eyes popped out, his long pink tongue turning black with blood, urine and excrement filling his pants.

". . . so I hope that if you have problems, if you need a man to talk to, you'll come to Virgil."

She waited for an answer. Hootchie-Cootchie faded. Virgil was hunched forward again, his face inches from Bobby's.

"You listen to your momma. I'll be there when you need me."

Bobby closed his eyes. Hootchie-Cootchie was gone. He opened his eyes and smiled. Laverne continued to squeeze his hands.

"It'll be all right," she said.

"That's the truth," Bobby said. "The truth."

The next day, Bobby drove over to Virgil's styling salon, Sheer Pleasures. The shop was located in a strip mall on Garrison Boulevard, between a Domino's Pizza and an H&R Block office.

A heavy silver-blonde woman, about Laverne's age, was trimming a mass of red hair, which was all that could be seen of the customer.

"Can I help you?" the silver-blonde said over her shoulder.

"I want a haircut."

"I got an empty slot when I finish here. Have a seat."

"I want Virgil Joy, the Reverend Virgil Joy, for the job."

The silver-blonde teased up a combful of hair.

"He'll be back in a little while. I don't know when though."

"I'll wait."

He seated himself beneath an aerial photograph of Graceland, which covered most of one wall. On the opposite wall, there were a few pictures of Elvis, but they were outnumbered by photos of Virgil as Elvis. Bobby was drawn to one in particular. Virgil, in one of his costumes, stood beside a woman who bore a strong resemblance to the silver-blonde. Bobby watched her as she dug into the red hair; from the back it was difficult to be absolutely certain that she was the same woman in the photograph. He was about to go over to the wall for a closer look, when Virgil walked in. His eyes widened when he saw Bobby. He quickly escorted Bobby to a small office in the rear of the shop.

"Well, what brings you down here today? Would you like some coffee? A Coke?"

"Elvis liked Pepsi better."

"Is that a fact? Been reading up on Elvis, I hear. Laverne tells me that you're real interested in the King."

"Yeah. That's right."

Virgil sat down, putting the desk between Bobby and himself. The office was decorated like the waiting room: more pictures of Virgil and Elvis. And not a single one of Laverne. Virgil rubbed his hands together and blinked nervously.

"I guess you came here for a reason," Virgil said.

"Sure did."

"About me marrying your momma? I want to tell you, son, I'm gonna treat your mother with respect. Respect! She's about the finest woman I ever been associated with!"

Virgil slapped the desk for emphasis and the pictures shook a little.

"I ain't here about that."

"You're not?"

"Naw. Something else . . ."

"I'm glad to hear you say that. You know, Laverne really loves you. She was so worried when you was in prison. We prayed for you at every service. I even composed a special prayer . . ."

"Something else. I want you to cut my hair."

"Cut your hair?"

Virgil sat back in his chair, less nervous, but still wary.

"I want it done special."

"How come you came to me?"

"You cut hair. Why else would I come?"

"Lots of people cut hair. Did you think I'd do it for free? Well, the best I can give you is half price, even if you are family, or almost family."

"The money don't matter. I came to you because I knew you'd get it right. I want it done special."

Virgil relaxed a little more.

"I'm flattered. I mean it. Never thought you had a real interest in hair."

"The interest came to me lately. This morning in fact. And I want it to look like this."

Bobby reached into his shirt pocket and produced a picture that he had torn from one of Laverne's books. He handed it to Virgil.

The picture had been taken early in Elvis' career, around 1954 or 1955, when Elvis was a Memphis thug, with his hair trained into an elaborate, slick monument. In the picture, Elvis reared up on stage, mike in hand, pointing into the audience. It was one of those early concerts, orchestrated by Colonel Parker, where Elvis revelled in the mass of teenaged, crinoline-clad bodies that writhed at his feet. His features were distorted with the force of the music, with his own sermon of power and lust. The real Elvis, Bobby had thought as he worked the page loose from the binding.

"How come you want to look like this?" Virgil asked.

"What man wouldn't want to look like the King?"

"You got a point there."

"And something else. I want my hair dyed jet black."

Virgil had warmed to the idea of the haircut by the time Bobby got into the chair. Virgil cut and combed there in the office so they could, as he said "talk in private". He chatted as he worked, describing how he discovered his calling.

"I preached in little holiness churches from the time I was sixteen. Hell and damnation. A little healing . . ."

Bobby watched the snippets of hair drift to the floor. It was his first haircut since prison, so Virgil had a great deal of material to work with.

"You healed people?" Bobby asked.

"No. Not actually. Some thought they got healed. That's just as good."

"Elvis believed he could heal afflictions."

"He could. In a way. Think how good he made millions of people feel. How he uplifted them, eased their burdens."

"Like Jesus."

"Yeah. Just like Jesus."

"Then how come so many people want to be like Elvis, and nobody wants to be like Jesus?"

Virgil carefully placed the scissors on the desk and sat down.

"You ain't finished are you?" Bobby asked.

"I'll get back to that. That's deep, Bobby. Very deep. Almost philosophical. Elvis was philosophical you know. Maybe I misjudged you. For a while it seemed like you weren't serious about any mission at the Temple."

"You mean when I tried to get some new songs in the service, or when I'd fuck up the music on purpose?"

"Ah yes. Today, though, I've seen a different side of you. Now, I'll ask you a question. Can anybody really be like Jesus?"

Bobby shrugged. Who would want to? he thought.

"See, when I was preaching, even before I got the call to found the Temple, I had this empty feeling. I could speak the words of Jesus, and maybe even heal some old lady of arthritis. But there was no way I could be Jesus. Then, back in '77, I was driving a truck for Coca-Cola. Preaching on the side. There really ain't that many preachers that make a living at it. Unless you hit it big, like Oral Roberts. Anyhow, I was loading crates on my truck, and it was that hot, hot August day. That's when a buddy of mine ran out on the loading dock and gave me the news. It had just come over the radio."

Virgil paused, his eyes resting on a point in the far distance. His voice was thick, husky. Just like at the Temple, Bobby thought.

"I heard of his death," Virgil finally said.

"The King's?"

"That's right. I heard about it, and a feeling went all over me. I had always loved Elvis. If he weren't dead, he'd only be a few years older than me. So I just left my truck sitting there, crying the whole time. The streets was full of crying people. Got right in my car, didn't even take off my Coca-Cola uniform, and drove straight to Memphis. To Graceland. I don't even remember driving. Didn't sleep. Didn't eat. Didn't need to. Prayed and cried the whole way. Thousands of other people was doing the same."

"The lines on Elvis Presley Boulevard was five miles long."

"I see you been studying hard. Good. And I waited in the dark of the night. In the heat. Memphis's got awful heat. And I was one of the lucky ones.''

"Lucky?" This is the best sermon old Virgil's ever preached, Bobby thought.

"I seen his grave. Passed right by it. Only a couple of years after I had seen him. In the living flesh. I got an award as the best route salesman for Coke and they gave me a trip to Las Vegas. I'll never forget it . . ."

"So you seen the grave?" Bobby did not want to hear about Las Vegas. The other part, the grave and Graceland and Virgil's journey, were what mattered.

"Yeah. I cried some more. It was the most beautiful grave that ever was. Right next to Gladys. His momma. He loved his momma mighty hard. And I cried some more, fell down crying. Somebody helped me up. Patted me on the back. Told me it would be okay. People was good to each other there at Graceland. Then I got back in my car and started back to Gastonia. And while I was driving, a feeling started to come over me. He had *entered* me. I knew it right off. And I was meant to carry on his work.''

"Elvis was in you?"

Bobby tried to imagine Elvis entering Virgil's body.

"Only a little of him. He's in the hearts and minds of others. I accept this. I got to admit I ain't the only one. What you do with the spirit is what matters, though. That's what's important. And you only need a little bit . . ."

Virgil picked up the scissors and went back to work, still talking as he cut and dyed Bobby's hair. He described how Elvis and Jesus were together within him; how Elvis spoke to him in the night and told him to go to hairdresser's school. How Jesus ordered him to pull off Highway 74 one afternoon in front of the shut-down drive-in restaurant that became the Burning Love Temple. How both Jesus and Elvis worked on the souls and minds of the loan officer at the United Carolina Bank and Trust to get the money that he, Virgil, needed to open Sheer Pleasures. How Elvis, through dreams, suggested both the name of the Temple, and then the shop.

"They give me all I want," Virgil said in conclusion, "and I will serve them. Come with me. I'm finished."

He led Bobby to the restroom and pointed toward a full-length mirror.

"How do you like it?" Virgil asked.

For a moment, Bobby could not speak. He was the picture, the twin of the early, wild Elvis.

"Is that what you wanted?"

"It couldn't be no better."

He almost felt a flicker of gratitude for Virgil. The feeling passed quickly. The gratitude was for Elvis alone.

He paid Virgil fifteen dollars and was quickly escorted to the front of the shop. Virgil's earlier nervousness had returned, and Bobby sensed he was to get out as quickly as possible. That blonde, he thought.

The silver-blonde was eating a McDonald's Quarter-Pounder and reading *People* magazine as Virgil hurried Bobby to the door.

"See you for a trim in a couple of weeks. Glad you came by. Be sure to use a good hair-spray . . ."

Virgil opened the door, but Bobby hung back.

"I'll be there tomorrow. It'll be a great wedding," Bobby said.

"Wedding? You getting married?" the silver-blonde said to Bobby. "That's nice. That a special haircut for your wedding?"

"Not me," Bobby said. "Virgil here. Ain't he told you? Gonna marry my momma. Laverne Snipes. Laverne Snipes Joy day after tomorrow. Come on down to the Burning Love Temple. Wednesday night. We gonna celebrate. Right, Virgil?"

Virgil opened his mouth, but the words would not come out. The silver-blonde had taken another bite of Quarter-Pounder. She shifted the half-chewed hamburger from cheek to cheek, like a plug of tobacco, before she started to sputter.

"Married?" she finally managed to say. Her eyes locked on Virgil's smile-rigid face.

"You marrying somebody's *momma*? You son-of-a-bitch! I never thought you'd *marry* her."

Virgil had gone gray beneath his permanent tan.

"I was gonna tell you, Arlene, I swear . . ."

"See you tomorrow, *Dad!*" Bobby said.

Outside, he could hear the high-pitched voice of the silver-blonde rising and falling. As he started the Vega, he heard shattering noises from within Sheer Pleasures. All the way home, he lovingly admired his hair in the rear-view mirror.

"Virgil can cut hair," he said as he turned onto Franklin Boulevard, "even if he is always trying to fuck me up."

They left for York early the next morning. Laverne wanted to be married as soon as the Courthouse opened. She was enthralled by Bobby's hair, and would not stop trying to touch it, until he told her to leave it alone. And then she had been disappointed when Virgil called the night before to tell her that he could not have dinner. He wasn't feeling well, he said. She had worried all evening about him, calling back three or four times. Finally, she was sure that he would be well enough for the wedding. Bobby ignored her and studied a new book. This one described the psychic experiences various people had with the King.

Virgil picked them up in his van. Laverne wore an orange organdy dress, and kept inquiring of Virgil as to whether it, and the Scarlet O'Hara style sun-bonnet, were right for the occasion. Virgil assured her that she was lovely, and she smiled all the way down to South Carolina. Virgil wore his white performance costume and a pair of heavy dark glasses which completely hid his eyes. Bobby sat in the back of the van. Virgil would not look at him, or speak to him.

Laverne could not keep still during the trip. She yammered and twisted and turned in her seat. Love was a word she used frequently that morning. She loved Virgil. She loved Bobby. She loved getting married. She loved the flowers that Virgil had presented to her—an armful of white roses that she kept clutched to her breasts.

A few miles from York, she requested that Virgil pull over so that she could go to the restroom. "All the excitement, I guess," she said. He found a service station, and for a few minutes, Virgil and Bobby were alone in the van. As soon as she went through the restroom door, Virgil spun around, whipping off his glasses. His left eye was swollen and blackened.

"See what you caused, you son-of-a-bitch," he hissed.

Bobby laughed, hard and toneless.

"I believe old Blondie musta done that . . ."

"She quit on me. Right there . . ."

". . . and don't call me a son-of-a-bitch."

". . . I'm gonna fire you."

"Momma wouldn't go for that, would she? On account of us being family. And because I might tell her how you got the shiner."

"You gonna pay for this."

"Okay. Let's get out. You can whip my ass."

Virgil put the glasses back on and stared out through the windshield. Signs, Bobby thought. I'm getting signs. Laverne came out of the restroom, tottering toward the van in her new yellow high heels.

"You gonna get married with them glasses on?" Bobby asked.

"You little . . . I have to."

"What're you gonna tell my momma? Think of a good lie."

Virgil did not answer. He was smiling again, leaning across the seat to open the door for Laverne.

"You could tell her you did it trying to kiss your own ass. Anybody that knows you would believe that."

Virgil's smile vanished and he flashed Bobby a final look of hate, which quickly turned back into a smile as Laverne climbed into the van.

"That's much better," she said. "You boys have a nice chat?" Bobby grinned and Virgil started the engine.

The ceremony, performed by the Clerk of Court, lasted less than five minutes. Virgil tried to keep his glasses on during the kiss that followed, but Laverne jerked them off, babbling about how she had to gaze into his baby-blue eyes. He yelped in pain, and Laverne shrieked when she saw what the silver-blonde had done. The Clerk asked them to leave if they were going to carry on in such a fashion. On the Courthouse steps, Virgil managed to calm her down and, Bobby thought, came up with a pretty good lie about his eye; he said that he had injured himself practicing a new move for his stage routine. Laverne kissed him then, and held him close, while Bobby snapped photos with Virgil's Instamatic.

They drove back to Gastonia, Virgil still not speaking to Bobby, Laverne crying and smiling, to have wedding brunch at Shoney's breakfast bar. Laverne had a sentimental attachment not only to the restaurant, but to the whole of the Eastridge Shopping Mall. She described to Bobby how Virgil took her there when they were dating, and how he told her he loved her over the seafood buffet. Virgil seemed to loosen up a little after a couple of plates of bacon, eggs, grits, and pancakes. He even glanced at Bobby a couple of times, and when the meal was over, he offered to take Laverne shopping. She agreed to go, but said that there was something that Bobby should know first.

"Son," she began, "now that me and Virgil are man and wife, we're going be living together . . ."

Bobby, who had been thinking about signs and all that was to come, whatever it might be, suddenly realized that she was speaking to him.

". . . and I'm going to move into Virgil's condo on Chester

Street. I expect I'll have my things out by next weekend. Of course I'll leave the La-Z-Boy—it reminds me too much of Raymond—and a few other things . . ."

"The house is going on the market," Virgil said pointedly, with satisfaction, to Bobby. "And we just don't have enough room for you in the condo. Anyhow, we can get thirty-five, forty thousand for Laverne's place at least."

"And you can stay there until it's sold," Laverne said quickly. "The real estate agent said that it might take a little while. Maybe a month or so. Now we'd love to have you come visit, but it's just like Virgil said. The condo only has one bedroom . . . do you understand?"

Bobby nodded and lit a cigarette. A month or so, he thought. A lot can happen in a month. Laverne kept on talking. She sounded relieved now.

"I hope you don't feel like we're trying to get rid of you. You'll still have the salary from the Temple . . ."

"Don't expect no raise though," Virgil said. "Times is hard."

"I'll be fine," Bobby said.

"That's wonderful," Laverne said. "I don't want you to think I'm just leaving you."

"One thing."

"What's that, son?"

"Leave me your Elvis books. And the T.V. and VCR and tapes until the place gets sold."

"Of course. And the refrigerator and stove, too. And I'll bring you donuts and coffee every day from the store. I think you're taking all of this real well."

"Don't worry about me."

She smiled and patted his hands. Virgil slowly chewed a mouthful of pancake and eggs.

At the Wednesday night rehearsal, Virgil, still wearing the heavy dark glasses, told the band about his marriage and the celebration. They congratulated him, although they showed more interest in Bobby's hair. Dean and Doyle asked Virgil if he would give them haircuts like Bobby's. Virgil told them that he would—at half price. Tommy did not ask for a haircut. As the band tuned up, he turned to Bobby and slowly shook his head.

"You ain't going Elvis on me are you?" Tommy asked.
"What if I did?"
"Elvis. Just think about it."
"I have."

Before Tommy could respond, Virgil declared that it was time for rehearsal to start.

At the beginning, the service was like all the others at the Temple. There was the usual dancing, and Virgil labored through a half dozen songs. After the collection was taken, however, Virgil dispensed with the sermon, and performed the wedding song, which was entitled "The Sacred Institution". It was a slow, turgid ballad, that described how kings need love, and how love, especially married love, was sacred to both Elvis and Jesus. Puzzled, the women barely moved to the music. After eight verses, Virgil finished the song, his head hung low, one leg thrust forward, his arms extended as if to embrace the congregation. Slowly, he raised his head.

"Laverne," he softly called, "come to the altar."

Laverne mounted the stage. She still wore her wedding outfit, and Bobby suspected that she might not have taken it off since the ceremony. Virgil took her hand in his.

"My wife," he said. "My bride. The First Lady of the Burning Love Temple!"

The band played "Love Me Tender" while Virgil and Laverne embraced and kissed. Then Virgil faced the congregation.

"We were married yesterday but I wanted all of you to find out as one. And, later, the caterers—Carolina Country Barbecue—will be here to ensure that we enjoy the finest wedding feast available."

No one moved or spoke. Virgil and Laverne remained rooted on the stage, their hands locked together, holding their smiles, awaiting congratulations. The silence turned thick. Virgil swallowed deeply.

"Me and Laverne want you to understand that the Temple will be the same as ever. We gonna be one with Jesus and Elvis. Together we can . . ."

"How come you married *her*!" April shouted. "I don't even see how come you messed with her like you done!"

She stood in the middle of the congregation. Her question filled up the whole temple. Virgil spoke rapidly, as if he could change their minds if he only produced enough words.

"We're in love. Love. And nobody messed with anybody else. That's unkind. We want love in this Temple. And kindness, too. When you feel love for another, you show it. And marriage is sacred. Like the wedding song says. Think about the words I give to you a minute ago. Wouldn't Elvis approve of them words? And Elvis believed in marriage! He married Priscilla, even if she eventually proved to be unworthy. We've . . ."

"We shoulda been told sooner!" a woman in a green pants suit yelled.

Many other members of the congregation nodded in agreement. Virgil raised his arms in supplication, and Laverne pressed herself against him, her mouth open in fury and astonishment.

"Ladies, please. It ain't Christian to say these things. And besides, I've gone to a lot of trouble for this service. The barbecue, the special song. I wanted all of you to be a part of this happy, joyous occasion. And so does Laverne. Ain't that right, honey?"

Before Laverne could reply, April shouted again.

"How come you married *her*!"

"Who should he marry?" Laverne screamed. "You? You bald-headed hog!"

April barrelled toward the stage, plowing through the women, who parted and gave way before her. Sheri and a woman in a gold tube-top grabbed for her arms, but held her for only a moment, as she surged forward, knocking both women into the falling, clattering chairs. She reached the edge of the stage, her face twisted into a hard, white fist, her breath coming in wild rasps.

"You done gone back on Elvis! You done ruined this Temple!"

She reached for Laverne's legs, but Laverne was too quick. She hopped backwards, knocking over a mike stand, sending a high electronic whine screaming from the P.A. system. April was halfway on the stage when Larry, Dean and Doyle tackled her and hurled her back, grunting and cursing, to the floor. With great effort and force, they managed to hold her down as Virgil, his priestly demeanor restored, went to her. She cursed and bucked, her eyes black with rage, her wig wadded beneath her bulk.

Virgil began to pray.

"Heal this woman. Drive out the demon of jealousy. Replace it with the love and power of Elvis, of Jesus . . ."

After a few minutes, as the congregation stood in silence and confusion, April's wiggling and cursing began to subside.

"You can let me up," she said in an even, reasonable voice.

Virgil nodded to the boys. They released her and backed away a healthy distance as she got to her feet and re-arranged her wig. She raised her eyes to Virgil, who had prudently resumed his place on stage. Her voice was a deep snarl.

"Heal me! You marry Laverne Snipes and you say you gonna heal me. You the one that needs healing!"

She took a step toward Virgil, who cringed and drew back. Then she turned and rumbled out of the Temple, picking up a three-layer chocolate cake on the way. Sheri followed close behind her. Neither woman looked back. Virgil, his voice full of confidence again, stepped to the mike.

"Those who want to go with April and Sheri are free to follow.

There ain't no hate in my heart for them. And you can tell them that they can come back any time. As long as they don't try to hurt me or my wife."

No one moved. There were mutterings, however; indistinct and low. The women no longer looked toward the stage either. Their eyes were downcast, their expressions furtive. Bobby studied them with the same energy he applied to the Elvis books. I'm learning some more good things, he thought.

"Well," Virgil said amicably, "now that all that's settled, we can get on with the festivities. The barbecue will be here soon, and we'll have us a real old-time get-together. Like Elvis would've enjoyed. Just like Jesus had at the wedding feast at Canna. Ain't that right?"

No one answered.

"That's right, darling," Laverne finally said.

Virgil turned to Dean.

"Play something. A fast one."

Dean, like the women, seemed frozen.

"A number, Dean! Come on!"

"What do you want?"

"Viva Las Vegas," Bobby said.

"That's fine. And rock out," Virgil said.

Dean hit the opening chords and the band chugged sluggishly into the song. Virgil sang, slightly off-key, as the women shuffled listlessly around the floor.

6

Wearing only the black leather jacket he had bought at Newburg's Mr. High Style, Bobby stood in front of the full length mirror. Outside, the afternoon was dark, wet and cold. The shadows fell across his face and crotch as he twisted from side to side, trying to catch the right look, to see if he was where he was supposed to be.

"Soon," he said to the mirror. His words echoed slightly in the nearly empty house. He turned from the mirror and glided from room to furnitureless room. The floors were littered with the books and tabloids. He had soaked all of it up, and was close to perfecting it, to reaching the place where he was always meant to be.

He stood by the living room window, staring at nothing through the sheets of gray, autumn rain. He did not care if anyone saw him there, nearly naked. He half hoped that he would be seen. That everyone, everywhere, would see and understand. This idea had come to him after the wedding celebration. The Temple had settled into only a semblance of what it had once been. There was still music, dancing, tithing and eating; the feeling had changed, however. It was as if the power had gone out of the women. They no longer flocked around Virgil as they once did, and the contributions to the food table had dwindled.

Bobby began to mingle with them after the service, and they touched him as they had once touched Virgil. Almost all of them, at one time or another, complimented him on his haircut, caressing it with their fingers. He could no longer go to Virgil for trims or fresh rinses of black dye. The styling salon at Eastridge Mall did just as good a job, however. And even after the other members of the band, except for Tommy, had Virgil work on their hair, the women only wanted Bobby. "Like Young Elvis," a woman in the prom dress said. Her name was Mildred, and she had five grandchildren and a husband retired from the mill. "You ain't nothing like my old man," she said, hugging him, as the other women waited their turn.

He was aware of how carefully Virgil observed him when he was with the women. Several times he caught Virgil watching as the women cooed and rubbed. He would smile and Virgil would return to the food.

He turned from the window and sat down in the La-Z-Boy. The naugahyde was cold on his bare legs, but he hardly noticed. Laverne had left a note a couple of days earlier that stated that the house had been sold; a young married couple, it said. Their first home. She had come by the next day and wanted to know if Bobby had any idea as to where he would live. He replied that he hadn't thought about it, but that he could stay most anywhere. She said that she hoped he would find a nice place and that she would leave some donuts and cigarettes for him when she got off work. But she never did.

The naugahyde gradually warmed up, and he reached for the Harmony Rocket, which was propped against the chair. He ran his fingers over the strings once, then put it down. He had not played with Tommy for a long time, and it was rare that he picked up the guitar when he was not on the job at the Temple. Tommy had asked him to come over a couple of times, but Bobby always found a reason to refuse. Then Tommy asked him if he wanted to be like Elvis, or like Virgil, and Bobby told him to get fucked. All of that was in the past, though. All of those people and things that had refused to understand, or had blocked him up, receded from him. He preferred to think about what was to come.

First, there was the pistol. He had paid Larry forty dollars for the .22, which meant that he would have to skip another car payment. He was already two payments behind, and the man at the Tote-the-Note Car Lot had sent him a notice. The .22 came first. It was crucial to all that would follow. And Tote-the-Note could have the Vega if they could find it. He kept it hidden in a vacant lot three blocks from the house.

Larry told him that the .22 would shoot straight up to fifteen feet. After that the bullets went wherever they wanted. The T.V. sets had been next. He had picked two of them up for ten dollars each at a used appliance store. They were heavy, old models, and Bobby fantasized that they might even have been in use when Elvis first became known to all creation; that they had once held his live, moaning image. Elvis would approve of what was to be, while Jesus would not. Of this he was sure. And it did not matter. No matter what Virgil said, no matter what was done in the Temple, Jesus was the rival of Elvis. And he was Bobby Snipes' rival too. Bobby laughed. Virgil thought people could not tell where Jesus ended and Elvis began. That was wrong. All wrong.

The rain came down harder. Bobby pushed the tape into the VCR and Elvis appeared dressed in a yachting cap, ascot and blue blazer. Bobby had seen the tape, and all of the others in Laverne's collection, over and over. She would come to claim them on Sunday, the day before Bobby was supposed to vacate the house for the new owners. He had no place to go, but that was unimportant. By Sunday morning, all would be as he wanted.

* * *

On Saturday night he slipped into the Temple and hid the two T.V. sets in the meat locker. Getting into the Temple was easy. After the Wednesday night service, he had flipped the lock on the back door as Virgil and Laverne were leaving.

Slowly, he lugged the big, boxy sets across the floor, sweating in the cold. The night was clear and moonlight washed over the Temple. Inside, however, he stumbled in the darkness, smashing his shins and arms against the sets. Despite the rising bruises, he felt no pain. He left the back door unlocked. He wanted to be there in the morning before anyone else arrived.

He returned to Modena Street and laid out his clothes for the next day. There was the leather jacket, of course; and the second-hand zip-up boots that he had stolen from the Piedmont Shoe Shop. The jeans were faded and so tight that it almost hurt to wear them. He would not need a shirt, no matter how cold it might be in the morning. He wanted them to see as much of him as possible, and had even considered appearing only in the jacket and boots. He had decided not to—for the time being.

After he laid out his wardrobe, he walked up to the Exxon Station on Franklin and phoned April and Sheri. The phone rang for a long time before April answered.

"Come to the Temple," he said.

There was a sharp intake of air on the other end of the line. "Who is this?"

"Bobby. Be there tomorrow. I need you. Sheri, too."

"I ain't going back. Virgil and your momma ruined . . ."

"Come to the Temple."

The line was silent for a moment.

"What's gonna happen?"

"Come and see. Something you been waiting for."

"I . . . I'll be there. We'll be there."

"Good. And act real quiet and meek at first."

"I ain't kissing nobody's ass, if that's what you want."

"You don't need to. That ain't gonna be part of it."

"Part of it?"

"Yeah. You won't see, if you don't come."

"I'll wear my best wig. And you better not be telling no lies."

He hung up and went to bed. He slept easily, deep and dreamless.

The Temple door swung open. He arrived an hour before the others. The room was cold and musty, so he turned on the space heaters and the lights. As he paced the length of the stage, his mind nearly boiled over; the purity of it all burned and bubbled. He wished that the stage was higher, a celestial platform.

The only sound in the Temple came from the taps on his high-heeled, zip up boots as he clattered back and forth in a hard metallic radiance. He paused before the mike stand and hurled himself in a spinning, three-hundred-sixty degree leap. He came down on one knee—laughing.

He was still on the stage when Doyle, Dean and Larry arrived. When they saw Bobby, they stopped dead.

"Damn, you . . . you look like . . . ," Larry stuttered.

"That's right." Bobby said.

"Virgil might not go for this," Dean said.

"That's right, too," Bobby said.

He executed another three-hundred-sixty degree spin, leaping from the stage, landing halfway across the dance floor and popping to his feet. The others drew back.

"I want you boys to help me," Bobby said.

"With what?" Doyle asked softly.

"You'll see. I'll give you the sign. And I guarantee that it'll be something real special."

Larry, Doyle and Dean slowly nodded.

A few minutes later Tommy showed up, yawning as he shuffled into the Temple. Like the others, he came to a dead stop when he saw Bobby. He was about to speak when Virgil and Laverne arrived. Laverne pretended not to notice Bobby's new self and fussed with the refreshment table. Slowly, Virgil approached him, sizing Bobby up as he came. Bobby waited for him in an arrogant slouch, his lip curled.

"Well," Virgil said. "That's some get-up."

"Elvis would like it. It is Elvis."

"A kind of Elvis. Not the solid, successful King. But I like it, even if it ain't consistent with the ways of the Burning Love Temple. Where's your leisure suit?"

"Cleaners. It stinks too much."

The suit was in a wad behind the T.V. sets in the meat locker.

"I don't understand . . ." Virgil began.

"They do smell right strong," Dean said, his eyes on Bobby.

"You been promising to get them cleaned for three months," Doyle said.

"I have. You're right. Laverne."

"Yes, honey?"

She did not look up from the table, where she was busy arranging a platter of eclairs and cream puffs.

"Make sure them suits is cleaned before Wednesday. We don't need a smelly band, do we?"

He laughed, but no one laughed with him.

They ran through the rehearsal, and Virgil was still a bit wary. He turned and regarded Bobby from time to time. Laverne, seated on the first row, watched him, too, her usual Temple-smile gone. Bobby said nothing, obediently playing along with the band. Virgil introduced a new song, one about Jesus and Elvis driving into Gastonia in a pink Cadillac. He said he had been inspired because he had just purchased such a car; a 1956 Coupe de Ville in mint condition. Laverne seemed to forget about Bobby when the car was mentioned. It was beautiful, she said, and a convertible, too. She had always wanted to ride in a Cadillac convertible. When the rehearsal ended, Virgil, as usual, disappeared into his dressing room, Laverne following him.

Bobby slipped out back and lit a cigarette. He shivered a little in the cold, and with the knowledge of what he would do. He was halfway through the cigarette when Tommy joined him.

"You gonna do something," Tommy said. It was the first time he had spoken to Bobby in a couple of weeks.

"Could be."

He lit another cigarette. He was covered with goose bumps.

"Could be's ass! That get-up you got on. Worse than Billy Idol. Or Elvis."

"Better, not worse."

"What ya gonna do?"

"You'll see."

They could hear the cars arriving out front. Dean peered around the back door.

"Come on. It's time," Dean said.

Bobby flipped the cigarette away and hurried inside.

About halfway through the service, after the song about the pink Cadillac, and while Virgil and Laverne passed among the congregation with the collection buckets, Bobby twisted the strings on his Red Harmony Rocket and ignited a blistering, howling version of "Jailhouse Rock". As he drew the chords out, Dean and Doyle joined him. Then Tommy came in on the second verse.

When the band started, Virgil had been blessing a mild, expectant April and Sheri on their return to the fold. He stood as if rooted to the floor, Laverne beside him, their faces tight with shock and anger. His bucket fell to the floor, the bills fluttering downward and coins jangling and rolling beneath the chairs.

The women danced, shouting out their longing. In tight formation, they shoved against the stage, chanting the names of Elvis, Jesus and Bobby Snipes. In their rush, Virgil had been knocked backwards by April's bull-like charge. She danced at Bobby's feet, moving in several directions at once. The wind had been knocked from Virgil, and it took him a couple of minutes, with the help of a chattering, weeping Laverne, to raise himself from the floor.

As "Jailhouse Rock" ended, Bobby immediately ripped into "The Plague". The first song was to show the living power of Elvis; the second illustrated that the power lived through Bobby Snipes, and no one else. It was as he had envisioned it, as it should be. He glowed with the multiple visions that rushed to him: the women; Virgil's mouth wide-open in protest; his words obliterated by the music; Bobby's image from the mirror holding dominion over all.

"The Plague" ground to a halt, and Bobby moved to the edge of the stage, his legs wide, the sweat flowing down his face and chest, the Harmony Rocket held loosely by the neck. Virgil and Laverne tried to force their way to the stage, but the women remained in their solid phalanx. Bobby thrust an arm forward, his finger aimed directly at Virgil.

"Your time is passed!" he shouted.

"I . . ."

"You! You forgot who Elvis was! And I'm here to get the Burning Love Temple back where it's supposed to be! I know Elvis! I'm with him! You mighta been with him once, but you ain't no more!"

"I'm the pastor here!" Virgil cried. "I made this Church!"

"Don't do this, son. Don't . . ." Laverne wheezed.

"I'm doing it!" Bobby snarled. "Boys, they's two T.V. sets in the meat locker. Bring 'em out."

Larry, Doyle and Dean, following Bobby's commands, quickly placed the sets along the wall next to Virgil's dressing room. The women whispered excitedly, like children at a surprise party. Larry plugged the sets in.

"Find me a pair of preachers!" Bobby shouted.

Larry adjusted the flickering, ancient sets until both revealed an evangelist in a white suit describing the end of the world.

Bobby told Larry to turn the sound low, and ordered the band members to pick up their instruments.

"What is this?" Virgil brayed, his words directed toward the women. "Is this what you want? A T.V. show where you could have the power of love and truth?"

Bobby's snake-like arm shot forward once more, and Virgil cringed as the finger found him.

"You're old! I understand the *wild*, young Elvis. He came out of nowhere, a poor boy. With nothing. Nobody ever heard before what he had to say, and there was them that tried to shut him up. Ed Sullivan, saying that Elvis couldn't shake it up. Scheming against him. All that schemed, all that doubted was turned to nothing."

"Who loves you?" Virgil begged. "What wants the best for you? Is it Bobby? I made him. Lifted him out of the gutter. Helped save him from prison. You know he's been in prison? And I gave him a job. I married his momma . . ."

"And you shouldn't have done it," Mildred said. The women made sounds of agreement.

"Wait!" Bobby bellowed into the mike. His voice froze them all.

"There's something you need to see. It's something Elvis used to do. He didn't like lies. He didn't want trash. When a thing offended him, he got rid of it."

Bobby jerked the .22 from the back waistband of his jeans, where it had been hidden by the leather jacket. When the gun was visible, the women emitted an ecstatic, pleased "Ahhh". He leaped from the stage and strode toward the television sets. Virgil and Laverne said nothing. The .22 had shut them up.

Bobby had read about Elvis and guns; how the King owned a large private arsenal; how, in addition to presenting complete strangers with Cadillacs and motorcycles, he often gave away expensive hunting rifles and custom-built hand guns. Most importantly, however, he had read of how Elvis blew out T.V. screens when he did not approve of a particular show. This act had intrigued Bobby more than anything else he had learned in his studies; so final, so extravagant.

The old sets popped and labored. The evangelist's face was divided by an enormous, white-toothed smile, much like Virgil's when he preached and asked for money. The congregation, the band, Virgil and Laverne all waited for the next gesture. Bobby turned and faced them.

"When you got something that ain't no good, YOU GET RID OF IT!"

He whirled toward the sets. He was about three feet away when he fired, shattering the screens and the evangelist with a single shot each, the glass from the picture tubes cascading about him like a shower of silver. Blue smoke, produced by the bullets and the sizzling innards of the sets, filled the Temple. Bobby stuck the .22 back in his pants, bounded onto the stage, and grabbed the mike.

"We're getting rid of things today! No more Reverend Virgil Joy! No more of my old momma! No more Jesus! From now on you got the real Elvis. And YOU GOT ME!"

Spontaneously the band churned out nameless, industrial-strength rock and roll. The women mounted the stage, pawing, kissing, and rubbing Bobby; their heat and hands made him drunk.

"BOBBY!" they called. "BOBBY!"

7

He moved into the Temple that afternoon. April and Sheri had loaded his few possessions into the pick-up while he examined himself in the bathroom mirror, which he tore from the wall and took with him. It had seemed natural that the women should work while he preened and glared. April's truculence had been replaced by submissive diffidence, at least when she addressed Bobby. She kept her eyes downcast, as if she were awaiting another gesture as divine as the exploding television sets.

The sets remained part of the service, although Bobby soon realized that if he shot screens every Wednesday night and Sunday morning, the gesture would grow stale, and its power would diminish. Virgil had never understood this, and neither had Elvis. It would not happen to him. He made the event unexpected, a special dispensation for the faith exhibited by his people. They waited for it, yearning. On occasion, he would allow as long as two weeks to pass before he brought forth the .22. And he had laid in a good supply of T.V. sets in the meat locker. April and

Sheri picked them up from the appliance store on Marietta Street, buying them with money gathered from a special collection.

There were dangers, though. Once a round from the .22 ricocheted off the back wall and passed through the snare drum. The repairs had run to fifty dollars. During a Wednesday night service, Mildred was struck in the heel by a stray shot. She suffered only a bruise, however, and was soon up and dancing. And Bobby found some resistance to a couple of his ideas. When he ordered Sheri to paint over the gold cross behind the stage and to remove the Jesus tapestries, some of the older women protested. He preached his first real sermon then, shouting and glowering, whispering and pleading, proving that Elvis alone was needed, and that Bobby Snipes was needed most of all. He ended that particular service by shooting two extra television sets. The women danced harder than ever that morning, the glass clicking and crunching beneath their feet.

He brought other innovations to the Burning Love Temple. Once, he stripped naked on the stage to prove to his people that he had nothing to hide. He encouraged not only the band members, but the women also to style their hair like his, and to dress like the wild, young Elvis. Soon a dozen of the women sported elaborate pompadours. April even managed to find a special wig that made her resemble the King in the twilight of his career. At other times, he would move into the audience, dancing with them, feeling their love and fear. And in addition to the sweets, he provided several bottles of Old Setter Bourbon and Orange Driver Wine on the tables in the rear of the Temple. With satisfaction, he noticed that he had to replenish his supply for nearly every service.

And new people began to attend the Temple. Doyle and Dean told a couple of their friends about the exploding television sets and the gun. The first to show up was a boy named Jerry. He wore the same spiked haircut once favored by Doyle and Dean, and a torn shirt that bore the slogan "Shit Happens". While his face was blank and his jaw slack, his eyes were watchful and darting. When the service ended, he approached the stage. Bobby saw him coming and waited, bare-chested, his legs spread wide.

"I'm glad you're here," Bobby said. "I been expecting you."

"I ain't never . . ." Jerry began, his face half-averted, mumbling. Then he turned and left.

The next week, Jerry arrived with four more boys. They stood in a motionless knot until Bobby shot the T.V. sets. Then they joined in the dance, grabbing the women, or jerking alone to the music. Eventually, there were more than a dozen boys, along with five or six girls. And they all styled their hair like Bobby's, or the wild, young Elvis.

As the weeks passed, he was a little surprised that he had not heard from Virgil and Laverne. Then the letter came to the Temple:

Dear Son [it began]:

I do not understand what made you do what you did. But you did it. And it destroyed my chances for real happiness and ruined the life of my husband. Ruined. That is right. He does not feel like he can honor the King anymore. He says that he has put away his costumes for good. For good. He sits in the living room and he does not talk for hours. He does not eat like he used to and has lost weight. A thing that has made me worry about his health which has been very good until now. He hardly goes into work and Beatrice, one of his beauty operators, quit on him after they had a fight which was her fault Virgil says. And he says he might cut his own hair which is one of the most handsomest things about him. I cry when I think of this. When he does talk he does not have anything good to say about you, a person that he helped so much. And to think of what you did to the memory of Elvis Presley, not to mention Jesus Christ, makes me sick to my stomach. Like my husband I can't eat and me and Virgil will never go back to Shoney's restaurant because you ruined that for us, too. I *never* thought that I would say this. I am sorry they let you out of prison in S.C. which is something any mother would not want to think about her son and you are a whole lot more like your daddy Raymond than you let on to people. But there is no way you can fix the bad things you have done because my husband Virgil does not even want to come back to the Burning Love Temple and you took my Elvis books and you can keep them because Elvis only makes us sad now. I want my T.V. and VCR and tapes back because there is no way I can stand you having them. Think about all this.

Your mother,
Laverne Snipes Joy

Bobby quickly read the letter and then threw it away. He was glad that Laverne had written it, however. It proved that Virgil could never be in competition against him, and that he had driven the old idea of Elvis out of Gastonia, if not the whole world.

One Sunday, a couple of hours after the service had ended and the worshipers had gone home, Bobby stretched out on his mattress, pleasantly fatigued from the music and preaching. He had spoken of Graceland that morning, the palace that the young Elvis had purchased for his mother. Bobby had recently begun to study a booklet that Virgil had bought at Graceland on the tenth anniversary of the King's death. It was a waste of time for someone like Virgil to go to Graceland, Bobby thought. Virgil, and Laverne, too, could never appreciate it, or understand the meaning of the musical gates, the memorial garden, and the special room where Elvis kept the television sets. He told the people that morning that Graceland was a special place, a place of mystery and knowledge. And he believed the words as he said them, as the women and the boys nodded and shouted approval.

His mind was still thick with Graceland when the front door opened and April and Sheri entered. He wished they had not come, for they broke his concentration. He would have to put the power of the Temple and Graceland away for a while.

"Can we sit down?" April softly asked.

He motioned them toward the folding chairs, sat up, and lit a cigarette.

"We seen him yesterday," Sheri said.

"Who? Seen who?"

"Virgil," April said. "Coming out of the Sears store on Franklin. And he was carrying a gun. A long gun, too."

Bobby smiled.

"So he got himself a rifle. Maybe he's gonna shoot some T.V. sets. Like if he acts like me, does what shoulda been done in the first place, he's gonna get back in the Temple."

"We didn't ask him. On account of how he don't have any use for us," April said.

"And I ain't never seen him dressed that way neither," Sheri said.

April leaned forward, her eyes widening.

"Rambo. That's how he was. He had on Army clothes. And his head was shaved. And his face was crazy. And he's got this new church. A girl I work with at the Burger King told me about it. Virgil closed down his hair salon and turned it into a church. Calls it the Cathedral of Combat and Love. Something like that. Don't but four or five people go to it. All of them dressed up in Army suits. That girl I work with, her brother goes there. He's just a pimply little old boy, about sixteen, seventeen. Plays video games all the time. She says he's a gun nut. Don't talk nothing but guns—all the time. Wishes he had gone to Viet Nam. My friend says that all the people at the church is like her brother. Young boys. All of them carry guns. Your momma dresses that way, too. Even got combat boots. And her own gun."

Bobby laughed.

"It ain't nothing to laugh about," April said. "We're worried."

"Don't worry about nothing. That shit don't matter. Virgil's just got another act. He tried to be Elvis. That didn't work. Now he wants to be this Rambo. That won't work either."

"A Rambo church," Sheri said in wonder.

April snorted.

"That can't be no kinda church at all. Who's gonna pray to Rambo? And you can't dance to Rambo neither. My girlfriend says that Virgil talks about rock and roll destroying America and how communists and queers is all the time messing with everything. Her brother told her. He believes it all. Virgil told him that the end of the world is coming."

"So you came here to warn me, huh? What do you think I oughta do?"

Her old power suddenly showed in her stolid face. She usually tried to keep it under control around Bobby, except when she was dancing and praising his name and that of Elvis.

"Go over there! Take them guns! I got a gun of my own. My daddy's old .30/.30 he shot hogs with in the fall. You got the T.V.-shooting gun. And Sheri can take a ball bat."

"Forget it. Virgil ain't important. He's never been nothing but talk . . ."

". . . he weren't close to the real Elvis. Like you are," April said coyly.

"Yeah. And don't tell nobody in the Temple about this. I don't want my people to get scared."

He had taken to referring to the congregation as his people. He liked the sound of it, and the congregation liked it, too.

April turned properly submissive again.

"Yes, Bobby. Only be careful. We don't want you to get hurt. You done become what we always needed. Ain't that right, Sheri?"

Sheri nodded.

"See?" April said. "Is there anything else we can do for you?"

She shifted heavily in her chair, leaning closer, drawn toward the mattress.

"No," Bobby said quickly. "Thanks for telling me, though. You and Sheri go on now. I got some thinking and planning to do."

April sighed deeply.

"Yes, Bobby. Whatever you say. But be careful. We love you so."

"That's right," Sheri added, smiling with manic desire.

After they left, he lolled about on the mattress, trying to concentrate on Graceland. A picture of Virgil, clad in fatigues and a beret, kept coming to him, though.

He heard no more of the Cathedral of Combat and Love and decided that Virgil was too cowardly to come after him. And Graceland stayed on his mind. Finally, after four months, his restlessness became overpowering. He hardly had time to think anymore. Too much was happening. When he was in prison, even when he was learning the guitar, learning about the world from Hootchie-Cootchie, there had been endless, eternity-like hours when he tried to learn how to think, how to fill up the blankness. He groped, always, for a way to translate his urges into the tangible. And it had come to be. There was the Temple, and the money; not much, but more than he had ever seen. He did not really need much for himself. And since he did not want to think about the money, he turned the Temple finances over to April, who was good at keeping up with the rent and the bills. She even took up the collections, making sure that everyone tithed properly.

Then there were his people. Although the congregation had

grown, it did not number more than ninety. In the cramped Temple, however, they seemed a multitude, gathered as others had once done for Hootchie-Cootchie and . . . The First Elvis.

The First Elvis. These words had come to him one night in a dream, blazing like a neon marquee in Las Vegas. He had leaped from his mattress, standing upright before he was awake. If there was a First Elvis, then there must be a second. And the second was meant to carry on what the first had started and been diverted from.

The next Sunday was the first really warm day of spring. In the heat of the Temple, Bobby had stripped off his shirt, and the men had followed his example. All waited for the next song, for his next gesture, as he held the brink of the stage.

"I'm going away," he announced.

"No!" a woman screamed.

"Don't do it!" someone begged.

An insect-like cheeping bounced back and forth from the cinderblock walls. Bobby did not speak. He would wait for the noises to cease. Gradually, the cheeping subsided. They waited now, awash in fear.

"I gotta go away. But I'll be back. And I won't be gone long. Maybe a week. Maybe two. No matter how long it takes, I'll come back to you."

"Where are you going?" April said. Tears ran down her cheeks.

Bobby maintained a long pause before he spoke again. Their faces, twisted with impending loss, pleased him.

"To Graceland," he said quietly.

"GRACELAND! LET *US* GO!"

He waved his hand and they were silent.

"Alone. I gotta go by myself. When I get back, I'm gonna tell you how things are, and how they gonna be."

He seized the guitar and the band followed him into "Baby, Let's Play House". After he blew out the T.V. screens, Jerry and some of his friends collected the fragments of glass. Souvenirs, they called them. They'll be worth a lot someday, Jerry said.

He had never been so far from home. With a wad of money jammed in his jeans, a change of clothes in a paper bag, and a Texaco road map on the seat beside him, he set out for Memphis. He hit I-40 at Asheville and the Vega crawled and lurched toward the state line. As he crossed into Tennessee, he nosed the Vega into a Welcome Center. He was hungry, and the women of the Temple had packed a cardboard box full of cakes, pies and sandwiches for the trip.

He leaned against the car, eating a ham sandwich. He watched as others pulled into the Welcome Center, a low brick building in the middle of a parking lot beneath a mountain. A tour bus disgorged forty elderly people who shuffled slowly toward the center, wondering out loud in New Jersey accents if the restrooms would be clean. A couple, stooped and white-haired, almost identical to each other, passed close to Bobby. The man grumbled that they were still at least ten hours from Memphis, not counting the stopover in Gatlinburg. Bobby compared the couple to Mildred, recalling how fast she danced. She was as old as they were, but she had something to look forward to. She didn't need Gatlinburg, Bobby snorted to himself. Laverne went to Gatlinburg every chance she got. That's where she got all those goddamn cloth pictures, he thought.

He finished the sandwich and a small piece of sweet potato pie before he went in search of the restrooms. When he came out, most of the tourists had drifted off toward the picnic grounds and the center was nearly empty. He drank long and deep from the water fountain. A mother and child, a girl of five or six, stood before a rack of brochures that advertised the sights and wonders of the State of Tennessee. The girl turned as Bobby raised his head from the fountain.

"Mommy! Mommy! Look!"

She glanced away from the brochures, half-smiling, as the child pointed toward Bobby.

"It's him, Mommy! It's Elvis!"

The child pointed from the brochure in her mother's hand, and back to Bobby. Bobby faced them, his hands held loosely at his sides, as if he might spring into song. The mother looked from the brochure, which proclaimed the mysteries of Graceland, then to Bobby."

"I don't believe it . . . Melissa! Don't point at people," she finally managed to say, her gaze never wavering.

Bobby walked over to the rack and picked up three or four copies of the Graceland brochure.

"I'm . . . I'm sorry." the mother said.

"Forget it. Happened to me before," Bobby smiled.

He held up the brochures.

"I always pick up a few of these. For my friends," he said.

"You do look like . . ."

"Elvis? No. The Second Elvis."

"The Second Elvis?"

The child listened quietly, gaping up at Bobby.

"That's right," Bobby said.

The woman did not seem to know what to say.

"Where are you going?" the child asked.

"Home. To Graceland."

He left then, leaving the mother and child, the air singing around him. If it's like this four hundred miles from Memphis, he thought, what's it gonna be like when I get there? He gunned out of the parking lot, trailing blue smoke, heading west.

He drove into the night, twirling the radio dial, impatient for the road to be behind him now. Every few miles the face of the woman at the Welcome Center returned to him. She might tell her friends that she had seen the King. To Bobby, this would be just like those articles he had read in *The Weekly World News* where people claimed they saw Elvis in McDonald's, or at a shopping mall, or that they picked him up hitchhiking in Texas. And, he thought, all of these people *could* be right. But not as right as that woman and her kid.

He tuned in talk shows, expecting to hear what people thought about the King, about how much they loved him and needed him. All he could pick up, however, were callers describing their financial problems to sympathetic voices that prescribed solutions. Other callers complained about taxes, or how the schools were ruining America, and how drugs had gotten out of control. Disappointed, he switched the radio off and drove in silence, trying to eat up time and space, trying to will himself to the gates of Graceland.

Toward midnight, when he was far beyond Knoxville and the mountains, he stopped to sleep in a rest area. He awoke near dawn, and, after washing up, he felt as energetic and clear-headed as if he had not spent the night in a '70 Vega. The last one hundred and fifty miles passed quickly, and before nine he was in Memphis' freeway traffic, searching for the final sign that would guide him to Graceland.

On Elvis Presley Boulevard, he cruised slowly past the souvenir shops and motels until he found a Burger King a few blocks from Graceland. He ordered a large coffee and slowly drank it as he consumed another ham sandwich and a chunk of lemon pound cake. He did not really feel hungry, at least for food, but he knew that he must keep his strength up for what lay ahead. And he could feel it—the presence of Graceland and its former owner all about him, their power working into him. Still chewing, he hurried the Vega into the traffic.

In a while, he found himself behind a tour bus which oozed diesel fumes. As he turned into the parking lot across the street from the mansion, he craned his neck for a glimpse of the gates and the musical notes, but he could not make them out. As he wheeled into a parking space, a guide, a teen-aged girl in a ranger-style uniform, appeared at his window and asked for fifteen dollars for admission. Bobby, taut, absently handed her the money and climbed from the car. Now he could see the trees and the house beyond, its white columns rising above the green lawn.

"That's it, ain't it?" he mumbled, as the guide handed him change from a twenty.

"Indeed it is!" she said brightly. "Graceland. Home of America's greatest entertainer. Memphis' most famous, most talented son!"

"He was born in Mississippi. Tupelo."

The guide did not respond to Bobby's observation. Instead, she directed him toward the crosswalk that led to the mansion's grounds. When he reached the far side of Elvis Presley Boulevard, he found his way blocked by the crowd that had arrived ahead of him. He halted as they surged ahead, laughing and chattering. Bobby had imagined himself arriving alone, a single pilgrim at the end of the quest. And now there were all these people. Far too many to suit him. One group among the crowd caught his eye. They were all, all the men at least, dressed like Elvis; or rather Virgil's version of what Elvis was supposed to be.

Most of them were middle-aged. Their hair was styled in the helmet-like configuration that Elvis had adopted a few years before his death. They wore the same kind of Las Vegas costumes that Virgil once loved, the rhinestones and zircons glowing above their beer bellies. They bore such an awful resemblance to Virgil, that Bobby felt his stomach, now acid-bursting with coffee, meat and sugar, rise into his throat. He dropped further behind the crowd, wishing that it would somehow vanish.

Behind the men in the Elvis costumes, came what Bobby guessed to be their wives. The women, fifteen or twenty of them, maintained a respectful distance, bearing Nikons, Polaroids and camcorders. And they were as heavily costumed as the men. Their hair was piled high, their make-up was heavy, and they wore frilly, little girl dresses. They were models of Priscilla; not the Priscilla of soap operas and commercials, but the original

Priscilla—the version that had been the child-virgin bride of the King. Their petticoats rustled as they passed, and they giggled like high school girls at their first prom.

Bobby watched them as they joined their men at the front door of the mansion. Another group came right behind the women. The Japanese were in the lead; seven or eight couples, even more heavily-laden with photographic equipment than the Priscillas. Three of the males wore clothes and hair which suggested their love of Elvis, although they could not compete with the first crowd. The English followed the Japanese. There were more of them, and they, too, adorned themselves like their idol. They spoke in thick Midlands accents, their hair, both male and female, slick with pomade. And there were more Americans, most of the men in baseball caps that advertised everything from Harley-Davidson motorcycles to the reptile farm in Bay St. Louis, Mississippi. Most of the women seemed to have purchased Elvis T-shirts recently, and they had packed themselves into jeans which accentuated the bulge and curve of their behinds. Many of them carried flowers. Their children raced ahead, scattering over the lawn.

They came, all of them, in a steady procession.

"It's something, isn't it?"

The voice surprised Bobby. The speaker was a short man, a bus driver. He had a flat, midwestern accent. His hair was thining and he combed it straight back from his forehead. His mirrored sunglasses reflected Bobby's image in a distorted, funhouse way.

"I bring them down every year. From Akron," the driver said.

"Who?"

There are so many, Bobby thought. And a lot of them are foreigners.

"That first bunch. They just about race to the house every time they come here. Hell, they're already inside. Call themselves the Upper Ohio Association of the Friends of the King. Last year we showed up at the same time as another crowd dressed like that.

Only the others were from some place in Texas. At first, I thought they might fight. That would be something to see, wouldn't it. All of them guys got up like Elvis fighting? They ended up being friends, though. Decided that they were all friends of Elvis, I guess."

Bobby had not imagined that there was a whole nation, perhaps a whole world of Virgils. The bitterness in his mouth was stronger now.

"They ain't really like He was," Bobby said.

"Don't tell them that. They're real touchy. Don't want any jokes about Elvis either. That drives them nuts."

Wonder what The First Elvis would think about them, Bobby thought. Probably about what I think. Ain't a one of them close to real.

"Took them to New York in '86," the driver said. "You know. When Reagan made a speech at the Statue of Liberty and they shot off all those fireworks. Whoever was running the show wanted two hundred Elvis impersonators there. Don't ask me why. Patriotism, I think. All those guys I brought down here tell me that Elvis was a real patriot. Loved America."

"I didn't know there was this many . . . impersonators," Bobby said.

The driver laughed, a short, nasty bark.

"They don't want to hear that word. Pisses them off."

"They don't know nothing."

"Hey, you sound like you take Elvis pretty seriously yourself. And you resemble him. A good bit. You know that?"

"People've told me."

The driver grinned slyly.

"Like when I was younger. I remember those old movies. *Love Me Tender*. You're not an impersonator are you?"

Bobby did not answer. He marched away from the driver and toward Graceland.

At the main entrance, near the white marble lions and the silver balls, he fell in at the rear of a group that was waiting for the tour to begin. He was glad to see that the impersonators were gone, and relieved to be rid of the driver. It was hard enough as it was, what with the crowds and the Virgils and the foreigners crawling all over the place; a place that was meant for him. A young woman, dressed like a hostess in a fancy restaurant, appeared on the portico, and smiled graciously.

"Welcome to Graceland. I'm sure that all of you know that Graceland was the home of Elvis Presley, the greatest . . ."

She rattled off the physical dimensions of Graceland and told of how Elvis had purchased it for his mother, Gladys. She described the various additions and improvements that were made on the house. Bobby tuned most of her words out. The important thing, he knew, was to get inside. There he could feel what really mattered.

The woman finished her introduction and the crowd followed her up the steps. As Bobby shuffled along with the others, he tried to make himself absorb the spirit that he knew was there. He strained after it, seeking an acknowledgement that a second King might also come. The spirit only flickered dimly as he passed over thick white carpets and down red and black hallways; past rooms stuffed to bursting with furniture, knick-knacks and relics of every sort. As the crowd paused before the dining room, Bobby sourly noted a painted porcelain shepherdess on a gleaming, ornate table. Laverne had had one exactly like it in the kitchen on Modena Street. She had bought it in Gatlinburg when Bobby was twelve. The more he looked around Graceland, the more it reminded him of Laverne, Virgil and the Upper Ohio Friends of the King.

At the foot of the main staircase, the guide said that the upstairs rooms were closed to the public. For Bobby, this was the worst of all the unpleasant surprises he had that morning. Most of all, he had desired the place where The First Elvis had died; if not the bathroom itself, and the toilet where he sat, then at least the master bedroom; the inner chambers of the King's mystery and passion. He imagined sneaking into these rooms, until he noticed the security guard stationed at the foot of the staircase.

The tour reached the recreation room, which boasted six television sets. Elvis had watched all of them at once. The crowd pressed into the room and Bobby worked his way to the front. The guide described how Elvis entertained his friends and visiting celebrities there: Natalie Wood, Nancy Sinatra, Tuesday Weld. The crowd voiced its approval at every name. Mr. Presley, the guide said, had a terrific sense of humor, and his quips during the television watching had cracked up his most famous guests. She finished her speech, and asked if there were any questions. Bobby's hand shot up.

"Is this where he blowed out the T.V. screens?"

The guide emitted a professional laugh.

"That's only one of the many, many rumors that circulated about Mr. Presley. I can assure you that it's untrue, like most other rumors."

"Then he did it upstairs? Where he died?"

The crowd was silent. The tour guide smiled, but her eyes were hard with anger.

"You are misinformed, sir. As with any world famous celebrity, there are untrue, and I might add, unkind, stories about Mr. Presley."

"You're lying now," Bobby said. "If you was Elvis, you'd be able to get rid of anything you didn't like. And he only shot the T.V. when a bad show was on."

The tour guide did not respond. She quickly directed the tourists down a short hallway that led to the memorial garden, and the tombs of Elvis and his parents. Bobby managed to drift away, lingering behind in the recreation room. He imagined The First Elvis, furious at some T.V. preacher, obliterating the offending screen. He was about to turn on one of the television sets when the guide returned. Her tone was controlled and firm, her teeth clenched slightly as she spoke.

"Your group has moved on, sir. I'd like to request that you do the same."

"I ain't in no group. I only want . . ."

"I'll call security. No one, not even you, would like an ugly scene."

"Elvis is in here, somehow," Bobby said, reluctantly drawing away, vainly seeking a sign.

"Whatever you say. Only get outside."

The tombs were thick with flowers, almost covering the flat gray slab above the King. At the head of the grave, a flame burned. Bobby stood at the fence that separated the crowd from the object of its veneration. The grave meant nothing to Bobby. All that mattered was the power, the spirit. And they had been hidden by the tour guides and guards, by all those who thought they were taking care of Elvis.

The people in the memorial garden were properly subdued. They spoke in whispers and with lowered voices, lingering by the tombstones, among the flowers. A tall, pock-marked man with long sideburns videotaped his weeping wife as she knelt in the gravel path. A couple in their fifties, lost and sad, held hands and prayed. Bobby took a last look at the gray slab. As dead as Hootchie-Cootchie, he thought. And there's so much confusion and bullshit that it's gonna be hard for people to know that the best part of him has come back.

Bobby turned away from the memorial garden, and followed another gravel path until he came to a place that would give him a good view of the house. He searched the upper floor, trying to find the right window, the room that held all of the secrets. There, he could have learned more, but the knowledge had been denied to him—for the time being. He guessed that there might be other, more difficult ways to discover it. The tour guide called for her group to form up for the visit to Elvis' fleet of cars and the racquetball court where he played on the night he died. Bobby ignored her orders, and headed toward the parking lot. He had seen what others would permit, and it was not nearly enough. They preferred lies to the truth. He was thinking hard about lies as he crossed Elvis Presley Boulevard. That is when he heard the noise.

Music was part of it, and it came from near the tour buses, where the Upper Ohio Friends of the King had cranked up twelve or fifteen cassette players, all blasting out different Elvis songs, all merging with the traffic into a disorienting fuzz. They had also set up card tables, from which they fed on Kentucky Fried Chicken, mashed potatoes and slaw. The women moved among them, making sure that their paper plates were filled with food.

Bobby unlocked the Vega, the muscle in his jaw twitching slightly. The bus driver waved to him.

"Hey, how come you leaving?"

"I've seen enough."

The bus driver took a bite from a chicken leg and swallowed.

"Most people want to stay all day."

One of the women filled the driver's plastic cup with iced tea.

"Who're you?" she yelled at Bobby above the noise. She was older than Laverne, her face sun-leathered and creased beneath the make-up.

Bobby almost said that he was The Second Elvis, but caught himself before the words came out.

"I ain't nobody," he said.

"You look familiar," the woman said.

"Like *King Creole*," the driver laughed. "Wasn't that an Elvis movie?"

"That's it!" the woman shouted to Bobby. "You're fixed up like Elvis was in *King Creole*. Jack! There's somebody you gotta meet!" She pointed toward Bobby.

One of the largest of the King's Friends detached himself from the crowd and ambled toward Bobby, grinning and nodding in his red jumpsuit, his face framed by a black cowl. Before he could reach the Vega, however, Bobby started the engine and began to back up.

"Wait!" the woman yelled. Jack, who carried a plate that was half-bent with the weight of the food, halted uncertainly. Bobby kept backing up, sliding past the bus, barely missing the stumbling Jack, slowly and deliberately forcing his way through the crowd, scattering the King's friends, ignoring their cries. With deep satisfaction, Bobby crushed several of the cassette players and tipped over a couple of card tables. He turned in an arc, trying to level the whole picnic, as well as any friends of the King who tried to stop him. It was the first, and only, real exhilaration he had experienced since his arrival at Graceland.

He threw the Vega into first gear and made for the gate. In the rearview mirror, he made out the pursuing squads of fake Kings, Jack now in the lead, their capes and cowls fluttering as they huffed after him, ignorant of the fact that they had been defeated by The Second Elvis. He made a quick right out of the gate and was gone.

8

He blundered through the unfamiliar streets, searching for the interstate, his eyes on the rearview mirror. Police cars passed a couple of times, and he tensed, expecting them to turn and follow. After stopping for directions at an Exxon station, he found I-40 and turned east, picking up speed, putting Graceland behind him. After about a hundred miles, he was able to relax and regard with deep satisfaction what he had done to the Upper Ohio Association of the Friends of the King. As he continued to think about the false Kings, the satisfaction gave way to an itchy, impotent anger. They had ruined that which was meant to explain all to him; and there were more of them than he ever imagined, standing bejeweled before him in their polyester costumes. His jaw worked in a slow, furious chewing motion, and his hands were whitely clinched on the steering wheel. He leaned forward, the empty interstate landscape whipping past him, trying to outrun time and space.

* * *

"They got it all wrong."

He pulled hard on the joint and handed it to Tommy. He had driven straight to the shack by the muddy creek, not bothering to stop, except for a short nap near Asheville. The grass hit the back of his neck and eased a little of the anger that had propelled him. Tommy handed him a beer. He popped it and drank deeply.

"What'd you expect?" Tommy said.

Outside, the rain came down hard. Tommy sat across from him in a chair he had found on the creek bank. The chair, like the rest of the house, smelled of river mud. The rain leaked in, a puddle forming in the kitchen. Tommy had been sleeping when Bobby pounded on his door near midnight, and his eyes were swollen behind his glasses.

"Not that. Not the way they have Graceland."

"You might be taking all this too serious."

Bobby took another hit from the joint and glared at Tommy.

"What you mean?"

"We've been over all this before," Tommy said wearily. "All this Elvis stuff. The Temple. It used to be just a joke. Only . . ."

Tommy paused.

"Only what?" Bobby did not want to hear anymore. Tommy had been talking like this for awhile. But he had to talk to someone, and Tommy was the only choice.

"Okay. I'll say it. You've gone too far. Virgil was one thing. He didn't do the women no harm, except for taking their money. And they probably would've given it to somebody about like Virgil anyway. There's a whole crowd with their hands stretched out waiting for money. Preachers, mostly. Politicians. Those kind. But you. You make them crazy, and then you come up with this pilgrimage, or whatever you call it. Mildred said it was like Jesus going to Jerusalem."

"I ain't got a thing to do with Jesus," Bobby said.

"I don't doubt that. And neither do you. Not much, anyhow."

Tommy stared at the floor and sighed.

"I been meaning to say this for a long time. So here it is. Give it up. Give up Elvis. Give up the Temple."

Bobby sputtered, choking on the smoke.

"You're crazy. What am I supposed to give it up for? You know so goddamn much. Tell me."

"The music," Tommy said evenly.

"I guess you forgot about Buddy's Lounge."

"That was one time. There could be others. And even if nobody ever knows your name, and you ain't got a crowd of poor crazy people dancing for you, or waiting for you to shoot T.V. sets, you still got talent. When you used to play, you were one of the best. The music's all that matters. The rest is bullshit. Ego trips. That's all."

"You got any more dope?"

"Right there on the table."

Bobby found another joint, and the smoke enveloped his head.

"What you got to say?" Tommy asked. "I'm trying to tell you the truth, and you ask for another joint."

The dope gripped Bobby, suspending him between anger and euphoria.

"I had a friend," Bobby said. "He was sorta like you. Hell, maybe he was a lot like you. Taught me the guitar and other things. He was the best. Best guitar player ever. He's dead."

"I'm sorry. Real sorry."

Tommy pushed his glasses up on his nose, and leaned toward Bobby, listening.

"I wanted to be him. First he tells me not to. Then he dies. And Elvis. Elvis is gonna live forever."

"Elvis is dead as shit."

Tommy jumped up from the chair and began to pace around the living room. The rain was heavier than ever.

"I'm The Second Elvis!" Bobby declared.

Tommy stopped pacing, and backed halfway across the living

room, up against one of the his big Fender amplifiers. "What're you talking about? You can't be somebody else! Alive or dead . . ."

"It's true," Bobby said, his voice now full of wonder. "He's in me. When I was at Graceland, it was like I was at home. Only the ones that ran it, took it from me. They took it from The First Elvis, too. Stuck him away, got his power . . ."

"You sound like the Reverend Virgil Joy," Tommy said.

Bobby came across the coffee table and stumbled toward Tommy. Tommy held his ground, his hands loose at his sides. His glasses had slipped down to the tip of his nose, and he looked like a plump, fierce ten year old boy. Bobby raised his fist then slowly lowered it.

"Don't ever say that," Bobby whispered.

"You can stomp my ass, but you better think about what I said."

Bobby slumped back on the couch, reaching for his beer.

"I'm right," he said. "I got Elvis in me. The real Elvis."

Tommy sat down and slowly shook his head. Neither spoke for awhile.

"It's supposed to rain all night," Tommy said. "The creek might flood."

"I wasn't gonna whip your ass," Bobby said.

Tommy laughed.

"I've had it whipped before. And I've whipped a few asses myself. It all works out about even, I guess."

A tremendous weariness settled in Bobby. Only the power of Elvis kept him awake. And the fact that he had declared his true identity. The Second Elvis. He opened another beer and regarded Tommy. He's a good boy, he thought, just like I saw when I met him. Only he ain't never gonna get anywhere.

"I gotta tell you another thing," Tommy said. "I'm leaving the band. I'm getting back with my wife. She stopped going to that damned church, and I'm gonna straighten up my act some. We about got things patched up. In fact, I'm moving outta here this weekend. Before it floods. I wanna be with her, and she wants me. And my kid. Hell, he was starting to forget who I am."

"A wife and a kid," Bobby mumbled. "You could still play at the Temple. Bring them with you."

As he spoke the words, Bobby knew that he did not mean them. It would be better if Tommy left, even if he was a good bass player. Bobby did not want to listen to him anymore.

"No. I'm through. I can't take the Temple no more."

"All right, go on. I give you a chance. Lots of people would be glad to play with The Second Elvis. And where you gonna play? You say the music is such a big deal. Where you gonna get a better chance than with me?"

"I can play wherever I want to. And I can find people that's still into the music."

"The *music*." Bobby's contempt was thick, almost a living thing.

"You're through with the music, and where you're going without it scares the hell outta me."

Bobby tilted the beer up. He was drunk and stoned on grass, beer, fatigue, and Elvis. There was no more room for words, especially words he did not want to hear. He listened to the rain. There was nothing left to say.

When he woke up, he was still on the couch, still exhausted, and fully clothed. Tommy had thrown an old musty-smelling quilt over him, but he ached with the morning cold and a hangover. He pulled the quilt around his shoulders and lurched toward the kitchen, calling for Tommy, sloshing through the water that had leaked in during the night. When he received no answer, it occurred to him that Tommy had probably gone to work. He leaned against the stove. The rain gurgled down, harder than ever. Tommy's right, he thought. There will be a flood.

His head felt swollen, distended with a vile liquid, and his mouth was foul-tasting. For a moment he thought he might vomit, but he steadied himself and filled the kitchen sink with cold water. He thrust his head into the sink a dozen times before the shock revived him. Dripping, he hoisted himself onto the greasy counter and lit a cigarette. He coughed hard and spit a wad of phlegm into a paper towel and felt better.

It was as if the water in the sink had removed some of the residue of Graceland and his encounter with Tommy. He recalled that he had told Tommy about Hootchie-Cootchie. He had not thought about Hootchie-Cootchie since before Virgil and Laverne's wedding.

And I ain't about to start thinking about him again, he thought. Waste of my time.

He finished the cigarette and lowered himself from the counter. He took a last look around Tommy's living room. The guitars and amps were arranged on one side of the room, the wires and cables properly connected; as if they were waiting for the music to start, or the creek to rise and wash all of it away.

And it wouldn't make no difference if it did, Bobby thought.

The Temple was as damp and dank as Tommy's place, but he did not care. The main thing was that he was back where he belonged, where no one could dispute what he said, or contradict what he had become. He sat on the mattress and ate from the box of food the women had provided for the pilgrimage. The sandwiches and cakes were soggy with moisture, but he ate them anyway.

When he finished, he turned on the lights and mounted the stage. The silence of the Temple longed to be filled—with him. Yet it was only Thursday, and he could not hold a service immediately. On Sunday, it would come, however. There would be the songs, but, more importantly, there would be his words. He would speak of falseness and of the false people who ran too many things, who turned too many heads.

All that falseness, he thought. The falseness was like a huge sore, an engorged boil or carbuncle, oozing filth, causing pain, blinding. There was a vast lake of falseness, and it threatened to drown the truth and The Second Elvis. He flipped the mike on, and was about to shout down the falseness, when the front door opened.

April appeared in her Burger King outfit and a blonde bouffant wig. She made for the stage, leaving the door open behind her, the rain blowing in. She pulled to a stop right at Bobby's feet.

"I thought you was here. I been riding by every day to see if you had come back. When I seen that Vega, I just had to stop."

He switched the mike off. Although the falseness was still with him, he saw that he must postpone shouting and singing. He sat down on the edge of the stage.

"What is it, honey?" April carefully asked. "Was you gonna sing? I wish you would. How about 'Only the Lonely' or one of your songs. Seems like I ain't heard you sing in so long."

"Don't call me honey. It ain't nothing. I'm tired. That's all."

She pulled a chair close to him and patted his knee.

"I understand. I hear it's a long way to Memphis, even if you wasn't gone as long as we thought you'd be. Everybody's gonna be so glad you're back. It musta been wonderful . . ."

"Wonderful. It weren't exactly wonderful."

"How couldn't it be? You was there wasn't you?"

"I was there. I said I'd go and I did."

"What was it like? Did you feel him? The King?"

"I'm gonna talk about that Sunday."

"Tell *me*! Come on!"

She reached for his knee again, but he avoided her, standing, moving away, lighting a cigarette before she could touch him.

"You'll hear about it. I told you. I got to do some thinking first. Got to get it right in my head."

April pressed her hands between her thighs and vibrated

slightly. Her eyes, big and moist with a thing a little like love, roved over Bobby.

"I missed you awful. So did Sheri. And everybody else. We come down here the other night. A few of us. Even if there wasn't gonna be no service. That boy Jerry brought a boom box, and we danced a little bit and spoke about you and Elvis. It was good, but not like when you're here."

"Yeah," he grunted.

"I told them about how I seen right off that you'd been sent here. They said they felt it, too. I was the first, wasn't I? When you came in with that red guitar . . ."

"Yeah. I remember."

". . . and you came to the trailer. That was real special to me."

Bobby dropped the cigarette butt on the floor and crushed it with his boot.

"You better get on to work. I got some stuff to do."

April's vibrations diminished. She sounded hurt.

"I don't need to be there for a while. I got a couple of things I need to tell you."

"Like what?" he said absently.

"I run into Virgil and your momma the other day. It was in the drive-through. The voice came over the speaker and it sounded familiar, but different, too. It ordered two Whoppers, two orders of fries, and two chocolate shakes. Then this Jeep came to the window and I seen it was them. That Jeep was painted up like it belonged to the Army, and they was wearing Army clothes and dark glasses and beret hats. And you could see the guns, too. One was a machine gun. Pistols. Rifles. And their faces. I wouldn't have recognized them. I swear. Virgil's face especially, on account of how much weight he had lost. His face . . . was like a mask of a skull. Like at Halloween. And your momma's wasn't no better. Just . . . *mean* . . . mean-looking. They scared me, and I don't scare easy. It was lots worse than that other time down at the Sears store. I asked for the money and give them the change, and they watched me real hard the whole time. It was like their eyes was boring into me. After I got their food, they sat there a few minutes. It was lunch time and there was a big line of cars behind them. Finally, Virgil says "Be Careful." Them was his words. And your momma said that you better be careful, too. After that they drove off, and I seen that the Jeep had 'The Cathedral of Combat and Love' painted on the side of it. And I wasn't no good for the rest of the day. Kept thinking about them. I musta messed up five orders during lunch."

"Forget about it," Bobby said.

"But you ain't seen them," April whined.

"I don't have to. Fakes. Did Virgil know what to do with Elvis?"

"Well . . . you said he didn't."

"Said! I showed it! Proved it!"

"That's right. Only them guns . . ."

"What's he gonna do with his guns and his Rambo shit? Tell me."

"My girlfriend at Burger King, the one whose brother goes to Virgil's church? Her brother says that Virgil's been preaching about getting rid of enemies. Dope fiends and abortionists. And you. He used your name. And your momma says the same thing. Don't that scare you none?"

Scare me, he thought. Just more bullshit.

"Well, don't it?" April asked again. "I used to wanna go over there and have it out with them. Not no more. They's something bad wrong with them people. Bad wrong."

"You right. They're fucked up and crazy. But they ain't important. What I seen at Graceland is worse. Lots worse."

"What was it?" April said with alarm. "Tell me, please."

"You gonna have to wait until Sunday. That's when it's gonna be said."

April sighed.

"They's something else."

"Don't tell me nothing about Virgil and Laverne. I'm sick of hearing about them."

April shook her head. She had released her hands and they appeared to be under control.

"This ain't about them. I swear. When we was down here on Sunday, a woman stopped by that we had never seen before. Said she heard about us from one of her contacts. She thought a service would be going on. Didn't know that you'd be gone to Graceland. Turned out she's a reporter from the *Gazette*. Wants to write about the Temple. And about you. She said you oughta call her when you get back. So she can do an interview."

The falseness receded.

"What's her name?" Bobby said quickly.

April reached into the breast pocket of her Burger King uniform and handed Bobby a slip of paper: Valarie Reynolds. *Gazette* Lifestyles. 867-4411. He read the name and the number over several times and rushed for the door.

"Where you going, Bobby?" April said, rising and following.

He did not answer. There was a phone booth at the Hospitality Motel. He splashed through the rain, dodging the traffic on Highway 74.

"And when did you first become interested in Elvis Presley?"

Valarie Reynolds was blonde, blue-eyed, young, and had a voice like the anchorwoman on the six o'clock news. She was the best looking woman that Bobby had seen since he left prison, and that made it even easier to answer the questions, although many of the questions struck him as being stupid.

After he arrived at the receptionist's desk, she had led him to an office, offered him coffee, and told him that she covered religion for her paper. Religion, she said with a perfect smile, is very big in Gastonia, and we try to examine it from as many angles as possible. She told him to relax, and when she spoke, he realized how stiffly he was sitting, how intent he was on making sure that she got the truth of The Second Elvis, the young, wild Elvis just right.

He had never been in a place like the *Gazette*'s offices, and was a little disoriented by the bright lights after the darkness of the Temple, and the grayness of the rain. April had wanted to come with him. He told her to go to work; this pilgrimage would be undertaken alone. Once he settled into the chair across the desk from Valarie Reynolds, he could feel that the interview could mean much more than the trip to Graceland.

She had switched on a tape recorder and produced a pen and pad for note-taking.

"Now that's a good question," he said. "I suspect that in a way I always been interested in Elvis. Being interested in a thing ain't the same as being that thing, now is it?"

Valarie Reynolds mustered a slightly ironic smile.

"Perhaps you would like to say a little more about that idea?"

She had already gotten him to describe the service, especially the blowing out of the T.V. screens. And how the congregation had grown. And how Elvis was important to so many people; the true Elvis, that is. Bobby's ideas about falseness had further congealed as the interview progressed, and he had related the truth about Graceland and those who controlled it. He omitted the part about his encounter with the Upper Ohio Association of the Friends of the King since he was not sure if the interview would be read as far away as Memphis. He described Virgil, too, and how Virgil had perverted the truth of the young, wild Elvis for his own selfish ends. He said that the Burning Love Temple now offered the one, true King; the Elvis who had changed the world, and would change it again. He spoke rapidly, barely aware of the words as they poured forth; the most words that he had ever spoken at one time.

Valarie Reynolds asked him about the music at the Temple. Was he a musician, she asked. He laughed and replied that he played the guitar, although he seldom needed it on stage any more. While the music was important, it was only a part of the mission of the Burning Love Temple. Yes, he said, I sing the songs once performed by Elvis Presley, and that the songs were a way of uniting with the King. She asked how many Kings there were. Two, he said. Two.

"Do you think that you . . . ah . . . are this *other* King?"

He leaned across the desk. She drew back slightly, still smiling.

"What do you think? I done told you about the falseness. If there's falseness, there's got to be truth. And I've found it."

"Then you say you're . . ."

"The Second Elvis. Right."

She did not seem to know what to say for awhile. Bobby smiled at her. She cleared her throat . . .

"Do you feel as if The First Elvis . . ."

"Would want it that way? He's got to. Don't you think so? He wouldn't want it any different, would he?" She concentrated on her note pad, not looking at Bobby, and asked if the congregation at the Temple felt as he did about the second King.

"If they don't now, they will soon," he said.

"I seen it all!" Bobby shouted. "What they let me see. The ones that think they own Elvis Presley!"

He paused. The congregation waited, as quiet as it had ever been. The music was low and ominous. Larry, who had replaced Tommy on the bass, thumped along clumsily. Valarie Reynolds, down at the far end of the stage from Bobby, took notes. The photographer she had brought with her snapped one picture after another, turning from Bobby to the congregation, to the band, and back again.

The Temple was packed. April had done a good job of spreading the word of Bobby's return, and of the crucial, powerful message that he would deliver. He held the mike close to his mouth, nearly kissing it.

"I bet some of you been there. And seen the fakes—worse than Virgil—that ruin what Graceland is supposed to mean. And you might remember how the guides and the rest of them paid fools blocked up the spirit of *The First Elvis*."

He paused once more, allowing them to contemplate the words. He nodded to the band, and the beat became more insistent.

"The First Elvis. You hear that? *I'm the Second!* I came here to get rid of all the lies, to take away the wrong that's done happened to the first King . . ."

He described the pilgrimage, and how he had vanquished the impostors; how he had been denied access to the death chamber of The First Elvis. As they listened, their collective breath quickened, and their beings were suffused with wonder and apprehension.

"We gonna *redeem* all that was good!"

Again, he nodded to the band. He began wailing out "Burning Love":

"Lord A-mighty feel my temperature rising
Higher, Higher, it's burning through to my soul . . . "

For an instant, the congregation was stunned by the words, by Bobby's revelation. Halfway through the first verse, however, they responded in a single motion, and pitched into the dance. The photographer stood on a chair, frantically aiming at all that came into his line of vision. Valarie Reynolds, her hair plastered with sweat to her forehead, gave up on taking notes and directed the photographer from one scene to another, vainly trying to catch it all. Bobby glanced in their direction. He had been acutely aware of them even as he shouted the words of truth. Their presence had propelled him. They'll never get it all, he managed to think.

It's too much. He worked his way to the photographer's end of the stage, making sure that there would be some good pictures of him in action. Then he headed in the opposite direction, where Mildred, Jerry and others that he could not even name, reached upwards toward him, calling out for The Second Elvis. He teased them with smiles, and an out-thrust leg, which they could not quite reach.

April and Sheri had arranged two television sets against the wall next to the kitchen, and tuned them to a grimacing evangelist. As April and Sheri returned to the dance, he ordered the band to stop playing. When the music ceased, he jerked the .22 from his jeans and fired from the stage. The evangelist's face disappeared. The congregation moaned. Bobby had never fired from such a distance, and to have both rounds hit dead center was more than they could ever have hoped for.

"We getting rid of all that old bullshit! We mixing what was once the old truth with the new truth. The Second Elvis is with you! Always!"

The words flamed as never before. He did not know what all of them meant, but he did understand that they throbbed and glowed with power. He dropped the empty, smoking .22 to the stage, and the band, without his orders, played hard. Like his people, he danced, hurling himself back and forth across the stage, howling above the music.

No one knew how long the dancing went on, consumed as they were with The Second Elvis. And no one was aware of the opening of the Temple door. Bobby had just completed one of his leaping, three hundred and sixty degree turns, landing on one knee. As he popped back to his feet, he saw them. Virgil was exactly as April described him: dark glasses, beret, and battle fatigues. There was an addition, however: a twelve gauge pump shotgun held at the ready. And April had not been wrong about Laverne either. She was dressed like Virgil, and her expression less face did not seem capable of ever having wept over the death of The First Elvis in *Flaming Star*. She held an M-16 at her hip, and Bobby saw the muzzle blast before he heard the sound. The first burst caught April, who had been dancing at the back of the crowd, full in the face. April staggered backwards, her feet still dancing, before she went down, taking a number of others with her.

Bobby never saw April fall. He had jumped into the crowd as Virgil raised the pump gun. He landed on his hands and knees, and a dancing foot drove itself into his mouth. In the second before the people closest to the stage became aware of the gunfire, their hands caressed Bobby. A woman kissed him. They tried to raise him to his feet, to tear him apart with love. He pulled away, crawling in a circle, spitting teeth, a red rage churning within. The falseness was in the Temple.

The congregation thrashed back and forth against the walls. Doyle and Larry fought their way through the back door, dragging Dean, who had caught the pump gun round meant for Bobby. Drums, mikes, amplifiers and guitars fell behind them. Wires and cables whipped through the air. Outside, they dropped Dean, his shoulder shredded, his teeth chattering, and ran to the Motel Hospitality to call for help.

Methodically, Virgil and Laverne raked the congregation. Some of the followers of The Second Elvis fought their way into the kitchen and took refuge in the meat locker, crouching among the television sets. Others pounded at the door, begging for refuge. Some escaped out the back, dashing, crawling for the cars; the wounded and the untouched, the gibbering and the silent.

Bobby squeezed himself beneath the stage. He had to lie flat since there were only a few inches of head room. The firing boomed off the walls, deafening him, making the .22 sound like a pop gun. Beneath the gunfire, he heard the wails and shrieks of the congregation. A man in a baseball cap and tank top, one of the newest members of the congregation, fell across Bobby's line of sight, blocking his already narrow view. The man did not move. Bobby crawled, inching his way closer to the point where Virgil had been when the shooting had started. From there, he could see a mike stand, a couple of more bodies, and Virgil's spit-shined combat boots, empty cartridges spread around them. The firing stopped. The fury bubbled, and he sensed that this was his best chance to get at the falseness. With a heave, he shoved himself from beneath the stage, bashing his head, blood running over his ears and neck. He did not feel the concussion. And he was out in the open and on his feet.

Virgil stood calmly on the dance floor, stuffing cartridges into the pump gun. Laverne was in the process of ramming another clip into the M-16, ready to fire again into the ball of wailing dancers jammed against the locker door. Bobby seized the mike stand and Virgil saw him just as he inserted the last round. But not in time to avoid Bobby's rush.

"You . . ." Virgil managed to say.

Bobby smashed the mike stand across Virgil's dark glasses. The minister of the Cathedral of Combat and Love folded to his knees as he dropped the pump gun. Bobby gave him another blow across the top of his head, bending the stand nearly in half. Without a sound, Virgil buried his face in the floor, his knees tucked beneath him.

Laverne was intent upon the dancers when Virgil went down. Someone shouted that The Second Elvis had come to save them, and she came about, firing. Bobby flung the mike stand in her direction, and dove to the floor. The bullets passed over him and struck the wall behind. Silently, she advanced on Bobby, the M-16 on automatic, churning up the concrete of the dance floor, thudding into the already dead and the wounded. She came on slowly and deliberately, Bobby crawling, trying to rise and run, just ahead of the bullets. His mind was a haze, impotent against the falseness.

A round nicked his shoulder as he belly-flopped onto the stage.

The back door was open and waiting, only she was too close. The wooden stage splintered around him. Then the firing stopped. There were shouts and curses and the sounds of things falling. He gained his feet. Automatically, he touched his shoulder. There was no blood, only a long, swelling contusion where he had been grazed.

Jerry and a couple of the other heavy metal boys had tackled Laverne from behind. They flailed away at her with their fists and boots, and were quickly joined by Mildred and several of the women, who spit and clawed and joined in the kicking.

The haze receded slightly, and he ordered Laverne's attackers to stop. Slowly, they backed off, laying on a couple of extra kicks as they went. He told Jerry and Mildred to keep an eye on Virgil, who was still in a heap on the dance floor. The others stayed in a loose circle around Laverne.

Bobby stood over her. Her face was a single, unified bruise. She lay on her back, her eyes aimed toward the ceiling, her arms at her sides, as if she were at attention. For a moment, Bobby thought that she might be dead.

"Momma," he said tonelessly.

"Name, rank and serial number," she whispered. "That's all I got to give. On account of being a prisoner of war."

Her voice was not her own. It was as if she was receiving a transmission from an unimaginable radio station. He picked up the M-16 and leaned it against the edge of the stage. The photographer, a sleeve torn from his jacket, reloaded his camera and resumed shooting. There were many subjects to choose from: the dead, the wounded, the shattered Temple, April's nearly headless corpse, Sheri weeping at its side. Before the photographer turned his attention to these subjects, however, he took half a dozen shots of Bobby.

"Hey, you're a hero," the photographer said, as he finished and turned his attention to the still-rigid Laverne.

"That's right," Mildred said. Her prom dress had been ripped down the front and a long cut traversed her face diagonally.

"The Second Elvis is a real hero—an American hero!"

She embraced Bobby. She smelled of perfume and blood.

He heard sirens in the distance.

April and five others were buried in a single ceremony in the new cemetery off Highway 273. The earth was orange and raw, as the cemetery's owners had not yet planted grass or trees. The only landmark that kept Green Lawn Cemetery from looking like a plowed field was a twelve foot tall statue of Jesus.

Bobby preached a graveside sermon and played a set on Dean's acoustic guitar. Dean would not need it any more. The shot that Virgil had meant for Bobby had paralyzed his arm. Bobby spoke of the truth and was genuinely grieved. He spoke, too, of The Second Elvis, although he frequently used the name of The First Elvis, too. He did not mention Jesus. That was the way April and the rest of them would have wanted it, he said afterwards to the T.V. reporter from Charlotte. He was pleasantly aware of the cameras and the fact that the reporter, like Mildred, referred to him as a hero, the hero of the Burning Love Temple Massacre. He sang "Love Me Tender", "All Shook Up", and "Suspicion" as the mourners wept and hummed along.

He was a little disappointed that the crowd was not larger. Then again, thirty-five members of the congregation were still in the hospital. As the television reporter said repeatedly, it was a miracle that more were not killed. And of those who were injured, only nine were still on the critical list. A boy named Tony, one of Jerry's friends, had been interviewed from his hospital bed. The doctors said that Tony would never walk again. Tony told the cameras that the doctors were wrong. Soon he would be up and dancing at the Burning Love Temple.

Despite the missing teeth, the cuts, and the crease across his back from the M-16, Bobby felt good. He had been interviewed numerous times since the massacre, and he enjoyed the power that came when the interviewers awaited his words or recorded his image. Valarie Reynolds, as it turned out, had gotten a great story for the *Gazette*. She had even been promoted to Feature Editor; and the photographer, a Yankee named Bruce, had a number of his pictures picked up by the wire services. One of Bobby appeared in *USA Today*. It showed him in Mildred's embrace. With his mouth closed, hiding his smashed teeth, he looked more like the young, wild Elvis than ever before.

He did not like everything about the interview, however. A reporter from the *Charlotte Observer* asked what it felt like to be shot at by his own mother. Bobby wanted to ignore the man, who waited with poised pen for an answer, but he told the reporter that it was all Virgil Joy's fault; that Virgil had ruined his momma. He also sensed that the reporters did not want to really hear about The Second Elvis. Every time Bobby began to expound upon his mission and to denounce the falseness, his interviewer changed the subject. All of them, the television reporters, the newspaper people, the man from *USA Today*, only seemed interested in the massacre; even Valarie Reynolds, who had heard about The Second Elvis before the shooting, kept running stories that emphasized the massacre. And she had even gotten a write-up in *Time*, describing how courageous she and Bruce were. Bobby remembered how she wet her jeans and could not speak when the firing ended.

Virgil was still in the hospital, his skull fractured, under twenty-four-hour guard. He would live, the doctors said, and would be able to stand trial when he recovered. And stories about Virgil and Laverne had almost pushed Bobby to the background. Fundamentalist Commandos, the press called them. Bobby scowled as he read about them in the papers. There was almost nothing about how they had tried to destroy The Second Elvis.

While Virgil would be in the hospital for some time, Laverne would remain in the Gaston County Jail for an indefinite period; the court had refused to set bail. "The Rambo Killers" was another term used to describe them. No one had yet called him The Second Elvis, and the television had even called him an impersonator, which made him consider giving up interviews.

Laverne had started to talk, apparently dropping any idea of sticking to her name, rank and serial number. According to the police, she still considered herself a prisoner of war; a war that was to be waged against all non-believers, abortionists, flag-burners, and the followers and leaders of satanic cults, including her son.

On the morning of the massacre, the police said, Virgil and Laverne had opened their church for services. Virgil was to preach on the message in the film *Red Dawn* and afterwards the congregation was to take its usual target practice at a secluded spot on the Catawba River near Mount Holly. They waited for an hour before they realized that no one would be in attendance that morning. The police had interviewed a couple of the members of the Cathedral of Combat and Love and discovered that all of Virgil's followers had stayed home to watch *Patton* on the TBS Sunday Morning Movie.

Unaware of this fact, Virgil declared that Bobby had stolen his people, just as he had done at the Burning Love Temple. He ordered what Laverne referred to as an "overt incursion" into hostile territory. They then cleaned and loaded their weapons, stocked up on ammunition, and drove to the Temple in the church Jeep, singing "The Star Spangled Banner" and "The Ballad of the Green Berets". Laverne told the homicide detectives that Bobby and selected members of the Temple were to be terminated, and that if anyone interfered with the incursion, they, too, would face termination. She added that both she and Virgil considered their plan to be humane, and that it only went wrong when Temple members attempted interdiction. She also said that she considered the plan a partial success. While her son was not terminated, a number of offending Temple members had been "removed".

In Virgil's condo, the police discovered three more M-16's, an Uzi, an AK-47, four high-powered sporting rifles, two shotguns, half a dozen handguns, and forty thousand rounds of ammunition. Laverne stated that the weapons were necessary for religious purposes. The condo had been stripped of all furnishings except for military-style bunks, a field radio, and boxes of canned and dehydrated food. Also discovered were numerous survivalist tracts and manuals; materials on how to construct bombs; pamphlets from the Liberty Lobby; copies of *Soldier of Fortune* magazine; video tapes of all of Sylvester Stallone's films; and a framed photograph of Oliver North. Evidence, the police called it.

The news people hurried away from the cemetery interview, and most of the spectators followed. Sheri lingered by April's grave, and knots of Bobby's people spoke in subdued voices. They came to Bobby, touching him, weeping, but after the interview he did not have anything left to say. They closed in around him, Jerry and Mildred, all of them seeming to want something. He felt as if they were drawing his breath from him.

"We love you, Second Elvis," a woman with jet-black hair said.

"We need you," said a bandaged boy in a Duke University sweatshirt.

They murmured around him. He nodded and patted them on the shoulders. But he had to get away. Slowly, he extricated himself from the congregation of the Burning Love Temple. He packed the guitar into its case and made for the Vega. He had some thinking to do.

There was the trial, of course. The homicide detectives had questioned him twice already, and he was scheduled to meet with the District Attorney the next day. The star witness, the detectives called him, which did not have quite the same ring as hero. They were blank, robotic men, like the ones that had worked him over in Horry County ten years before. And they knew all about his prison stretch, treating it as a kind of a joke. But they had been a little surprised that he was so willing to testify against his own mother. It would not look good, they said. They could not guess that Bobby had decided that during the trial he might be able to fully get across the fact that he was The Second Elvis. He was not sure, however, that the judges and lawyers would allow this. They were as false as Virgil and the owners of Graceland. Then, too, he had to figure out what to do about the Temple. The band was finished. And many of those in the hospital might never come back. All of it seemed a burden, even as the prospect of a nearly empty Temple filled him with bleakness.

"Mr. Snipes?"

Bobby had reached the Vega when he heard his name being called. The speaker was a man of about his own age. He wore an expensive, conservatively cut suit, a subdued tie, and highly polished bluchers, which had picked up a film of dust from the cemetery.

"Mr. Snipes?" the man repeated in a blandly personable tone.

"Yeah. That's me."

Bobby leaned the guitar case against the Vega. He had always been suspicious of men dressed like this one. The man offered his hand and Bobby gingerly shook it.

"I'm Brent Collingwood. With Ayers, Mullin and Ralston in Charlotte."

"You a lawyer?" Bobby knew that he was. He had lawyer all over him.

"I'm an associate with the firm. I've been asked . . ."

"I'm supposed to talk to the D.A. tomorrow. I ain't making no other statements."

The lawyer smiled as blandly as he spoke.

"You don't understand. I'm . . ."

"You Virgil and my momma's lawyer? I've done told the truth

and I ain't changing a word of my story. If you wanna talk to me, you better see the D.A. If I get ordered to talk to you, I will. Understand?''

Collingwood laughed. The condescension was thick.

"Oh, no, no. Let me explain. My firm doesn't even *handle* criminal matters. In fact, we represent Mr. Maurice Short. We take care of all his legal affairs in this area. By the way, I enjoyed your singing. I'm a jazz fan myself, though."

"Maurice Short?"

The lawyer seemed to expect Bobby to know the name.

"You've never heard of him? Excuse me, but I find that hard to believe."

"Well, it's the truth. Why should I have heard of this guy?"

"He's very wealthy. Very important."

Collingwood waited for a response. Bobby placed his hand on the Vega's door. He considered leaving. There was too much bullshit crowding in. Collingwood went on.

"Land mostly. Development. Entertainment. He was one of the original backers of the Hornets . . ."

Bobby had heard of the Hornets. A ball team in Charlotte.

". . . and he's known for his philanthropic endeavors. The Short Foundation? He contributes significantly to colleges and libraries, and . . ."

"What's he want with me?"

Collingwood handed him a card. It bore the name of Maurice Short and an address in Myrtle Beach. Bobby started when he saw the address. The detectives had known all about Myrtle Beach. He flipped the card over. A second address was handwritten on the back; the Marriott Center Hotel in Charlotte. A telephone number was scribbled beneath the name of the hotel.

"A proposition," Collingwood said. "One that you might be very interested in."

"What kind of proposition?"

Bobby stuffed the card into his shirt pocket.

"Business. I can't say because I don't know. He wants to see you. Personally. I can tell you that the proposition will be to your advantage."

"I don't get it."

Collingwood's smile grew blander by the second.

"He'll explain. You should call first. The number on the back of the card. And I suggest you do so as soon as possible."

"Is that right? You suggest. I'm going to have to think about your suggestion."

Collingwood shrugged.

"That's up to you, Mr. Snipes."

"He sent you over here from Charlotte to tell me this?"

"He wanted to make sure that you were notified personally."

"How come he didn't come himself?"

"Why don't you ask him? I've got to go. Have to be in court at three. It's been a pleasure."

Collingwood waved as he drove away in a blue BMW. The card felt heavy in Bobby's pocket. As he started the Vega, the weight increased. He took the card out and read it once more, staring at the words as the engine idled.

Sheri appeared at the window, bobbing up as if in a dream. She still wore the effects of the massacre. She had a black eye, and a number of Band-Aids criss-crossed her face. She limped a little, too. Someone had fallen across her leg when the shooting started.

"I'm gonna miss her bad," Sheri said, leaning in the window, her face inches from Bobby's.

"Who?" Bobby said absently, startled from his contemplation of the card.

"Why April! And the rest that . . . it ain't ever gonna be the same at the Temple. Every time we start to dance, I'm gonna think about her . . ."

"You're right. It won't be the same."

"And I been so lonesome at the trailer. If you ain't too busy tonight, I thought maybe you'd like to come over. We could order Pizza from Domino's and listen to music from The First Elvis, and . . ."

"Not tonight. I gotta take care of business."

He did not recall that The First Elvis and Virgil had often spoken of taking care of business.

"Well, then, tomorrow night . . ."

"I gotta go."

She was still talking as he put the Vega in gear; the most talking he had ever heard from her. She limped back awkwardly as Bobby started for the cemetery gate.

He found a pay phone just over the Mecklenburg County line, on Highway 74, heading for Charlotte. The phone range once, and a kindly voice, a voice rich in all things, said hello.

9

"My business brings me to Charlotte only about five or six times a year, but when I'm here the suite is a real necessity. So I maintain it year round. Of course, I do the same in other cities: Atlanta, Miami, New York. Expensive, but I know you'll agree that we need proper surroundings for our work."

Maurice Short began talking the moment Bobby entered the top-floor suite at the Marriott Center Hotel. The early afternoon sunlight flooded through the open draperies, forcing Bobby to squint. Despite the fact that Bobby had been in the suite for nearly an hour, he had yet to discover why Mr. Short had summoned him. And he had hardly had a chance to speak. The rich voice that he had first heard on the telephone had been operating non-stop since his arrival. It was a curious voice. Most of the time it sounded as if it belonged on television; like that of a soap opera character. Beneath the television polish, however, there was a rough, country accent. Mr. Short sounded as if he were taking a speech course and had not yet completed all of his assignments.

Despite all of the words, he had not said very much. He mentioned the weather, golf, the growth of Charlotte, the local basketball team, and two or three other subjects that Bobby was completely ignorant of, or had no interest in.

Mr. Short leaned back in his chair. He was about sixty, a tall man, heavily tanned, and graying at the temples. He was probably considered handsome when he was younger. Now, his face was puffy, and he possessed a growing waistline. He wore a purple jogging suit and running shoes. Bobby did not know if rich men always did business in such clothing, or if Mr. Short even wanted to see him for business reasons. It was not what Bobby had expected at all. Rich men, men with voices like Mr. Short, were supposed to wear expensive suits and sit behind massive desks, like the record producers The First Elvis encountered in *Jailhouse Rock* and *Loving You*. They were supposed to be hard-headed and tough, not chatty. And they were supposed to want all they could get their hands on.

What Mr. Short seemed to want was an audience. Bobby had not been an audience for anyone since his days with Hootchie-Cootchie. Twice, he nearly interrupted Mr. Short to ask why he had been summoned. Both times, however, Mr. Short had changed the subject before Bobby could get the words out, and Bobby had lapsed into a kind of paralysis.

Besides Mr. Short's voice, the suite and the hotel had a hold on him. It was all too sleek and beautiful, from the lobby where the angelic women paraded about, to the expensive looking pictures on the cream colored walls. As the leather couch where he sat enfolded him, his eyes grew heavy. The Temple, the funeral, the shoot-out all belonged to another world. There was only Mr. Short's voice, brimming with the weight of money, and the empty blue sky and merciless sun through the window.

"I was impressed, quite impressed, with the accounts of your actions during the incident at your Temple. Tragic as it was, such events often bring out the heroic in us."

Bobby stirred from his torpor, aware that Mr. Short was speaking, finally, about him. He was sick of the shoot-out. Everyone acted as if bashing in Virgil's head was the only important thing about The Second Elvis.

"Anybody woulda done it," Bobby sighed. "It was him or me."

"Self preservation? No. It was more, much more than that. In saving yourself, you saved others; an idea that has always been one of my guiding principles. In business, for instance, if you do well for yourself, others will rise with you. Don't you think that's an idea that has made America what it is?"

"Yeah. I suppose you're right."

Bobby was not sure what Mr. Short was getting at. It seemed best to agree with him, for now.

"All of the really great things that have been achieved in this country started with the vision of the individual. Take Henry Ford. Take Thomas Edison, Ross Perot, Carnegie. And take Elvis Presley."

The torpor dissolved. Bobby, who had felt as if he were being sucked into the softness of the couch, sat straight up. Mr. Short focused tightly on him, his hands folded beneath his chin, a half-smile fluttering about his mouth.

"Elvis. I'm the Second . . ."

"I know," Mr. Short said gently. "I could sense it, meeting you like this; even if I had never heard any of the news reports. You are *very close* to Elvis. I must say that the papers have not treated your claims accurately or fairly."

"That's right!" Bobby nodded vigorously. "My people at the Temple, they saw. And now some of them are dead, and others got laid up in the hospital. Them reporters won't listen! I tell them who I really am, and they forget . . ."

"Reporters forget many things. A blessing and a curse. Could you do something for me?"

Mr. Short's tone was seductive, filled with all sorts of promises. Bobby forgot what he wanted to say about truth and falseness.

"Ah . . . what is it you want me to do?"

"Sing."

"Here? I ain't even got a guitar. Not that I really need one. You got to have . . ."

Mr. Short laughed good-naturedly.

"No, Bobby. I mean Second Elvis. I'll take you to a place where you can fully exhibit your talents. And I hope you don't mind if I videotape you."

"I don't mind. Only . . . how come?"

Bobby was wide awake now, excited, yet a little suspicious of what might come.

"I can see that you are your own man. Yes. You have a right to ask questions. And I respect you for it. Deeply. The reason that I want to tape you, and to see you perform, is to confirm what I already suspect."

"What do you suspect?" Bobby said warily.

"That you are the right man for the job."

"What kinda job? I had one job, and it weren't so good. I worked for that damn Virgil Joy . . ."

Mr. Short chuckled coyly.

"More about the job later."

He glanced at his enormous Rolex watch.

"We're due at the studio in twenty minutes. I'll call for the car."

The driver's name was Clarence, and he was an albino. He stood about six-five, and was costumed in a black cowboy outfit, complete with a very tall Stetson, and heavy, silver-framed sunglasses. He did not speak as he expertly guided the stretch limo through the traffic. Mr. Short more than made up for Clarence's and Bobby's silence. He was back on The First Elvis again; how

The First Elvis had been poor, but had risen to wealth and worldwide acclaim and veneration; how talent, of whatever kind, is always recognized in America. Bobby felt nearly as dizzy as when he rode the elevator up to Mr. Short's suite. He wanted all of it, the words, the drive, the events to come, to slow down so that he could have a chance to think. Instead, he was carried along in Mr. Short's expensive car, and by the soothing, cooing voice.

Clarence parked behind a low brick building that bore the sign: Tornado Recording Studios. Bobby followed Mr. Short into the building. Clarence, silent and expressionless, remained in the car. Mr. Short was still chattering, recalling how The First Elvis made his initial recording at Sun Records in Memphis. He did it for his mother, Gladys, Mr. Short said. And everything that followed in his life had come from that single gesture of love.

Bobby had never been in a studio, and had never been recorded, expect for the tapes done by the college students in Columbia when he played in Hootchie-Cootchie's prison band. That was nothing compared to what he saw when he entered Tornado Studios. Wires, cables, and connections ran in every direction. A drum kit and guitars sat waiting. Mr. Short led him into the recording room, which was filled with banks of switches and blinking dials. Two men, who Bobby guessed were engineers, met him and Mr. Short as they entered the room. They were deferential, almost obsequious. A third man, a mini-cam on his shoulder, was introduced a moment later. The names of all three of the men quickly escaped Bobby. His mouth was dry and his palms had begun to sweat. I can't sing, he thought. I'm gonna mess up, and Mr. Short will get somebody else for the job. But what is the job? What if I ain't really The Second Elvis? Mr. Short had used that name when Bobby was introduced. The engineers and the cameraman did not seem surprised by the name.

Before he had time to dwell on these unsettling ideas, three more men appeared. Mr. Short introduced them as the band. They were clones; all three were of medium height, younger than Bobby, dressed in T-shirts and jeans. They were tanned and well-groomed, and Mr. Short said they were the house band in one of his establishments at Myrtle Beach. A place, Mr. Short noted, where young people could go to listen to their favorite music and dance in a clean, wholesome, drug-free environment. As one, they smiled at Bobby.

"What do you call yourselves?" Bobby said.

"Excitement," one of them answered.

"Thought of the name myself," Mr. Short said.

Excitement began to tune up, still smiling.

"What do you want me to do?" Bobby asked Mr. Short.

Mr. Short patted him on the shoulder, squeezing a little, testing Bobby's flesh. Bobby was glad that Mr. Short grabbed the shoulder that had not been grazed by Laverne's bullet.

"I want you to be what you already are, or what I am ninety-nine percent sure you are."

"I ain't rehearsed or nothing."

"That doesn't matter. I only want you to do four songs: 'Mystery Train', 'Teddy Bear', 'Suspicious Minds' and 'Burning Love'. The band is ready, so don't worry about them. And I'm sure that these songs aren't new to you, are they?"

"No . . . it's just that . . ."

"Just what, Second Elvis?"

"It's too quick. I'm used to being with my people."

"From your church."

"Well, it ain't exactly a church. See, they know about . . ."

"About who you really are. Consider this: There is a chance, an excellent chance, that the entire world will know who you are before too much longer. Does that interest you?"

Mr. Short squeezed tighter.

"All right," Bobby said. The whole world, he thought. He was ready to sing.

* * *

An hour later they were back in the suite. A security guard wheeled in a television and a VCR. The draperies had been drawn, and the tape began. Mr. Short played it over and over, stopping to make notes, never commenting on Bobby's performance. He had room service send up sandwiches and freshly squeezed orange juice, which he claimed was his favorite beverage. Bobby barely touched the food. He had never seen himself on television before. His face, battered as it was, enthralled him. In the space of a minute, he was sullen, joyful, defiant, childlike, world-weary, as he worked through the songs specified by Mr. Short.

Once the music had started, his doubts had disappeared. He had immersed himself in the songs, filling the studio and the tapes with himself. By the time he began "Teddy Bear", he was leaping and hopping just as he did at the Temple; or as much as he could in the cramped space of the studio. As he moaned the banal, absurd lyrics of "Teddy Bear", a part of him was intent upon what Mr. Short might be thinking. When "Burning Love" ended, Mr. Short announced that he was satisfied. No one, the band, the record engineers, or the cameramen, spoke to Bobby. Magically, they disappeared, leaving Bobby alone with Mr. Short, whose benevolent smile rose majestically. For once, he did not speak. He smiled all the way back to the Marriott Center, the video tape resting on his lap. As they pulled into the parking garage, Bobby nearly asked him what he thought of the performance. He changed his mind, in fear that Mr. Short might reject The Second Elvis.

Mr. Short froze Bobby's face on the screen. Bobby's head was tilted back slightly, his eyes closed, his upper lip curled like The First Elvis, revealing where his teeth had been kicked out. His jet black hair was mussed, and sweat ran down his cheeks. Both Bobby and Mr. Short stared at the image for a good five minutes. For Bobby, his own huge face was beyond life itself. Mr. Short pressed a button on the remote control and the screen went dead. He opened the draperies and Bobby blinked in the harsh sunlight.

Mr. Short stood with his back to the window, framed by the sun and the sky. He spoke in that drawling, deep accent that cut through the tones of wealth.

"You know, I loved Elvis, too. I started out in radio, before I went into marketing and real estate. A little old thousand-watt station in Goldsboro. I grew up down in Goldsboro. Daddy was in tobacco. Not me. I gave that up when I was old enough to say no. No future in it. Anyhow, I played Elvis music all day long. For hours. I coulda gone to college, but I was too restless. Wanted something big to come along, and pretty soon it did . . ."

The sun shone around Mr. Short's head. Bobby could barely make out his face.

". . . I went to Elvis' earliest shows. Back before he became world famous. In fact, I met him. Interviewed him right here in Charlotte. Took me a week to convince the station manager to send me down from Goldsboro. He said I'd never get to talk to Elvis. The next year, *I* was the station manager. And don't ask me how I got in to see Elvis. Luck, I guess. Right after that I started making it big. Both me and Elvis started coming to the top at the same time. Back in the fifties, when life was sweeter. It was a different country in those days . . ."

"You met him?" Bobby said. The enormity of such an experience was overwhelming; it dwarfed entering the bedroom of The First Elvis at Graceland.

"Backstage, after a show. He had the finest manners of anyone I've ever met. We wrote to each other a few times over the years. I visited twice—once in Las Vegas. One in Memphis . . ."

"Did you see his bedroom?" Bobby blurted.

Mr. Short was a little annoyed by the interruption, but he went on in his now dreamy drawl.

"I don't recall. The first time I saw him up close was the one that mattered. He didn't have a lick of false pride. He was so sincere. Down to earth. I felt like . . . we could've been brothers. Do you know what he told me? He took my arm, and drew me to one side, right there in the dressing room and said 'Maurice, I got to use my talents for others. Not just for myself. Not just to make money.' That's what he told me. And I'll never forget it.''

Bobby waited for Mr. Short to say more, to describe the wildness of The First Elvis, and how he made people rave for him. Instead, Mr. Short sank into contemplation, silent in the sun. After a while he spoke, returning to his carefully cultivated voice.

"You have it. It's so thick I could cut it with a knife. I strongly suspected it from the stories in the media. I had to be sure, though. Your performance this afternoon is all the additional proof I need. I can inform Beverly that she no longer needs to search."

"What have I got?" Bobby said, holding his breath.

Mr. Short appeared not to have heard him.

"I'm going to give you a gift. I'm going to harness the power of The Second Elvis. I've had a vision, a powerful vision. And when I've followed my visions, I've transformed them into reality, success and deep, deep gratification. Beverly will be a little difficult perhaps. She did not want me to contact you. Once she sees the tapes, though . . ."

"Beverly? Who . . ."

"My daughter, my only child," Mr. Short said quickly. "And my closest business associate. Absolutely brilliant. Literature, politics, marketing. You name it. An expert in every field. It took me a good while to bring her to Short Enterprises. It was only when I explained my latest project that she consented to join me. You'll meet her—if you decide to come with us."

Mr. Short sat down and leaned close to Bobby. His expression was that of a man on the verge of making an important purchase. Bobby felt as if he were close to bursting. Dizzy again, the words came in a rush.

"What you want with me? I *gotta* find out. You bring me up here, and you got me to sing and . . ."

"You're a wonderful performer. You catch the essence of *Him*."

"I ain't no impersonator. Them impersonators got it all wrong. You read about Virgil Joy. Said he wasn't an impersonator, but he really was . . ."

Mr. Short raised his hand. Bobby stopped speaking.

"I understand what you're saying. You go beyond mere impersonation. Now listen to me. Have you ever been to Graceland?"

"Hell, yes! And it weren't like it was supposed to be."

"About six months ago, I acquired a house, a mansion actually. It's located about ten miles from Myrtle Beach. Can you guess what is special about this house?"

Bobby shook his head. He wanted to tell about the falseness he had seen in Memphis, but Mr. Short once again emptied his mind of words.

"It is an exact replica of Graceland."

Mr. Short went on, not waiting for the idea to register with Bobby.

"At least from the outside. The previous owner was a life-long admirer of Elvis, and had the house built to match the original. When the house became mine, the owner owed me a good bit of money, I set to work to make it as authentic as possible. My decorating consultants made numerous visits to Memphis, consulted the available literature on the subject, and now they have completed their work. And, Second Elvis, you can't tell the place from the original!"

Mr. Short slapped Bobby's thigh for emphasis and smiled.

"Another Graceland," Bobby said slowly. "Has it got a T.V. room? Where The First Elvis shot the sets?"

Mr. Short nodded, his smile competing with the sun.

"And the bathroom where he died?" Bobby asked. "And the extra big bed?"

"And the white carpets. And the kind of furniture the King loved. And the most powerful central air-conditioning system available. And the lions on the front portico. We even have copies of his favorite books. And a kitchen stocked with his favorite foods: Cotton States brand bacon, institutional size jars of peanut butter, and plenty of bananas. There is only one thing missing."

"What's that?" Bobby whispered.

"Elvis."

The Temple was dark except for the single light bulb above Bobby's mattress. He read over the letter he had just composed. The survivors of the congregation would find it in the morning. They, and the Temple itself, were distant now; as if they had been part of someone else's life. He scanned the words once more, to make sure that they were right. Mr. Short had helped him think of the ideas. He was sure, however, that the words were his own.

My People,
    I have gone to a better place. A trip that won't ever stop. Don't try to find me. I am still with you. Don't be afraid. Virgil and Laverne will never come back. The Second Elvis is part of you. Even if you can't really see him. Don't give in to the falseness.

                                              Second Elvis

He had packed his belongings, and would tape the letter to the door when he left. Mr. Short had taken care of the rest. He had given Bobby two hundred dollars for expenses, and a plane ticket to Atlanta. The plane would leave in two hours. Bobby had asked Mr. Short why he had to go to Atlanta when Graceland-by-the-Sea, which is what Mr. Short called the house, was at Myrtle Beach. Mr. Short said that Bobby must undergo training and modification before he took his rightful place as The Second

Elvis. When Bobby asked what was meant by training and modification, Mr. Short was as friendly as ever, but vague. You will find out in time, he said.

Besides arranging for the trip to Atlanta, and Bobby's training and modification, Mr. Short had taken care of other matters as well. Before Bobby left the suite that night, Mr. Short informed him that it was no longer necessary for Bobby to meet with the Gaston County District Attorney; that it had been arranged so that Bobby did not even have to testify at the trial. Bobby was glad that his interview with the D.A. had been canceled. And now that he was to be properly enthroned as the new King, it was no longer important that he try to explain the mission of The Second Elvis to a courtroom full of ignorant, skeptical reporters and lawyers. They would never understand the truth anyway. He asked Mr. Short how he was able to fix things up with the D.A.'s office. Mr. Short replied that it was all a mere technicality; that the criminal justice system, because of its liberal-induced corruptions, was quite flexible in some matters. He also told Bobby that he no longer need concern himself with the trial. As The Second Elvis, he should only concentrate on fulfilling his mission to the world.

There had been a lawyer, however. Bobby had returned to Mr. Short's suite the next morning to, as Mr. Short put it, ". . . make our association legal and binding, for both of our benefits." As soon as Bobby arrived, Collingwood materialized, and handed Bobby a thick, official-looking document. The contract, he said. Collingwood went through the contract, glancing at Mr. Short now and then for approval. Bobby pretended to read along with him. He already knew what the contract said, however; that he was to have his own Graceland; that he was to live as the new King. He skimmed over the incomprehensible words as he tuned out Collingwood's voice. And he signed. Collingwood disappeared, and Mr. Short gave Bobby a fatherly hug.

Bobby taped the letter to the Temple door, then hoisted himself on to the still-wrecked stage. For the first time, he realized how small and dirty the Temple was, smelling of blood and gunpowder, the floor covered with glass, garbage, clothing, and shoes, the chairs smashed and over-turned. Even in the near-darkness, it was all clear to him. The Temple was one of those places, like his prison cell, that had hemmed him in; a place to escape from. And the people had started to hem him in, too. They were always after something, he thought. Like Momma and Virgil. Maybe even Hootchie-Cootchie. I beat all of them, though.

He left the Temple stage for the last time. He did not bother to lock the door. The front of the Temple was briefly illuminated in the car's headlights. He took one last look and was gone.

He left the Vega in the long term parking lot at the airport, the key still in the ignition. He had been ordered to do this. One of Mr. Short's associates would see to it that the car was properly taken care of. Mr. Short had been very explicit in his instructions. Bobby was to take nothing with him to Atlanta, and he was to leave nothing behind in the temple. Bobby had placed his clothes, the .22, and the books that had helped him become The Second Elvis in the trunk. The Red Harmony Rocket and its amplifier were in the back seat.

Inside the terminal, and after a confused search, he found the place where he was supposed to present his ticket. He had never been in an airport, much less flown, and he concentrated on remembering all that Mr. Short had told him. He was relieved when he found the correct gate. He sat down in the waiting area, nervously jiggling one leg. He glanced at the clock that was suspended above the check-in desk. His flight would not leave for nearly an hour. Then he remembered he had passed a lounge during his search for the proper gate.

At the bar, he ordered a beer. There were a few other people there, most of them huddled around tables, reading paperbacks and newspapers. He slowly sipped the beer and lit a cigarette. The television above the bar blared away. It was the local news. The anchorman spoke in an urgent voice.

"In a late-breaking story, Virgil and Laverne Joy, the alleged Rambo killers, have pleaded guilty to first-degree murder. Channel Three only received news of this development in the last hour. Laura Chase is on the scene at the Gaston County Courthouse. Laura, what's the latest on the Burning Love Temple shoot-out?"

A woman holding a microphone stood in front of the courthouse, the Confederate monument behind her.

"The attorneys for Virgil and Laverne Joy stated late this afternoon that their clients had accepted the District Attorney's plea bargain arrangement. This news comes as a shock to the community, where expectations were that the trial would not begin until early next year. It was also expected that the Joys' attorneys would mount an insanity defense. Apparently, that is not going to happen. The Joys can expect to receive consecutive life sentences, or the death penalty, although it is believed now that the District Attorney's office will recommend that the court show mercy . . ."

The reporter described the shoot-out as the screen flashed to still photographs of the Temple, complete with the dead and wounded. Those pictures were soon replaced by the faces of Virgil and Laverne. Virgil's head was still swathed with thick bandages, and Laverne's expression was empty, nearly dead. Then the picture of Bobby and Mildred, the one taken after the shoot-out, the one that was in all the papers, flashed onto the screen. The reporter said that efforts to contact Bobby Snipes, the so-called Second Elvis, for his reaction to the news had been futile so far. It was hoped, the reporter said, that his comments would be available for the eleven o'clock newscast.

Bobby discovered that he was sweating. He took a long pull at his beer and lit another cigarette. Mr. Short can do anything, he thought. And he picked me.

ALPHA OMEGA

"That's something, isn't it?" the bartender said. She was a stout, lacquered blonde in a frilly blouse. "They kill a buncha people and don't even get tried for it. You want another beer?"

Bobby shook his head. The anchorman had gone to another story; something about an explosion in one of the textile mills. He envisioned Virgil in prison, and wanted to laugh. And momma, too, he thought. Well, she did try to kill me. And she blowed April's head off. And neither her nor Virgil will have to smell the gas up in Raleigh. Mr. Short sure is something.

"You from around here?" the bartender asked.

"No. Passing through."

Mr. Short had told him to say as little as possible about who he was or where he was going. In due time, Mr. Short had said. All will be revealed in due time.

"You look like you were in a hell of an accident," the bartender said.

"Car wreck." He was pleased with the lie.

"Well, you look familiar. Did you hear about the shoot-out? It was over in Gastonia. I'm never surprised at what comes outta there. One bunch of nuts killing another crowd of nuts. There was a preacher that was real cute. He tried to be like Elvis, if you can believe that."

"Is that right?"

Bobby drained the rest of the beer and laid a couple of bills on the table.

"I know I've seen you before," the bartender said as she picked up the money.

Bobby shrugged.

"Maybe. And maybe you'll see me again."

As he walked out of the lounge, he never felt more like The Second Elvis.

10

"This is Dr. Anders," Mr. Short said.

The doctor wore a white clinician's coat, and his speech and appearance were foreign, like one of the villains in *Harem Scarum*. As they shook hands, the doctor carefully scrutinized Bobby's face. The doctor then asked Bobby and Mr. Short to take a seat at the conference table. In the exact center of the table sat a large, official-looking binder. After they were seated, the doctor continued to gaze at Bobby, which made him nervous.

The Anders Clinic was located in a medical park in an Atlanta suburb. The building, and all of the furnishings and equipment, were new and shiny, as if they had recently been purchased. Bobby understood that he was in a doctor's office, and that he was in Atlanta. Beyond that, he knew nothing. Clarence had met him when the flight arrived, and, without speaking, had driven him through a confusing maze of interstate highways to a small, but luxurious hotel. Mr. Short had welcomed him, announcing that he had procured a special suite for Bobby, in addition to the rooms that he usually maintained. An elaborate meal, consisting of foods that Bobby had never before seen or imagined, was laid out. Mr. Short, clad, as usual, in his jogging outfit, consumed several glasses of orange juice, squab, strange-looking vegetables, and a thing called strawberry sorbet, which reminded Bobby of the snow cones at the Gaston County Fair when he was a boy. The sorbet was the only thing that tasted good. After the waiter cleared away the remains of the meal, Mr. Short excused himself; there was an important call that he had to make to Beverly in Myrtle Beach. Before he left, he reminded Bobby to get a good night's sleep; they would have a busy day tomorrow, he said. Not a moment was to be wasted. There was much to do, he went on, and the doctor charged extra high rates for a Sunday consultation. Mr. Short disappeared before Bobby had a chance to discover why they had to visit a doctor.

Despite Mr. Short's admonition, Bobby lay awake for a long time. He was on his way; this much was clear. But why a doctor? He was not sick, and had always been healthy—even in prison where almost everyone had some physical affliction. And there were those words of Mr. Short's: *modification* and *training*. When he finally fell asleep, the words tumbled over and over in his head, clueless and enigmatic.

"Dr. Anders is a plastic surgeon," Mr. Short said. "One of the best in the nation."

Dr. Anders cleared his throat.

"A reconstructionist, actually. I specialize in the human face."

"It would be fair to call him an artist," Mr. Short said through one of his benevolent smiles.

"True. Like all artists, I am concerned with the materials I must work with," Dr. Anders said.

"How come you bring me to a plastic surgeon?" Bobby asked. He had heard of such doctors. In prison, another inmate, a car thief named Benny, had his face smashed to pieces in a fight over a carton of Marlboros. Benny had been worked over with iron pipes, and there had not been much left of his nose and jaw. He was sent to a hospital on the outside. When he returned, he had a kind of face. He was mostly lumps and dead-white scar tissue. Benny made constant sucking noises when he tried to breath through his new, monstrous nose. And no one called him Benny. Frankenstein was his new name. And it fit.

"I ain't gonna be no freak," Bobby said. "I've seen what can happen when them plastic surgeons get their hands on you."

Dr. Anders stiffened as Bobby spoke. Mr. Short turned his smile up full blast.

"No, Second Elvis. You don't understand. Dr. Anders is only going to provide a few cosmetic adjustments. That's all."

"I thought you had prepared him for the procedures," Dr. Anders said. "If he is unwilling to co-operate . . ."

Mr. Short wheeled his smile around on the doctor.

"You have to understand that Second Elvis has been through a great deal. He narrowly escaped death. His bruises and missing teeth should tell you of his ordeal. And you must admit that the idea of even cosmetic adjustments is not to be taken lightly."

"This is true . . ."

"Especially when it's my face you're talking about," Bobby said. His apprehension had eased a bit when Mr. Short referred to him as Second Elvis, although the image of Frankenstein's face was still with him.

"Perhaps if we could discuss the procedures?" Mr. Short said.

"I assumed that was one of the purposes of the initial visit," Dr. Anders said with professional dignity.

Dr. Anders opened the binder, which contained candid photographs of The First Elvis. It reminded Bobby of Hootchie-Cootchie's scrapbooks; the ones he kept under the bunk. Instead of Hootchie-Cootchie's life, the binder overflowed with the King's images, mostly close-up shots of his face. Dr. Anders slowly thumbed through the plastic-covered pages, commenting on the shapes of ears, the configurations of noses, chins, and cheekbones. His main interest in The First Elvis was purely structural. The pictures were all from The First Elvis' Las Vegas period; before he grew fat and died. In all of the photographs, The First Elvis wore a seductive, yet kindly, vague smile; as if he had no idea where he was.

"I particularly like this one," Mr. Short said, pointing to a profile shot.

"A classic," Dr. Anders replied. "And we have the material here to achieve a final product that could be quite close to the original. The nose will present the greatest challenge, although the chin will need lengthening and sculpting."

"This ain't right," Bobby declared.

Mr. Short and Dr. Anders were startled by Bobby's voice. He had not spoken since the binder had been opened.

"Is there a . . . problem, Second Elvis?" Mr. Short said.

"None of them pictures is the wild Elvis. The one that changed the world. That book there is nothing but Las Vegas. You can't hardly tell him from one of them impersonators."

Dr. Anders closed the binder.

"Perhaps your associate," he said slowly and carefully to Mr. Short, "is not prepared for the gifts I can provide. I will be in my office when, and if, you are ready to proceed."

Dr. Anders seized the binder and swept out of the room, the door slamming behind him. Mr. Short started in before the door's echo had died.

"Have I mistreated you? Have I offended you? I bring you to Atlanta, introduce you to one of the giants of the medical profession, and promise, no, *guarantee* that you will be the living embodiment of a great American. That you will reign over the new, improved Graceland. And yet . . . you resist. Please tell me what I've done wrong."

"I . . . I'm grateful for all them things. And I want to be the King. Want it more than anything. The Elvis in that book, the one you want me to be, I ain't that way. See, I studied and learned before it came to me that I'm The Second Elvis. It weren't no overnight thing. Maybe I ain't meant to be the rich Elvis. That's what Virgil Joy tried to do. I can't. The Second Elvis is against falseness. And you seen me perform. You got that tape. Now, I want to look right. I do. But I got to be The Second Elvis."

Mr. Short folded his hands beneath his chin, contemplating Bobby's words. Bobby was nervous now. Averting his eyes from Mr. Short. Mr. Short had not spoken since Bobby started his speech.

"I think I understand. You want to maintain the essential spirit of Elvis. Am I correct?" Mr. Short said.

He understands, Bobby thought with relief.

"The First Elvis, he went wrong. Other people got a hold of him . . ."

"Second Elvis, the last thing I want to do is change that spirit. It is the source of your unique gifts. I understood that from the first, even when others did not. There are other considerations, though."

"What you mean, considerations?"

"The people. The American people. They will be drawn to Graceland-by-the-Sea by the thousands. They will pay their hard-earned money for a chance to commune with you, The Second Elvis. By communing with you, they will arrive at a deep and holy contact with the spirit and the truth of the past, present and future Elvis. For you will be all of them at once."

Coming to me, Bobby thought.

"You don't strike me as a selfish person, or foolish either. Of your sincerity, I have no doubt. Therefore, we must return to these considerations. The people want reassurance above all things. What would reassure them more than a living manifestation of The First Elvis? We are not talking about impersonation. Both of us are deeply opposed to such a notion. And Dr. Anders can put you in a position to triumph over all the impersonators in the world. He can give you the truest Elvis face; a visage that encompasses, yet goes beyond the young wild Elvis you speak of. You will be the *Eternal Elvis*. This is the Elvis that now lives only within you and through your performances. We are going to bring him out—so that he will live twenty-four hours a day. Once the modifications are made, you will be complete. And the people will love you."

"The Eternal Elvis. That means forever and ever, don't it?"

"Absolutely!"

Dr. Anders measured Bobby's face and head, kneading his flesh like a baker working over dough. The doctor also took a large number of photographs and viewed the videotape of Bobby's performance at the Tornado Studios. After lunch, he put Bobby through an exhaustive physical. He drew blood from Bobby's arm, administered an EKG and a CAT scan; Anders tested for hernias, hemorrhoids, and respiratory problems. Finally he put Bobby, naked except for his ragged underwear, on a treadmill, and made him stay there for almost an hour while lights flashed off and on, and a long computer print-out spilled to the floor. Mr. Short remained with Bobby throughout the examination, solicitous and kindly, urging him to be patient. When the physical was over, Mr. Short and Dr. Anders conferred alone for a long time while Bobby cooled off from the treadmill. When they returned, the doctor said that Bobby was in good shape, although he must give up cigarettes. He added that Bobby was a perfect subject for reconstruction, one of the best that he had ever seen. The doctor even managed a slight smile.

"When can we start, Doctor?" Mr. Short asked.

"Tomorrow. The entire process can be undertaken here at the clinic, just as you wished. I project a two week stay. Then he will need monitoring for at least a month—until he adjusts to the modifications."

"Good, good," Mr. Short said. "Any questions, Second Elvis?"

Bobby shook his head.

"Let's get it over with, I guess. I want to get on down to Myrtle Beach and be . . ."

"The Eternal Elvis?" Mr. Short said.

"Yeah. Eternal."

He was given a gown, and a nurse led him to a windowless room that contained a hospital bed, a night stand, and a chair. The nurse was the only other person he saw in the hallways of the clinic, and he had the feeling that the place was empty. The nurse pulled back the sheets and left. She returned a short while later with a meal of consommé, crackers, and tea. She watched him eat, and when he finished, she produced a syringe, which she jabbed into his hip. He asked her what the shot was for. "Sleep," she said, as she glided noiselessly from the room.

The shot took effect, dissolving his tension. He relaxed for the first time since the shoot-out. It was difficult, in his floating, disconnected state, to realize that he had once crawled and scrambled for his life. He imagined the survivors of the Temple, reading the note, wailing, calling out for him. Guilt drifted through his consciousness. Would they ever learn that he was the Eternal, as well as The Second Elvis? Perhaps they would find him at Graceland-by-the-Sea; Mildred, Jerry, Sheri, and April. Then he remembered that April was dead, and that the others would not be able to recognize him.

A voice called his name. Mr. Short stood beside the bed.

"How are you feeling, Second Elvis?"

"Sleepy."

"Good. Rest is important. You understand that the operation will take place in the morning?"

Bobby nodded. He had nearly forgotten about the operation.

"I won't be with you when you come out of anesthesia. Must return to Myrtle Beach. Beverly says that there are a number of important matters that I must attend to. My signature is required for certain documents. She wants me to get a first-hand view of the construction. That sort of thing. Dr. Anders will see to your needs, and I will be back before the bandages come off."

Mr. Short appeared to be far away, and smaller than usual. His words, as always, were perfect and sweet, obliterating doubt.

"Second Elvis?"

"Yeah, Mr. Short."

"I'm proud of you. Almost as if you were my own son. I don't have a son, you know. Beverly is my only child. In a sense, though, I am your father."

"That right?" These were the only words that Bobby was capable of. My father, he thought. Daddy to the wild, Second, Eternal Elvis.

"Don't fathers create their sons?"

Mr. Short evaporated. Bobby tried to concentrate on what he had said, but failed. He closed his eyes and washed into a warm, slow stream.

He was awakened near dawn. Three nurses hustled into the room and went to work. One of them cut his hair down to the scalp and shaved his head back to the middle of his skull. He wanted to scream for them to stop, but they had given him another shot; and it was much more powerful than the one he had the night before. He barely felt the prick of the needle as they hooked him to the IV, and he was so limp it took all three of them, along with a male attendant they had summoned, to shift him from the bed to the gurney. As they wheeled him toward the operating room, he thought he was laughing, although he could not be sure.

When he came to, the first thing he was aware of was the thick surgical wrappings. They covered his entire head, except for his eyes and two small openings at his nostrils. He gasped, and instinctively pulled at the bandages. Firm hands grasped him, and held on until he ceased his struggle.

In bed, in the windowless room, attached to the IV, he lost track of time. He recalled that Anders said that the wrappings would stay in place for two weeks. The doctor visited twice a day, peering beneath the dressings, poking and prodding. Bobby watched for signs that the bandages would come off, that he would have the face of the Eternal, Second, Wild Elvis. The doctor never spoke, and the wrappings around his mouth kept Bobby from asking any questions.

And then there was the pain. It radiated upward from his chin, swallowing his head. In the beginning, he thought he could endure it. It was too much, however, and the heavy throbbing felt strong enough to dissolve his features. He buzzed the nurse for shots six or seven times a day. Usually, he fell asleep almost as soon as the needle left his arm. On some occasions, he had the sensation of dreaming while awake. He knew he was in bed, in a room, that he would possess the eternal, forever face. He concentrated on what the face would mean until other images intruded. Two or three times Hootchie-Cootchie was seated in the chair next to the bed in the exact spot where Bobby had last seen Mr. Short. Bobby wanted to howl, as Hootchie-Cootchie mournfully regarded the white wrappings. Virgil and Laverne also appeared. They did not want to kill him, even if they did frighten him a good deal. Instead, they were incapable of any action at all. Clad in combat dress, they posed stiffly at attention, like life-size cardboard cut-outs of themselves. Bobby closed his eyes and they vanished. He was grateful. Sheri and April came to him, like that day at the trailer. April shimmied before him, her white breasts vibrating. Sheri did the pony like a sixties go-go dancer. Together, they chanted the name of The Second Elvis. Bobby made wet sputtering sounds against the bandages until the nurse arrived with the syringe.

Mr. Short returned the day Bobby had the bandages removed from his mouth and the IV needle taken from his hand.

"When am I gonna get the rest of these bandages off?" Bobby said as Mr. Short entered the room. Bobby had asked Dr. Anders the same question as soon as the wrappings were gone, but, as usual, had received no answer. Mr. Short pulled the chair close to the bed and sat down.

"It won't be long. Dr. Anders says that you're making tremendous progress. You can even have solid food. That means that your jaw and lips have responded nicely. Lunch will arrive any minute."

Bobby sat up. He was not interested in food. And it occurred to him that he did not need a shot, at least for the moment. The pain had withdrawn for awhile. A nurse arrived. She placed a tray, containing a huge fried peanut butter and mashed banana sandwich and a Pepsi, on the bedside table. She reappeared a couple of minutes later and handed Mr. Short a tray. On it, a plate was heaped with fried chicken, mashed potatoes, collards, and a large glass of orange juice. With great enthusiasm, Mr. Short began to eat. Tentatively, Bobby bit into the sandwich. His lips, still partially concealed, were numb, and he gagged on the hot, heavy sandwich filling.

"What's the matter?" Mr. Short asked.

"I got to get used to eating again," Bobby said, swallowing.

"It was the King's favorite snack. I ordered it especially for you."

Mr. Short sounded hurt. Bobby took another bite. The sandwich tasted better. And, at least, he was no longer chained to the IV.

"Do you like it?" The hurt was gone from Mr. Short's voice.

"It's fine. Fine." Bobby sipped the Pepsi. It was too sweet, but he figured he could stand it.

"I'm sorry I couldn't be with you sooner. Business. I thought I would be gone for only a few days. And here it is nearly two weeks since I've seen you. I've called every day to check on you. Beverly insisted I stay in Myrtle Beach. We had to hammer out the contracts with the gift shop people. And Beverly has completed the final arrangements with the Presley Estate. Clearances on everything, for a fee, and a percentage of the profits, naturally.

She worked out a great contract. She's smarter than any of my lawyers.''

Gift shops, Bobby thought. What's that got to do with The Second, Eternal Elvis? Laverne loved gift shops, and he could, despite the brevity of his stay in Memphis, remember that there were dozens of shops on Elvis Presley Boulevard. I guess it ain't none of my concern, he told himself.

Mr. Short chewed a steaming hunk of white meat.

"This is my kind of food. I was raised on it. Eastern North Carolina barbecue, turnip greens, pecan pie. I eat that other stuff; French cooking, nouvelle cuisine and all that. For business reasons mostly. Makes some people think that you're sophisticated. I still love my downhome food though."

Mr. Short's country accent had come out in full force. He smacked his lips and drank orange juice.

"I growed up on french fries," Bobby said.

Mr. Short laughed. His face trembled with good humor.

"I like that. That's you. Blunt. Honest. The way Elvis is supposed to be."

"When am I going to Graceland-by-the Sea? I'm ready now."

Mr. Short's country-boy accent disappeared.

"In due time. That's what Dr. Anders says. And his word is final as long as you are in recovery. After all, he's in charge of the medical element in the production. Now, you have been here longer than originally projected. And that's nature's fault, not the doctor's. Healing takes time."

"He don't tell me nothing."

"His work will be his only comment. He's an artist, a real perfectionist. Which means that you'll be a work of art."

Mr. Short laughed again, slurping collards.

"Once you leave the clinic," Mr. Short continued, "you'll have to undergo a few other modifications."

Bobby sighed. He was sick of modifications.

"There's the oral surgery. Replacement of the teeth you lost during the unfortunate affair at the Burning Love Temple, and caps for the rest. I've arranged for the very best man in Atlanta to work with you. And we'll start the day you leave the clinic. He's cleared his appointments, and he can complete the job in two, three days at the most. You can expect a little discomfort."

Mr. Short's fork sliced into a large piece of lemon pie.

"And you'll be measured for a new wardrobe. No expense will be spared in that department, I assure you. Beverly has contracted with the designer who did a number of the King's Las Vegas costumes. He's flying in for the fittings . . ."

"I gotta wear them suits? Like Virgil Joy?"

Mr. Short's pie-filled fork paused halfway to his mouth.

"The people expect it. It has nothing to do with Virgil Joy. And besides, you'll look wonderful for the shows."

"The shows? Then I'm gonna be performing, too?"

Bobby had nearly forgotten that he would be on stage. No one had mentioned performing since the video was made.

"Certainly," Mr. Short said with some astonishment. "At the music hall, which is almost completed. Beverly has hired a director. Top-rated, I believe. The sound system is being installed now. Musicians and singers are being auditioned. All will be ready for the Fourth of July Grand Opening. Which gives us less than two months. Do you think you'll be ready?"

A music hall full of people, Bobby thought. A band. Probably spotlights, too. And me. Right in the middle of it. It'll be bigger than The First Elvis' '68 comeback.

"Well? What about it?"

Mr. Short scraped his fork on the plate picking up the last bits of pie. He eyed Bobby.

"You've seen me. Once I get on that stage, I'll show you that you picked the right man for the job."

"Of that, I have no doubt. And the way you conduct yourself

at the mansion will be as important as the shows. Believe me. Beverly will be personally instructing you in that area, by the way.''

Bobby hoped that he would get to blow out some T.V. screens. He would ask Beverly about it. She sounds smart, he thought. Maybe she's done set it up already. Get me a .357 magnum. That would be a whole lot better than that shitty old .22.

Mr. Short daintily wiped his mouth and fingers.

''I've been examining your past,'' he said as he tossed the napkin on the plate. ''Prison. Ten years without parole. Unfortunate. Very. It can't be helped, although that, too, has been taken care of by Beverly.''

Bobby lost the fantasy of the screens and the .357. He shoved away the remains of the sandwich. Slowly, the pain was coming back. It was weaker than before, but it was still there. He would need a shot soon. But not before he found out what Beverly had done.

''People read about it in the newspapers,'' Bobby said. ''The law up in Gastonia knew all about it, too.''

''True. If it is never mentioned again in the media, it will cease to exist.''

''I ain't ashamed of it.''

''You don't have to be ashamed. Merely silent. By the way, Beverly is also in charge of your grammar and diction lessons. You don't have to sound like Lawrence Olivier, and God knows we don't want you to lose that natural, unvarnished style, but you could stand some improvement. Beverly is perfect for the job. Majored in English. That was one of her majors. She had four. Phi Beta Kappa at Chapel Hill. As for prison, consider how the public would react.''

Mr. Short smiled. The pain crept up from Bobby's chin.

''They might not like it?''

''Yes. But Beverly has seen to it. Don't think that we didn't have to expend a lot of energy and money on this segment of the project. Some members of my organization were even opposed to your selection because of your past. Of course, I had final say. Records had to be removed and destroyed. And while Beverly was at it, she had your driver's license, Social Security and school records expunged. Officially, you don't exist. I envy you. You can start over."

"And you made sure that Virgil and Momma didn't get tried neither."

"That wasn't as difficult as your records. Records have a life of their own. By the way, how did you find out?"

"I seen it on T.V. before I flew down here."

"Naturally, there was a public outcry. We were successful in containing the condemnation of the District Attorney's office up there. That was part of our understanding. A couple of articles about the miscarriage of justice and so on. After that, the shootout was strictly back page until it died. T.V. was easier. It usually is. There were a few angry letters about your mother and stepfather . . ."

"He ain't my stepfather." The pain grew. Soon he would have to ring for the nurse and her needle.

"Beverly will have her work cut out for her. You know, English was Elvis' favorite subject in school. Anyway, your mother and Virgil Joy won't pay with their lives, as atrocious as their crimes were. I'm in favor of capital punishment, except in certain instances where the greater good will be served. In this case, the American people will have an Eternal Elvis, uncontaminated by sordid courtroom scenes. As with all such incidents, the public, will forget quickly enough. Speaking of the public, your public, there was the slight problem with your church."

"They was the first to understand that I was The Second Elvis." The pain held dominion over most of Bobby's skull. It was mixed with the guilt he felt when he thought about the congregation.

"Sad. I wish there had been some way to ease the shock of

your disappearance. There *was* no other way, I'm afraid. And the people who followed you are potential patrons of Graceland-by-the-Sea; plain simple Americans. The sort who loved Elvis.''

"And The Second Elvis, too," Bobby said quietly. He had to have that shot.

"One of my representatives has been in contact with them. While no one can really take your place, your congregation has been provided with a substitute."

"What you saying! A substitute . . ."

"Calm down. He's a young man named Johnny. I've viewed a tape of him. He's clumsy, and lacks your power. He does possess energy, though it's doubtful that he'll ever be more than a competent impersonator. My representative discovered him in a lounge in Jasper, Alabama, and brought him to Gastonia. Your people have gotten used to him, although he can never replace you."

"He don't call himself Second Elvis, does he?"

"Johnny Love is his name. Do you consider him a threat?"

"Goddamn impersonator."

Mr. Short laughed.

"You can't be jealous!"

Bobby dropped back onto the pillows, laboring to erase a picture from his mind. He envisioned Johnny Love, to him a jailhouse pussy-boy type, prancing and strutting on stage, the women dancing and shouting. He pressed the buzzer for the nurse. The shot had to come now.

"I don't understand how come you got this impersonator."

"An investment, and not much of one. Beverly's idea again. Johnny gets a weekly salary and, as a gift, we gave him a few thousand to pass on to the Temple. For repairs and renovations, you understand. There are good reasons. First, if your old followers are satisfied, then they won't search for you . . ."

Bobby had to admit that Mr. Short had a point. Johnny Love, he thought. What kinda dumb ass name is that?

". . . and, secondly, an impersonator will keep them happy. I love to provide happiness. They deserve some compensation for being blown to pieces and having The Second Elvis disappear from their lives."

"I guess you're right. Only, why did you tape him? I thought you'd only taped me."

"I scout all my talent. Never buy a pig in the poke. Come on. Don't let this upset you. We simply have to figure all the angles to ensure that you emerge as the Eternal Elvis, embodying the ultimate mystery of the King."

"The mystery."

Bobby enjoyed the sound of the word, and the fact that it now applied to him.

"You're in our hands, and you'll have what no one has ever had before. Except for the original Elvis. And we've taken another step to safeguard the mystery. You have a new name. You'll no longer be either Bobby Snipes or Second Elvis."

"If I ain't Second Elvis, then who am I? I was meant to be him. What name could be better?"

"Alpha Omega!"

Mr. Short nearly shouted in triumph.

"I ain't never heard of a name like that."

"Alpha means first. Omega, the last. The beginning and the end. It's from the Bible. Beverly thought of it. What do you think?"

Softly, Bobby uttered the name. The beginning and the end.

"I . . . I can get used to it," he finally said.

"I'm sure you will. The Presley Estate approved it. We couldn't get away with calling you The Second Elvis, or Eternal Elvis; although those are your unofficial names. There were contractual and copyright problems. So we had to find a suitable alternative. It costs us enough just to get the use of Graceland's name."

Mr. Short glanced at his watch.

"Got to go. Expecting a call from Beverly. She demands punctuality. Don't know how we'd get along without her," he said automatically.

The nurse arrived, syringe in hand, and Mr. Short departed. As the pain killer took effect, it occurred to Bobby that he had so many names that he hardly knew what to call himself anymore.

The next time Bobby saw Mr. Short was in an examination room on the day the last of the bandages were removed. The room was equipped with a dozen mirrors, which had been strategically positioned to provide multiple views; like mirrors for evaluating merchandise in a clothing store.

A nurse led Bobby into the room, where he was greeted by myriad Mr. Shorts and Dr. Anderses. He halted at the door, blinking, confused. The nurse guided him to an examining table.

"This is it, Alpha," Mr. Short said. "What all of us have waited for."

The nurse stepped back, reverent and expectant, as Dr. Anders went to work. The doctor slowly unwound the dressing, making Bobby's unveiling as dramatic as possible. Bobby shivered in the air-conditioning as each layer was drawn from his head. He reached for his face, but Dr. Anders caught his hands.

"In a moment," Anders said. "Only a moment more."

The bandages were gone, and Bobby's hands went up to his face. It was without feeling. He rubbed harder, as if he could massage the face into life. Anders grabbed him again.

"We will, directly, discuss the sensory and tactile consequences of the operation. First, he must have a thorough going over."

"Let me see it," Bobby begged. Anders had successfully imposed himself between the closest mirrors. Bobby turned his face from side to side, and caught a glimpse of his hair, mostly blonde stubble. Anders seized his head and held it.

"Relax, Alpha," Mr. Short said. "It couldn't be any better."

"No one," Dr. Anders said, "expected an exact reproduction of the original. It does seem that we have achieved total replication on ten of the twelve major points. I really wish I could do a professional paper on this one."

Bobby had ceased his struggles. He breathed deeply. Anders grip was strong, and it felt as if he might never let go.

"Remember our agreement, Doctor," Mr. Short said.

"Yes, yes. Total confidentiality. A pity."

"Your work will have to be your monument."

"It's like he's come back to life," the nurse said.

"I gotta see my face!"

Dr. Anders bore down harder, squaring himself before the mirrors, obstructing a full view. Twice, Bobby tried to peer around him. Anders ordered him to remain absolutely motionless.

"It won't be long, Alpha," Mr. Short said.

At last, Anders stepped aside. Bobby's breath came sharp and deep as he met Alpha Omega. The lips were fuller—petulant and sexy. The cheekbones appeared to have been raised, providing a slightly American Indian cast; like The First Elvis in *Flaming Star*. The nose was thinner; almost an exact duplicate of the original; a Royal nose. And the chin was royal, too. They belonged to a King.

"God Almighty damn," Bobby said in stunned wonder. "God Almighty damn."

There were no other words for it. He had encountered himself—perhaps. And perhaps not. All of it, the nose, chin, lips, were cold with a deep down chill which had nothing to do with the air-conditioning. Frozen and numb. He wet his lips with his tongue; a caress of alien flesh.

"I can't feel nothing. Not with my hands. Or even with my tongue," he said, turning and facing Dr. Anders. "What the hell is wrong?"

The doctor radiated professionalism.

"I suppose we can discuss the sensory and tactile consequences

I mentioned a moment ago. Your reconstituted visage is composed of rearranged bone material and implants."

"What's implants?" Bobby asked as he gently rubbed the cheekbones.

"Small deposits of putty, silicone. First used for the physical enhancement of topless dancers, I believe. A crude, hit-or-miss procedure in those days. It has been refined and improved considerably since its introduction."

"That don't tell me how come I don't feel nothing."

"In time some feeling will return," Dr. Anders said curtly. "Do not expect your face to be as it was. A number of the nerve endings may never re-connect."

"The price of beauty," Mr. Short said.

Bobby returned to the mirrors. The face came at him from everywhere. It was his face—perhaps. How could he be sure?

"What if I want to go back to the way I was?"

Dr Anders, who was washing his hands in a stainless steel sink, whirled about.

"Go back? This is not possible! This face is one of my finest creations. The idea is an insult . . ."

The doctor gave up and furiously dried his hands. Mr. Short wrapped an arm around Bobby's shoulders.

"Alpha, you'll come to love this face. A gift from all of us to you. No other living person has such a face, and only one, no longer among us, had a face which was as . . . stunning. Do I need to speak his name?"

Bobby shook his head. It was all in the mirror. He was part of Elvis, part Bobby Snipes, and all Alpha Omega. All at once. All those beings with The Second Elvis whispering inside.

"I ain't ever seen any face but my own."

"Think of Graceland-by-the-Sea," Mr. Short said. "Think of your kingdom and all who will gather there."

"I'm going to be thinking of all that," Bobby mumbled. The face, devoid of expression, stared into him. He wished he could turn away. Instead, he was immobilized, surrounded by himself in all of his manifestations.

"When can we check out?" Mr. Short said. He was in a hurry, all business.

"Immediately, if you wish," Dr. Anders said. "He has mended well. I doubt that he will need a follow-up for at least three months. And my colleague in Myrtle Beach is competent enough for that. I imagine that only a little polishing will be required. If you will permit a little vanity, I believe this to be my finest transformation."

"Even better than the Jimi Hendrix back in 1980," the nurse said.

"And that was a masterpiece," Dr. Anders said.

"A work of genius," the nurse said.

Mr. Short paid no attention to Anders and the nurse. He was too busy evaluating the face.

"I must say, I've gotten my money's worth," Mr. Short said.

Bobby concentrated on the mirrors, turning first one way, then another, the face contorted in its efforts to apprehend itself.

Mr. Short provided Bobby with a hooded, purple jogging suit, new underwear and socks, running shoes and a pair of dark glasses. It only took a few minutes to check out of the Anders Clinic. The stretch limousine and Clarence waited for them at the door. The sun was bright and high, and Bobby was glad for the glasses and the heavily tinted windows of the limo. Clarence roared through the traffic. The swaying of the car nauseated Bobby. He had been in bed far too long.

"Keep the hood up at all times," Mr. Short said.

Bobby leaned back and closed his eyes. The nausea abated a little.

"How come? My head's been covered up for weeks."

"The mystery, Alpha. The mystery. You will be revealed at the proper time. Now, we're on our way to the oral surgeon. Get those teeth just right."

"That's good . . . I guess." He did not want to go anywhere else, except perhaps Graceland-by-the-Sea. And he had never liked dentists. I'm only gonna hurt some more, he thought.

"You guess? This oral surgeon will make you perfect. Then the tailor. A complete wardrobe; costumes, pajamas, jogging suits, all types of leisure wear. Actually, everything but the costumes has been ordered and shipped to Myrtle Beach. The costumes must be specially fitted. You'll be exquisite. The total, final, Eternal Elvis—Alpha Omega. When the vision of Graceland-by-the-Sea first came to me . . ."

Mr. Short became more excited as he spoke. Mr. Short is about the smartest man I ever met, Bobby thought. That's why he talks like that. Half listening to Mr. Short, sick and exhausted, he tried to make out the city through the sunglasses and the darkened windows. Instead of people and buildings, he only got a dulled, blue-black image of the face.

The oral surgeon was as good, or at least as fast, as Mr. Short claimed. The procedure took two days, ten hours at a stretch in the dentist's chair, and there was new pain when the novocaine and nitrous oxide wore off. When the surgeon finished, the teeth glowed, exactly as Mr. Short predicted; they were nearly as unearthly and detached as the face. Mr. Short took care of the pain, as he had taken care of all things. When Bobby told him he hurt like a son-of-a-bitch, Mr. Short handed him a bottle of pills. Some were pink, some were blue, others red, and a few were multi-colored. Each night, after a day of endlessly gaping open-mouthed, Bobby took two of each type of pill, and hit the bed fully clothed, almost as soon as Mr. Short said good-night.

The tailor, a short, dark man, expertly and methodically took Bobby's measurements. Bobby stood in the center of the room as the tailor worked his way around him. Mr. Short was on the telephone, engaged in animated conversation with Beverly. It must be daytime, Bobby thought. Then maybe it ain't. What difference does it make? It had taken Mr. Short a long time to wake him up. When Bobby came to, Mr. Short lectured him about the pills. He gave Bobby a couple of red ones, which Bobby swallowed at once, and pocketed the bottle. The pain that came on waking was replaced by a slightly, fuzzy disorientation.

The tailor completed his measurements, and opened a large satchel that contained cloth and jewelry samples, and sketches of costumes bound in a loose-leaf notebook. Wordlessly, he handed the notebook to Bobby, who had floated into a chair. Bobby opened the notebook and perfunctorily examined the sketches. He closed his eyes. I can't think about that shit right now, he decided, tossing the notebook onto the bed.

"Beverly, I've got to go. Mr. Chagaris wants us to make some decisions. Yes. Your flight leaves at six. Clarence will meet you. Don't worry so much."

Mr. Short hung up.

"The concession stands are ahead of schedule. That means we'll be able to get the landscapers in a week early. Beverly pushed the construction people pretty hard, but she doesn't demand any more of others than she does of herself."

Mr. Short immersed himself in the notebook. Bobby watched as the tailor arranged the pieces of cloth on the bed; velvet, blends, gold and silver lamé; materials that would inspire the fiercest jealousy in the Upper Ohio Friends of the King and Virgil Joy, or at least the old Virgil Joy.

"What kinda stands?" Bobby said absently. Gloomily, he understood that he would be expected to wear costumes made of these fabrics. He saw that he would have to think about the pictures in the notebook whether he wanted to or not. The tailor spread out a selection of fake diamonds, rubies and sapphires.

"Concessions," Mr. Short said, as he reviewed the sketches. "Food and drink. Non-alcoholic. We are family-oriented. We must satisfy all the needs of the people while they are our guests.

We've even developed a series of Alpha Hot Dogs; from small to super-jumbo."

Before Bobby had a chance to learn more about the Alpha dogs, Mr. Short closed the notebook and moved over to the bed. He fingered the cloth and matched it with the jewels.

"I'll take two of each costume in each of these fabrics. I'll leave the designs up to you. I suppose the usual will do? Sunbursts, thunderbirds, stars?"

Mr. Chagaris packed his wares, and told Mr. Short that the costumes would be ready in three weeks. Bobby noticed for the first time that Mr. Chagaris had an accent similar to Dr. Anders'. Maybe they kin, Bobby thought.

"You make many of these suits?" Bobby asked. Mr. Chagaris paused at the door, surprised that Bobby had spoken to him.

"I do. From all over the country. And Europe, Japan. Big demand for Elvis suits."

"You ever make any suits for a guy named Virgil Joy up in Gastonia, North Carolina?"

"Joy? Could be. Yes. I have not had an order for some time. He never bought top of the line. I sold him a couple of my specials. I make them for the commercial market. Why do you ask?"

"I used to know him."

Mr. Chagaris nodded courteously and departed.

"I believe our operations would be better off if you omitted references to your past," Mr. Short said.

"I don't see no harm in asking. All that stuff Mr. What's-his-name brought reminded me of Virgil."

"The less you think about the past, the happier you'll be."

Mr. Short opened a briefcase and tossed something soft and black on the bed. Bobby picked it up. It was a wig.

"Try it on. It's the finest available. You'll only have to wear it until your own grows back. And we've lined up a terrific stylist for you. He'll be working on permanent salary."

ALPHA OMEGA

Bobby stood in front of the mirror and adjusted the wig. It gave him that First Elvis Las Vegas look. He frowned.

"Is there a problem?" Mr. Short asked.

"It ain't me."

"Alpha, you are no longer you. You are Alpha Omega, almost. You can't expect to become perfect overnight. Perhaps we have pushed things. Once the training starts, things will improve."

"I been hearing a lot about training." The wig perched on Bobby's head like a small furry animal.

"It will start tomorrow. The training is in Beverly's department. She insisted. She arrives tonight, and in the morning we start for Graceland-by-the-Sea. She's driving up with us so she can begin observing and coaching you as soon as possible."

"Like a ball player."

Mr. Short laughed merrily.

"Something like that."

Bobby's mouth started to throb.

"I need some more medicine."

Mr. Short shook out a couple of blue pills. Bobby swallowed them immediately, without even going for water.

"We leave early. And you should relax. The training is nothing that you can't handle. I'd say you were born for it."

"I'll be glad to get going. And to get out of here."

Bobby's teeth ached mightily. And the face was still cold.

"Good boy!" Mr. Short said.

"One more thing. Did that doctor say when I'd be able to feel my face? How many days?"

"He . . . ah . . . wasn't specific as to an exact time. I would guess that your face will grow to fit you almost before you know it."

"That's good. I been worried."

"Alpha, your worries are nearly over!"

163

11

They left in the warm darkness, long before dawn, quickly clearing Atlanta, bound east on the interstate. Clarence held the limo at a steady eighty, driving without regard for the speed limit or the possible attentions of the Georgia Highway Patrol. Mr. Short had given Bobby a couple of pills before they departed. He watched the sun begin its ascent, hot and red; he drifted, suspended between sleep and drugs. Bobby and Mr. Short sat in the back seat. Beverly was up front, beside Clarence. Both she and her father had trained small reading lamps on the piles of paper which they balanced on their laps. Beverly moved efficiently from one document to another, forcing her father to concentrate on the material. Her speech was brisk, cultured, without a trace of her father's latent accent.

"The landscapers are waffling on the completion date. On Monday, I had a conference with Walters. I think he understands. If the grounds aren't ready a week before opening, he stands to lose forty percent of the contract price. He whined, but he brought in three more crews . . ."

Mr. Short listened attentively. He ain't saying much, Bobby thought. That's a new one.

"Will the sprinkler systems be in place?" Mr. Short asked.

"They better be ready by the time we get back."

The more Bobby listened to Beverly, sizing her up, the more he stirred into consciousness. She had awakened him with a phone call at three a.m. and ordered him to be ready to go in fifteen minutes. Those were the first, and only words that she had spoken to him. She was good-looking; attractive in a way that Bobby was not used to. She reminded him of the rich girls back in high school; the ones that never had anything to do with him. They had a bubble, made of money and privilege, around them, and he had hated them because they were unapproachable. Other than the phone call, Beverly had only acknowledged his existence once; that occurred when he staggered, still nearly asleep, into the car. She had given him a quick, indifferent once-over before immersing herself and her father in the papers. Bobby had asked how she was doing, and had not received a reply. He had shrugged and closed his eyes. Friendly as hell, he thought. Maybe she don't appreciate who I am—yet.

He listened to her; facts and figures and how she forced somebody to do exactly what she wanted them to do. A goddamn rich bitch, he thought. And Mr. Short says she's gonna train me. He wanted to snarl, but did not.

The sun climbed higher. The day was already hot. Clarence had provided coffee for everyone when the trip started, but no one had mentioned breakfast. Not that Bobby wanted to eat. The teeth, the face, and the pills had obliterated most of his appetite. Still, it was unusual for Mr. Short to miss a meal. That was this Beverly, Bobby thought. She put her old Daddy right to work. Then it occurred to Bobby that it was odd that they should be driving to Graceland-by-the-Sea. Mr. Short had mentioned during one of his monologues that he owned a couple of planes. Probably another one of Beverly's ideas, Bobby thought.

"Alpha here is making good progress," Mr. Short said. "He's ready to go to work. Aren't you Alpha?"

Bobby was suddenly aware that Mr. Short wanted a response. "Ah . . . sure. I'm ready when you are."

"Perhaps. We'll get to that soon enough," Beverly said. "First we need to go over the salary figures for the ride operators. I've had a difficult time getting top-flight crews. The best ones are at Disney World, and they won't leave. Year-round work, good benefits. They're spoiled. I've checked into the crews at Kings Dominion, Carowinds and Six Flags Over Georgia, and I think I've lined up some very good roller coaster operators . . ."

Roller coasters, Bobby repeated to himself. Goddamn. I don't have to pay no attention to that. She's got The Second Elvis, Alpha Omega, riding with her and she's going on about roller coasters, and who knows what else. He closed his eyes again. Don't have to listen to no rich bitch.

Somewhere west of Savannah, the limo left the interstate and connected with a two-lane highway that ran north. Clarence never slowed down. The road was an old one, seldom-traveled, and the fields, tobacco sheds, and solitary farm houses raced past. After about half an hour, Clarence slowed the limo in front of a low dilapidated building; a kind of gas station-store-house combination. Clarence knocked on a side door. An elderly man, white-haired and shriveled, answered. He embraced Clarence and Mr. Short as they entered the building. Bobby followed Beverly inside. From the rear, in her expensively tailored suit, she looked almost more distant, desirable, and hostile to Bobby, even if she did walk like she was on her way to a business meeting. She had stuffed the papers in an expensive briefcase which she carried with her. I bet she even takes that fucking thing to bed, Bobby thought.

He found himself in a low-ceilinged room, which was jammed

with all sorts of cast-off furniture. There were three couches, too many chairs to count, end tables, chests-of-drawers, and a refrigerator that was at least twenty years old. It could have been a warehouse, or a second-hand store, if it were not for the enormous breakfast that had been laid out: scrambled eggs, a large pot of grits, country ham, biscuits, toast, a pitcher of orange juice, and a pot of coffee. There was enough food for ten people. Clarence and Mr. Short were already seated, steaming plates in front of them. Clarence did not bother to remove his cowboy hat. Instead, he pushed it back from his forehead. There was a distinct, extra-white ring where the hat normally rested, as if it were rarely taken off.

The old man was joined by a woman, who was about his age. Except for the clothes—he wore Exxon coveralls and she was clad in red slacks and a University of Georgia Bulldog T-shirt—they could have been twins. Both were bent, shuffling along, their breath coming in long rasps. They smiled timidly and continuously, like they were afraid they might offend someone.

"More coffee," Clarence said. His voice was high, eunuch-like. These were the first words Bobby had ever heard him speak.

"Yes, son," the woman said, creaking out of the room. Bobby sipped coffee and ate a couple of mouthfuls of grits. The mouth still hurt too much.

"So that lady's your momma?" Bobby asked, genuinely curious.

Clarence did not respond. Instead he shoveled in more eggs, making soft slurping noises. Just like the rich bitch, Bobby thought. Won't say nothing.

"That's correct," Mr. Short said, as he buttered a biscuit. The old man stood behind Mr. Short's chair like a servant awaiting orders.

"And this is Clarence's father, Mr. Aubrey Witherspoon. Shake hands with Alpha Omega."

Mr. Witherspoon's grasp was weak. The old woman returned with a fresh pot of coffee and refilled the cups. Neither of the Witherspoons ate. Clarence gobbled on.

"This is my wife, Maynon." Mr. Witherspoon's voice was as feathery as his grasp. Maynon smiled at Bobby. She reminded him of Mildred, except that she had fewer teeth.

"You're handsome. Like *He* was. The spitting image. I seen him on T.V. every chance I got. Yes sir. What did you say you call yourself?"

"I'm . . ."

"Alpha Omega," Beverly said. She had been methodically eating a piece of toast, while she read through the papers.

"I can say it," Bobby said irritably. He wished that Beverly was on T.V., and that he had his old .22, ready to destroy her image.

"You can say it. But does that mean you can *be* Alpha Omega?" Beverly asked. She resumed reading without waiting for an answer.

"Now, now. Let's enjoy this wonderful breakfast," Mr. Short said, his voice well-fed and expansive. "It's the most important meal of the day. How have you and Maynon been?"

"Fine. Except for getting old." Mr. Witherspoon glanced eagerly around to see if anyone had laughed at his joke. No one had, not even Maynon, who was still mooning at Bobby. "Mother had the flu in the winter, but she's better now. Ain't you?"

Maynon nodded, fluttering her eyes at Bobby. Well, at least somebody here sees what Alpha Omega means, he thought.

"Business ain't been too good," Mr. Witherspoon went on. "Guess you can see that nobody's buying the furniture. I hauled all of it to the flea market in Savannah last month, and didn't sell but one couch. Had to haul it all back. We do okay on the groceries and gas, though. The main thing is, we're glad you're here. Honored, you could say. When we heard you was coming, we decided to go all out on the eats. You and our boy deserve the best. We're so glad to see him. It ain't often son gets home anymore."

"My name ain't son, and I seen you last Christmas," Clarence said.

"I believe it was two Christmases ago," Mr. Witherspoon said softly, almost as if he were afraid Clarence would hear.

"You wrong, as usual," Clarence said. His face was devoid of expression, bisected by the silver sunglasses.

"You were with me last Christmas, Clarence," Mr. Short said. "In Atlantic City. We were guests of the Trumps, remember?"

Clarence refilled his plate.

"If you say so, Mr. Short."

"Sit down, sit down," Mr. Short said to the Witherspoons. "You've gone to all the trouble of preparing this lovely, down home breakfast. Rest, relax."

They dragged chairs from the pile near the refrigerator, and perched on the edges, still waiting for orders.

"Is Clarence sending you money?" Mr. Short asked.

"He's a good son . . . a good boy," Mr. Witherspoon said carefully.

"I keep track of such matters." Mr. Short chomped into another biscuit. "A man's got to respect his parents, help them out. Too many today have forgotten that old commandment: Honor Thy Father and Thy Mother. It's a question of values. There are too many today who sneer at decent family values. You aren't going to forget your Momma and Daddy are you, Clarence?"

Clarence shook his head as he lit a cigarette. He blew out a cloud of smoke and belched. He appeared to be satisfied with the breakfast. Beverly started at the noise, grimacing. She don't like burping and farting, Bobby thought. And not much else either.

"Clarence sends us that money every month. Like you told him to. And you been good to us, too, Mr. Short. Taking our boy in the way you done."

"Don't mention it. Besides, Clarence is a valued employee. The best driver I've ever had. Trained him myself."

Mr. Witherspoon spoke quickly, turning to Bobby.

"Mr. Short took Clarence in when nobody else would. On account of him being an albino and all . . ."

"Shut up," Clarence barked, his voice higher than usual, like a heavy object had fallen on his foot. "Go on out and service my car. And fill up the tank. And take Momma with you. I'm sick of the two of you."

The Witherspoons did as they were told. When they were gone, Mr. Short spoke in a stern, fatherly manner.

"I'm surprised at you. I really am. Using such language to your parents. Especially since I've warned you before."

"I'm sorry," Clarence said.

"Don't tell me. Go to your poor old Momma and Daddy. Say it to them. And mean it, too. I'll ask them later if you did as you were told. And send them an extra hundred this month. And remember this; it's *my* car—not yours."

Clarence lumbered from the room. Mr. Short freshened his glass of orange juice.

"Clarence was only a boy when he came to work for me. I'm afraid he still has some rough edges. His Daddy is right. It must have been difficult being an albino when he was growing up. Apparently, other children tormented him. Such cruelty. I guess you could say I have a soft spot for the downtrodden."

"It's called sentimentality," Beverly said.

"I'll admit I have a streak of sentimentality and nostalgia. I'll never apologize for it. If more people were in touch with such emotions, this would be a better world."

"Don't apologize," Beverly said as she leafed through the papers. "Sentimentality and nostalgia are valuable commodities—in any number of ways."

What the hell is all that about? Bobby thought.

ALPHA OMEGA

* * *

Clarence and his parents returned, and Mr. Witherspoon swore that the limo was running as good as a brand new Singer sewing machine. Mr. Short ordered Clarence to help his parents clean up the remains of the meal as further penance for his harsh words. When the dishes and food were gone, Mr. Short told Clarence to drive his parents over to the produce mart in Thunderbolt for some fresh peaches and tomatoes. He was to be back in an hour.

"You may as well go along," Beverly said to her father. "I need to confer with Alpha Omega—alone."

"But honey . . ."

"Go. You need a break. You've been working very hard. Besides, it won't be long until we begin the field test. I want you sharp so that you can assist in the evaluation."

"Well . . . whatever you want."

Mr. Short stopped at the door. The Witherspoons were already luxuriating in the limo's back seat. Clarence waited impassively at the wheel.

"Now you listen to Beverly, Alpha. This is where your training begins."

Bobby tried to accept being alone with Beverly. He could not. It was too close to those times he had to face his father, or the police, or the prison guards. He did not even want to look at her. Neither spoke until the sound of the limo's engine vanished down the road toward Thunderbolt. Bobby had an acute awareness of a clock ticking in another room, and of the bacon grease, closed-in odor of the Witherspoon's house. Carefully, Beverly deposited the papers in her briefcase. She laid a small notebook and a silver Cross pen on the table, perfectly aligning them. She does every goddamn thing right, Bobby thought.

"Alpha Omega," she said. She attempted a smile, but was unsuccessful. Bobby could see that she could not have much in common with her father, if smiling was so difficult for her.

"I created the name," she said.

"That's what I heard." And it's my name now, he thought, no matter who dreamed it up.

"You heard correctly. The doctors certainly earned their fees, outrageous as they were. Daddy insisted, though. He adores re-making people. Clarence is a good example. He was nearly feral when Daddy came across him. It was during one of his trips, years ago. He also adores visiting grotesque shit holes like this place. Part of the real America, he says. He may have something there. Anyway, Clarence was about fifteen, and his parents couldn't control him. All you have to do is look at them to see why. Half the time, he lived in the swamps. I understand that a few of the locals actually thought he was Big Foot. People yearn for that sort of magical experience. But Daddy trained him. He's made remarkable progress. And Daddy's money has given you your . . . appearance. I wonder if you and Clarence aren't brothers . . . in a sense, of course."

She did smile then, tight, without showing any teeth. Bobby drank cold coffee. Rich bitch, he thought again. Got all the fucking answers.

"And magical experiences are one of the many items that Short Enterprises has to offer, most especially in the case of Graceland-by-the-Sea. That is why it is important to initiate your training immediately. From this point on, you are to consider yourself my student."

"Is that right?" Bobby said slowly, his voice full of jailhouse insolence. Here was falseness, and he welcomed the rage he felt against it. "What're you gonna train me to do? I'm already Alpha Omega. What're you gonna do to make me better?"

"Attitude is a very important part of training. *Your* attitude needs radical improvement."

She was composed, despite his rage, her voice calm and analytical. Bobby finished the coffee. It was bitter and brackish, and he wanted to spit.

"What're you gonna do if I keep this attitude? The people want me. Your Daddy said so. I'm the closest thing to The First Elvis you're ever gonna find. I done gone way past him. Hell, I had my own Temple. All kinds of people come to see me. I'm The Second Elvis. Don't you know that?"

She jotted something in the notebook. Her writing made Bobby nervous, and his rage, for some reason he could not name or grasp, was mixed with confusion.

"What you writing?"

"So you've come out of your delusion long enough to take an interest in the outside world?"

She handed the notebook to him. The handwriting was neat, perfect. *Ignorant prick*, it read, underlined three times. Bobby tossed the notebook across the table. Hatred rose like a steaming, iron shaft.

"I have nothing to hide from you," she said matter-of-factly, more composed than ever. "We may as well be honest. What you see on the page was, by the way, my initial judgement. It has proven correct—so far. As for the Temple, I commissioned some research. You never drew more than a hundred people to a service. Your replacement, Johnny Love, brings in at least one fifty, which is quite good for one of Short Enterprises minor concerns."

"That don't mean shit," Bobby grunted.

"I have the figures. And you should understand this. You were hardly my choice for the Elvis figure."

"What the hell is an Elvis figure?" The term filled Bobby with an ill-defined alarm.

She laughed, mechanical and triumphant.

"You are the Elvis figure. An important prop. Probably indispensable and replaceable at once. Daddy would disagree. For some reason, which I'll never understand, he wanted you from the first. Usually, I can make him listen to reason. Not this time. I think he is obsessed by the conception of total transformation, uniting past, present and future. The Eternal Elvis is the term he keeps using. So it is done, and can't be helped . . ."

"It's his money, ain't it?" Bobby's hatred simmered now. She ain't got as much say-so as she thinks.

"You're an ignorant prick, but you're obviously not stupid. There are remedies for ignorance, and I believe that we can actually harness the power of your delusions for the benefit of all . . ."

"If a delusion is what I think it is, you dead fucking wrong. I *am* The Second Elvis . . . I'm Alpha Omega . . ."

". . . don't use that term to me, that Second Elvis nonsense. You are the Elvis figure, as I said, and for better or for worse. I've trained all sorts, and the possibility exists that you can be made to function, despite the flaws in your nature."

Bobby's teeth hurt. He had clenched them tightly since the limo left, and wide bands of pain slithered through his head. He wanted pills, and they were with Mr. Short in Thunderbolt. The teeth ground together. He could not stop them. Mercilessly, she went on.

". . . before your media exposure, I had auditioned the best impersonators in the business. I recommended one who was so close to the original that I doubt even Priscilla could tell them apart. Unfortunately, he turned out to be gay, which eliminated him from consideration. Gay or not, he was more trainable than you appear to be. The question is whether or not you want to be trained so that you can become worthy of your position."

Bobby rolled the thick mug around in his hands, struggling to unclench his teeth. It would do a lot of damage if he smashed it against her ear. He forced himself, instead, to think of Graceland-by-the-Sea.

"All right. Train me, goddammit." He released his grip on the mug.

"I hope that you're sincere. If you aren't, I'll find out quickly enough."

"I said okay." What the fuck does she want, he thought. The pills were far away.

"Good. When we get to Myrtle Beach, you will be given an operations manual, which I have personally written and developed. You must familiarize yourself with every section. There are also copies of texts that were important to Elvis Presley. You will also be expected to read them, although they are not as vital as the manual."

"The First Elvis," he said through his teeth.

"Very well. The First Elvis it is. I can accept a few of your whims. I believe my father has informed you about the grammar lessons. On the positive side, you have a number of potential strengths. Musically, you are at least adequate . . ."

"Singing. I'm good . . ."

"I've seen the tapes. Yes. You can sing. Now, will you please let me finish?"

Again, he considered using the mug on her. Perhaps then the pain would go away. He restrained himself. Even if she had a grip on him, it could not last—once he got to Graceland-by-the-Sea.

"Your height and weight are nearly perfect, and you possess that unexplainable redneck sexual allure that was the trademark of Elvis . . . The First Elvis."

"Thanks, I guess."

"And you are not without a certain primitive irony, I might add. The First Elvis also put that trait to good use. Are there any questions so far?"

"I can't think of none. You got all the questions and all the answers."

"I can see that you're already making progress. Today, we conduct the field test . . ."

The field test, as Beverly called it, was to take place at a Tasti-Freeze a few miles from the Witherspoon's store. Beverly equipped Bobby with a small cassette recorder; the type police informers used in gathering evidence. She said that the recorder was vital for monitoring the responses of Bobby and the subjects. He wondered who the subjects were supposed to be. She ordered him to hoist up his sweat shirt, and she strapped the recorder on him herself, her long, cold-white fingers wedging it into Bobby's armpit, then taping the wire down nearly to his hand. The straps cut into him a little, and her touch gave him goose-bumps.

As the limo moved north, Beverly drilled him on the procedures. His materialization would be most important. Bobby was to keep his remarks to a minimum. The reaction of the test subjects could be better judged that way. Mr. Short, who had loaded down the back of the limo with produce, listened raptly. It will be miraculous, he said at one point. Only if it works, Beverly said.

Clarence slowed down. They entered a small town, which consisted of a few fly-blown stores, a red light, and an abandoned cotton gin. In the heat, the town appeared dried-up, utterly dead and gone. Despite the fact that it was not quite one o'clock, there were no people on the street. The only sign of life that Bobby saw was a couple of large sleeping dogs, their tongues lolling against the sidewalk in front of a pool room.

"How are we doing this . . . field test here?" Bobby asked.

"Most sightings of The First Elvis are in small towns," Beverly said. "I believe it was Hume who noted that most religious hallucinations are experienced by peasants. Not noblemen and philosophers. The same principle applies here. I've done a complete search of sightings as reported in both the tabloids and mainstream newspapers. Eighty-three percent occur in places like this. Now, once more . . . what are you to do?"

The Tasti-Freeze was in sight. It stood beside a small skating rink on the outskirts of town. Beyond, the blazing highway seemed to go straight into infinity.

"I go up to the window. Order a large Pepsi. Keep the hood

up on account of the wig. If anybody asks my name, say Alpha Omega. If anybody gets too excited, get back to the car. Walk. Don't run. Don't wave when we drive off. If anybody chases us, don't look out the back window."

"And what is important, most important, for this test?" Beverly said.

"Mystery."

About ten cars were out front, and a small line of customers was at the window. Clarence kept the engine running, the car parallel to the road for a quick get-away. Bobby took his place at the end of the line. His teeth still hurt, but not as bad as earlier. Beverly told Mr. Short not to give him any pills until after the test; that Bobby's head had to be completely clear. Bobby had shouted helplessly then. They ignored him. Now, however, the pills did not matter as much. A tenseness, an excitement had nudged away some of the pain.

The sweat ran down from beneath the wig and over the numb, cold face. The line moved slowly. Two teenaged boys in Clemson baseball caps were in front of him, and they waved to and flirted with the girls who worked behind the plate-glass front of the Tasti-Freeze. In front of the boys, a middle-aged housewife paid for a banana-split. She licked ice cream from a long red spoon as she made her way back to her Chevrolet Blazer. She paused, the spoon before her face, the ice cream falling in white drops to the asphalt, and started for Bobby. He saw her coming, and held his place in line. That goddamn Beverly's watching, he thought. I'm gonna show her.

The two boys had ordered hot dogs all the way. As one of the girls handed them their order, her mouth fell open. She remained poised, a hot dog in each hand.

"Gimme my hot dog, Starla," the taller of the two boys said.

"Look there," Starla said in a faraway voice. "Right there in line."

The middle-aged housewife was at Bobby's side. He pretended

not to notice her. Starla called to the other girls, who abandoned work on hamburgers and hot fudge sundaes. The boys forgot about the girls and the hot dogs.

"Excuse me," the housewife said. She had a worn, sweet face, as if she had been married too long and had too many children. She pushed the hair back from her damp forehead, primping, unconsciously trying to arrange herself.

"Excuse me," she repeated, her voice shaking. "I don't mean to be nosey . . ."

Bobby gave her the teeth and the face. He smiled. She took two steps backwards.

"Yes, ma'am?" he said courteously.

"I . . . I don't mean to be rude or nothing . . ."

"You're not."

"I seen *Blue Hawaii* on the T.V. last night . . ."

Her hands fluttered helplessly. She was nearly immobilized.

"One of my favorites," Bobby said through the teeth.

Starla had stuck her head halfway through the low window where the orders were placed. The other girls pressed their faces against the glass, whispering and giggling.

"You fellows through?" Bobby said as he stepped past them.

Starla, who was redheaded, high school cute with plenty of make-up and MTV hair, cast an upward look of wonder with her big blue eyes. The hot dogs sat untouched on the ledge below the window.

"Yeah. I mean, yes, sir," the taller boy said.

Bobby could feel the housewife behind him, and he heard car doors slamming. He did not turn around. That would spoil the mystery. He handed the hot dogs to the boys.

"Enjoy your lunch," he said uncovering all of the teeth. The boys grinned back at him, holding on to the hot dogs as if they were talismans.

"What'll you have, sir?" Starla asked, her voice reverent, virginal.

"I heard one of your friends here call you Starla. That's a pretty name."

"Thank you. Thank you *so much*."

"Starla, all I need is a large Pepsi with plenty of ice."

The girls inside the Tasti-Freeze rushed toward the drink fountain. Starla was the quickest, however. Her hands shook as she drew the Pepsi.

"It's my favorite drink," Bobby said to the housewife.

"Mine, too," she said. "I love a good Pepsi." She began to giggle and it sounded as if she might never stop. Starla held the Pepsi out to Bobby, and their hands touched as he took it from her.

"What do I owe you?" Bobby asked, pitching his voice low and sexy.

"That's . . . uh . . . that's . . ." Starla was without words. He gave her the smile, understanding that it was magic.

"Never mind. Here's twenty. You and the other girls split the change."

He held the bill out to her. Giving away money was Mr. Short's idea. Beverly said it was a nice touch. The First Elvis had been recklessly generous.

"I couldn't . . . we couldn't," Starla stammered.

Bobby took her hands, and pressed the bill into them.

"Sure you can, honey."

She held up the twenty, examining it like she had never seen money before. Bobby drank deeply from the sweating Tasti-Freeze cup. The ice did not even hurt his teeth, and the sweetness of the Pepsi eased his parched mouth. He had not realized how thirsty he was.

He faced the crowd. The cars were empty, their owners abandoning their ice cream and sandwiches, drawn toward the hooded figure with the large Pepsi in his hand. They clustered around him, then made way as he walked toward the limo. Before Bobby could get in the car, the housewife tugged gently at his sleeve, right where the wire rested. He took a last swallow, and handed the remains of the drink to her. Greedily, she chugged it down, Pepsi running from the corners of her mouth. The banana split had long since melted and run down the hood of her Blazer. Someone told her to pass it around, and she did. The Pepsi went from hand to hand, mouth to mouth, until only the ice was left. When it was gone, she demanded the cup, which was reluctantly handed back to her.

"Where did you come from?" she asked.

Bobby only smiled.

"Where're you going?" a man said in an impressive bass voice. He wore a blue polyester blazer and yellow checked pants.

"That's a good question," Bobby replied.

"What's your name?" Starla asked. She and the other girls had abandoned their stations in the Tasti-Freeze.

"Alpha Omega," Bobby said solemnly.

"The beginning and the end," the man with the bass voice said. "I'm Reverend Harland Bowaters of the Antioch Primitive Baptist Church."

"Pray, Reverend," Bobby said. That's a good one, he thought. Even old Beverly hadn't counted on a preacher.

"That's my job," the Reverend said with dignity.

"And I'll bet that you're real good at it. Pray that we get rid of all of the falseness."

As the preacher contemplated Bobby's admonition, the housewife, quick as a snake, kissed him on the cheek, and Starla hugged him around the waist. Bobby pulled away from her—regretfully wishing that she could hug him more, and do other things. The crowd pressed in closer, begging him to stay. He darted through them as the rear door of the limo swung open. Clarence stomped the accelerator and they broke free into the void of the highway.

As soon as the town was behind them, Beverly demanded the recorder. Bobby was glad to be free of it. He threw back the hood, pulled off the wig, and waited for the air-conditioning to revive him. Beverly punched the tape on, and feverishly took notes. It was easy, he thought; a lot easier than she made it out to be. I didn't even have to act. He was about to ask Mr. Short for a pill when another realization came to him. There was no pain. The mouth, his mouth, no longer hurt. The tape ended.

"You were great!" Mr. Short whooped. "Even better than I imagined. Did you see the way they swarmed around him? All sorts of people. They cut across all the demographic lines. There were even three blacks, and blacks could hardly be called fans of The First Elvis. Too bad we can't go back. I'll bet the whole town has turned out."

Beverly snapped the notebook closed.

"I'll make a more thorough evaluation later. On the surface, I'd say you were about ninety percent successful. You stayed a little too long. Another couple of minutes, and they would've been all over you. Or that housewife, or the girl, might've found the wire. Did you think about that?"

Bobby was too absorbed with the absence of pain to pay much attention to Beverly's criticism.

"No," he finally said.

"Concentrate now, Alpha," Beverly said. "I don't conduct critiques just to hear myself speak."

"She's right, you know," Mr. Short said.

Beverly rewound the tape and started over. Frequently, she pressed the stop button.

"The voice inflection is good. No problem. Watch the religious references. That must be strongly implied, not directly stated. I like the passing of the Pepsi. Shows good instincts."

She offered criticisms and pointers after almost every one of Bobby's utterances. He was elsewhere, however, even if he did seem to be paying attention. He thought of the adulation, the naked craving of the people at the Tasti-Freeze. They were no different than the people at the Temple. There was a whole world waiting out there, and it had been waiting for years. Something is happening, he thought. Something is starting right now.

He touched the face.

It was no longer cold, even in the wind of the limo's air-conditioning. The lips, cheekbones, and nose all responded, welding themselves to him for all time. His fingers probed the features. They were his. It was as great as the moment in which he became The Second Elvis. He laughed, a hoarse, unfettered bellow.

"What are you doing?" For once, the distanced composure was missing from Beverly's voice.

"It's MINE!" Bobby roared.

Clarence slowed down to seventy.

"Are you sick?" Mr. Short said.

"I ain't never been better. It's mine! I own the face!"

He hurled himself halfway over the seat, lunging toward the rearview mirror, hungry for the sight of himself. Clarence swerved, fighting at the wheel, while Beverly and Mr. Short tried to pull Bobby back. Desperately, they held to him as he drank in what he could from the mirror. It was no longer the face of a stranger.

12

He laughed until the tears rolled down what had finally, and permanently, become his face. Mr. Short tried to give him some new pills of a type which would render him serene, but Bobby shook his head in refusal. Curiously, Beverly agreed to his refusal. You could have predicted this, she said. We'll have him in proper shape soon enough. She wrote something in her notebook, and Mr. Short reluctantly put the pills away.

In the late afternoon, they reached Myrtle Beach. The limo raced past the hotels, the T-shirt shops, the gooney golf courses, and the seafood restaurants. If he had been able, Bobby might have recalled the last time he had been in Myrtle Beach. For the time being, however, he was beyond memory. What had been was temporarily canceled. As the limo turned away from the coastal highway and onto a two lane road that cut through miles of pine trees, Mr. Short said that they were nearly there. Bobby understood that he was almost home, and gave out a final, long howl of ecstasy, the first sound that had come out of his mouth since the laughter.

Clarence swung the limo off the road and through gates that materialized from nowhere. When Bobby saw the gate's musical notes, he felt no need to howl. He had mastered and channeled the electricity. He could see the whole world as never before in his life.

They cruised through the acres of new parking lots which covered the flat, baking land on either side of the road. Tall metal poles supported a variety of signs that described how to reach the ticket windows, where the shuttle buses could be found, and other information which would be vital to those who would come to Graceland-by-the-Sea. Beyond the parking lots were the ticket booths. A guard opened a gate to the right of the red brick booths, and the limo rolled onto a new single-lane road. Mr. Short said they had set up thirty stations, although they could expand to fifty easily enough. Chain-link fences ran on either side of the booths, sealing off Graceland-by-the-Sea from the parking lots, from the rest of the world. Beside the narrow road, gangs of men, the landscapers who Beverly had pressed so relentlessly, labored in the heat, sodding the raw, sandy earth, planting lines of trees and shrubbery. Despite their efforts, the place had a bare, scalded appearance, like a new subdivision.

The roller coaster, which had been named the Mystery Train, towered above the other rides: two ferris wheels, a Tilt-a-Whirl, bumper cars and a waterslide which had been christened Paradise, Hawaiian Style. Next came the gift shops, which would offer T-shirts, statues, commemorative plates, ash-trays, dolls, tapestries, and all the other wonders of the Eternal Elvis and Alpha Omega. Beyond the gift shops were the concession stands where visitors could slack their thirsts on giant Pepsis and feast on Alpha Dogs, hamburgers, Love Me Tender chicken, and fried peanut butter and banana sandwiches. There was also a wax museum, devoted to, according to Mr. Short, the life of The First Elvis. The wax museum was of pre-fabricated metal construction, like the music hall, a big barn of a building still thick with construction workers. In the shadow of the music hall lay two small, white-washed frame buildings. The first was a small chapel, an exact duplicate of the little church in Tupelo which The First Elvis had attended with his parents, Gladys and Vernon. The second building was a replica of the shotgun house where the original King was born.

Mr. Short lectured on the wonders of Graceland-by-the-Sea. Bobby cared nothing for the rides, the stands, or even the music hall. He had yet to gaze upon what really mattered. Without warning, however, the road, which had been straight as a knife, curved away from the rest of the park.

"My house," he said. The mansion had sprung up at him—right out of the ground.

"Graceland-by-the-Sea," Beverly snapped. "A Short Enterprises Production."

Her words were of no importance to Bobby. The white columns, the lions, the portico. All of it was right. Clarence parked at the rear entrance. Mr. Short lead him through the gleaming, stainless steel kitchen, down a corridor, and into a large office which was all glass, leather and oak paneling. He fought back the desire to race from room to room, caressing the furniture, rolling on the carpets, wallowing in his Graceland. Beverly motioned for him to take a seat, as Mr. Short installed himself behind a massive desk and phoned for dinner. She handed Bobby a book entitled "Operations Manual for Principal Figure: Graceland-by-the-Sea".

"Beverly has put this manual together for our mutual benefit, and I have approved it. If The First Elvis had owned such a document, he would still be in business."

Bobby opened the manual to the table of contents: Tours,

Performances, Code of Conduct, Attitude and Behavior Toward the Public. He flipped through the pages, reading here and there.

> Section 5 (a): The principal figure shall refrain from the use of drugs, alcohol and tobacco . . .
> Section 9 (c): The principal figure is to be courteous and sincere with all members of the public. Under no circumstances, however, should the principal figure fraternize excessively with visitors, especially in such a way as to reflect poorly upon Graceland-by-the-Sea . . .
> Section 13 (a): When not performing in the Music Hall, or engaged in tour activities, the principal figure will remain in the upstairs portion of the mansion. This will be done so as to ensure the essential mystery of the principal figure's character. Absence from the mansion or the Music Hall will only be allowed with prior approval of the management, and in the company of another employee or employees of Graceland-by-the-Sea or Short Enterprises.

Bobby closed the manual.

"You have much to learn, don't you?" Beverly asked.

"Looks like you thought of it all," Bobby said. With or without the book, Beverly could not interfere with the electricity. Then something came to him. He was surprised he had not thought of it before. *I'm gonna use it against her. I'm gonna get it so right, I'll shut her up for good.*

"You'll have to absorb all of it, Alpha," Mr. Short said. "We open five weeks from today. Now, the field test proved what I said all along; that you are the best, the only real choice for the principal figure. Still, Beverly and I agree that you are not yet complete. However, total perfection is within our grasp."

"That remains to be seen," Beverly said.

She can't get at me, Bobby thought.

"We want you to rest tonight. Read through the manual. Your instruction begins tomorrow," Mr. Short said.

"Probably the most difficult job in the entire operation," Beverly said.

"For a smart lady like you?" Bobby asked.

After dinner, Mr. Short showed him around the mansion. Beverly excused herself, claiming that she had important matters to attend to. It is Graceland, Bobby thought. He compared the mansion with what he recalled of his abortive visit to the original, and the pictures from Laverne's Elvis library. When he reached the television room, he could almost see himself back in Memphis, arguing with the tour guide—she could have been Beverly's sister—hearing her lie about how The First Elvis never shot T.V. sets. Despite his resentment, the clarity, the electricity, did not weaken. And he no longer wanted to stroke the furniture or leap through the gilded rooms. He was cool, dignified.

Mr. Short led him upstairs; to the very heart of Graceland, to that which had been denied him.

"And here is the master bedroom," Mr. Short said, pushing open a door.

A double king-sized bed filled much of the space, although the room was large enough to hold most of Bobby's old home on Modena Street. The heavy draperies were closed, barring any trace of natural light. A massive television, complete with a VCR, was mounted on the wall opposite the bed. A stack of books rested on the night stand. Bobby picked up a copy of *The Late, Great Planet Earth*.

"These very books were in The First Elvis' room the night he died," Mr. Short said. "We overlooked no details. Beverly saw to that."

I'll bet she did, Bobby thought. He glanced at the titles of the other volumes: *The Complete Works of Madame Blavatsky; The Shroud of Turin; The Tibetan Book of the Dead.*

"I knew The First Elvis owned these books," Bobby said. The books smacked of falseness, but at the same time, he had a curiosity as to what they might reveal.

"Beverly wants you to read them. The manual comes first, however."

Bobby picked up a few of the video tapes that were stacked beside the VCR: *Doctor Strangelove: or How I Learned to Stop Worrying And Love the Bomb ; Monte Python's Flying Circus; Dirty Harry.* All those films had been beloved by The First Elvis.

"I gotta watch these movies, too?"

"Correct." Mr. Short flopped heavily on the bed. Bobby could tell that something was bothering him.

"That Beverly's real smart, ain't she?"

"I couldn't have done it without her."

"College. All that stuff."

"She had to be at the top of her class." A trace of a southern whine crept into Mr. Short's voice. "Even back in the first grade. Had to make a hundred on every test. She'd have a fit if she didn't. Cute as could be, though. I can still see her stomping her little feet and flouncing around when she didn't get what she wanted. Which brings us to a delicate subject; I've sensed that there is . . . friction between you two."

Bobby sat down in an ugly, Spanish-style chair. The clarity was strong.

"I don't want you to worry about such things, Mr. Short. Me and Beverly's gonna get along fine. I'm gonna do whatever she says. You can bet on that."

Bobby's words pleased Mr. Short, and the whine subsided.

"I feel better, hearing that. Once you get used to her methods, you'll find that she's really easy to get along with . . ."

And shit don't stink, Bobby thought.

"Tell me about her," Bobby said.

"Her mother was the smartest woman I've ever known. Cultured. Read books all the time. I loved her very much."

"Where's her momma now?"

Bobby enjoyed asking about Beverly. If she only knew I was talking about her, he thought.

"We were divorced when Beverly was ten. She married again. Almost immediately. The director of several multi-national corporations. He dropped dead of a heart attack at the Bohemian Club in San Francisco. It was during a fund-raiser for Richard Nixon, back before the '72 election. She likes to travel; Europe, the far East. Anywhere she pleases. She gives benefit balls in Washington and New York. Owns a horse farm in northern Virginia. You can read about her in the social columns in the *Times* and the *Post*."

"Who raised Beverly?"

"Gloria, that's my former wife's name, had custody of Beverly. I was traveling an awful lot then. That was before I made Myrtle Beach my permanent headquarters. Almost the only time I saw Beverly was during holidays. And I had to fight to see her then. Gloria . . . Gloria looked down on me. Said that I did not have the proper background or instincts to raise her child. 'Her child,' she said. Not ours. She said I wasn't civilized. Perhaps I wasn't, by her standards. I improved myself, though. Why, do you know I hired a world-famous professor from the University of Chicago to help me become cultivated? I paid him top dollar, five summers running. He's the head of academic development for the Short Foundation. A brilliant man. I loaned him to the White House. For helping in the creation of cultural policy papers . . ."

"What about Beverly?" Bobby had grown impatient with Mr. Short and his professor.

"Oh, yes. Gloria tried to say that I would turn Beverly into a cheap, flashy, homecoming queen type. That only shows that she never understood her own daughter. When she was sixteen,

Beverly went to Chapel Hill. Two years early. Gloria demanded that she go to some fancier school up North, but I got my way on that one. I even bought Beverly a house there. I still use it when I go to basketball games. Beverly made A's in every course she took. Got all kinds of awards. Then she went to graduate school at Harvard. An MBA, of course. And a communications degree from Penn. She studied in France, too . . ."

Big goddamn deal, Bobby thought.

"She been married?"

Mr. Short sighed deeply.

"For two years. To a professor at the Sorbonne."

"Have a kid?"

"No. And I've wanted grandchildren more than anything else. Even more than Graceland-by-the-Sea. She left the professor. He was supposed to be important in his field. Some kind of literary criticism, Beverly said. I never met the man. She won't even talk about him. He is, however, considerably older than Beverly."

"It musta been hard on her." Ain't nothing ever been hard enough on her, Bobby thought.

"It didn't seem to affect her at all. After she left Paris, she worked for Ronald Reagan."

"The President, huh? I bet you was real proud of her."

"Naturally. She went to work for President Reagan during the 1980 campaign. She was one of his media co-ordinators. Mostly, she devised television strategies, developed commercials, that sort of thing. Later she moved to speech writing. The President loved her work. Said so many times. He urged her to stay on, but she resigned after the first term. She's so restless, so inventive. Wants to try new things all the time. When she left Washington, Disney Productions made her a wonderful offer. In two years, she became the top vice-president for public relations."

"Mickey Mouse?" Bobby was puzzled. Mr. Short smiled.

"Not simply Mickey Mouse. No. She articulated and defined. Those were her contributions to Disney World and Disney Productions; which is, as you must know, one man's vision of adventure, decency, fantasy and truth. All absolutely essential American qualities."

"How come she left?"

"For me. It was like a dream come true. One day last year I called her and told her of my vision. And without my even asking, she said that she must work with me. And now we're a team."

Sure you are, Bobby thought. The electricity was so strong, Bobby thought that its crackle must be audible to Mr. Short.

"Sometimes it's hard for me to realize that she's my daughter."

"But she is." And you can't get out of it, Bobby thought.

"I'm a lucky man."

"You can say that."

Mr. Short stood up.

"I've got to go now."

"Gonna see Beverly?"

"Yes. More details to attend to. Mainly, though, I want to let her know about our conversation. I feel much better now that we've cleared the air."

"Hey. We're all in this together."

"How true, Alpha. How true."

Mr. Short's voice was touchingly husky with love.

She drilled him from eight to ten hours every day, with half an hour for lunch. She never ate with him. Instead, she disappeared, and returned in exactly thirty minutes, to pick up where they had stopped. If Mr. Short had spoken to her about the conversation in the master bedroom, Bobby could not tell it. And it was not difficult for Bobby to tell that she still detested him. He sensed, however, that she was surprised by his enthusiasm and energy.

That first night at Graceland-by-the-Sea, he spent several hours on the toilet, the manual in his lap. He was consumed by the idea of being in the exact spot, almost, where The First Elvis died. And he was also consumed with knowing the material in the manual so that he could show Beverly up. When they met the next morning in the office, he was able to describe in detail all of his duties and obligations. From her expression, he could tell that she had been prepared to humiliate him, to lead him like a child. He enjoyed denying her the pleasure. Once, on that first morning, she paused and asked if he objected to the numerous restrictive rules that the principal figure must observe. Clearly, she was not used to seeking the opinions of others. And the rules were restrictive. When he was not leading tours or performing, Bobby was to be confined to the mansion. "If it's for the good of Short Enterprises and allows Alpha Omega to keep that mystery of his, then I'll do it," he said. And he was only half-lying.

From the beginning of the training, Beverly stressed the importance of the tour. It took precedence over what she referred to as "the musical experience" because the patrons would be closest to Alpha Omega at the mansion, where contact would be practically on a one-on-one basis. A guide would assemble the customers in the foyer, limiting the group to no more than fifty members. The patrons would have to pay an extra ten dollars above the regular admission price for the full Graceland-by-the-Sea experience, and they would expect a good return on their money. Once the group was in place, Bobby would descend the staircase, and recite a short welcoming speech. At the conclusion of the speech, he would conduct the group through the house and grounds, describing the activities he enjoyed as master of Graceland-by-the-Sea: go-cart racing, horseback riding, racquetball, extended T.V. watching, and "hanging out with the guys." However, no provision had been made in Beverly's plan for the importation of male friends who would correspond to The First Elvis' Memphis mafia.

For two weeks, she drilled him on tour procedures, concentrating on posture, language, and memorization. The grammar lessons were conducted in the evening and lasted for two hours. Bobby did not mind the lessons as much as he thought he would. Beverly was a good teacher. As she explained subject-verb agreement and the avoidance of double-negatives, it was obvious that she would have been at home in front of a high school English class. If Bobby was fifteen, he might even have gotten an erection as he watched her pace authoritatively back and forth.

When the lessons ended, she left quickly, and he retired to the upstairs. There, he watched the video tapes, the volume turned up as high as it could go, and read the books from the nightstand. He could make little sense of them, except for *The Late, Great Planet Earth*. The text spoke of the return of Christ to earth, and the signs that had been given to the faithful to prepare them for that coming. Bobby had not studied a book so hard since he first discovered the Elvis volumes. If Christ is coming, he thought, then Elvis can, too. As he read the feverish, logic-leaping prose, he substituted the name of Elvis for that of Jesus. Christ was transformed many times, and so was The First Elvis. It all made sense to him. And the book, like the Bible in the Free Will Baptist Church, promised a millennium of peace and happiness for all who believed. The people who would come to Graceland-by-the-Sea would enter a parallel paradise, with Alpha Omega reigning over all. The more Bobby read, the more he realized that his training with Beverly was like the time of tribulation spoken of in the Bible. Beverly was only a tool, a way to achieve heaven. With this fact in mind, it made even more sense to go along with her schemes. As he read, his face became a beatific, all-accepting mask.

The music director's name was Jonathan Kalo. He was a tiny, nervous man, his pale, city face framed by an expensive haircut and a well-trimmed mustache. Beverly introduced Kalo to Bobby in the music hall. Kalo called her Bev, and they apparently had known each other for a long time. They laughed and chatted, and told private stories, as if Bobby were not even there. Beverly said that Kalo was the best in the business. He had done six Miss America pageants, three Republican National Conventions and dozens of Broadway shows. Accompanying Kalo was a seventeen piece orchestra, which had been recruited among penniless New York musicians. In addition to the orchestra, there was a chorus—three tall, handsome black sisters who called themselves the Gospelettes—and a back-up rock and roll band. The band was the same bunch that had backed Bobby in the recording studio in Charlotte, but they no longer called themselves "Excitement". Now they were The King's Court, although they were still bland and collegiate-looking.

Beverly showed Bobby and Kalo around the music hall. Not nearly as much money had been spent there as on the mansion. The floor was concrete, and the walls were sheet metal, inside and out. And it was hot inside, despite the big fans that blew from each end of the building. The stage was high, however, the sound-system first-rate, and twenty-foot neon letters, spelling out Alpha Omega, were installed at the rear of the stage.

Once the rehearsals were underway, Beverly cut back on the tour practices and reduced the grammar lessons to every other night. Bobby and the musicians worked together from eight in the morning until late afternoon. Kalo had selected six of The First Elvis' early songs for the show. Bobby heard him tell Beverly that he was sick to death of hearing them, but they were a necessity, he guessed. Three of The First Elvis' old Las Vegas numbers were included: "Polk Salad Annie", "American Trilogy", and Frank Sinatra's "My Way". Mr. Short had insisted on including "How Great Thou Art". There were other songs that were new to Bobby. One of these, "Send in the Clowns", was the worst Bobby had ever heard, but he kept his opinion to himself.

The old numbers presented no problems for Bobby. He had learned them all, and the corresponding stage acrobatics, at the Burning Love Temple. He was not encumbered by the guitar, and when he was allowed to jump and spin, he experienced a touch of power that was to come once the tribulation was over. The other songs did not come as easily, even after he learned the words. Kalo kept at him during the rehearsals. Put some feeling into it, he squeaked, frisking about like a toy poodle. Bobby was at his humblest, his most co-operative then. He clung tightly to the electricity, and spent even more time with *The Late, Great Planet Earth*.

Beverly came to every rehearsal. She watched Bobby constantly. He could feel her, even when he was dancing and bouncing around the stage. He was curious about her half-smile when Kalo berated him. After ten days even Kalo had to admit that Bobby was more than passable on the Broadway show tunes.

"Okay," Kalo said after a particularly grueling rehearsal. "That's enough. We're getting counterproductive here. Be back in the morning at the regular time."

Kalo and Beverly remained at the back of the hall, reviewing the rehearsal. The orchestra, heat-stricken northerners, dragged themselves up the aisle. The King's Court bounded past them, apparently impervious to eight hours of Kalo and his rehearsals. Bobby, exhausted, yet serene, was about to leave when the tallest of the Gospelettes approached him. The Gospelettes made him uneasy. A part of him still appreciated how good they were, with their high tight gospel harmonies. People like that can cause trouble, he thought. For them, the music was everything. He had never spoken to any of them; or, for that matter, to any other members of the show.

"I'm Towanda Shelton," she said.

"I'm Alpha Omega."

"I *know* that," she laughed. "I can see those big lighted letters. That's some name to carry around."

"I guess so."

He backed away from her. It was nearly time for tour practice. More importantly, however, her luminous eyes seemed to peer right into him.

"Can you play, or do you just sing?"

Her words brought him to a halt.

"I can play . . . I used to play."

She pointed to one of the guitars left by the King's Court.

"Let me hear you."

"Alpha," Beverly called. "You're due back at the mansion."

Without quite knowing why, and going against all he had learned at Graceland-by-the-Sea, he plugged the guitar in. Beverly called to him again as he ran his fingers over the strings. The calluses were soft, like the hands of a beginner. He ran through an E-chord progression, and hit a blues run. He was stiff and self-conscious, but he could approximate what he wanted. Then, before he could really work into the sounds, he made himself stop. The guitar hung from him, heavy and threatening.

"Not bad," Towanda said. "How come you stopped? You got a real familiar sound. Like some of my Daddy's old records."

"ALPHA! IT'S TIME!"

Beverly's arms were folded across her chest, and her face was rock-hard with professionalism. Bobby placed the guitar on its stand.

"It ain't . . . it isn't anything," Bobby said.

"You're sure about that?" Towanda asked.

He could not think of an answer, so he hurried from the stage. Don't talk to her again, he thought. Never.

He did not touch the guitar again during the time remaining before the grand opening, even though Towanda Shelton asked him to play a couple of more times before she gave up, shaking her head. Once she left him alone, rehearsals no longer required concentration or thought. And once he no longer had to think or feel the music, he had become what was expected of him. Beverly and Kalo offered their congratulations the last day before the opening. You have my complete confidence, Kalo said. Beverly nodded her approval, still watchful, still judging. The final grammar lesson also came that day.

"You've made good progress," Beverly said after grading his last multiple choice test. "Ninety-two. I wouldn't have thought it possible."

"I took some English in prison."

"But you didn't learn much there, did you?"

"Maybe not."

"At any rate, you've worked hard—in all things. And you've kept your mind on your duties."

Towanda Shelton, he thought. She would not even look at him.

"Perhaps you need some recreation."

"What kind of recreation?"

He was immediately suspicious. It was not at all like Beverly to bring up such a subject.

"Perhaps an arrangement can be made. I'll speak to Clarence."

"Why him? What does he know about recreation? He don't . . . he doesn't seem like much fun to me."

"We'll have to see what Clarence knows about fun, won't we?"

Rehearsal ended early that evening. Kalo drove them through a complete run through. It was the first time Bobby had worn one of Mr. Chagaris' costumes. As the orchestra played "Thus Spake Zarathustra", he moved awkwardly onto the stage. The costume choked him at first, impeding his movements through the opening number, Kalo hissing at him all the while. With the first lines of "Polk Salad Annie", he forgot the suit. By the time the show ended with "American Trilogy", he was doing all that Kalo wanted him to do.

He barely had time to change after the run-through. Beverly pounded on the dressing room door and told him to hurry; that he had to meet Mr. Tony. Mr. Tony turned out to be the hairdresser that Mr. Short had promised. Bobby's hair was of sufficient length for styling, and Mr. Tony, a fat, soft young man in tight jogging shorts and a tank top, worked for a couple of hours, dyeing, trimming, shaping and snipping, until the hair was perfect. Mr. Tony chattered while he worked; about his cats, and the weather, and how Myrtle Beach was the swingingest town he had ever been in, if a fellow knew where to look. When Mr. Tony was finished, he told Bobby that he would be beautiful for the opening.

"I'm on call twenty-four hours a day, if you need me," Mr. Tony said. "And I'll be back for your regular trim in two weeks. Good night . . . Alpha Omega."

After Mr. Tony left, Bobby did not bother to check out his new haircut. He knew what it represented. Nor did he contemplate the fact that the haircut had erased any remaining traces of the young, wild Elvis. There were other, more important tasks to attend to.

Bobby put on a pair of green pajamas, sat down on the toilet, and opened his copy of *The Late, Great Planet Earth*. In the bedroom, the VCR featured Clint Eastwood slaughtering hyena-faced gangsters and defying lily-livered bureaucrats. Bobby read of how Russia was the seat of the Anti-Christ, and how the end of the world was at hand. He was concentrating on these ideas when there was a knock at the door. A woman in a very short mini-skirt and a T-shirt stood before him.

"I'm supposed to say I'm your recreation," she announced.

She was about forty, and a pro. She was a good-natured sort, and expertly performed her duties before Bobby could even ask them of her. She called herself Mona. When Bobby asked if that was her real name, she laughed and said her Momma had named her Betty. Her momma was dead now, and she could call herself whatever she wanted. Her laugh was loose and throaty. Bobby rummaged through a drawer until he found a few of the pills that Mr. Short had left for "emergencies". She swallowed a couple of the green ones, and said that she had been paid for all night, or as long as Bobby wanted her, so they may as well enjoy themselves. When the pills began to flow through her, she filled the bathtub.

"You don't want none of them downers? They're good."

"I don't need anything."

They lowered themselves into the water.

"You believe that there can be more than one of somebody?" Bobby asked her after they had squirmed into a comfortable position, facing each other. Thoughtfully, she soaped his penis.

"I don't know what you mean by that, now."

"I've been reading up on it. Jesus is supposed to come back. Somebody else could come back if they were strong enough."

She cackled, her eyes unfocused, her jaw slack. Her cackle irritated Bobby.

"It ain't . . . it isn't anything to laugh about," he said grimly. "How come you think that's funny?"

She smiled lopsidedly.

"I don't know. Jesus was special. Nothing like us. I remember that much. I ain't laughing at Jesus. Never have. Jesus is serious. And I ain't laughing at you. What I thought about was my ex-husband. Herman was his name. Drove for Carolina Freight. Got smushed in a wreck near Beeville, Texas. If he came back and saw me now . . ."

She laughed again.

"Who do I look like?"

She stopped soaping him.

"I been paid not to ask you about that. The guy in the cowboy suit . . . the one who left me at the door to your room."

"Bleached-out looking dude?"

"That's the one. Scared me. He said if I asked too many personal questions, that he'd get me in trouble with the law. I had to wear a blindfold to get in this place, wherever it is. I don't even know where I am. I can tell that it ain't nothing like the usual places I work. Motels, bars. You know. Out on Highway Seventeen.''

She resumed the soaping.

"Last week I had to trick with two guys at once. Right down beside a Datsun pick-up at the Fiesta Club. That was a first, Baby.''

"You haven't answered what I asked you. Who do I look like? Nobody's gonna hear you. It'll be between us.''

"You won't tell? I can't afford to go to Court no more. I'm still on probation. Damn District Attorney called it a crime against nature.''

"Who do I look like?" Bobby was more insistent now, his voice edgy.

"It's silly.'' She tried to laugh his question off.

"You gonna say it. You gonna say it now.''

She grasped his penis tightly, as if in fear.

"Okay. Don't get mad. We're here to party.''

"Who?''

"Elvis, Baby. The King, You know it, and I know it. So why do I have to tell you?''

Bobby leaned back. His face had been inches from hers. His fierceness dissipated a little.

"*That* Elvis is in me. Sure enough. That's how he's come back. Same as Jesus will. Only Elvis got here ahead of Jesus. I used to not think that they had anything to do with each other, but I learned. I'm learning all the time. Did you love The First Elvis?''

"Every woman loves Elvis. I cried when he died.''

"He ain't . . . he *isn't* dead. I told you. He's in me. I'm Alpha Omega. And I'm here. Right *now*.''

"Looking at you, I can believe it.''

"Then you see the truth? See through the falseness.''

"Baby, I'm right in there with every word you say. Sure, I see. Alpha Omega . . .''

She sounded too high to be frightened.

". . . I've heard that name someplace. Yeah. I can see it. I mean, you're right here in this tub with me, ain't you?"

She rolled his penis back and forth in her hands and gazed into his face. His penis was red, heavily lathered. She giggled.

"Alpha Omega, you probably got the cleanest tool in Myrtle Beach."

They rocked and heaved. It was hard to keep his seat, but he had to try. The First Elvis had died on the toilet and now he would be redeemed and transformed. Mona fell off a couple of times, but did not hurt herself. Gamely, she climbed back on. The soap made wet, sucking noises where their flesh met.

"Baby . . . goddamn . . ." Her words and breath came in gurgles. "I bet Elvis never done it . . . this way."

"Alpha Omega," he panted. "Say it."

"Alpha . . . Omega."

"Keep saying it."

"Alpha . . . Omega . . . Alpha . . . Omega . . ."

Bobby joined her, hardly knowing where his voice left off, and where hers began.

"Alpha . . . Omega."

"Alpha . . . Omega."

13

"Here he comes!" Mr. Short yelled, his voice nearly obliterated by the deep, bass clatter of the helicopter engine. The helicopter hovered like a nightmare insect before it descended from the hot, blue-white sky. The prop blast stirred up clouds of dust and grass seed into a mist, undoing much of what the landscapers had accomplished. As the rotor blades slowly came to a stop, a squad of men in dark glasses and somber suits strolled toward the landing site. The men assumed watchful poises, covering every angle of approach around the helicopter, as an honor guard from the local Air Force base formed in welcoming files beside the main hatch.

"Come on!" Mr. Short yelled, his voice giddy and loud in the new silence. "It's time to welcome him!"

"Remember what I told you," Beverly said to Bobby as they made their way through the settling dust and seed. "Act naturally, and say as little as possible."

The crowd, selected politicians, reporters and local dignitaries, fell in behind Bobby, Beverly and Mr. Short, joking and complaining about the dust and the early morning heat. Bobby had been introduced to a few of them before the President's arrival. There were Marine and Air Force officers, resplendent in full-dress uniforms, the Mayor of Myrtle Beach in yellow Sansa-belt slacks, and a number of men and women who appeared to be wealthy, perhaps even as rich as Mr. Short. Beverly had made sure that Bobby had a special brief meeting with two United States Senators, who Bobby had never heard of; Beverly had assured him that they were powerful and important. One of the Senators was probably the oldest man that Bobby had ever met. From a distance, he appeared to be distinguished and vigorous. When he attempted speech, however, it was obvious that he was on the edge of senility. He spoke in a slow, nearly indecipherable jumble, with long pauses between word clusters. He looked puzzled during the pauses, searching for the appropriate cluster before he could go on. He was accompanied by a much younger, once-pretty wife. Part of her duties included supplying the Senator with the necessary word that would allow him to connect with the correct cluster. As he shook Bobby's hand, the Senator began his agonizing attempt to communicate.

"The weather is mighty . . ."

The Senator paused, swallowing hard.

"Warm, Drum," the Senator's wife said cheerily.

"Yes, warm. I don't know when we've had such a hot . . ."

The Senator craned his neck, swerving his head from side to side as if the word might appear out of the air.

"Summer?" the wife ventured with a desperate smile.

"Yes, summer. Dry, too . . ."

The word cluster had locked in, and the Senator's speech became more animated. He spoke of how it was not nearly so hot when he was a boy, and about how he went fishing and life was good. He worried that children today did not get a chance to enjoy all those things that he had loved so much in his youth.

And did Mr. Omega realize that he had a number of children of his own?

"Eight," the Senator's wife said patiently. "Three by Irene and five of our own."

"Irene?" The Senator did not recall the name.

"Irene. Your first wife."

"Oh yes. She's *been* dead. Years and years. She was a good woman, too. Anyhow, we try to raise our children, except for the grown ones who are already raised. And doing quite well, I might add. We try to raise our children so they don't get polluted by all the pornography and terrible things that have . . . uh . . . uh . . . uh . . ."

The Senator's speech had run down to a mystified gulping.

"Infused?" the Senator's wife said, taking him by the arm. The Senator's aide, a squat, earnest looking man, nervously coughed into his hand.

"Infused," the Senator shouted happily. "That's it. Thank you, Missy."

"Infused," he repeated with solemnity.

The second Senator was rumpled and chinless. Through his thick glasses, he fastened his myopic, distrustful gaze on Bobby.

"You sing that Rock-and-Roll?" the chinless Senator demanded in a phlegm-filled southern frog voice.

"Alpha Omega performs only *traditional*, early rock and roll music, Senator," Beverly said before Bobby could respond.

"Traditional rock and roll? I didn't know there was such an animal," the Senator sniffed. "As long as it's not satanic, I suppose people can listen to it. It won't hurt anything, I guess. I been wondering; where'd you find a get-up like that?"

"Alpha Omega's costumes are made especially for his performances and occasions such as we have today," Beverly said. "They are exactly like those worn by the late Elvis Presley."

"Is that a fact?" the Senator said dryly.

The white costume with the eagle on the chest had been laid out for Bobby that morning. It was uncomfortable in the heat, but he was glad that he wore it, since the Senator did not approve of it. After registering his displeasure, the Senator, whose name Bobby had immediately forgotten, moved away, posting himself beneath the awning by the mansion's rear entrance to await the President's arrival. What the hell is he so high and mighty for? Bobby thought. He ain't nothing like Alpha Omega.

When the Senator reached the awning, he had been surrounded by younger, pudgy men. Frequently, they drew him to one side. They whispered to him, and the Senator would nod or shake his head, setting his thin mouth in a gloomy pout. Bobby tried to imagine what the pudgy men told the Senator. Nothing worth hearing, he decided. Maybe he's a kind of old queen, Bobby thought. The Senator reminded him of an old-time lifer in prison, a tall, bloodless man named Lester. Lester had traded in cigarettes and candy and coaxed the young inmates to run up big tabs. Then he would take it out in trade. Lester kept a couple of weight-lifters on his payroll for enforcement purposes.

The hatch opened and a small ladder was lowered. More men in dark suits alighted, glancing vigilantly to the left and right, speaking into walkie-talkies. The airmen snapped to attention and presented arms as a trim, almost boyish figure sprang through the hatch and strolled hastily toward his hosts. As the figure, who Bobby took to be the President, drew closer, his arms extended in expectation of an embrace. For a moment, Bobby feared that the hug was intended for him. Can the President be a queen, too? he thought. The President, who was deeply tanned and whose teeth were nearly as imposing as Bobby's, instead made straight for Beverly.

"Bev, you look great!" The President had a slightly nasal, Yankee accent, which irritated Bobby.

"Gosh, it has been a long time!"

"Too long, Mr. President," Beverly said. "And you look great, too. How's the First Lady?"

"Terrific, couldn't be better. She sends her regrets. She had to be at the opening of a new animal shelter in Boston. Committed to it a long time back. And you know how she feels about animals."

"The country knows, too," Beverly said with sincerity.

Who the hell did he come to meet? Bobby thought.

Beverly presented Mr. Short to the President who, for the first time since Bobby had known him, wore a conventional business suit instead of a jogging outfit. And, for once, Mr. Short was nearly speechless.

"I . . . it's a great honor. I swear it is . . . I'm enthused to have you at Graceland-by-the-Sea. You're something. The way you handled those A-rabs . . ."

Unaccountably, Mr. Short's down home speech pattern had burst forth. He lapsed into an awed silence. The President slapped him on the back.

"Thanks for saying so. Without the support of the American people it would not have been possible. The Middle Eastern thing has been . . . difficult. But we will pull through. Thank God. The worst of it appears to be behind us. Senator, how are you?"

The old Senator had pulled even with the President.

"Mister President . . . Mister President," the old Senator huffed, slightly out of breath from walking through the dust cloud. His head bobbed up and down like a broken doll's as he once again commenced his struggle for the right word cluster.

"Mr. President," he repeated, "I'm . . . infused with overjoyment that you are back in South Carolina!"

The Senator's aide and Missy were obviously relieved that something approaching the proper phrase had come out of the Senator's mouth.

"We hope you enjoy your visit," Missy said.

The chinless Senator and his young men thrust themselves forward and offered greetings. Then the chinless Senator launched into a recitation of his troubles; the liberals were smearing him again in the *Washington Post*, and his home state papers were, as usual, against him.

"I'm sure, Mr. President, that their dirty tricks are nothing new to you," the Senator concluded.

"Absolutely, Senator. Absolutely. There is no end to the irresponsibility in certain quarters. Stay the course, though. As if I have to tell you that."

The chinless Senator was about to resume his complaints when Beverly took the President's arm.

"And this, Mr. President, is Alpha Omega."

At the mention of his name, Bobby stepped forward and shook the President's hand. About goddamn time, he thought.

"A real pleasure," the President said. "So you're the young man that has been the source of so much mystery. The T.V. spots. The newspaper ads. Beverly's work, I imagine. And first-rate, too, from what I hear. Not that I get a chance to pay as much attention as I would like to events outside the White House. Duties of the office and all that."

"Yes, sir. I guess so. Glad that you're our guest here at Graceland-by-the-Sea."

He does sound like a queen, Bobby thought. And what the fuck is he talking about? Commercials. Ads.

The President turned to Beverly.

"I must say, he looks exactly like Elvis Presley. Sounds like him, too. You've done a marvelous job. Then again, you were always one of the best."

"Elvis doesn't compare to me," Bobby said firmly.

The President's eyes widened, perplexed by Bobby's observation.

"I'm sure."

"Daddy?" Beverly said. "Will you conduct our guests to the dining room? It's time for breakfast."

Mr. Short and the President led the procession toward the mansion. Cameras clicked and minicams ran through yards of tape.

"Alpha," Beverly said. "One moment."

Bobby was right behind the President, who blithered away at Mr. Short about the great golfing and fishing at Myrtle Beach. Beverly waited until the guests were out of hearing range.

"No more about how you are greater than The First Elvis," she hissed. "I've told you: humble. Humble and mysterious. Do you understand?"

The dust and seed drifted all over.

Fifty special guests settled down for a Presidential breakfast, while the rest of the welcoming crowd remained outside. Buffet tables had been set up in the dining room, along with the instruments, speakers, and the mikes of The King's Court. Bobby was expected to perform a short set after the eating and speaking had concluded. Beverly directed Bobby to his seat, which was at one end of the head table. She sat to his right, placed between him and the most important guests. The President sat in the center, flanked by the two Senators. Mr. Short had been installed next to the old Senator, and he had regained his composure, if not his smooth, polished accent. He babbled at the old man about the marvels of Graceland-by-the-Sea, and the pair then dug into their Eggs Benedict before the lesser special guests could be seated. The President sipped orange juice and listened intently as the chinless Senator resumed his monologue. Occasionally, above the clatter of silverware and the buzzing voices, Bobby heard the words and phrases that made no sense: NEA. Marxist-Leninists. Ultra-liberal.

"I hope you're ready to perform," Beverly said.

"Kalo run . . . ran me through the new songs."

"Your grammar still slips far too often. Perhaps we can find time for more lessons. Now, when your performance is over, the formal pictures will be made. After that the President will be off. The story should hit the major networks in time for the six p.m. news. The best free publicity in the world."

"That President said I've already been on T.V. And in the papers, too. I don't remember any of that."

"We're not going to discuss that now."

Missy sat next to Beverly. She openly listened to their conversation, her child-like face devoid of intelligence or malice.

"That's a lovely outfit, Beverly."

"Thank you. You're lovely, too. Especially for such an early hour, on such a warm day."

Bobby heard the sound of Beverly's lie in her voice. Sometimes he was able to tell. Apparently Missy, who was clad in a white, frilly, bare-shouldered dress, could not.

"How nice of you to say so! Last week Drum took me to a fabulous little shop in Washington. Told me to get anything I wanted. So I did!"

She giggled like a school girl. Beverly's half-smile locked down.

"Your taste is exquisite."

Another lie, Bobby thought. And this old girl's married to a guy that calls himself Drum. What a name.

"Mr. Omega?" Missy politely inquired. "Can you do a request for me?"

Bobby was about to say yes, but Beverly spoke first.

"Alpha Omega has a set schedule, Missy. And as you know, the President's time is limited. I'm sorry . . ."

"When you come back to Graceland-by-the-Sea, I'll sing it for you," Bobby said before Beverly could continue. I'll bet Beverly will like that, Bobby thought.

"What a kind offer. Really," Missy said.

"Yes. Kind," Beverly said. "And what's the name of this song?"

" 'It's My Party.' Leslie Gore used to sing it. It always reminds me of when I first met Drum."

Missy told her husband of Bobby's generosity, and dabbed a glob of hollandaise sauce from his chin. The Senator nodded in Bobby's direction. Bobby had never heard of 'It's My Party.' It can't be any worse than 'My Way', he thought. And I sing that one all the time.

"A goddamn white sundress," Beverly whispered. "Like a tea dance forty years ago."

Missy carefully cut her husband's English muffin into bite size pieces while the Senator and Mr. Short condemned flag-burners.

"My compliments," Beverly said. "You handled her pretty well."

"You taught me, didn't you?"

"True enough. As true a statement as you'll ever utter."

Bobby drank coffee while Beverly and Missy, who had seen to Drum's needs, went on about life in Washington and how the blacks had just about completely ruined the city. He wished he was upstairs, reading *The Late, Great Planet Earth*, especially those passages that described the terrible fate of the unsaved.

When the meal was more or less over, the old Senator made a speech. For ten minutes, he went on in a syrupy, incoherent monotone, with long pauses as he searched for word clusters, while Missy whispered the cues to him. Drum said that the Fourth of July was important, and that all Americans should be happy to have a man like the President in the White House. He began a story about when he was a young lawyer, just beginning his practice and was appointed by the court to defend two brothers on hog-stealing charges. Before he could describe the fate of the brothers, whose names were Donnie and Lonnie, he abruptly launched into an account of how his grandmother's house had burned down on the Fourth of July. He would never forget that fire, he said, even if he was only six years old when it occurred. For years afterwards, he said, he thought that his grandmother's house was supposed to burn *every* Fourth of July. The Senator was then taken with a coughing fit and sat down. The speech appeared to be over. Missy held his hand as the cough gradually died down.

Bobby thought that the old Senator was dumb, but good-natured. The speech did not make any sense, but Bobby had never been able to listen to other people for more than a couple of minutes; Hootchie-Cootchie, and now Beverly, being the only exceptions. The chinless Senator's speech could hardly be described as good-natured.

He warned the special guests of alien influences and powers that were subverting the character of the American people. He condemned a conspiracy between the ultra-liberals and some other people called humanists to destroy the national soul. Bobby had never heard of ultra-liberals or these humanists. He did know that they had nothing to do with Alpha Omega, however.

The chinless Senator concluded by proclaiming the Fourth of July as good a time as any to commence a crusade devoted to "stern decency", as he put it. When he finished, he folded his arms across his chest, and his dark magpie-eyes darted around the room, daring anyone to disagree with him. No one did. Bobby could tell that the special guests were a little afraid of the chinless Senator. That voice of his is what done it, Bobby thought: that mean-ass, old-con voice; like he was telling a chicken-shit car thief what was gonna happen if he didn't come up with ten cartons of Winstons by next week. It was all bullshit, though. The chinless Senator might think his words was powerful. But they weren't close to "Mystery Train" or even the worst songs that Kalo picked for the show.

As the President began his speech, Bobby yawned deeply. Beverly kicked him beneath the table.

"My friends, we are gathered here to inaugurate—one of my favorite words, by the way . . ."

The special guests chuckled appreciatively, happy to hear even a bad joke after the chinless Senator's speech.

". . . to inaugurate a great undertaking: Graceland-by-the-Sea. As has been noted, it is of symbolic significance that this undertaking has its official birth on the Fourth of July, the two hundred and fifteenth birthday of our nation. And here, today, we are present at a kind of rebirth, embodied in flesh and stone, of one of our greatest entertainers. No. I'll change that. One of the greatest Americans of this, or any other century . . ."

When's he gonna say my name? Bobby thought. He stifled another yawn, impatience and boredom competing within him.

". . . Elvis Presley was the personification of American youth, spirit and optimism. And, I might add, of our sense of playfulness and fun. Are we too serious today? Do we need a healing dose of the sort of fun that Elvis Presley gave, and continues to give, to us? Indeed we do. You know, some of my critics might not think so, but I'm a fun guy."

The President paused, his smile radiant and impish with measured delight.

"It's true though. If you don't think I'm a fun guy, just ask the First Lady!"

Unrestrained glee burst forth. All the special guests laughed in unison; all except for the chinless Senator and Bobby, who could not figure out what was supposed to be so funny.

"And believe it or not, I can rock and roll with the best of them!"

A roar shook the dining room, and reverberated throughout the mansion. Applause followed. The President beamed until the tumult subsided.

"Seriously, Elvis Presley means a great deal to me, and Graceland-by-the-Sea will mean much to all Americans. Here is a chance to permanently experience what the world thought was lost with the untimely death of the man called King. And now, let us enjoy ourselves. Let us regain our playfulness. Let us unite in a common sense of fun and joy. Let us rock and roll!''

Bobby could not understand why the applause lasted so long. He twitched with resentment. No one had uttered the name of Alpha Omega. Sullenly, he waited as the senators and Mr. Short congratulated the President. Bobby might have remained in a permanent state of frozen anger if it were not for Beverly.

"Get up," she said, jerking at his arm. "It's time to sing. Get going. We're on a schedule."

Inertly, The King's Court awaited him. He picked up the mike and nodded to the band. The first song was "I'm Proud to Be an American", which Bobby dimly recalled from the open-mike night at Buddy's Lounge. It was a terrible song, but Beverly and Kalo had ordered him to do it. And he was not yet ready to go against their orders. They said that "I'm Proud to Be an American" had been the President's theme song during the last election. As Bobby sang about God blessing the good old U.S.A., the President listened gravely to the chinless Senator, whose mouth was twisted into a yellow-toothed hole. Hell, he ain't even paying attention to this shit, Bobby thought. He moved closer to the central table, the mike cord uncoiling behind him. He tried to meet the President's eyes, to wordlessly accuse him of dwelling in falseness. The President finally looked at Bobby, the chinless Senator's mouth still working away in his ear. Bobby could not tell whether the President's eyes were blue or brown. Like dead stars, they reflected no light, giving nothing back. Bobby backed away from the central table. The man is et up with falseness, he thought. No use in trying to get through to him.

After "I'm Proud to Be an American", Bobby did two fast early Elvis numbers, dancing and sliding around as much as he could in the table-jammed dining room. In the middle of "All Shook Up", Missy grabbed one of the chinless Senator's pudgy young men and forced him to dance. The man moved like a human sponge, and at the first opportunity he excused himself. Alone, Missy stayed on the floor, gyrating, the other special guests trying to ignore her out of politeness. Her husband, his belly full, had fallen into a head-drooping stupor, unaware that his wife was dancing her way toward Alpha Omega.

"Come on, Mr. Omega!" she shouted. "Let's work it out!"

She was panting a little, throbbing to the music, and her elaborate hairdo, piled into a lacquered cone, had partially collapsed. She thrust her arms out, imploring Alpha Omega.

"Come on!"

Bobby hesitated until he saw Beverly nod. He left the mike and The King's Court played on automatically.

"You're good!" Missy said. The sundress had fallen away from her terminally-tanned shoulders. "Just like *he* was!"

Bobby took her hands as the band played "Only the Lonely." Missy braced herself against him, holding him close, her body welded to his. Her face was transfixed with an innocent carnality as they slithered around the floor, bumping into tables.

"Isn't he something?" Mr. Short said to the President.

"Wonderful," the President responded. "Wonderful."

The chinless Senator peered malevolently at Mr. Short, offended by the interruption.

Missy and Drum disappeared after the photographers completed their work, although she insisted on a shot of her kissing Bobby on the mouth.

"Don't forget 'It's My Party!'" she cried, blowing Bobby a final kiss. Drum smiled indulgently and inquired as to the location of the nearest bathroom.

After Missy and Drum were gone, a series of shots were made of Bobby and the chinless Senator, who, with great effort, was able to work up a weak grin as he shook Bobby's hand. Then it was the President's turn.

Beverly arranged Bobby and the President on the black naugahyde couch in the T.V. room. Bobby wondered if this dumb ass

President would like to have his picture made upstairs, in the secret chamber of the bedroom. He concluded, however, that the President was not worthy of such an honor.

"Look natural," Beverly commanded. The President, who had been smiling into space, sprang into action.

"You certainly have a great deal of energy," the President said to Bobby. The two of them appeared to be in deep conversation as the cameras clicked and popped.

"Thank you, sir."

"Where do you get all that energy?"

He's the biggest dumb ass in the whole world, Bobby thought. Instead of expressing this idea to the President, he remembered what Beverly had told him to say.

"From within, Mr. President. Deep inside, something is inspiring me." And that ain't no lie Bobby thought.

"Well . . . Alpha, that's very fine. That's very fine, indeed. There is one thing I'm curious about. In fact, many others share my curiosity."

On Beverly's command, they turned for a profile shot.

"What's that, Mr. President?"

"Is Alpha Omega your real name?"

Bobby did not have to remember any of Beverly's special instructions.

"Sir, it's the *realest* name I've ever had."

"That's . . . that's a wonderful statement. It really is."

The photographers were ushered out, and one of the dark-suited men said that it was time for the President to leave.

The helicopter engines were warming for take-off, and those who had not been permitted at the breakfast feast cheered as Bobby and the President emerged from the mansion and into the swirling dust.

"Where's your next stop, Mr. President?" Mr Short shouted, once again trying to compete with the engines.

"Camp Lejeune," the President said soberly. "To honor the remains of our boys lost in the Middle East. I must be there to meet them."

"A sad occasion," Beverly said.

"Sad. Very. No one could say, however, that their sacrifice was in vain."

"Never," Mr. Short said.

The President shook hands all around, and embraced Beverly once more.

"A pleasure, Alpha. May I call you Alpha?"

"Sure . . . Mr. President." Bobby did not know the President's name and had not cared enough to find out. The main thing is he's leaving, Bobby thought. And I can get back to doing what I'm supposed to do.

"You have a wonderful talent. I hope you use it for the good of all," the President said.

"I'm gonna use it. Yes sir, I'll do that."

The helicopter rose higher and higher, an ever-growing column of dust trailing it far into the sky.

14

It was nearly ten when Beverly finished her critique. The gates would soon open, and Bobby's first tour would begin at eleven. Beverly sat on the edge of Mr. Short's desk, notebook in hand, brisk and efficient as ever. Bobby had often thought that she enjoyed these critiques, as she called them, more than any of her other duties.

"I thought you handled Missy very well. It's hard to tell what an airhead like her can do to a photo opportunity. As it turned out, we got some good tape of your little dance number. The spontaneous, fun-loving side of Alpha Omega."

"Playful, just like the President said," Mr. Short added. He had swapped his business suit for a jogging costume as soon as the helicopter was out of sight. "The President's simply terrific. Plain as an old shoe."

"A regular guy," Beverly sneered. "He's gotten better at P.R. I'll give him that, even if he doesn't understand it as well as Reagan. There's no one in Ronnie's league. Even the Kennedys were mere amateurs in comparison. Ronnie's instinctive. God knows, he'd never be able to *describe* what he does. But if you say the word, he's ready for any sort of dog and pony show.''

"I think you're too hard on George," Mr. Short said aggrievedly.

"George, is it? I'll bet he told you to call him that. The common touch. He works pretty hard on it, even if he still looks and sounds like an old-time floor-walker at Bloomingdales.''

"He's sincere, traditional American," Mr. Short said.

Beverly rolled her eyes toward the ceiling.

"And our man, too. Let's not forget that.''

"I gotta ask you about the papers and T.V.," Bobby said. "Like the President told me about when he landed. Is all that true?"

"Certainly it's true," Beverly said. "You don't think we would undertake a project like this without a full-scale marketing campaign do you? We started selling Graceland-by-the-Sea last winter.''

"But you didn't even know me then," Bobby said.

"Haven't we been over the question of your supposed uniqueness before? We didn't need to know you. It was enough to know that there would be someone like you.''

"There isn't nobody like me," Bobby said.

"Sure, whatever you say. I refuse to discuss this point with you.''

Beverly returned to her notes.

"Did I tell you that I was on the Today show?" Mr. Short said.

"Nobody's told me nothing," Bobby said.

"*No one's* told me *anything*," Beverly said, jotting something in her notebook.

"Me. On national T.V.," Mr. Short went on. "And they ran segments on the mansion, the water slide. All of it.''

"How about some pictures of me," Bobby demanded. "That President said there were pictures of me.''

"There are . . . have been all along," Mr. Short said slowly.

"With the face blocked out by a question mark," Beverly said. "It's more mysterious that way. Daddy, show him a copy of the ad."

Mr. Short searched in a desk drawer and handed Bobby a Xerox of a full page advertisement from the *Los Angeles Times*. In the center of the page was a figure in a performance costume. The question mark was exactly where Beverly said it would be, and the copy read:

ALPHA OMEGA IS NEAR!
DISCOVER GRACELAND-BY-THE-SEA
MYRTLE BEACH
JULY 4TH, 1991

"Nationwide," Mr. Short said. "We've been nationwide for months."

Beverly ordered Bobby upstairs. He was told to rest so that he would appear fresh and natural when the first tour began. Once in the secret chamber, however, he was too keyed up to relax. Automatically, he went over the instructions: act natural, but mysterious. Be like one of the people, yet seem unattainable. Create closeness, while remaining separate, somehow divine. Be ready to ad lib if necessary. You can never tell what sort of geek might be in the crowd. Beverly's teachings revolved over and over in his cramped, nearly bursting skull, mixed in with the seven-headed beasts and the notions about the end of time that he had absorbed from *The Late, Great Planet Earth*.

He could not sit still, so he dressed. An informal outfit had been laid out for him: tight white slacks, red shirt, paisley ascot, pointed boots, and blue blazer. When he finished dressing, he sat on the edge of the bed, his hands dangling between his thighs, one leg pumping with nervous energy. After remaining in this position for a few minutes, he rushed to the bathroom, where he tried to read *The Late, Great Planet Earth*. Even on the toilet, he could not focus his mind on anything solid. The book dropped to the floor, and he hoisted his pants. He had to see them; those who had really and finally come to Alpha Omega.

The thick carpet muffled his footsteps as he stole along the corridor with slow, exaggerated movements; an intruder in his own palace. He tried the door on one of the rooms that faced into the front of the mansion. It was unfurnished and nearly as large as his own bedroom. He carefully parted the draperies.

They were there, spread out below him: the Fourth of July pilgrims to Graceland-by-the-Sea. They came to him as he once went to Memphis: to see, to feel. His lips parted in a reverent, erotic sigh as he pressed his face to the warm window.

The line for the first tour had formed, extending back toward the water slide. There were more pilgrims than Bobby had ever imagined; far more than he remembered from the Graceland in Memphis. They bustled in and out of the gift shops. They chewed on chicken wings and swallowed gallons of Pepsi, while balancing armloads of children, tapestries and souvenir plates. Whole families, from grandparents to three year olds, drifted through the heat. An exhausted mother, her cloud-like hair billowing upwards, spanked a small child, her hand rising and falling in slow motion, the child's mouth a perfect, silent, wailing oval. A shirtless man about Bobby's age, his shoulders already blistered, watched the woman flog her child, and ordered a sno-cone. His tongue worked methodically against the ice in long, rapid strokes. A crowd of teen-aged boys and girls, all wearing cut-off jeans and black T-shirts, obscured the licking man, the mother and the child. The boys and girls were followed by tattooed bikers, servicemen with boot camp haircuts, ordinary middle-class families, shambling retirees, college students, every kind of American. Beverly and Mr. Short had called to them, and they had responded, pouring forth from every corner of the land. Bobby nearly cried out with rapture. They covered every inch of Graceland-by-the-Sea.

A hush greeted his descent. He came down slowly, stately; the way Beverly had taught him. He did not see her, but her presence was strong in the mass of faces that greeted him. He paused four steps from the foot of the staircase; close enough to be among them, but still elevated. The tour guide, a pert, cheerleader-type in her early twenties, stood to one side, allowing a full view of the master of Graceland-by-the-Sea. She had led them to the source. Now it was Bobby's duty to comfort, to reveal. He leaned against the banister, shifting from stateliness to slouchy elegance.

"It's him," a wonder-struck male voice declared.

"He's not dead. Lord, he's not even fat!" a woman shouted.

Bobby smiled, and the pilgrims pressed in.

"I am Alpha Omega, and welcome to my home. You are my guests. And I treat my guests with respect and love."

The words were Beverly's, but at that moment Bobby fully and absolutely believed them. There was hardly a breath in the tightly-packed foyer as the pilgrims stood on the brink of the blissful experience that had been designed for them. Bobby descended the final steps, and they parted before him in loving waves. He halted, his back to the dining room.

"Most of you probably know that our President was here this morning. I had breakfast with him. He's a fine man, and I was honored to have him in my home. But it's just as great an honor to have all of you with me, too. All of us, me, you and the President, are part of the business called America."

They followed Bobby into the dining room, which had been cleaned up and rearranged after the Presidential breakfast.

"This way please," the guide said. "Make room for everyone."

The pilgrims pushed in, bumping against the furniture, pushing against the walls, surrounding Bobby.

"This is where I do most of my entertaining. When my friends visit Graceland-by-the-Sea, I always have at least one big meal here. It's especially nice during Christmas and Thanksgiving. Lots of times, though, we eat informally, over in the T.V. room, which we'll come to later in your visit."

"What do you like to eat?" a tow-headed Huckleberry Finn-looking boy of about nine said. His father, a lumbering man with a face like a broken boulder, seized the boy's arm.

"Hush, Troy," the man said in a strangled, embarrassed voice.

Bobby laughed good-naturedly.

"That's all right, Troy. When I was your age, I mostly thought about supper, too."

Troy's father released his arm. The pilgrims laughed as one, turning to each other as if to say: "See. He's just like us. He loves children. He loves food."

"But for the record, Troy," Bobby said, once the laughter subsided, "I enjoy a traditional dinner for the holidays. Turkey, and dressing and cranberry sauce. The same kind of dinner your momma and grandma fix for you, I bet."

"It's good, too!" Troy peeped. The father laughed then and Bobby playfully rubbed the child's head.

"He's all boy," Bobby said. The electricity fed into all of his circuits. It was worth it, he thought. Even them operations. Even Beverly Short and that damned President of the United States.

"What else you like to eat?" said a thin, insolent teen-aged boy. The teenager wore a Hard Rock Cafe T-shirt, and an early-Elvis pompadour, his face blotted by acne and a smirk. Somehow, he reminded Bobby of an impersonator.

"Let's see now," Bobby said genially. "There's fried peanut butter and mashed banana sandwiches. Crisp bacon. Chocolate layer cake. Popsicles. Cheeseburgers. About the same things you would like."

"I don't eat none of that stuff," the teenager said, his smirk growing bolder and challenging.

A gasp arose. Bobby chuckled. Beverly, who had prepared him for children, had also instructed him about smart-asses.

"Maybe you should try an Alpha Dog. They taste real good and have been known to improve a man's disposition."

The pilgrims laughed as Bobby pulled a Graceland-by-the-Sea token from his pocket and flipped it to the surprised young man. Beverly had provided a handful for situations such as this.

"How come you giving me this?" the teenager asked, as his smirk disappeared.

"One free Alpha dog. And if it doesn't improve your disposition, let me know and I'll tell the man at the counter to put more mustard on the next one."

"Thanks, Alpha. Thanks," the teenager said.

"Enjoy yourself. Now don't all the rest of you act like you're in a bad mood—I'll run out of tokens, and I won't even get my own Alpha Dog!"

They were Bobby's, fully and completely.

He led them back through the kitchen. There were more questions: how big was his staff? Where did he keep his private plane? How much money did the house cost? Bobby rattled off the answers that Beverly had supplied him with. He had no idea if any of them were accurate. The pilgrims accepted his words, oohing and ahhing when large sums of money were mentioned. He hated to admit it, but Beverly had proved that she really knew what she was doing, at least when it came to giving the pilgrims what they wanted.

In the knick-knack choked living room, a basset hound-like man in Bermuda shorts pushed his way to the front of the crowd, his wet lips moving before the words came out in a question. Bobby had spotted the man as he started elbowing his way forward, and he calmly regarded him despite the annoyed looks of the other pilgrims.

"I got to ask you a real personal-type question," the man finally said. "Do you still miss your momma?"

Bobby withdrew his smile for the moment. His voice was tinged with controlled loss. Beverly would have been pleased.

"Everyday . . . I wish that I could see her again. That we could sit and talk and just be together. But I have accepted the fact that we will never set eyes on each other. At least not in this life."

"She'll fix you something good to eat in heaven," the man said earnestly.

"I suspect so," Bobby answered. "A better place than this, as marvelous as Graceland-by-the-Sea is. I wish she was here."

"Gladys," someone said, amidst a great deal of throat-clearing and feet-shuffling.

As the pilgrims exited the mansion, the tour guide herded them toward a spot near where the Presidential helicopter had landed.

"Ladies and gentlemen," she said, "If you wish, you may now purchase autographed photos of Alpha Omega at four ninety-five each. We also have available Graceland-by-the-Sea memory books at twelve ninety-five. Mr. Omega will also be happy to autograph both the pictures and books for you."

Bobby seated himself behind a table that was piled high with neat stacks of photographs and books. The memory books contained color pictures of all the downstairs rooms, with Bobby posed in each. Bobby began to sign as soon as he sat down, while the guide collected the eagerly offered money and directed the pilgrims into line.

The sun, burnished and cruel, beat down upon them as they patiently moved forward. Bobby scribbled the name of Alpha Omega, smiled, and answered some more questions. What did he do for fun? What was his favorite car? Did he ever visit Michael Jackson? Was the President as handsome in person as he was on television? Did he ever have any contact with Priscilla? Did he mind how people used to lie about his taking dope? With each pilgrim, bearing their photos and memory books like sacred relics, the questions came.

Bobby had just informed a disappointed computer programmer from New Haven, Connecticut that he would not be singing "U.S. Male" during the evening show, when he became aware of some sort of disruption in the middle of the line. The pilgrims, money in hand, backed away from a prone figure; a woman, collapsed in the dust and seed. Bobby sprang over the table, nearly knocking down the computer programmer. The guide and a man knelt beside the woman. The acne-faced teenager with the token for a free Alpha Dog, fanned her with his memory book.

"She fainted, I guess," the guide said, with the proper concern.

"Give her room," Bobby ordered. "Back up and give her room. Please, my friends. Do as I ask."

The woman was fifty or fifty-five, and her face was puffy, dead-white. The crowd shifted its position, but not enough to suit Bobby. They stared at the woman, like people viewing an especially bloody and interesting traffic accident.

"She's gotta have some room," Bobby shouted. The crowd moved further away.

"You, too," he said to the man and the teenager. Slowly, they backed off as Bobby sat in the dust and took the woman's head in his lap. He stroked her hair. It was thin, brittle and wire-like with hairspray and years of permanents. Her eyes opened at his touch.

"You're gonna be okay," he said. He was sure that she would be. He was Alpha Omega, and this was his Graceland-by-the-Sea. What's Beverly gonna think when she hears about how I handled this one, he thought.

"Get some water and call first-aid," he said to the guide. "And a damp towel. And hurry!"

The woman remained rigid, nearly catatonic. Bobby continued

to stroke her hair and she smiled weakly. The guide returned, and Bobby placed the towel on her forehead. He held a souvenir cup of water—the cup bore his own face—to her lips. The woman whose head was beginning to weigh heavily in Bobby's lap, drank deeply. A trickle of water ran from the corner of her mouth.

"She's coming around," the guide said.

"Where's first aid?" Bobby demanded like a general in the midst of battle.

"They're on the way. They had to treat somebody who choked on a cheeseburger."

"They better hurry. This lady is my special guest."

The woman's face had regained a bit of color, and she maintained a quivering smile. Bobby held the cup to her mouth, but she shook her head.

"I'm . . ."the woman began.

"Don't talk," Bobby said gently. "You passed out, but you're gonna be okay. I'm gonna take care of you."

He held her until the two medical attendants arrived. They checked her pulse and heart rate, and asked her general questions about her health as Bobby and the pilgrims, united as they were, waited breathlessly for a verdict.

"She'll be fine," an attendant said. "A fainting spell, that's all. She'll need to rest and stay out of the sun."

The woman was alert now. She stroked Bobby's hand in a gentle, insistent rhythm.

"What's your name?" Bobby asked her.

"Hazel Carothers, and I'm from London, Kentucky."

"Hazel, do you think you can stand up?"

Slowly, with the help of Bobby, the guide, and the first-aid men, she raised herself from the dust.

"You say she's got to stay out of the sun?"

"Yes, sir, Mr. Omega," a first-aid man said. "No more sun for her today."

"Does she have to go to the hospital? As long as she's inside and she's cool, wouldn't she be all right?"

"Sure. If she could rest for a while, she wouldn't have a thing to worry about."

"Hazel, I want you to rest in the T.V. room until you feel well enough to enjoy your visit. And I'll make sure that you get a refund on your tickets so that you can come back tomorrow."

Hazel embraced Bobby. The pilgrims broke into spontaneous applause.

"Wish I'd fainted," a woman said.

A man, stoop-shouldered with years of some sort of pointless, heavy labor, stepped forward. He had been kneeling by Hazel Carothers when Bobby first came to her rescue, and he had hovered nearby while Bobby ministered to her.

"I'm Buck Carothers, and I want to thank you for what you done for my wife. Lord, I just lost my head. If it weren't for you, Mr. Omega . . ."

"Don't say another word," Bobby said. "You two just go on into the T.V. room. I'll make sure that you and Hazel get some Pepsis, and free photos and a memory book. Autographed, too. When you feel like eating, I'll send for a little Love Me Tender chicken."

"How about an Alpha Dog?" the once insolent teenager said. His voice was all love and wonder. Bobby laughed, his teeth leaping forward.

"You and those Alpha Dogs!"

The pilgrims guffawed with Bobby, and the teenager basked in his union with the great Alpha Omega. Hazel wrapped her arms around Bobby.

"It's a miracle!" she yelped.

"A miracle!" responded dozens of voices.

Both shows went exactly as Kalo and Beverly wanted them to. As Bobby came on the stage, the big electric letters flared in the darkness, the orchestra played "Thus Spake Zarathustra", and a disembodied voice proclaimed the name of Alpha Omega. Dutifully, Bobby worked his way through the act. Even as he sang Kalo's songs, he concentrated less on the music than upon those who had gathered for the long-desired second coming. Their presence swelled in the warm darkness of the music hall, just beyond the lights. Bobby reached for them with all that was in him. And it was, he knew, even greater than anything in *The Late, Great Planet Earth*. No one, not the President of the United States, not even Beverly Short, could touch him.

He sang "My Way" to conclude each show, tossing cheap, sweat-soaked scarves to the audience. Disembodied hands added new scarves as the others fluttered downward over the end of the stage into the crowd below. The First Elvis, the dead Elvis, had created this gesture. And no one had dared to dream that the gesture would live again in flesh and blood.

It was all a miracle.

15

Much that came after the Fourth of July confirmed Bobby's beliefs. The crowds were even larger after opening day, brimming with love and salvation, secure in the fact that all they had ever believed was true, and all that they had ever wanted stood before them. There were others like Hazel Carothers, men and women, young and old, who wrote letters to Bobby, who were interviewed by reporters. Few claimed any direct physical miracles, although a retired salesman from Monroe, Michigan, assured *The Weekly World News* that his arthritis improved considerably after Alpha Omega shook his hand. The testimony of those who had experienced Alpha Omega were delivered to the offices of Short Enterprises at a rate of several dozen a day. Alpha Omega changed my life, they said. He lives again. I will treasure my autographed Memory Book forever. The new Elvis, Mr. Alpha Omega, has made me so happy. My family will return every year to Graceland-by-the-Sea.

Beverly allowed Bobby to read a few, selected letters, although she warned him that their contents should in no way divert Bobby from his tour scenario or any other assigned purposes. Bobby did not need to read the letters, however. He understood what his people felt as she never could.

Despite the five tours and two daily shows, he never tired. He sweated barely enough to anoint the scarves that he tossed to the audience. Mr. Short, during one of their weekly meetings, remarked on Bobby's energy, and inquired as to whether Alpha Omega had access to a new type of medication. Bobby shook his head. He rarely spoke, and when he was not conducting a tour or singing, he was quiet most of the time, responding only to direct questions.

He ate only enough to maintain his strength, and allowed himself only the sleep required to be fresh for the next day's schedule. In his bedroom, he no longer viewed the videotapes, and he seldom pondered the messages in *The Late, Great Planet Earth*, although he did sit for hours on the toilet clutching the book. He needed nothing, and no one could touch him. Beverly's critiques and caustic asides went unheard. If he had been more aware of her presence during their meetings, he might have seen that she sometimes regarded him in a bemused, quizzical way; as if there were a new factor in her equation of Graceland-by-the-Sea that she had yet to master.

She and Mr. Short said that Graceland-by-the-Sea was prospering far beyond their best expectations and projections. Through July and August and now, into early September, they had accommodated an average of a hundred thousand visitors a week. The surge of Americans to Myrtle Beach had become so great that the resources of the park were strained to the limit. Mr. Short had been forced to double the size of his staff and to keep the park open until eleven o'clock each night. Expansive with success, and what he called "pure happiness", Mr. Short took a step that was unheard of in the history of American theme parks. Graceland-by-the-Sea, he proclaimed in a press release, would remain open year-round, although the rides and water slide would be closed from October to April. However, the food concessions, the souvenir shops, the wax museum, the mansion, and the music hall would be open in order "to give the American people exactly what they want and need." Mr. Short asked Bobby if he would mind continuing the tours and shows without any break, as long as it was for the good of the organization. Bobby nodded.

"I knew you'd come through!" Mr. Short said.

For a smart man, he asks some dumb-ass questions, Bobby thought.

One night after the second show, Bobby sat in one of the bedroom's Spanish style chairs, still clad in his performance costume, before the recently installed full-length mirror. The mirror was the only thing that Bobby had asked for since his arrival at Graceland-by-the-Sea, and Beverly could not think of a good reason for refusing him.

He examined each segment of his reflection, gladdened with the rightness of all that he saw. That night, as had happened one or two other times since the mirror was placed in the bedroom, he was inadvertently stricken with memory. He had not been at memory's mercy since his recuperation at the Anders Clinic, when Virgil, Laverne and Hootchie-Cootchie had appeared to him.

He saw himself this time, back on Modena Street, nearly naked in Laverne's emptied-out house, examining himself as the Young, Wild Elvis. That Elvis was as dead as the original King, transformed and replaced. He felt a slight, uncertain tug of nostalgia. He could never have seen all that would follow from that moment in that cold, dingy house.

"I've even gone way beyond myself," he said to the mirror. These were, he knew, the truest words he had ever spoken. And they would become truer every day.

"And I did it all," he told the mirror.

Others thought that they were responsible. Doctor Anders believed that he made Alpha Omega by making the face. Mr. Short thought that his money did it. Beverly said that she had formed Alpha Omega with her planning, bitching, and training.

"They all wrong," he told the reflection. Pleased with his perception, he changed into his pajamas. The session with the mirror had been highly satisfactory, and he wanted to leave it that way. The memory of Laverne's house should not be dwelt upon. He understood that if he concentrated too much upon the past, he could harm Alpha Omega's sense of serenity.

As he buttoned his pajama top, there was a knock at the door. He slowly opened it, irritated over being disturbed in his moment of renewal. Before him stood Mona, her blindfold in place. She pulled it away as Bobby led her into the room.

"Back again, Baby," she said, as she sat on the bed and pulled off her shoes.

"Glad to see me? The cowboy found me over at the Grand Strand Lodge. Caught me just in time, too. I was about to sign on for an all-nighter with a real ugly Canadian. Sunburned all to hell. Claimed he played ice hockey. Mostly, looked like he played with himself."

She patted the spot next to her on the bed.

"Sit down, Baby. Cowboy said he'd be back in two hours, on account of you needing your sleep for them shows of yours. You about the biggest thing ever in Myrtle Beach. See you on T.V. all the time. Hear about how everyone loves you and all the things you do for them. Saw you with the President back on the Fourth. He's cute, ain't he?"

She let out a robust yawp. Bobby remained standing.

"I'm getting paid extra, lots extra to say nothing about how famous you are. But, shoot. How am I gonna do that? Me and you are friends."

Still standing, Bobby took her hands in his, pressing them gently together. He was close to bursting with kindness.

"Mona , I don't need to do those things we did before."

He squeezed her hands, trying to make her understand.

"You ain't gone queer on me have you? A man like you going queer. That's hard to believe."

He left her and sat down on the other side of the room. He gave himself a quick restorative glance in the mirror. He had not been prepared for Mona, and he saw that he had to explain.

"No, Mona," he said with an all-knowing smile. "I'm not a queer. Being a queer, or not being a queer, none of that matters to me."

"What's that mean? If stuff like that don't matter, what does? And you sound different. Like you're way off somewhere. Not really even in this room. Kinda . . . kinda scary."

"Don't be afraid. Let me tell you some things. Important things."

When he began, he stuttered and paused; he was not used to saying so much to a single person. Then it was as if a powerful, emotional laxative had taken effect; the words poured fourth. He told Mona of the second coming, and of the many second comings. He assured her that he had been chosen to eliminate falseness. Nearly shouting, he revealed his connections to The First, Dead Elvis. As he spoke, he paced the room, waving his arms, checking himself in the mirror. He told all of it: of his time at the Burning Love Temple, of his journey to the first, now false Graceland. He broke into a sweat, more copious than he ever produced for a show.

". . . and now I'm at Graceland-by-the-Sea. And what I do here is for everybody. The whole world. Not just me. Do you understand?"

He sat down as he finished his speech. The electricity and power were strong. He waited for her to respond. She stared at him for a least a full minute, while he returned to the mirror.

"I sure ain't never seen nobody like you," she finally said. Her voice was low, filled with astonishment and apprehension.

"And I've seen them all. It's like you're a special, superfine preacher . . ."

"*Not* a preacher," he said quickly, turning from the mirror. "Don't mix me up with a preacher." He was on his feet again, his fists clinched.

"Okay, Baby. You're not like that. I didn't mean nothing. I *believe* you. I do."

She came to him and chastely embraced him. Bobby moved away from her. He had stopped sweating.

"I'm with you," she said.

"Do you mean it? You better mean it. If you could see the people at the tours. And the shows, too. You know, everything I said was the truth."

"I've seen them on T.V." Her voice dropped even lower. "Some say you can heal people."

"I can. I never planned to do it. It just happened. You believe it happened, don't you?"

"I ain't got no doubts."

Lightly, he touched her cheek, quickly drew his hand away, and darted into the bathroom.

"I want to give you a gift," he said when he returned. He thrust his dog-eared copy of *The Late, Great Planet Earth* toward her.

"Here. Take it. Read it. Every word. Think about what I told you."

She took the book from him, turning it over in her hands, examining it.

"A book? You giving me a *book*?"

"Not just a book. It matters a lot to me, but I got out of it all I can. Now I'm passing it on. This book don't . . . doesn't explain all of it. None of them do. It can help you get started, though. Listen and watch for me. And all the things that're in the book."

She stuck the book into her overflowing tote bag.

"The last time anybody give me a book, it was a Bible from my grandmother when I was twelve. Don't know what happened to it. Things get lost." Her tone was wistful, a little sad.

"Don't lose this one," Bobby commanded.

"I won't. Will I ever see you again?"

"You can count on it, only I don't know when or how."

"Can I come back up here to see you?" she begged.

"I gotta be alone. Alpha Omega needs to get off by himself so that he can figure out the best way to keep putting out the truth, and fighting all that falseness."

She kissed his cheek, like a sister with a brother.

On a Sunday evening, a few days after Mona's visit, Mr. Short invited Bobby to dinner at Sun Shores, which was the name of Mr. Short's private estate just south of Myrtle Beach. Clarence picked Bobby up in the limo, which, as always, shone with a fresh wax job. As they turned onto the main highway, Clarence cleared his throat.

"You like her?" he asked. His high voice sounded rusty from lack of use. Bobby did not hear him. He was preoccupied with the dinner at Mr. Short's. The invitation, which was, in fact, a command, had disturbed him. He did not want to leave the mansion, and the mirror, for any reason. The very idea of being removed from the park grounds filled him with a queasy dread. After a couple of miles, Clarence tried again.

"I said, do you like her?"

Bobby then realized that Clarence had spoken to him. The fact that Clarence wanted to communicate with him was almost as irritating as the dinner invitation. He had hardly spoken to anyone since the outpouring of words during Mona's visit.

"Like? What are you talking about?" Bobby said.

"*Her*. The woman I had to go out and get for you. The whore."

"Name's Mona. And she ain't, I mean she isn't a whore."

Clarence snorted. You a nasty son-of-a-bitch, Bobby thought.

"If she ain't a whore, I ain't never seen one," Clarence said. "And I got her, too. Right after you did. It weren't nothing special."

"Is that right? You knew how to do it?"

"What's that mean?" His hard, pink eyes flashed at Bobby from the rearview mirror.

"Think about it."

Neither man spoke during the rest of the drive to Sun Shores.

Bobby heard the surf beyond the live oaks that stood between the house and the shore. The house itself was long and low, the various wings and sections winding among the trees and around the tennis courts and outdoor pool. Bobby could not tell where Sun Shores began or ended.

Beverly greeted him, and Bobby started when he saw her. She did not wear her usual business suit; instead, she undulated toward him in a slinky black cocktail dress that clung to her in a way that her suits never could. Her half-smile held a touch of recklessness which only increased Bobby's anxiety.

"Alpha Omega himself," she said gaily. "Welcome."

Bobby followed her into the house which was decorated in various shades of white. There were plenty of plants, many of them flowering, and their cloying, heavy smell, reminded Bobby of a funeral. The furniture was sleekly modern, and, to Bobby's eyes, uncomfortable-looking.

A man, who had been seated on a couch, came forward to shake Bobby's hand. He was older than Beverly by at least ten years, and wore a dark blue suit, white shirt, and red tie. His rich man's face and cultured northern accent reminded Bobby of the President of the United States—that President who would not say the name of Alpha Omega. The man's name was Richard Aldrick, and he sported an amused, superior smile.

"What would you like?" Beverly asked Bobby. Bobby did not reply. He was still trying to figure out why Beverly was dressed that way, and why she would want him to meet someone like this Richard Aldrick.

"What would you like to *drink*," Beverly said impatiently. "A common question among the civilized," she laughed.

"Gimme a beer," Bobby said.

"What brand? There are all sorts of beer."

"It . . . it doesn't matter."

"How typical of you. Juan?"

A servant, a short, black-jacketed Mexican, appeared.

"Yes, Miss Beverly?"

"A beer for Mr. Omega. Make it foreign. Expand his horizons."

Juan turned on his heel. When he returned, he handed Bobby a glass of something dark and foamy. It tasted funny, but Bobby liked it. He stood, stiffly holding the glass to his mouth until most of the beer was gone.

Beverly had arranged herself on the couch, squeezing close to Richard Aldrick. The hem of her dress was hiked up to reveal a formidable stretch of her slim, perfect legs. She sipped white wine, and Bobby realized that she had put away quite a bit before his arrival.

"Sit down, Alpha," she said.

Bobby perched on the edge of a chair opposite the couch. He drained off the last of the beer, and felt pleasantly light-headed. He remembered the last beer he had before this one. Charlotte, he thought. The airport. Before I was Alpha Omega. Even before the face was mine. Juan appeared a moment later with a fresh glass.

"There he is," Beverly said, pointing to Bobby. "The one, the only Alpha Omega." She laughed, and Aldrick laughed with her. Funny as hell, Bobby thought, gulping the fresh beer.

"He certainly does stay in character," Aldrick observed. "The appearance is uncanny. Almost the genuine article."

Aldrick's remark propelled Beverly into a spasm of delighted giggles, and she choked slightly on her wine. I wish you'd die, Bobby thought. He said nothing, however, and his face remained impassive.

"How was the show this afternoon?" Aldrick asked.

"All right," Bobby said, as he finished his second beer. Juan, as if summoned by a high-pitched dog whistle, presented Bobby with another glass. The alcohol had started a slow, steady, burning within him. If I'm gonna be in this shit, I may as well drink, Bobby thought.

"I plan to see your show tomorrow," Aldrick said. "In action, so to speak."

"There's nothing like it," Beverly chortled.

"So I understand. How did you come to this . . . profession?" Aldrick asked.

"What you . . . what do you mean?"

"How did you become what you are?"

Before Bobby could answer, Beverly joined in.

"Alpha Omega was created by Short Enterprises, with some help from a reputable plastic surgeon. And despite what you've heard, his grammer has actually improved."

Juan materialized and refilled Beverly's glass.

"What are you?" Bobby asked Aldrick, curling his upper lip, his high, dead-Elvis cheekbones tinged with red. Aldrick raised an eyebrow. I bet you practice that, Bobby thought. Whatever you are.

"What Alpha Omega means, dear, is could you state your occupation," Beverly said, resting a hand on Aldrick's arm.

"Where should I begin?" Aldrick smiled.

Bobby wondered if this Aldrick had fucked her. He could not imagine her fucking, even if she was dressed for it.

"Mr. Aldrick is a lawyer . . ."

"Cambridge, '72," Aldrick interjected.

"An advisor to presidents. A marketing genius . . ."

Aldrick laughed modestly.

". . . and an all-around grand fellow," Beverly concluded. The pair of them laughed as one, and her hand dropped to Aldrick's knee.

"Bev and I go way back," Aldrick said. "I suppose where we really came together, where I had the opportunity to witness *Bev's* genius at work, was during the '80 campaign. We collaborated on Ronnie's rejoinder to poor, sad, Jimmy Carter. During the debate."

Bobby did not know what Aldrick was talking about. Beverly, Mr. Short and Kalo went on about Ronnie, or Reagan, or whoever he was, all the time; like he was some kind of second coming himself. Bobby turned up his glass and belched. Beverly and Aldrick obviously wanted another sort of response.

"Don't you remember?" Aldrick said, his voice slightly less wealthy and assured. 'There you go again.' When Ronnie uttered those words, he simply destroyed Carter. The election was as good as over."

"One of the most important phrases in American political history," Beverly said proudly. "Richard and I worked for two weeks on that one. And it came across exactly as we planned it. Spontaneous perfection, pure and total."

"I don't pay any attention to stuff like that," Bobby said with beer-fueled satisfaction. "Never have."

"I have a personal note from George Will thanking us for our work," Beverly said stiffly.

"Who's he?" Bobby asked.

Aldrick arched both of his eyebrows this time, but before he could explain any more American political history to Bobby, Mr. Short entered the room. Juan arrived at the same moment and handed Mr. Short a glass of orange juice. He also handed Bobby a fresh beer, which tasted even better than the first three, now that Aldrick had shut up.

"I've been on the phone with the president of Galaxy Productions," Mr. Short said. "They can have forty-thousand of the new design Alpha Omega T-shirts by the end of the month. No sooner, I'm afraid. What we don't sell over the counter by the end of November, we can mail-order. Provided the Graceland-by-the-Sea catalogs get off the press in time."

"I'm familiar with Galaxy," Beverly said. "They do excellent work. We used them at Disney World. And they were the first on the market with the Beijing Massacre Memorial shirts. Naturally, they've done Iraq, NASCAR, and most of the NFL teams."

"Beijing, huh?" Aldrick said. "That must have been a risky one. I mean with the speed of events there, they might have taken some tough losses."

"They sold over two hundred thousand units in ten days," Beverly said. "And when China went to the back pages, they weren't even stuck with excessive inventory."

"And how are you this evening, Alpha?" Mr. Short inquired kindly.

"All right."

"Has Juan seen to your needs?"

"He's been doing good. Only I need another beer. And this time, I gotta have it in the bottle." He was drunk and it had felt good to tell Beverly and Aldrick the truth about their politics. Juan handed him a long necked bottle that had foreign words on the label.

"In the bottle," Aldrick said. "Exactly. The perfect detail."

"Yes," Beverly said. "Every day Alpha Omega comes closer to being a real work of art."

Bobby had two more beers before dinner, downing them quickly like he used to when he was sixteen and wanted to get ferociously drunk as fast as possible. At dinner, he kept drinking, pouring down the wine that Juan served with each new course. He also refused to speak, and no one asked him any more dumb questions or spoke as if he were a thing and not Alpha Omega.

Most of the conversation was between Beverly and Aldrick, and Bobby's befuddlement and contempt grew as he listened to them.

"I simply don't understand why you stay down here," Aldrick said.

"I need her. That's why," Mr. Short said, quickly looking up from his plate. Aldrick ignored Mr. Short, and Bobby saw that Short did not like it.

"I appreciate filial piety," Aldrick said, "but you're wasting your talents. The White House, to name one place, would love to have you. All you have to do is call."

"Richard," Beverly said as she lowered her wine glass, "we've discussed this before. We have differing theories, modes of operation."

Aldrick shook his head, and an eyebrow shot up.

"I know, I know. You want to operate at . . . what do you call it? An emotional grass-roots level? Populist fantasies and all that . . ."

". . . isn't that what we did back in '80 and '84?" It was Beverly's turn to raise an eyebrow. Through the haze of beer and wine, Bobby almost laughed. They could probably shoot them eyebrows up and down all night long, he thought.

"Perhaps," Aldrick went on. "Only, this isn't the same. I mean a theme park, for Christ's sake. The power base isn't there."

"What's wrong with a park?" Mr. Short asked.

"We're expanding," Beverly said. "Besides, the potential power base is enormous. And consider this: we aren't subject to the kinds of restrictions you work with in politics. Elections, polls, the law and so on."

"That can change."

"Not quickly enough for me. Richard, you're a traditionalist, a member of the Harvard-Republican-male power block. I've seen the future, and it's here, at Graceland-by-the-Sea. There are virtually no restrictions in this field unless you make the mistake of going into the religious entertainment branch.''

Aldrick laughed. Bobby gulped down more wine. He especially hated Aldrick when he laughed.

"I heard," Aldrick said, "PTL tried to get you back in '87, didn't they?"

"The Bakkers," Beverly said. "My God, you should've seen them. Jim interviewed me personally. What an ordeal. Said I could save his ministry. He cried, of course. I couldn't get out of Heritage Village fast enough. He had disaster written all over him. So did the whole operation. As for taste, well, they were beyond redemption. At least Graceland-by-the-Sea has a certain authentic, honest tackiness that I find refreshing."

"Tackiness?" Mr. Short said through a mouthful of raspberry sorbet.

"Like Lourdes?" Aldrick said, straight-faced.

"Trust Richard Aldrick to put it just so. Yes. A Lourdes right here at Myrtle Beach if you will. A perfect icon that defies time and space," Beverly said.

"What's a Lourdes?" Bobby asked. He had broken his silence, but he had to find out what a Lourdes was, and how it could be like Graceland-by-the-Sea. Aldrick and Beverly nearly bent double with hilarity.

"He's astonishing," Aldrick said once his laughter subsided. "Where did you ever find him?"

Bobby never found out what a Lourdes was, and because of the laughter, he did not ask again. Instead, he stared at his dessert and tried to think of the mirror. He was thankful when the meal was over and Mr. Short offered to show him around Sun Shores. He was numb with alcohol but he acknowledged the paintings that Mr. Short claimed were priceless originals.

"Beverly picked them out over in Europe," Mr. Short said. The paintings did not make any sense to Bobby. They consisted of fuzzy, out-of-focus representations of fields, trees, and dim figures in old-fashioned clothes. He was relieved when Mr. Short stopped praising the paintings and going on about who did them and how much they cost. Mr. Short spent almost as much time, however, praising the other features of his estate: the indoor pool; the outdoor pool; the antique furniture; the new, specially-designed contemporary furniture; the sky lights; the jacuzzi. All of it was expensive, or custom-made, or one of a kind.

Mr. Short led him past the "great room" as he called it, where Aldrick and Beverly were still yakking away and laughing. Bobby could not make out what they said, which suited him. At least I don't have to hear that shit for awhile, he thought. He followed Mr. Short down a corridor near the kitchen. A heavy wooden door swung open.

"My game room," Mr. Short said. "I thought you might be interested."

The room was narrow, but large enough to contain a full-size pool table, a bar, and a refrigerator. It was also plain, lacking Beverly's decorative touch. The only ornamentation was a large photograph of a beefy, handsome young man behind a microphone. Mr. Short handed Bobby a beer, an Old Milwaukee. With a sudden, involuntary wrench, Bobby saw Tommy Aycock pulling an Old Milwaukee from beneath the front seat of his van the first night at the Burning Love Temple.

The game room was frigid with air-conditioning, but Bobby began to sweat. He did not want to be beset by Tommy's image. The music, he thought, nearly saying the word out loud. And for some reason, he experienced a jerking ominous recollection of Towanda Shelton and her sisters. They had, to Kalo's amazed rage, quit the show. It had happened a couple of weeks back, and Bobby, immersed in the truth of Alpha Omega, had not thought about it. Before a rehearsal for a couple of numbers, and in front of the entire cast, Towanda told Kalo that her conscience would no longer allow her to perform; that the show, and Graceland-by-the-Sea, were cruel jokes. Towanda and her sisters walked out of the music hall, Kalo cursing and threatening them. She had ignored Kalo, but as she strode across the stage, she nodded to Bobby like there was some secret about him that she understood. Kalo replaced the Sheltons in twenty-four hours with three perfectly complacent blondes who sang whatever they were told. With a nervous jerk, Bobby turned the Old Milwaukee up, chugging nearly half of it.

"That's me," Mr. Short said, pointing to the young man with the microphone. "That was in September 1955, right after I interviewed The First Elvis. I know I told you about it. One of the greatest experiences of my life."

Bobby gaped at the young Mr. Short. The beer had formed a thick knot in his stomach, but he drank the rest of it down anyway and opened another. He wanted to be rid of Towanda and Tommy, and The First Elvis, too.

"Would you like to shoot?" Mr. Short asked. Bobby pulled a cue from the rack on the wall. Yeah, he thought. No more of them. No more of Beverly and her goddamn friend either.

"Good," Mr. Short smiled. "We'll play for fun. No bets. It seems like none of us around here do anything for fun anymore."

The cue was thick and cumbersome in Bobby's hands, like a tree trunk.

"I ain't . . . I haven't shot in a long time," Bobby said.

"I'll break," Mr. Short said happily. He had a strong, smooth stroke, and the balls spun prettily across the green felt. A striped ball, the eleven, dropped into a corner pocket.

"Eight ball's the game," Mr. Short said. He lined up the twelve and touched it in. Mr. Short was good. As he surveyed the table, lining up each shot, he seemed to grow younger. It occurred to Bobby, as he desperately worked on his beer, that Mr. Short was old most of the time. Back in Charlotte, and Atlanta, he had been full of life, full of ideas and power. When Beverly showed up, he changed, and started to fade into the background. Mr. Short sank the thirteen, and had a good angle on the fourteen, which he also made. He smiled at Bobby.

"Don't worry, Alpha. I'll miss in a minute." But he did not.

There was something about Mr. Short that reminded Bobby of those old guys who hung around the pool halls back in Gastonia when he was a kid. They looked harmless enough, but they always turned out to be hustlers. If you got sucked into a game with them, they cleaned you out. Whatever you had, they would get. Then they would pat you on the back and wish you better luck the next time.

Mr. Short made a difficult shot on the nine, the cue ball just kissing it into the side pocket. Mr. Short took unfeigned delight at his skill. He looks like Santa Claus, Bobby thought. The man with all the toys. Finally, Mr. Short missed, a tricky double bank shot on the fifteen ball.

"Thought I had that one," he said, clicking his tongue. Slowly, and with all the concentration he could muster, Bobby chalked his cue, then aimed at the one ball, which was positioned directly in front of a corner pocket. He scratched, the stick jumping in his hand like a living, untameable thing.

"Out of practice," Mr. Short said, with sympathy. "I'll get you a table over at the mansion."

Who would I shoot with, Bobby thought. Mona and Clarence? At the mention of Graceland-by-the-Sea, he wanted to rush home. That did not seem possible, at least until Mr. Short, or Beverly, decided that he should go. Mr. Short slammed the fifteen in, and then the eight ball, and the game ended. Bobby tried to rack for another game, but he had a hard time manipulating the balls. Mr. Short finished the job for him.

"I'll order it tomorrow," Mr. Short said as he made two balls on the break.

"Order what?" To Bobby, Mr. Short sounded distant, indistinct.

"The pool table, Alpha. You know, some of the best, most relaxing times I spend are right here in this room."

Mr. Short's down home accent was in full operation. He even sounds like them old sharks back in Gastonia, Bobby thought.

"When Doctor Kaplan was down here the last few summers, I taught him the game. And he swore it was an even trade, which is a real nice compliment when you consider all I learned from him. I must've mentioned the doctor to you. A fine man. Real smart. A professor at the University of Chicago. Wrote that famous book on how culturally illiterate American college students are."

Mr. Short banged the seven ball in. He was shooting the solids this time.

"Beverly told me about him. It seems that the liberals ruined our colleges, like they did everything else. And Doctor Kaplan—he's a Ph.D. not a medical doctor—blew the whistle on them. Anyhow, Beverly said I should contact the professor to teach me about all those things I missed when I was younger. Well, I spoke to the man, and we became friends; and we set up the Short Institute. To promote traditional values and western civilization to our universities. Teach the right things. Have respect for the American system. That sort of thing. I'm sure you would understand."

The six ball careened off the rail and into a pocket. Mr. Short stopped speaking as he measured his next shot. He then hit the five ball in.

"Like I was saying, Doctor Kaplan set up the Short Institute. Part of his job, and I was real clear on this, was that he had to tutor me. You know, in what Doctor Kaplan calls the standard, accepted works of western civilization. Especially Plato and those Greeks. And Shakespeare, too, even though he wasn't a Greek at all. He was English."

The four ball fell, leaving Mr. Short an easy shot on the three.

"I hadn't had Shakespeare since *Macbeth* when I was fifteen. Heck, I'm only a high school graduate, but after three summers with Doctor Kaplan, well, I *know* some things."

Bobby tried to follow Mr. Short's words, but once he had started in on Doctor Kaplan, Plato and the Short Institute, Bobby gave up. He leaned against the wall for support, his face level with the photograph of the young Mr. Short. He did not know how much longer he could stand erect, but he did know that he was still drinking Old Milwaukees. Mercilessly, genially, Mr. Short went on.

"So after I wrote a paper on Plato, Aristotle, and Shakespeare, just like in college, I told Doctor Kaplan that it was time for him to learn how to shoot pool. By the way, I got an A on the paper. Now Doctor Kaplan grew up in this very cultured home in New York City. Started the cello when he was nine. Read Spinoza when he was ten. Spinoza's another philosopher, but he wasn't a Greek. Doctor Kaplan loves Mozart. Did I tell you I listened to Mozart during the summer sessions? Beethoven, too. And Schumann and Richard Strauss. Strauss is where we get the 2001 introduction for the show. Did you know that, Alpha?"

Aware that Mr. Short had asked him a question, Bobby nodded. He was afraid that if he said no, Mr. Short would try to explain.

"You do? Well I'll be. Not that I think you're uncultured or anything. But back to Doctor Kaplan. Before he came to Sun Shores, he had *never shot pool*. Can you believe that? So we started coming down here after our evening sessions to play eight ball. Doctor Kaplan got to be pretty good. And you know what? He thanked me. Said I was a natural teacher. Coming from a man like Arthur Kaplan, that's some compliment. And he said something else I'll never forget: 'Maurice', he said, 'shooting eight ball makes me feel like a real American.' "

Mr. Short finished running the table.

"Guess I'm lucky tonight. I'll rack them again, Alpha."

"Whatever . . . yeah," Bobby grunted.

* * *

Bobby did not know how many games they shot. He stumbled around the table, muttering to himself, and he could not make a single ball, even when Mr. Short started missing on purpose in an effort to create a little excitement. Mr. Short kept on winning, and he also kept up his monologue. He finally tired of Doctor Kaplan and the Short Institute, and turned to his favorite subjects: Beverly and Graceland-by-the-Sea. Beverly projected that in a year, at most, Short Enterprises could begin construction of a giant hotel and music hall complex, which would be greater than anything in Las Vegas or Atlantic City. Then Bobby would have a proper venue for his talents. And Beverly was going to get the park another front page story in *USA Today*, as well as a write-up in *The Wall Street Journal*. And Alpha Omega would appear in another clip next month on *Entertainment Tonight*. And more and more people would come to the park, and there would be a general, universal happiness. Mr. Short won another game and placed his cue on the wall.

"That's enough for tonight. We should rejoin Beverly and Richard. They probably miss us. And we really ought to do this again. Oh, I think I should apologize."

"Apologize," Bobby repeated. He was supporting himself with both hands, leaning on the end of the table. He's still going at me, Bobby thought. His stomach rose and flopped on itself, and his throat felt constricted, dried-up.

"For Beverly and her friend. The way they acted at dinner."

Bobby could not raise his head. The green felt wiggled and shimmied before his eyes.

"She's brilliant," Mr. Short said, oblivious to Bobby's wobbling knees. "And she tends to be impatient at times. Still, I love her and . . ."

"Bitch," Bobby mumbled.

"What's that, Alpha?"

Before Bobby could repeat himself, a freshet of vomit spouted from his mouth and spilled over Mr. Short's pool table. The unending stream, all those foreign beers, all that wine, all those Old Milwaukees and rich, silly food, ran down the side of the table, over Bobby's hot pink shirt and tight black pants, to spatter Mr. Short's two hundred dollar running shoes.

"My God, Alpha!"

Bobby dropped to his knees. The chin, sculptured to perfection at the Anders Clinic, struck the edge of the table and he was out cold.

There were many voices. One belonged to Juan, who was accompanied by a couple of other servants, their Hispanic accents strange in Bobby's ear. They argued as they tried to lift and drag Bobby from Mr. Short's private hideaway. Beverly drunkenly cursed, as Aldrick tried to calm her.

"Alpha was out of his element. Perhaps he was nervous."

"It's your goddamn fault, Daddy," Beverly said, her voice cold and deliberate. "Inviting him here in the first place. I told you . . ."

"He seemed so lonely up there . . ."

"In his mansion? That's where he belongs. You put him up when you don't need him, and bring him out when you do. It's simple. As simple as can be. The way I designed it. And the chin. What if he fucked it up? And right as we've extended the season. You let him get drunk . . ."

"I didn't!" Mr. Short whimpered. "I only wanted him to have a good time. I've checked the chin. It seems okay."

". . . what about the fact that he has five tours and two shows tomorrow. Look at the bastard."

As much as he had ever desired anything, Bobby wanted to come up off the floor and give her one to the face. But he could only raise himself halfway there, his fist clenched, before he fell back into the vomit.

"Disgusting," Aldrick said.

* * *

After the voices came the freezing water. Bobby kicked and bucked against the web of arms that held him in the shower. When the water ceased beating against him, he was carried and dragged to bed. He cursed whoever held him, whoever had taken control. There were several of them, all without names, and they stood around his bed until he fell into a deep, beer sleep.

His shoulders shook so hard that his head flopped up and down on the pillow.

"Wake up. Now." It was Beverly pulling at him with a furious strength. He pawed the air until he grabbed her wrists and held them until the shaking stopped.

"You can let go," she said.

He released her. She had shaken him so violently, he thought he might vomit again. He took a couple of deep breaths, and his head cleared a slightly. His mouth was fetid and he retched dryly. He sat up and discovered that he was naked.

"I want you out of here," she said.

Bobby nodded. He did not want to speak to her if he could help it.

"Put this on," she said, dropping a royal blue jogging suit into his lap. "It's Daddy's, but he won't mind. Don't bother to ask for shoes. You ruined yours, so you can do without. You're lucky I don't make you go home bare-assed."

She waited while he pulled on the suit. It was at least three sizes too large, and he had to hold the waistband up as he followed her through the dark, quiet house. Clarence was nowhere in sight when they reached the limo. The night was warm, and the thick, salt wind blew in from the Atlantic.

"Where's the cowboy?" he asked.

"Asleep, I guess. I'm driving. Do you think I want anyone else to see you this way? Too many have already. Get in."

A few minutes later the limo hit the main highway, Beverly

driving as fast as Clarence would. She carried a drink with her, and still wore the slinky party dress. Bobby took one look at her, and turned away. He lowered the window and let the wind wash over him. Despite the wind, he was soon nearly asleep, the hum of the well-tuned engine lulling and caressing him. When Beverly turned onto the road that led to Graceland-by-the-Sea, he was relieved. Soon he would be in his room. Soon he would rise and greet the pilgrims. When Beverly spoke, she seemed to be in the far distance.

"Perhaps I've been too hard on you. That's what Daddy says. Of course he's sentimental. He told me once that you're the closest thing he's ever had to a son. What an idea . . ."

Bobby did not reply. He only wanted to get home.

"He could be right, about how hard I've been on you that is. After all, you are, in a sense, only human. And I have made you what you are. I've noticed, too, how quiet you've become lately, even when I try to goad you. And except for your . . . being ill tonight, you even have a kind of, well, dignity. Something like a noble savage. I haven't decided whether you've achieved perfection as a central figure, or whether you've gone catatonic on us. I think that you're close to perfection, if I had to choose. Richard disagreed."

Her speech ended, to Bobby's relief. In a moment, however, she started again.

"So what do you think of the job I've done with you? I'm sure you have an opinion."

Bobby stirred toward consciousness. He opened his eyes, but kept his head in the wind. She had never asked him for anything. What is this shit? he thought and closed his eyes. Myrtle Beach was far behind them and the only illumination in the thick darkness came from the dashboard and the headlights.

"What about it?" There was a small, pleading note in her voice.

"I . . . I don't have any answer for that." I got an answer, he thought. If you could understand about second comings.

"You mean you won't tell me?"

He sat up, fully awake now, distracted and a little amused. What's she want, he thought. Probably don't know. Still drunk. About as drunk as I was. They passed the entrance to Graceland-by-the-Sea, the limo racing down a two-lane blacktop that pushed into the sweltering, early Indian summer countryside. The salt wind was gone, and the backroad air congealed in Bobby's lungs.

"How come you didn't take me home?"

"We need to talk. I'm trying to unravel my feelings about you."

"I wanna go to bed. I gotta see my people in the morning." He was immediately sorry for what he said, and he cursed himself for being caught off guard.

"So it's your people. That's how you think of them. I never would've guessed. And it's perfect. Perfect."

He could tell that she was pleased with herself, although he was not sure why.

"When did you discover that they were your people?"

He wanted her to stop the car so that he could flee, to run back to his room. But Mr. Short's pants would keep falling down, and he did not even have any shoes.

"Don't want to talk about it."

"I see. Yes. The essential mystery. I inculcated you with the mystery even more than I thought. Talking would spoil it, right? Like a great writer growing garrulous over a work in progress."

"I don't know what you're saying." He was a fool for giving her even the slightest clue about the second coming.

"Perfection. How blind I've been to the awful, splendid power I've brought forth."

She laughed, and when she did, Bobby dared to look at her. In the green dashboard lights she was smiling, and not with the victorious, half-smile that he hated. His palms began to sweat. She frightened him; her laughter and her smile were all wrong.

He was even more alarmed when she pulled to the side of the road and cut the engine.

The lights stayed on, shining into the void. Millions of bullfrogs and crickets made their night noises. Beverly laughed once more, and Bobby sweated harder, the thick cotton of Mr. Short's jogging suit clinging to him. The laughter halted abruptly, but the smile floated in the undersea light of the dashboard. She came across the seat at him, pulling the shoulders down from the slinky dress, hoisting her father's sweatshirt, and kissing Bobby's damp chest. He did not, could not, move. Paralyzed, he prayed to himself.

"I'm a second coming," he groaned, nearly splitting with loathing and desire. She wrapped her arms around his neck, the smile floated in his breath.

"You are, my dear, my perfection. Greater than all of my other creations. Supreme over all that I have molded."

She crawled on him, rubbing and squirming, her tongue diving into his mouth in an effort to consume all that was Alpha Omega. He remained paralyzed in the green light, amid the crash and boom of the bullfrogs and the chirpings of summer's last crickets.

16

Bobby was positioned before the mirror, trying to find himself. He had searched every night after the episode with Beverly on the two lane blacktop, obsessed with how she had devoured him. She was still correct and professional, as if nothing had ever happened between them. But, he felt her eyes. It was as if she were evaluating him in some new, unexpected way. They had not touched each other since that night, yet she was all over him.

At their last meeting she announced the purchase of a mint condition 1956 pink Cadillac convertible.

"What do we need with a '56 Caddy?" Mr. Short had asked Beverly. "I'm not questioning your judgement, but . . . ."

"The atmosphere," she had said. "The First Elvis gave one to his mother. Isn't that right, Alpha?"

Bobby had nodded.

"Alpha has an encyclopedic knowledge of The First Elvis. Now I present the Cadillac to him; a symbolic object, in line with the essential mystery of Graceland-by-the-Sea."

She's saying she's my mother? Bobby thought.

The Cadillac was parked behind the mansion, in the very spot where the presidential helicopter had landed on the Fourth of July. Mr. Short had seen to it that Bobby was photographed behind the wheel. Beverly made it clear, however, that Bobby would never be able to drive the Cadillac. That would be too dangerous, although she did point out to him that the car held all sorts of other possibilities.

He concentrated on the mirror. She was still there. He felt her around him all the time, but most especially when he was alone and did not have to lead tours or sing. He longed for her to go away, to leave him in the solitude of Alpha Omega. Yet, he also wanted her there, with him, perhaps appearing suddenly in the mirror behind his image.

He abandoned the face of Alpha Omega, and Beverly's imminent materialization, and paced the room until he noticed *The Tibetan Book of the Dead* on the nightstand. He tried to read it, but the words meant nothing. He regretted giving Mona his copy of *The Late, Great Planet Earth*. He needed the book badly; he needed a way to get back to the second coming.

What's that Cadillac mean? he thought. There were the photographs, which sold even better than the other glossy eight by tens. There he was; one hand raised in a jaunty, care-free salute, the other on the wheel, his special teeth pressed together in a world famous smile. Beverly had squeezed his hand after the photo session. "*Our* beautiful car," she said.

Soundlessly, familiar with every inch of Graceland-by-the-Sea, Bobby glided toward the ribbon of light that shone from beneath the kitchen door. There was a telephone in the pantry off of the kitchen, although he had never used it. There had never before been anyone to call. He swung the door open, and blinked rapidly in the hard, fluorescent light.

"Who's there?" an alarmed male voice demanded.

"Alpha Omega."

Bobby stepped into the spotless, seldom used kitchen. The owner of the voice was a mild-looking, middle aged man in an ill-fitting security guard's uniform. He held a cup of coffee in one hand, and a sandwich in the other. A thermos and a .38 revolver in a holster rested on the counter. The man placed the cup and the sandwich beside them.

"It *is* Alpha Omega," the guard said, grasping Bobby's hand. He pumped hard until Bobby eased his hand away.

"I'm Howard Dunn, Mr. Omega. This is something. Boy, it's something! Wait 'til I tell Fern, she's my wife. She loves you. Like she loved Elvis. I mean this is a real pleasure."

"Can you help me?"

"Anything. How about some coffee? Something to eat? There's all kinds of food here. Hardly any of it gets used up."

"No. I need a telephone."

"There's one in the pantry. Let me show you."

"I know where it is. And I gotta have the number for Mr. Short's house."

Howard Dunn pulled a notebook from his jacket and thumbed through it until he found the number. The pantry was stocked with many of the necessities of American life: untouched crockery, crystal, platters capable of holding a twenty-pound turkey for a happy family's Thanksgiving feast. All of it appeared to have just come from the box; untouched, almost, by human hands. Bobby picked up the receiver. Howard Dunn stood beside him, smiling.

"You alone?" Bobby asked.

"Yes, sir. I have the eight 'til four shift. Then another man comes on. A woman comes in at seven and fixes some food—for you I guess."

"Don't say that you saw me. It's a secret."

"Not even Fern?" Howard Dunn sounded disappointed.

"Nobody."

"Yes, sir. You can count on me."

"And this is gonna be a private call."

Howard Dunn shuffled back to his coffee and his sandwich. Bobby held the receiver, unable to dial the number. He might have raced back to the mirror to find where he was supposed to be, but then, as if another had taken hold of him, he slowly dialed Sun Shores.

"I knew you'd call," she said as she pointed the Cadillac north. "It took a little longer than I thought it would, but you called just the same." She drove fast, and as expertly as Clarence. She held a quart of Jack Daniels between her thighs, and every couple of miles she took a deep pull, before passing the bottle to Bobby. The roof was down and the breeze was cool, cooler than it had been for months. Bobby nipped at the bottle and handed it to Beverly. Her hair whipped around in the wind, and although Bobby thought she was beautiful, he still hated her.

"As I said, the Cadillac has other uses."

"You like to . . . do things in cars?"

She laughed. "Do things? How prissy, Alpha! Do things in cars. Part of my Southern upbringing. I suppose I do. Cars are signs of power, although relatively minor ones. Still, they remain the most visible power symbols for most people."

"How come you're laughing at me? Like you did at your Daddy's house?"

"Perhaps because you're so serious. Or because you're such a perfect, splendid fraud."

"A fraud!" he screamed into the breeze. The call was a mistake. He saw then that it was dangerous to hurdle through the darkness with Beverly.

"Take me back!" he shouted.

"Back to Graceland-by-the-Sea? That's not possible. Not yet, anyway. First we have to go to a special place."

"I don't wanta go. I was wrong to call you up."

"Wrong? The call was inevitable. Calm yourself. I meant no insult when I called you a fraud. I'll explain my theories on fraud after you've become a bit more educated. Going back to that night at Daddy's, I'll admit I was a trifle harsh. I drank too much, and Richard was there. He can bring out the worst in me. We used to hoot together when we were in the White House. Richard's unchecked wit, by the way, has kept him from rising higher than he has; which is still high enough, for him anyway."

"You ever fuck him?" Bobby gave up on going back to the mansion, even if he was not sure why he was riding in the Dead Elvis' Mother's car with a woman who tormented him. All of this is gonna lead to some kinda sign, he thought. But he had no idea from what direction the sign would come.

"You're *not* prissy. As far as Richard, we dallied occasionally in cabs. Between stop lights, you might say. Very 1920s. F. Scott Fitzgerald sort of stuff."

"Does a rich smart-ass son-of-a-bitch call it a dally?"

Beverly laughed and pounded the steering wheel with the flat of her hand.

"Even rich boys know the difference between dallying and the real thing."

The road narrowed from four lanes to two, and the pink Cadillac crossed over the state line into North Carolina. It was the farthest Bobby had been from Graceland-by-the-Sea since the day of his arrival.

"I do like to fuck in cars," she said. "I'm a real American—in that sense at least. I've done it in pick-up trucks, old Fords, Mercedes. A Volkswagen with a poor, but very good-looking grad student at Penn. A Rolls Royce. Never in a pink 1956 Cadillac convertible, though. I also like what my gay friends refer to as a rough trade. Have you ever heard of rough trade before?"

"I was in prison for ten years."

"Since your transcendence to Alpha Omega, one tends to forget such facts. Were you a jailhouse punk?"

Bobby wanted to strike her, but she was at the wheel. She was in control.

"That ain't any of your business."

"I think I find you more alluring when you're ungrammatical, at least at times like this. So much more in character. More authentic, too; like the original, hot, burning Elvis. Rougher."

"It still ain't your business."

She lifted the bottle to her face.

"So here we are in the car again. Our most intimate moments are taken on the fly, which is more exciting. But going back to the original question, you don't have to answer. I'll just guess. As for myself, I could provide you with a list of rough types, starting with a couple of good old boys who worked for my Daddy when I was a kid. Right up to Travis Washington."

"Who's he?" Bobby still watched the road and the sky for a sign, half-dreading, half-enamored at what might come.

"You've never heard of Travis Washington? I guess you didn't watch the NFL on Sunday there in prison. Too busy with the guitar, and whatever else you did in there."

She flashed a triumphant half-smile, and he looked away.

"Travis. What a guy, as all real guys might put it. The star running back for the Dallas Cowboys. America's Team, or least they were at one time. Travis made lots of money with the football, and invested it wisely. A multi-millionaire. One of the first important blacks to endorse Reagan in 1980. You can still see him on T.V. He does commentary for the games. Total blather, of course. And he plays in benefit golf tournaments. Makes personal appearances. A real American success story, as Daddy might say. Travis even studied with Professor Kaplan, Daddy's boring friend. Have you heard of Kaplan? Head of the Short Institute? One of Daddy's projects, and a good tax shelter. Kaplan is full of blather, too, but Daddy and Travis and people like them eat that shit up. I can tell that you never would. When Kaplan was through, Travis had achieved a highly polished veneer. Travis could have passed for the United nations representative from Kenya. Behind closed doors he was entirely different; a man-child from Greenwood, Mississippi. He still calls me, married or not. Naturally, our relationship has become platonic. Daddy says that he's a credit to his race."

"And I'm like him?"

"In certain refreshing ways. I never created Travis in the same full, complete way I created you."

She keeps saying that, Bobby thought. About creating me. The heat radiated across the front seat, and the Jack Daniels had made him light-headed. The pink Cadillac slowed down.

"We've nearly reached my special place."

They left the main highway and crossed a long bridge into a small, nearly-deserted beach town. A few minutes later they turned down a sandy road that was marked with a no trespassing sign.

"This is mine," Beverly said. "I bought it years ago with the money Mother gave me when I graduated from Chapel Hill."

Beverly expertly nudged the pink Cadillac down the narrow road.

"Your mother's still in prison. She tried to kill you."

"That's something else I'm not gonna talk about."

Beverly giggled. Bobby especially hated her when she giggled.

"I suppose I can see why. You defeated her though, didn't you?"

"I never thought about it that way."

"Why not? I love to remember all the defeats I've inflicted. I have a list of names that I go over at night when I can't sleep. It comforts me."

They bumped along the road until it met the beach. The early autumn moon was big and low, its light silver-white across the water. Beverly cut the ignition and they sat in silence, the Atlantic wind blowing in on them. Bobby had heard the ocean when he was at Sun Shores; he had not seen it in ten years, not since he had wandered drunkenly away from a flaming motel room. It was living, shifting, metal, its thick, fecund smell rising in his nostrils. There's a sign here somewhere, he thought. His quest for a sign was abandoned when Beverly slid across the seat and began to unbutton his shirt.

When they finished, when the pink Cadillac ceased rocking, she, still naked, grabbed the Jack Daniels and headed for the shoreline. At the edge of the tide, she sat with her legs splayed out on the wet, hard-packed sand, and drank deeply. He remained in the back seat for awhile before he wandered down to her. She handed him the bottle, but he did not drink. He stood there naked, facing the sea, the bottle dangling at his side.

"Sit down, Alpha."

He did as he was told.

"She's dying. My mother, I mean. Cancer. It's all a big secret. Even Daddy doesn't know. She spends most of her time in her apartment in New York. She's on some sort of painkillers, and all she does is read one best seller after another. Blockbusters only: family sagas, exercise books. Volumes on how to make money and to become a loving, creative individual. Autobiographies of famous actors and politicians. Her apartment is filling up with books. Jesus. In fifty years books will be curiosities. Like stone axes in museums."

"I tried to read that *Book of the Dead*. It didn't make sense. *The Late, Great Planet Earth*, that was something else now. See, it tells about the end of the world, and the second coming . . ."

Beverly went on as if she had not heard him, her speech slightly slurred with Jack Daniels.

"After I left Francois—he was my husband—my intellectual professor husband—I spent a few months working for a publisher in New York. I was sick of Francois' cultured and elegant ways, and his theories about everything. I was sick of Paris and the French, too, although I admire the way they systematize their ideas, even if the ideas are mostly empty horseshit. Americans are incapable of systematic thought . . ."

Bobby wanted to tell her about the second coming, but he knew that he could not. Her voice had taken on a commanding, unearthly quality that drowned out all other voices. He watched the surf, the waves breaking on top of each other forever.

". . . by the time I left Francois, I had been pumped absolutely full of shit. My husband, and all the other professors I had ever known had seen to that: deconstruction, Marxism, feminism. What shit. What silly, unadulterated shit. Even if it was systematized and mostly French. Theories. Francois and all like him are incapable of anything other than talking and writing ridiculous books for each other. When I got to New York, I began purging myself of that nonsense. I sat in my little office at the publisher's and these manuscripts would pour in. I read them for hours, or I read at least part of each one. A small part was usually enough. Do you know what I appreciated the most about that otherwise stupid job?"

Her voice mingled with the beating waves and swallowed him whole. She did not seem to expect any sort of response from him.

"The best part was rejecting manuscripts. I had the power to do that. And I did. Over and over. It was an important, wonderful experience. I decided who would succeed and who would fail. Who would be given a voice, and who would remain silent. The publishing house was necessary. It led me to all the other places I've gone. Imagine getting people to buy into what you put in front of them, even if it was only the small, literate element of society."

The command in her voice was tinged with a trace of nostalgia.

". . . back in those days I turned down Southern novels about lovable, eccentric families; Jewish coming-of-age novels; Vietnam novels; the whole range of moth-eaten contemporary fiction. Some of what I rejected was better than the stuff we published, if it is possible to speak of better or worse when discussing books . . ."

He squinted toward the horizon. If he watched long enough,

he might find a sign: the sign would be important and would have to do with the second coming. It would offer an explanation as to why he was here with Beverly and what might happen next.

". . . at this very moment," she said, all traces of nostalgia rubbed away from her voice, "I have the capability of making millions of people do what I wish. You're living proof of that."

She wrapped an arm around his waist and snuggled close to him. Her warmth was distracting, and he tried to steady himself and concentrate on the horizon. Almost absentmindedly, she took hold of his wind-shriveled penis.

". . . and I could make them hop on one foot and fart 'The 1812 Overture' at the same time."

The horizon was still there, unyielding. She released his penis and took the bottle from him.

"I'll never build here. This place must stay untouched. So few are. Do you know that you're the first person I've ever brought here? Not even Daddy knows that it's mine. It'll be our secret."

She grasped his penis again and stroked it in a slow, distracted way. He gave up on the horizon. Anything that mattered was elsewhere. There would be no signs. Inside was what mattered. Most of his days were spent on the inside, one way or another. That had to be where everything was. He became conscious of her hand, and pulled away. She pressed closer, talking, talking again.

". . . Alpha Omega. An image for all time. Pure. Forever."

"I hate you," he said calmly.

"You're bound to it. Part of us hates who, or what made us. I'll bet you hate The First Elvis."

It's true, Bobby thought.

"I hate his ass bad."

"And you love him, don't you?"

"Yes." The horizon was a world away. There was no reason why he should have expected anything there.

"And you love me, don't you?" She was absolutely sure of the answer.

"Yes. I love you."

"You can't help it. You loved me from the first, as you were meant to."

The first, he thought. When was the first?

She visited the mansion at least two nights a week. An unfailing routine developed: wordless, grinding sex, followed by a drive in the pink Cadillac and Beverly's monologues on power, illusion and the absence of truth in the world. She had the power, a power greater than his. She had made him, after all; and he did love, and hate her.

They visited Beverly's secluded beach two or three more times, until the weather turned colder and they could no longer go naked. During the day, while leading tours or performing, Bobby's mind was nearly empty, imprinted only with the words love and hate. He seldom thought of the second coming, and wished he had another copy of *The Late, Great Planet Earth*. He passed the mirror as if it were not there. It was all Beverly now, and he was, finally, her work of art.

One morning, he listlessly conducted a tour. The groups were smaller now than he had encountered during the summer, although they were large enough to justify Short Enterprises' decision to keep the park opened year round. To him the pilgrims were a vague, undefined mass.

He descended the stairs, exhausted from the night before. Beverly had visited for what she referred to as a "special consultation with the principal figure". As they coupled, he had howled like a dog, while she, giggling, urged him on. He howled until Howard Dunn pounded on the door and asked if anything was wrong.

The faces in the group were the same as all the other faces he had seen: innocent, lumpy American visages. Beverly spoke of them with a kind of fond contempt, while Mr. Short said that he loved them for their values and the plain, home truths by which they lived. Bobby was too wary to ascribe any qualities to them. They were simply there.

The tour guide, the blonde that worked the morning shift, introduced him as he reached the foot of the stairs.

"Welcome to my home, ladies and gentlemen. Graceland-by-the-Sea . . ."

As he had done for five times a day since July, he lead them from room to room, mouthing his lines and his jokes. They laughed when they were supposed to, and were properly respectful when he spoke of his mother or money. He was thankful when the tour ended and he took his seat behind the autograph table. Love and hate welled up within him as he signed the mementos; relics that would be pressed into scrapbooks, or, once framed, would hang above mantles or in family rooms. Bobby's childlike scrawl spread across his face, across the pink Cadillac, and through the memory books, which the obedient pilgrims pushed at him. When everyone in the group had passed by, he pushed his chair back from the table and took a deep breath. Love-Hate-Love-Hate. The words flashed back and forth.

"I'm not spending a dime on that stuff."

The voice was familiar, and frightening.

"I told you. It was dumb enough to come here in the first place . . ."

It was Tommy Aycock. He was arguing with a slender, dark-haired woman about his own age. She clutched the hand of a small boy who possessed Tommy's round face and myopic squint. The boy struggled to free himself from his mother's grasp.

"Let me go! I wanta see Alpha!" the boy cried.

"Wait a *minute*," the woman said. "Tommy, I promised momma that we'd get a memory book. It's the only thing she wants for Christmas. And you said you'd buy her one."

"A memory book. Goddamn."

"Now don't cuss. Mr. Omega might hear you."

"Mr. Omega? What the hell if he does hear?"

The tour guide, ever vigilant for the unusual, advanced toward Tommy and the woman. The boy broke free, dashed to the table, and plopped down into Bobby's lap.

"I seen you on T.V.!" the boy piped. "I seen you sing, and seen pictures of you in that big pink car. Like these pictures."

The boy held up a photograph of the pink Cadillac and grinned at Bobby. He looks like Tommy, he thought. And the woman was the wife that Tommy had spoken of with such bitterness. Tommy slowly trailed along behind her, his hands thrust deeply into his pockets, not looking at Bobby. The boy prattled on and hugged Bobby, who patted him on the head.

"I'm sorry," the woman said. "He's got so much energy. And he's so excited being here. Every time he sees your picture, he goes 'Alpha, Alpha, Alpha'. It's the cutest thing."

"Nothing to be sorry about," Bobby said. He don't know me, Bobby realized with relief and an odd floating sensation. The guide positioned herself, arms folded, by the table.

"Do you need me, Mr. Omega?" she asked.

"I'll call you if I do." Bobby waved her away, leaving himself momentarily alone with Tommy and his family.

"Where you folks from?" Bobby asked, directing the question to Tommy.

"Near Charlotte," the woman said. "Gaston County, North Carolina. I guess you've never heard of it."

"Sure I have. Gastonia. Been a long time . . . I mean I've never been there, though."

"It ain't much," Tommy said through lips that curled surprisingly like those of The Dead Elvis.

"Oh, Tommy. He's always going on like that. Nothing's ever good enough. It took me weeks to get him to come here . . ."

"I'm so glad I came," Tommy said. "The wax museum. The three dollar hot dogs. Boy, what a deal . . ."

"Stop, Tommy," the woman said.

"My Daddy plays the guitar!"

"Is that right?" Bobby wanted to draw Tommy in, although he was not sure why. "I play a little myself," Bobby said.

"Oh, Tommy just messes around with his rock and roll," the woman said.

"That's what you call it," Tommy grunted.

"Where you play?" Bobby asked.

Tommy's eyes met his for the first time. The floating feeling intensified as Tommy looked away, speaking to the ground.

"Clubs. Bars. Wherever I can."

"That's where a lot of us got started," Bobby said.

"Tommy's not really serious, except about spending money on new guitars and amps and all that stuff."

"You don't know what serious is," Tommy said. "Come on. We got to get going."

"Why?" the woman blurted. "Everybody but you is having fun . . ."

"Let this . . . let Alpha Omega do his job. I mean, you got a job to do, don't you?"

He ain't changed a bit, Bobby thought.

"Don't talk that way," the woman said.

"I don't take offense," Bobby said. "I wish you luck with . . . the music."

He wished, too, that he could talk to Tommy alone to tell him about the second coming. He wouldn't understand, but it might help cut through the love and hate.

"You folks gonna be here for the show this afternoon?"

"I wouldn't miss it," the woman said.

"We already paid for it," Tommy said. "Couldn't get in this place without paying for it."

"Oh, Tommy."

"I want you folks to have something to remember me by." He also wanted to return Tommy's money to him, although he knew that was impossible. It was easy to see that Tommy had nothing, that he still scuffled and pissed along, busting his ass in some shit job. That on weekends he hooked up with others who were at least as unsuccessful to play in stinking bars and in each other's garages and living rooms. The music. For an instant, he forgot about Beverly, love and hate. He quickly signed two memory books and four or five photographs. When he finished, he shoved them toward the woman.

"Here. On me," he said.

"We *couldn't.*"

"I want you to have them. I mean it."

Breathlessly, she scooped up the souvenirs and pressed them to her body.

"Thank you! Thank you so much! You don't know what this means to us. Come on, son."

"No," the boy said, clinging to Bobby. "I wanta stay with Alpha."

"No. Do like your momma wants. We got to listen to our mommas."

"All right. If that's what *you* want me to do, Alpha." The boy jumped from his lap and ran to his father.

"Let's get out of here," Tommy said, hoisting his son to his shoulders, marching away from Alpha Omega. The woman kissed Bobby's cheek. She blushed mightily.

"Come on!" Tommy demanded.

"I hope you don't mind," she said. "I got carried away."

"My pleasure." Beverly had instructed him to use that phrase when he was kissed by impulsive pilgrims.

"*Let's go!*" Tommy yelled. He was nearly around the side of the mansion, disappearing with his son.

"Good-bye, Alpha," the woman called, her voice reedy with emotion. She half ran to catch up to her husband and child.

"Come back to Graceland-by-the-Sea," Bobby called to the vanishing Tommy. "Come back."

He found that he was standing, ready to pursue them. Then the guide reappeared and reminded him that another tour would start in ten minutes.

His afternoon musical performance went badly. He missed several cues and once, during "Send in the Clowns", he came to a mute, dead halt. The musicians kept right on without him as he tried to remember the lyrics. It was Tommy's fault. Bobby could feel him, still judging, out there in the darkness. For a single, clarity-stricken moment, he considered seizing a guitar and plunging into one of the old songs, one of his, or a Hootchie-Cootchie original.

He stood bolted to the center of the stage, statue-like in the cone from the green spotlight. The music stopped as Kalo, in the control booth, cursed and ripped the earphones from his head. He signaled for the orchestra to play anything. Before they could begin, the moment had passed for Bobby, and he had an acute terrifying awareness of his audience, of its gigantic bafflement and consternation.

"Sorry, ladies and gentlemen . . . I . . . I'm sorry. Let's start over."

The opening bars of "Send in the Clowns" began and he worked numbly, with even less feeling than usual, through the rest of the show. The pilgrims, their alarm now past, sat back and enjoyed all that they had expected. He left the stage quickly following "American Trilogy" and the distribution of the scarves. Kalo accosted him as he reached his dressing room.

"What the hell did you think you were doing out there?" Kalo demanded in his tiny, furious voice. Bobby brushed past him into the dressing room. Beverly was waiting for him.

"Why, Alpha," she said. "Our musical director says that there are some problems."

Kalo followed Bobby into the dressing room.

"You're damn right. He stopped. Right in the middle of 'Send in the Clowns'. A song he's done hundreds of times. Hundreds, Bev.''

Bobby sat down at the make-up table. The mirrors held the face, his face, multiplied a dozen times. He found a towel and rubbed away at the sweat and the make-up. Love and hate were back in force, and it now seemed impossible that he had considered singing one of the old songs.

"Calm down, Jonathan," Beverly said. "Even the principal figure is entitled to a mistake now and then."

"But . . ."

"It won't happen again. And if it does, we can surely repair the damages. I don't understand why you were so alarmed. I got here in time to see most of the show, and it was fine. Pure Alpha Omega. Don't worry so much. Now, why don't you run along? I have to discuss some important business with our principal figure."

"All right, Bev. But I work hard. You know how seriously I take my job, for God's sake. I'm a professional. I have my reputation. And if this moron . . ."

"I . . . I'm not a moron," Bobby said without turning around. He was afraid of the mirror, but he could not stand to look at Kalo even at the best of times.

"Alpha's correct. He's not a moron," Beverly said firmly. "and your professionalism hasn't been compromised. And I do require privacy."

Kalo slammed the door and Bobby pressed his face into the towel. Beverly would talk now, and he would want to grab her and rut, rut until the love and hate were gone. That was, he knew, impossible; as impossible as picking up the guitar and playing one for Tommy. Tommy was outside somewhere, leading his wife and child toward his old van. Eventually Tommy would get back to his dead end world, and the truth of Alpha Omega would never be known to him.

ALPHA OMEGA

Beverly locked the door and stood behind Bobby, massaging his shoulders.

"My, we're tense tonight. What happened?" She sounded like a mother consoling a small boy after a school yard fight.

"Nothing. Got lost for a minute. That's all."

"You can't afford to be lost. You're the one and only Alpha Omega."

"That goddamn Kalo . . ."

"Jonathan is artistic. High-strung and excitable."

"I'm gonna stomp his ass if he ever calls me a moron again."

She gripped his neck, massaging deeply, pressing his head back into her stomach as she worked on his shoulders.

"That would never do, would it Alpha? Anyway, it's just as well that Jonathan called me. We have a special project in the works."

Bobby pulled away from her and stretched out on the couch, the towel draped over his face. The very words "special project" made him apprehensive.

"I hope that President of the United States won't come back," he said through the towel.

"You don't like the President?" she laughed. "What sort of American are you? We couldn't get him for this one; and besides—it's bigger than the grand opening. So big that Daddy wants you to come to Sun Shores tomorrow for a meeting."

The name of the Short estate put him even more on guard. The last time he was there had led to the diminishing of the second coming.

"What kinda meeting? Why can't we have it at the mansion?"

"Daddy considers the security stronger at Sun Shores. Clarence will pick you up at five-thirty. You'll be back in time for the second show."

"You gonna tell me what this meeting's about? Like I asked you?"

"We are out of sorts today. Are you sure nothing happened?"

He did not answer. Tommy was a secret. She bent over the couch and planted a chaste, ironic kiss on his forehead.

"I'll be by tonight. And we can take a little drive."

She left him on the couch, his face still covered by the towel.

17

"We've called you here for a very important discussion," Beverly said.

Beverly, Bobby and Mr. Short were seated in the great room at Sun Shores. Juan had provided them with freshly-squeezed orange juice, but Bobby's glass sat on the coffee table, untouched. He was nearly immobilized by love and hate. The night before he had pleaded with Beverly; tell me about this meeting, this goddamn meeting, he whined. It will be a surprise, she said. Don't you like surprises?

". . . we've formulated a policy decision of far-reaching consequences . . ."

She paused. Bobby chewed his lips.

"Should we tell him?" she said to her father.

"Don't keep him in suspense any longer," Mr. Short laughed. "The poor boy might come apart on us."

"And we wouldn't want that. I'll be direct. You are to be married."

Bobby gripped the arms of the designer chair, his jaw working, the grinding of his splendid teeth audible in the silence that followed Beverly's declaration. Married. To her. Love and hate twenty-four hours a day. He wanted to run, but love and hate had welded him in place.

"What are your feelings, Alpha?" Mr. Short inquired. "What do you think of marriage? Having a home? Raising children?"

"We'll get to that later," Beverly said.

"You . . . uh . . . you . . . uh," Bobby stuttered.

"The idea may take some getting used to," Mr. Short said soothingly. "I'm glad to see that you don't take marriage lightly. Far too many do . . ."

"Daddy, could I have a few minutes alone with Alpha? Perhaps a woman can help him gain a proper perspective. Why don't you shoot some pool? I'll call you when we're through."

After Mr. Short left, Beverly patted the spot next to her on the couch. He shuffled over to her and sat down. She rubbed his helmet of dead Elvis hair, which had recently been trimmed by Mr. Tony. Bobby could not look at her.

"I understand your feelings," she said with kindness. "Perhaps you're confused?"

"How come you want to marry me?" he groaned.

"You don't seriously believe that *I* want to marry you? I'm insulted. If our marriage was the reason I brought you here today, I would expect you to be a little happier, instead of looking like a pole-axed goat. Actually, we've approached someone else, and she's agreed to our offer."

"I don't understand . . ."

"Then you'll have to listen and let me explain. First, you should rest assured that our evening training sessions will continue. More discretion will be necessary, though; purely for security reasons."

"What you trying to tell me is . . ."

"Let me finish. Please. This marriage will be undertaken purely with the needs of the organization in mind. Specific duties will be required of you, but those duties won't interfere with your role as principal figure, or my role as learning facilitator. Do you see?"

He nodded. He felt like a lump of old, spoiled dough, but he was relieved that he would not be Beverly's husband.

"I'm glad you accept the plan." She kissed his cheek and snuggled close.

"I'm only thinking of you, my perfection," she whispered.

Mr. Short was summoned from the billiards room. He entered complaining that he did not have a chance to finish running the table.

"Is it settled?" he asked, as Juan handed him more orange juice.

"Quite satisfactorily," Beverly said. She handed Bobby a photograph: Stacy, the tour guide.

"Your bride," she said. Bobby glanced at the familiar, sunny face, and returned it to Beverly.

"Her?" And why not, he thought. After all the love and hate, and being a perfection, why not.

"You might show more enthusiasm," Mr. Short said. "She's a lovely girl. I'm sure that the two of you could develop a deep relationship. You know, when we approached Stacy with the proposition, she was thrilled."

"She wept," Beverly said. "Tears of joy."

Then Bobby saw why. It all fit.

"You want me to do this on account of The Dead Elvis marrying Priscilla?"

"Good, you're learning," Beverly said. "A pure, innocent bride for the new King. And her virginity has been medically verified. The parallel with The Dead Elvis is real enough; however, duplicating the First King's life is only a part of what we hope to accomplish. We feel that the essential mystery of Alpha Omega has been firmly established in the national consciousness. The time has come to humanize him—to a degree."

"Marriage is a sacred institution," Mr. Short said. "Since we have been called to entertain the American family, we want our patrons to identify more strongly with you, to feel more comfortable. And you can provide a wholesome role model."

"While maintaining the essential mystery," Beverly said. "The marriage of The First Elvis created huge interest. The female fans were jealous of Priscilla. Think of it: for years they dreamed of having The First Elvis as their own. After the wedding, they developed fantasies about stealing The First Elvis away from his wife. The male fans took one look at Priscilla and developed their own fantasies. And it's a truism of my art that celebrity marriage creates extended media interest and publicity. So does celebrity divorce. Further down the road, let's say five, six years, we plan for you and Stacy to split up. Think of the present divorce rate, and how many people identify with a failure that is so similar to their own. Divorce is as American as baseball."

"A national tragedy," Mr. Short solemnly intoned.

"Thanks for the editorial, Daddy."

"Is that all of it?" Bobby asked, hoping that they would demand no more.

"There is another major element to consider," Beverly said. "There must be a child."

"You saying that I got to knock her up?"

"Exactly, although you might phrase things more delicately. There shouldn't be any problem in this area, however. Stacy's been tested, and she's as fertile as they come. The doctor says that she can have fifteen children without ever breaking stride. I might add that she is fervently opposed to abortion, and was chairperson of the student Pro-Life organization at Liberty University, her Alma Mater. We think that a son would be in the best interests of the organization, although I personally prefer a female child. We don't have much control over that end of things, though."

"That's up to God," Mr. Short said.

"The romantic element is also to be considered. And that's my department," Beverly said. She opened a notebook and began to read.

"The love story of Stacy Cooper and Alpha Omega has a fairy tale ring to it, not unlike that of Charles, Prince of Wales, and Lady Diana Spencer. Like the Royal couple, the love that Stacy and Alpha share for each other is not of the overnight variety. It grew from friendship and mutual respect, and is both deep and wide. Stacy is a professional, an accomplished tour guide at the world-famous mansion at Graceland-by-the-Sea. Twice named employee of the month, she works daily with Alpha Omega. Together, they have done much to create the dream that means so much to so many people. It was through serving the American public that their relationship began to blossom. At first, there was mutual respect, although, Stacy, it may be candidly said, worshipped Alpha Omega from afar. As time passed, he came to realize that she was more than a valued co-worker; and she came to understand that beneath the mystery and glamour of Alpha Omega, there lives a caring, warm, loving individual; a man who she could live and grow with. Finally, their bond, their love, evolved into what it is today. After a performance by Alpha Omega at the world famous Graceland-by-the-Sea Music Hall, a performance at which Stacy was his special guest, he proposed . . ."

Beverly read on, describing the particulars of their love, including favorite foods (Love Me Tender Chicken, fried banana sandwiches), favorite colors (black and hot pink), and favorite pastimes (watching television, singing, just being together). The details of the wedding came next. The ceremony would take place on Christmas Eve at the mansion. Celebrity guests, including Pat Boone, Wayne Newton, Senator and Mrs. Drum Snead, Charlton Heston, General William Westmoreland, Professor Arthur Kaplan, and a host of others would be in attendance. Alpha Omega would sing seasonal numbers, "Silent Night", "Santa

Claus Is Coming to Town", as well as "The Hawaiian Wedding Song" and "How Great Thou Art". Portions of the ceremony would be aired during Ted Koppel's *Night Line*. Beverly closed the notebook.

"That's only a working draft. The final copy will be smoother. I'll finish by tomorrow and get it to the media geeks for the weekend press conference."

"You've been mighty quiet," Mr. Short said to Bobby. "I know you've been given a lot to digest, and you might even be taken aback by all of this. But if you've got any questions, ask us. We're here for you, Alpha."

"She's not in love with me, is she?" More love and more hate would, he knew, make him sicker.

"Not in the least, although she does love the idea of Alpha Omega. And she is one of our most loyal and devoted employees," Beverly said.

"Then what's she getting out of this?"

Beverly glanced at Mr. Short, who coughed nervously.

"A thousand a week. And we've arranged a small role for her in a soap opera on the Christian Broadcasting Network. 'A Balm in Gilead' is the name of the show, I believe. She'll use the name Stacy Omega, which can't hurt business. She doesn't have to produce a child for two years, which will give her plenty of time to establish her career. And I'm sure that she'll be a big success. You know, I've always had faith in the dreams and talents of the young. Like you, Alpha . . ."

"So I won't have to see her much, right?" It was clear that Mr. Short was prepared to go on at length about his vision for America's youth, but Bobby had to find out how much his wife would be inflicted upon him.

"Correct," Beverly said. "She'll work on 'A Balm in Gilead' Monday through Friday. On the weekends, we'll have her here. I'm working up a special routine for the two of you for the Saturday and Sunday tours. Something like 'At Home with the

Omegas at Graceland-by-the-Sea'. She'll do a housewife number, like bake chocolate chip cookies while you lead the customers through the kitchen."

"That's a great idea," Mr. Short said.

"Isn't it? You should know, Alpha, that there is one, final necessity: we need a sperm count to make sure that you can do your part in producing the child. A mere precaution."

"How do you get one of those sperm counts?"

"Nothing could be easier for you. A simple and natural procedure. Dr. Wise, our fertility expert, will drop by tomorrow between shows for a sample. He'll explain all that is required of you."

The next morning, before the first tour, Bobby found Stacy in the kitchen. Beverly had told him to get better acquainted with his future wife, and he knew that she sometimes waited in the kitchen until the tours began. She was alone, seated at the table, sipping a Diet Coke.

"Hi," she said shyly.

"Uh . . . hello. I talked with Beverly and Mr. Short yesterday. You know what about, don't you?"

"Yes, Mr. Omega," she said softly.

"Call me Alpha. On account of us getting married and all."

"Okay, Alpha." She smiled, all sweetness and hygienic cuteness.

"What you think—about this wedding?"

"It's a wonderful opportunity. Ms. Short . . ."

"Beverly?"

"I have to call her Ms. Short. All the staff people do. Anyway, Ms. Short has arranged it so I can get a real break. On television. We'll still do tours . . ."

"She told me."

"Oh. Well, I'm so happy. I've always wanted to be on T.V. At Liberty—that's where I went to college—I was in lots of the drama department productions: *Barabas*—I played Mary Magdeline. And *Oklahoma!*; I didn't have a big role in that one, but I was only a freshman. I studied voice for twelve years, and sang in the choir in the Reverend Falwell's own church. Ten solos my senior year, and Reverend Falwell himself said I had the finest soprano voice he had ever heard. Oh, yeah. I've wanted to tell you for a long time what a great job you do on 'How Great Thou Art'."

"Thanks. That's Mr. Short's favorite song. I'm gonna do it at the wedding, too."

"Really? And I was a feature baton twirler at Tarboro High School. Only Liberty doesn't have baton twirling, so I couldn't perform at the halftime of the football games. I still practice, though. I could show you sometime, if you want."

"I'll think about that. What I gotta find out is what you think about being married. Beverly told you everything she wants?"

She modestly lowered her eyes.

"You mean about the children?"

"That's one thing. Yeah. And I was told there's gonna be one child. No more."

"I hope it's a boy. Alpha Omega, Junior. Think of that."

"Real nice."

"You'd be the daddy and I'd be the momma."

He could hardly imagine touching her. It would be like having sex with a pretty, life-size doll.

"We're going to procreate," she said. "Like it says in the Bible. I take procreation very seriously."

"What do you think about me?" he asked. From the look on her face, he could tell that the question had never occurred to her.

"Let's see. You make lots and lots of people happy. And you do your job. And you dress well."

"You never thought about me being greater than the old Elvis? Anything like that?"

Thoughtfully, she drank her Coke.

"I'm too young to remember Elvis. I was only nine when he died. I've seen a couple of his movies, and heard some of his songs. Is that what you mean? You know, I like Christian contemporary music. Have you ever heard . . ."

"No, I haven't. We don't need to talk about that now."

How could she not know about the dead Elvis? he thought.

"You ever heard of the Second Coming?" he asked.

"Sure. The end of the world. It could happen any time. My mother says that we're living in the last days. I've heard about the Second Coming since I was real little, and the Reverend Falwell used to preach on it. He said we have to be ready to go at any time."

"You don't mind having a kid in such times?"

"Children are sacred, no matter when they're born. They're innocent, without sin. Did Ms. Short tell you about my fertility test?"

"That you could have as many kids as you could stand?"

Stacy blushed.

"I always do well on standardized tests. I made 1352 on the SAT."

It's good she's gonna be gone five days a week, Bobby thought.

"Anything about me bother you?"

She tapped the Coke can with her fingernails and blushed again.

"I've heard a couple of stories. You know how stories get around."

"What kinda stories?"

"About . . . I don't know if I should tell you . . . about this woman who visits you at night. I don't mean Ms. Short. She told me that she has to come here on business. There was supposed to be this other woman who looked sort of . . . trashy."

Mona, he thought. Clarence did this.

"My sister," he smiled. "A good woman. She's had some hard times in her life. She travels for the Lord, singing in little churches. Stops by Myrtle Beach when she's down this way."

"I'm so relieved. I hated to bring it up, but since we're going to be man and wife, I had to ask."

"Who told you about my sister?"

"Clarence. Mr. Short's chauffeur. He's asked me for dates, but he scares me."

"Clarence is fulla sh . . . I mean, he got it all wrong."

"I'm glad to hear that. I really mean it. Maybe I could meet her someday. What about the rest of your family?"

"Dead. Just me and Ruth are left."

"My dad is the football coach in Tarboro. He won the State 3-A Championship this year. I was so excited for him. My mom's a homemaker. And I have a brother who flies jets for the Navy. He has his own F-14! Claude Junior is my little brother. He's cute, but a real brat. Daddy spoils him."

Before Bobby could think of a way to stop her, she whipped out her wallet and pushed a snapshot of her family into his hands. The father's broad shoulders filled the picture. He owned a fist-like, brutal cop's face. The mother was a heavier version of Stacy, and the brother, in his dress blue uniform, reminded Bobby of all the jocks who ran his high school. Claude Junior was clearly a smart-assed little punk.

"They look real nice," Bobby said, as he handed the snapshot back to her.

"They're looking forward to the wedding. They'll all be here, except for Jesse, my older brother. He's on the *Saratoga*. I hope your sister can come, too."

"It would be something if she did."

"I guess you can tell that we're Christians. And after we get married, I hope you want a Christian life-style. I believe that the husband should lead in the marriage, don't you?"

"That's in the Bible, about the man leading, right?"

"In the Holy Word."

She glanced at her watch and leaped up.

"Good grief! We've forgotten about the time! The first tour

starts in five minutes. And I've got to fix my make-up. It's been nice talking to you, and I can't wait until we're married. We should sit down and talk like this again soon."

She squeezed his hand, and hustled prettily from the kitchen.

That afternoon Dr. Wise came for his sample. The doctor was trim and athletic, wore luminous lime-green slacks, and said that he had just come from the golf course. He slowly and carefully described what was needed from Bobby. After a few minutes work upstairs, Bobby returned and handed in his sample.

"I'll have the results in the morning and pass them on to Mr. Short," Dr. Wise said at the door.

"I guess you know what you're supposed to do with it," Bobby said, turning away, feeling the love and hate coming back at him.

After lunch the next day, Clarence burst into the mansion and told Bobby that he had to get out to SunShores for an emergency meeting. The remaining tours, and both shows were to be canceled. Emergency, my ass, Bobby thought as the limo roared toward SunShores. When are they—when is Beverly—gonna let me get back to being Alpha Omega?

Beverly, Dr. Wise, and Stacy were waiting. Clarence followed Bobby into the Great Room, and Dr. Wise started spouting off confusing medical terminology before Bobby could sit down. The doctor's jargon flowed on and on; all about high counts, low counts, spermatozoa, ovaries, and high profile conception potential. What is this shit? Bobby thought. He did not notice that no one in the room would look at him, except for Clarence, who wore a delighted grin.

". . . the condition is known commonly as 'hot testicles.' Because of an imbalance of body heat in that area of the genitals, conception is a virtual impossibility. To put it bluntly, the subject is sterile."

Doctor Wise cleared his throat and turned to his audience.

"Any questions?"

"None, Doctor. Thank you for your time," Beverly said.

After Dr. Wise left, Beverly sat beside Bobby and took his hand.

"What's all this? What's this 'hot testicles' stuff?" Bobby demanded. "How come you canceling my tours? And the shows?"

"Your count is low. Far too low," Beverly said.

"So what?"

"You and Stacy could labor at procreation forever and nothing would come of it."

Mr. Short entered the room. Without acknowledging Bobby's presence, he lowered himself heavily into an armchair.

"I just got off the phone from Gastonia. The test results were completely favorable."

"Good," Beverly nodded. "We're covered."

"What the hell is this about?" Bobby said, jerking his hand from Beverly's grasp. "Mr. Short, nobody will tell me a thing. Except about 'hot testicles'."

"There can't be a marriage," Mr. Short sighed. "At least between you and Stacy. A marriage without children is an empty, barren thing."

Bobby was relieved. It was hard enough living with the love and hate, and trying to get back to really being Alpha Omega, much less being married.

"We've been forced to make arrangements," Mr. Short said. "Beverly will explain."

Beverly left Bobby's side and began to walk back and forth like a general addressing troops before a battle. Something ain't right, Bobby thought.

"It's a good thing we discovered the sperm count problem when we did. Otherwise, we'd have ourselves in a rather tricky situation . . ."

"We gonna get back to normal now?" Bobby asked.

Beverly gave him a look that said she had never visited the mansion, or ever ridden in the pink Cadillac.

"Our back-up system has worked well. And, as Daddy told us, Johnny Love has limitless potential for fatherhood. Can we have him here tonight?"

"He's leaving Gastonia within the hour," Mr. Short said.

"Excellent."

"Johnny Love? From the Burning Love Temple?" Bobby asked.

"Correct."

"Them I'm going to marry an Alpha Omega after all?" Stacy said, her voice rising with hope.

"That's right," Mr. Short said.

"I hope that this one's a little bit taller. I like tall men. Like my daddy," Stacy said.

"Thank God we caught this in time," Mr. Short said.

"Hold on," Bobby said. "This Johnny Love. He's coming here to take my place?"

"I wouldn't put it quite in those terms," Beverly said. She had ceased pacing and stood in front of the very low couch where she and Richard Aldrick once laughed at Bobby. "The image. The songs. The Elvis Presley-Messiah experience will be the same. That's what's important. There's absolutely no reason why Johnny Love can't start the tours tomorrow. He's seen the instructional tapes, and I'm sure that Stacy can help him over the rough spots, can't you dear?"

"I'll do my best. Ms. Short, is he a Christian?"

"He'll be fine in all respects. What he doesn't know, he'll learn on the job. And we won't have to make any more ticket refunds. Naturally, he's more than familiar with the musical components, and I doubt even a mother could tell the difference between the old Alpha Omega and the new one. After all, Anders did the work on both of them. And if Johnny, or as I should say, Alpha, doesn't work, we can bring in that kid from Nevada.

Anders finished with him last month. I suppose I would have to give him a crash course, but it could be done."

Bobby was on his feet, tottering slightly, dizzy with all of it.

"You getting rid of me . . ."

Beverly raised her hand in a gesture of peace and reconciliation.

"Wait Bobby . . ."

"Alpha, you mean. You could get a baby without putting me through all this." His voice was alien in his ears, unnaturally high, as if it belonged to another.

"This must be authentic," Beverly said. "A child conceived and nurtured by Short Enterprises. For some time, I've wanted to raise a child, a girl. Boys are such nasty beasts."

"You raising a child?" Bobby squeaked.

"She'll have all the advantages. As for you, you won't be forgotten. You can keep the clothes we gave you, except for the performance costumes. The new Alpha will need them. Daddy has generously agreed to provide you with three hundred a week for the next year, or until you find a suitable situation. I've been told that you have some slight musical talent, and there may be a place for you in the entertainment industry."

"My goddamn place is at Graceland-by-the-Sea."

"I'm glad you mentioned that. You are, following this meeting, barred from all premises owned and operated by Short Enterprises."

"You fucking cunt . . ."

"Now wait a minute," Mr. Short shouted. "There's no need . . ."

Clarence, his grin growing broader, eased toward Bobby.

"You stinking, fucking cunt," Bobby screamed. "And your big fat-assed daddy."

"Sit down, Bobby," Beverly said firmly.

"Your language is awful," Stacy said.

"Do what the lady says," Clarence said.

Bobby remained standing, love and hate boiling away.

"Very well," Beverly said, "stand if you want. As I was saying, we require you to sign a release which states that you will no longer refer to yourself as Alpha Omega, or make public or private statements to the effect that you were ever employed by Short Enterprises. You must also refrain from appearing in any capacity as an Elvis Presley impersonator . . ."

"I never been any impersonator."

". . . or to take on the name of Elvis Presley, Alpha Omega, or Graceland-by-the-Sea. There are other, relatively minor items included in the release, but we don't need to cover those."

She crossed the room, extracted some papers and a pen from a briefcase, and handed them to Bobby. He slapped them away, the papers drifting slowly, noiselessly around him.

"I hate you," he said. His voice had lost its piercing quality, and had subsided into something more ominous.

"I take that to mean that you won't sign?" Beverly asked pleasantly.

"I love you too. But I won't sign."

"We don't need this unpleasantness," Mr. Short said. "We can work out an arrangement. Do you want more money, son? Is that it? Can we hire a band to play with you?"

Beverly shook her head.

"We've been generous enough. More so than Mr. Snipes deserves. If he doesn't sign, he'll get nothing. And we'll still throw his redneck ass out into the street. It's as simple as that."

"I'll go to the T.V. To the papers," Bobby said, although he knew he never would. Through his puffing rage he at last saw that Short Enterprises, or its friends, owned the T.V. and the papers. They owned everything.

"And what will the media say?" Beverly crowed. "Even if by some miracle they accepted the story of a psychotic, deluded figure like you, how could they prove that we substituted one principal figure for another? Would it even matter?"

She stepped toward him, a half-smile of victory in place.

"No matter what, the essential mystery will be preserved. You've never understood; you're only a part of my masterpiece. Except for your hot testicles, you were, to be sure, a perfect part. Parts can be replaced. Do you think my creation extended only to you? And come to think of it, any confession you make could actually be good publicity."

"I'm sorry that you won't get to be Alpha Omega anymore," Stacy said politely. "And what's your real name again?"

"Bobby Snipes," Beverly laughed. "Bobby Snipes forever and ever."

The quivering started in his thighs, racing to his hot testicles, his eyes, his brain. Without a word, without a sound, he lunged for Beverly, his hands locking neatly around her throat, as if they were always meant to be there. They fell together as Stacy wailed and Mr. Short begged Bobby to release his daughter, his only child. Beverly's eyes were huge with astonishment, and what Bobby hoped was terror.

"This has got to be," he told her eyes. "Just like the goddamn love and hate."

Her face changed colors, even as her eyes remained fixed on a thing she never imagined. He wanted to remember those eyes for a long time. Then hands grasped his hair and jerked his head backwards. He fought to maintain his hold, but the pain slowly forced him to surrender his grip. The pain stopped for a moment, and he bore down again on Beverly's throat until something hard and round crunched down on his head, then across his face, over and over. Dr. Anders' work gave way as the face, its moorings lost, slid up and down in his skull, back and forth across his cheekbones. Someone stronger than he was, he guessed it was that bastard Clarence, pried at his hands, forcing them from Beverly's throat. Clarence picked up the poker and administered one final blow across the bridge of his nose.

"Look at his face!" Stacy screamed.

Bobby pulled himself to one knee, feeling for where his teeth used to be, testing the chin. It wiggled under his fingers, and his hand came away bloody. He was still astride Beverly. She lay still, her arms at her sides, her eyes still overflowing with surprise.

"Good." The words hissed through his destroyed lips. "Love and hate . . ."

As he tried to stand, Clarence grasped the poker with both hands and brought it down across the long gone, dead Elvis, first Alpha Omega, styled-by-Mr. Tony, hair-do.

"That ought to hold the fake son-of-a-bitch," Clarence said, his rusty voice full of pride and accomplishment.

18

It took him a long time to get to his feet. As he pulled himself up, he flexed his arms and paused to rub his legs. The pain was general. He was thirsty and the room was dark. He thought he was in a hospital until he felt his way around the walls and discovered a light switch: a motel, cheap and old, complete with a vividly colored print of a mounted cowboy above the broken Magic Fingers bed. The room even smelled old, and he felt the ghosts and dreams of all who had slept, copulated or wept there.

In the bathroom he found another light switch next to the mirror, and he also found out why he had difficulty breathing. The nose was a series of lumps and ripples. He pressed a thumb against a constricted nostril and blew. A clot of phlegm and black blood splatted into the sink and his breath came easier. After solving that problem, he returned to the rest of the face. There were no solutions there.

The bruises—deep purple, black, and red—ran the length and breadth of Dr. Anders' masterpiece. Then there was the chin. In sleep, it had been pushed far to one side, like a rubber ball beneath a blanket. Slowly, carefully, he worked the mass back to its approximately correct position. It was easy to see that unless he visited Dr. Anders or another plastic surgeon, the chin would forever roam around the lower portion of the face.

Most of Mr. Tony's perfect dead Elvis hair had been shaved away. He discovered this as he unwound the bandage which covered the top of his head and counted the twelve stitches. The sideburns remained, as did most of the hair on the back.

"I'm a monster now," he said to the mirror. "A Frankenstein." He backed out of the bathroom, no longer needing mirrors.

Except for socks and jockey shorts, he was naked. In a quick search of the room, he discovered some T-shirts and a couple of pairs of jeans. He also found the Red Harmony Rocket, the small amplifier, zip-up boots, and a paper grocery bag: all of the belongings he had left in the trunk of the Vega at the Charlotte airport a long, long time ago. His things were in a pile, as if whoever had deposited him in the motel had done so in a frantic rush. He pulled on a pair of jeans and sat down. Beside the bed sat a large prescription bottle and an envelope. He opened the bottle: big pills of some sort, a final gift from Mr. Short.

"Goddamn nice of you," he said, swallowing three of the pills, waiting for them to work. When the pain slackened, he opened the envelope. It contained five new, crisp one hundred dollar bills, a set of car keys, and a letter. He turned the keys over in his hand, remembering, before he peered out the musty-smelling draperies. The Vega was the only car in the parking lot. Across the street he could make out a gift shop, a gas station, a McDonald's and the rest of Myrtle Beach, all under a stale gray sky. I bet I ain't that far from Graceland-by-the-Sea, he thought. Only about a million fucking miles.

The letter had been composed by Beverly, and he was disappointed and amazed that she still lived.

"After all that choking," he said to no one. He read quickly, the phlegm and blood welling up again in his face and throat.

Dear Mr. Snipes,

Despite the fact you rejected our severance offer, Mr. Maurice Short, President of Short Enterprises, has generously presented you with this gift of five hundred dollars. He did so against my recommendation: a fact I wish you to take note of. You will also note that Short Enterprises has returned all of your possessions, excluding any clothing, jewelry or other items you made use of while in our employment. This is in accordance with the conditions we discussed at our final meeting, and any offers of continued support from Short Enterprises have been withdrawn. As to the release, you may only examine that document, which is signed in your hand, with the permission of Short Enterprises. It is expected, as is described in the release, that you will leave Myrtle Beach as soon as you are physically able. Do not try to contact the office of Short Enterprises, or enter the premises of Graceland-by-the-Sea.

                              Yours,
                              Beverly Short
                              President for Operations

P.S. The doctors say that no permanent damage was done during your attempt on my life. The brace is uncomfortable, although it will be removed soon after the first of the year. I should regain full use of my voice within the next two months. Alpha Omega is working out very well, as I'm sure you would wish to know.

He read the letter over twice before tearing it up. There was no more love in him; only a mashed-down, impotent hate.

Between the pills and the pain, it took him a while to summon up enough strength to pack and leave. He had to find a place to think, even if that meant running from Myrtle Beach and doing what was commanded of him by Beverly and Short Enterprises. After about an hour of sitting on the edge of the bed, he was able to move. He dressed and tossed all that he owned into the car. Before he closed the door, he glanced around the room to see if he had forgotten anything. He spotted the paper bag: a toothbrush, deodorant, a pack of Winstons, his wallet, a box of shells, and the .22 pistol he once used in the services at the Burning Love Temple. He sat down again, opened the cigarettes, lit up and turned the gun over and over in his hand. By God, he thought, this means something.

He stowed the .22 under the front seat, and slowly walked over to the motel office. The pills had a good grip on him and he was almost comfortable now, even if it did hurt some to put one foot in front of the other. The owner was behind the desk, watching an old John Wayne movie on a tiny black and white television. He was engrossed in the Duke, who was busy slaughtering Japanese, and did not hear Bobby come in. Bobby drew down more phlegm and blood and spit into the trash can. The owner looked up and jumped when he saw Bobby.

"Didn't mean to scare you," Bobby said. "How much I owe?"

"You . . . uh . . . not a thing. It's been taken care of."

"Mr. Short pay my bill?"

"I'm not supposed to say."

"That figures. A big albino guy in a cowboy suit bring me here?"

"I'm not supposed to say that either. He a friend of yours?"

"Almost my brother. Only he don't know it. When did I get here?"

"Like I said, I'm not supposed to say."

"Getting paid extra not to? And they've already given you the money?"

"Maybe it won't hurt anything. You seem to know a lot anyhow. You've been here three days and two nights. A doctor came by twice, along with the fellow in the cowboy suit. You been sick?"

"Not a thing wrong with me. You know Mr. Short?"

"Not personally," the owner said uneasily. "Everybody knows what Maurice Short has done for Myrtle Beach."

Bobby pushed his chin back in place. Speaking made it move around.

"You gonna call his office when I leave?"

"How do you know that?"

"I know Mr. Short pretty good. That's how."

The owner stopped watching Bobby's chin and smiled.

"You know Mr. Short? That's really something. That Graceland-by-the-Sea has helped the economy so much. The only reason I'm open in the winter is because we get some of the tourist trade year round. People coming for the theme park, you know. A first in the history of Myrtle Beach."

"Pilgrims."

"Who?"

"Graceland-by-the-Sea is world famous. You tell Mr. Short I'm going home. Or somewhere. I ain't real sure of my destination."

"I'll call as soon as you're outta here."

"That'll make Mr. Short happy."

"You look familiar. If you weren't . . ."

"So tore up?"

Bobby lobbed more phlegm and blood into the trash can. The owner vigorously scratched his left ear and looked away.

The Vega's gas tank was full, and it started easily. Bobby guessed that Mr. Short had probably ordered Clarence to tune it up. That was mighty kind, he thought. All those people at Short Enterprises are big on cars. For the first time since he left prison, he had no idea where he was going, or if he could find a place where he could figure things out. Once in the traffic, and after only a couple of aimless miles, it came to him that he should eat. Eating was a basic thing, and basic things should come first. Many of the beautiful teeth were gone, but he would find a way to manage.

The Steak 'N Egg Kitchen was nearly empty, and the clock above the counter read one forty-five. He had not known real time for a good while, since he became Alpha Omega, and the clock, like the prospect of food, gave him a point to start from. He ordered eggs, grits, toast and coffee, foods that were easy to chew. The waitress, a girl about Stacy's age, loitered at the far end of the counter while he ate. He caught her staring at him, and when he smiled, she turned away. He was carefully gumming the last piece of toast when someone sat down beside him.

"I thought it was you," Mona said. "Only something bad wrong has happened."

Mona lived in a pale-orange frame house a few miles from the ocean. Her place, consisting of four cramped rooms, was neat and clean—frilly white curtains, a sagging couch, and a paint-by-numbers portrait of a German Shepherd above her double bed. Mona, in her old Monte Carlo, had led him there, and he followed without a word or a thought. They sat on the couch and drank beer, and he gave her one of Mr. Short's pills so that she could feel like he did.

"I love Darvocets," she said, swallowing the pill with a swig of Old Milwaukee. "And Valiums. And Darvon, even if the codeine likes to kill my stomach. I can't do that speed no more. Used to take it and work. I could make three hundred a night on speed. If you ask me to take any of that Dilaudid, I'll tell you to kiss my ass. I've seen what that stuff can do."

"I don't have no Dilaudid. Only those things. I didn't even know what they were until you told me."

"I'm real knowledgeable about your prescription drugs."

She lit a Salem. Her house smelled like millions of cigarettes had been smoked there, and that gallons of ammonia and air freshener had been splashed down in an effort to wash the smell away.

"You gonna tell me what happened?" she asked. "About who done this to you?"

Bobby squeezed the beer can and the aluminum buckled slightly.

"No."

"It was somebody pretty mean."

"I guess so."

"I hardly knowed you. If I wasn't *real* familiar with you, I woulda swore you just got out of a bad car wreck."

"I don't wanta hear that."

"Sorry. Only how come you ain't over at Graceland-by-the-Sea?"

"My count was too low. That's what I got told."

"What's that mean?"

"I don't know. I still don't have it figured out."

"You do seem kinda . . . stunned."

"Leave off on that."

Mona shrugged and went into the kitchen, returning with a fresh pair of Old Milwaukees.

"I won't ask you no more questions if you don't feel like answering them. I've thought lots about the last time we was together: all that stuff about the second coming, and The First Elvis and Alpha Omega. Made me think. Really. I even tried to tell a couple of my clients about it. I don't believe that they paid much attention, though. You can't tell a horny man a damned thing. But you said we'd meet again, and here we are. Was that a kind of . . . prophecy?"

"I'd forgotten I'd told you that stuff."

"It's like it was meant to be, us meeting up at the Steak 'n Egg Kitchen. And I started to go on down to the Waffle House. It's giving me goosebumps to think about it. The only thing is, you ain't Alpha Omega no more."

He squeezed the can until the beer sloshed over into his lap.

"I'll *never* stop being Alpha Omega. I'm gonna . . . come back. All I need is a little time to think on things."

"I'm sorry. I just said it the wrong way. See, last night on the news I seen this other Alpha Omega. He looks exactly like you, or like you used to be. I thought it was you until I seen you there at the counter. From the back you ain't changed a bit. This other Alpha Omega is getting married to a real pretty girl, and when I saw her I got jealous. Figured for sure that I'd never see you again."

"She's named Stacy."

"That's right. You know her?"

"Met her."

"They're getting married on Christmas Eve. It's a big deal for Myrtle Beach. Wayne Newton, Miss America, Pat Boone, a bunch of famous people are gonna be there . . ."

"Don't tell me."

"Okay, Baby." She moved closer to him and took the crumpled can from his hand and placed it on the floor. "I understand. Bad shit has come down on you. Relax. You're with me, and I appreciate who the second coming really is."

"You mean that?"

"Sure I mean it. I even tried hard to read that book you give me. Only I got scared of the words. Kept going on and on about the end of the world and all."

"I need that book."

"I'll get it," she said rising. He pulled her back down to the couch.

"Not now. I need some other stuff."

"I'll give you whatever you want." She smiled, nestling against him.

"I wanta stay here for awhile. I got money, and you can have most of it. I don't need much. A little bit for when I get my head straightened out. I won't be here long."

"I guess that'll be all right. How much you gonna give me?"

He handed over four of the hundred dollar bills. Mona was delighted.

"Baby! You can stay here as long as you want. Now I hope you understand that I'll be working and won't be here much in the evening. And every so often I bring customers back here, usually for all nighters or when they get paranoid about being seen going in and out of motels. You won't mind that, will you?"

"I don't care. I gotta sit still, right here in Myrtle Beach. Close to where I used to be."

"That's settled. You still not doing sex?"

"I don't know."

"I ain't got a secret chamber, but I change the sheets regular."

It took a couple of days for Mona to work him into bed. He tried because he thought it might give him a sign of what to do next, and that it might make him feel less like Frankenstein. When it did not, she gave up and told him that when he was really ready to let her know. He said that he would, although he could not foresee a time when he could take advantage of all Mona had to offer. She seemed disappointed over his failure, but the four hundred dollars had made her happy. She immediately spent half of it on six new outfits from the Target Store at the Ocean View Mall. She modeled them for Bobby. He told her that she looked nice, and kept eating Darvocets and drinking beer.

They drifted into a routine. She left at sundown, either to meet her telephone customers, or to work the sparsely populated off-season bars. Business was slow during winter, and some nights she drove over to I-95 to troll the truck stops. She returned near dawn, and Bobby was grateful for the solitude.

After three or four days, the pain was gone, except for his mouth when he forced down whatever Mona had time to cook or bring in from the fast food franchises out on Highway 17. The bruises faded to pink and blue, and tiny tufts of hair sprouted around the scar on his head. He convinced Mona to cut the stitches out for him—he had no intentions of going to a doctor's office, or leaving the house for any reason. He had to stay out of sight, hidden away, while the picture of what was to come took shape.

He read through *The Late, Great Planet Earth* several times, copying out key passages, especially those pertaining to the terrible punishments awaiting those who doubted the divinity of the Messiah. Every afternoon he loudly declaimed these passages to Mona as soon as she got out of bed. As he read, she yawned, smoked and drank coffee. When Bobby finished declaiming, he would ask her what she thought. That's real interesting, Baby, she would say.

Once, while Bobby read of false saviours, she rummaged around in a closet until she found a two foot plastic Christmas tree, lights, and ornaments. With energy and purpose she went to work, frowning when Bobby refused to help with the decorating. It's Christmas week, she said. He returned to his book, and wished that she would pay attention to the truth.

After the tree was completed, she stepped back to admire her handiwork.

"Don't you love Christmas?" she asked.

Bobby closed *The Late, Great Planet Earth*. The tree twinkled atop the television set. He hated it. It reminded him of Mr. Short, and Mr. Short reminded him in turn of Beverly. All day he had dwelled upon The Dead Elvis and how he had ruined himself; and such thoughts led him to the disfiguration and abandonment of Alpha Omega.

"Don't even think about it," he said. Mona babbled too much. He understood that his attempts at educating her had failed. She would not even pretend to listen when he spoke of the love and the hate. Lately, she had taken to reminding him that most of the four hundred was gone. Why don't you go back to Graceland-by-the-Sea and get some more, she had said. They'll give it to you for old times sake. When he refused, she asked if he had to have that last hundred. It wasn't doing anybody any good stuck in his wallet.

"You're a grouch sometimes. I swear you are," she said straightening the star that topped the tree. He wished that she would leave for work so that he could temporarily erase her from his consciousness. Instead, she fetched a beer and turned on the T.V.

"How about that!" she yelped. Reluctantly, he looked up at the screen. There he was; or rather there was the way he used to be.

"The gala event, scheduled for Christmas Eve, will include a star-studded celebrity guests list, and will cost in excess of half a million dollars to produce. A spokesperson for Short Enterprises stated that the wedding of Alpha Omega will unite America's couple . . ."

The screen flickered with Johnny Love, and Bobby found that he could not look away from the false Alpha Omega. There were his own lips, his chin, his nose; the whole face that he had explored nightly in the mirror of the secret chamber. The face was luminous, transcendent, as if it had never been re-arranged with a poker. The quivering, which he had not experienced since that last day at Sun Shores, blew up his spine.

"That's amazing, ain't it?" Mona said. "I can't tell him from you. I mean the way you used to be. Hair, clothes. He's a teenie bit taller. That's the only difference. How'd they get a guy like that? Hey. You're shaking."

"It's nothing."

Johnny Love kissed Stacy on the cheek, and Bobby grabbed the arm of the couch and tried to stop quivering.

"Let me hold you. You must be cold," Mona said. Bobby shoved her away. She retreated to the far end of the couch and lit a cigarette. She was furious, but Bobby did not notice, consumed as he was by his stolen face.

The wedding of Alpha Omega and Stacy was replaced by pictures of dirty, foreign-looking men who the announcer described as war criminals. Mona turned the set off.

"We got to discuss some things," she said.

"Discuss what?" All he wanted was for the face to return.

"You're hard to get along with. I set up the Christmas tree and try to make you feel better and you act like a son-of-a-bitch. What's wrong with you?"

"If you was me, you'd know."

"I understand about your face and all, and about how things ain't like they used to be for you. You got to live, though. All you do is sit on this couch, writing down crazy shit from that book and boring me with it. You ain't no fun. You don't even take Darvocets any more."

"You can have them. I ain't hurting like I was."

"You mean that? Thanks. I hope you don't mind, but I took a couple of them already. They help me at work."

"They're yours, all of them."

The quivering stopped and he drifted into a calm, peaceful sort of hate; a hate that held a slight promise of deliverance.

"I wish I could help you," she said. Liar, he thought, but not as bad as most of this world's liars.

Obsessively, he watched T.V. after that, going from channel to channel for news of the wedding. Despite his initial fury at the sight of Johnny Love, he watched for him as he had once watched for himself. He hoped also to catch a glimpse of Beverly, although she was sure to stay out of sight because of the brace. He sat through soap operas, afternoon talk shows, cartoons, evangelists, and ball games all during Christmas week. Eventually, he was rewarded by the commercials for Graceland-by-the-Sea, and the featured news stories on the wedding. His hate was at its most intense when he listened to the words, however; the off-screen voice as it described Alpha Omega's adoration of his bride, and how together they would serve the American people. Bobby knew that the words belonged to Beverly. She's got all the words sewed up tight, he thought. But I still got the truth, and the hate. He no longer quivered with the image of Johnny Love. He took this as a good sign.

Mona was alarmed by his extended television viewing. "That's all you do," she said. "Why don't you take a walk? As long as you're inside all day, you could clean up this place. At least take out the beer cans," she said. He never answered her; he hardly moved at all, unless news of the wedding came into his line of sight. Then he lurched forward, intent on the screen, his face transformed by a broken, wolf-like smile.

On Christmas Eve Day, she gave him a gold chain. A present, she said. She confessed that she had stolen the chain from a trick at the Ramada Inn. The trick was rich and would not miss it, and she wanted Bobby to wear it for the holidays because it was so pretty. He clutched the chain in a fist and focused on the screen.

"Ain't you gonna thank me," she said, "or say Merry Christmas?"

"It's tonight."

"What's that mean? I give you a nice gift, and you say 'It's tonight'. What in the hell are you talking about?"

"The wedding. What else is there?" He lit a Winston and watched Wiley Coyote pursue the Roadrunner through a cartoon desert landscape.

"That's what you been thinking about? There ain't a thing you can do!"

"You don't know shit. Leave me alone."

She vanished into the bedroom. An hour later she emerged, showered, made-up and packed into a metallic blue slit skirt; one of the outfits from the Target Store. He grimaced at the powerful odor of her perfume. Without a word, she arranged herself on the far end of the couch and crossed her legs. She lit a Salem, one leg jiggling in mid-air, and loudly exhaled toward the ceiling.

"Am I supposed to ask if you're nervous or what?" Bobby said, his eyes on the screen. Wiley Coyote had failed once more and was replaced by the President of the United States; the one that Bobby had met at the mansion. The President wished the nation a Merry Christmas and said that everything was fine, despite the carping of media critics. The President's message ended, and "The Flintstone's Christmas" began.

"Let me tell you how it's gonna be," Mona said.

"They didn't show that fucking Johnny Love, or give out any of Beverly's words. Maybe later."

"Did you hear me?" Mona sprang from the couch and placed herself between Bobby and the screen.

"You're in my way."

"It was goddamn bad enough with the book—now this."

She slammed the set off.

"What the fuck you doing?"

"You're gonna listen, Baby. Things is changing. I felt sorry for you. I did. You were up there at one time. At the top, I guess. Being like Elvis . . ."

"Elvis my ass . . ."

"I ain't going into that. So I took you in. You gave me money. That's true. And I'm grateful. Only you done got too weird for anybody to stand. I've had to turn down four or five tricks lately because I was afraid they'd see you. And not because you look so fucked up either. Or not just because of that. You done turned into a zombie of some kind. Sitting there all day. Not moving. Not changing clothes. Then I come home and try to relate to you, and the only thing I get is that chin moving back and forth, which makes me sick to see.''

"How about turning the set back on? I might miss them."

"In a minute. Here's what I really need to say. I'm going out today with Colonel Earle Bascom. He's an old customer. Used to be in the Air Force and retired to Myrtle Beach for the golf and the fishing. So he called me yesterday. He's lonely. It's Christmas. And his wife is in a rest home with the Alzheimer's, whatever that is. Colonel Earle has promised to take me out to buy any Christmas gifts I want. Then we're going to a very nice restaurant for a fine Christmas dinner. After that we're coming back here, and I'm gonna give Colonel Earle his Christmas presents, if you know what I mean. He won't take me to his house because he feels funny on account of his wife . . .''

"Turn the T.V. on. I don't give a shit what you and this Colonel Earle do."

"Listen. I don't want you here. Not when me and Colonel Earle come home, and not after that neither. Baby, you have outstayed yourself. You got to go someplace else to get straight, and I ain't got no idea where that could be. After you're better, come back. I'll be happy to see you. But I can't help you no more."

She was out of breath when she finished. I bet she practiced them words, Bobby thought. Goddamn words.

"What else you got to say?"

"Nothing. Not a damn thing," Mona said.

She bustled to the door. The dress was too tight in the rear, and her perfume would hang heavy in the air for a long time after she was gone.

"Don't be here when I get back."

As the door slammed behind her, Bobby reached for the power button on the T.V. Soon he was rewarded with Fred Flintstone and Barney Rubble singing "Santa Claus Is Coming to Town."

ALPHA OMEGA

* * *

Bobby fetched the .22 from the Vega. It was the first time he had been outside since Mona had taken him home with her. He did not linger; the sunlight was sharp and painful. Back inside, Fred and Barney were gone and the First Annual Victory Bowl football game, live from the Hoosier Dome in Indianapolis, was about to begin. Bobby loaded the pistol as a team in red helmets bashed at another team in blue jerseys. He was not quite sure why he had gotten the gun, although he vaguely toyed with the idea of shooting Mona's T.V. set: a kind of Christmas present. Like back in the old days, he thought. He checked his wallet to see if Mona had lifted the last of his money. The hundred was still there. He tried to imagine a place to go; nothing came to him. Then, too, he would not have to make any decisions for awhile. Mona would not return for hours. Hell, he thought, I might even be here when her and Colonel Earle get back. Somebody scored a touchdown and thousands cheered.

The first quarter of the Victory Bowl was nearly over when he heard the front door open. Whoever was there paused in the tiny foyer, then slowly and carefully crept toward the living room. Bobby slid the .22 under a cushion and waited. It ain't Mona, he thought. She barges into places. Bobby faced the foyer, his hand beneath the cushion, firm on the .22's grip.

"Well, if it ain't Clarence, the albino motherfucker," Bobby said.

Clarence stopped. He looked the same as ever, except for the baseball bat he clutched in a black-gloved hand.

"Ain't baseball season over?" Bobby said. "You preparing yourself to try out for the freak team?"

"You the one that ought be on the freak team. You seen yourself lately?"

Bobby rubbed the .22.

"I didn't think you'd have an answer," Clarence said. "You ain't laughing neither."

"What're you doing here?"

"Seeing to you, that you do what you're supposed to."

"What am I supposed to do? All I been doing is watching T.V. and eating dinner with Mona."

"That's how I found you. Followed her yesterday morning and peeked in the window. See, I had this feeling that you hadn't done like you was ordered. Played my hunch."

"You on orders? From Beverly and old Short?"

"They don't know about this. Got too many important matters on their minds without worrying with shit like you. In fact, they ain't spoke of you since I saved Miss Beverly's life."

"You're a hero."

"That's true. And you know what? They let me drive the pink Cadillac when Alpha Omega don't need it. Mr. Short said I could have anything I wanted for saving Miss Beverly's life. And the Cadillac was it."

"Me and Beverly used to sport around in that Caddy. Driving and fucking all the time."

Clarence lumbered toward him.

"That's a lie."

"No lie, Clarence. That was back when I was all eaten up with the love and the hate. Just hate now. She's got good pussy, if you can believe it."

Clarence raised the bat above his head.

"You gonna work me over some more? Pissed because she didn't give you any?"

"They was good to you . . ."

"And now they're good to you. Why don't you go ride around in the Caddy and leave it at that. Go on now."

"You the one that's going, like you was told. Get up, get in that Vega, and get outta Myrtle Beach. And I'm gonna follow you to be sure this time."

"You love her and her daddy, don't you? I bet you love Johnny and Stacy. And you love the pink Cadillac. And you come after me because of all that love."

Clarence lowered the bat.

"Something like that."

"I could see it in your face. Beverly and Mr. Short are like your real momma and daddy. Only Beverly would never give you any pussy. That's because you a ugly, fucking monster."

The bat rapped sharply against Bobby's boot.

"I'm gonna forget you said that. Move."

Bobby laughed. He had not felt so good since before Beverly drowned him in love and hate.

"How about a beer Clarence? Get me one too. You're a good errand boy."

"You got shit in your ears? Move. I'm through fooling with you."

"Don't want a cold Old Milwaukee? You never were sociable. Not enough training. Beverly trained me up fine."

Bobby pulled the .22 from beneath the cushion and fired. Clarence grasped his knee and dropped to the floor, tipping over an end table, shaking the windows, the Christmas tree, the furniture. Slowly, he sat up, feeling his knee.

"You . . . you shot me!"

"That's true. Didn't know about this little old .22, did you? Carried it all the time in the old days before I got trained, before I got smashed up. Take that damned cowboy hat off. I've never seen you without it on."

"Not my hat."

"Yeah. The hat."

Clarence was bald, as bald as April at The Burning Love Temple. He had lost his sunglasses, and his watery yellow eyes made him look like a large, surprised rabbit. He tried to get up, but the wounded knee would not support him. Gasping, he sat back down.

"Knew a bald-headed woman once," Bobby said happily. "She was a whole lot prettier than you. Yes, she was. Even if she was a monster, like me and you, Clarence. I bet you can't guess what happened to her."

Clarence watched Bobby and the .22 while he rubbed the knee. The blood had given a sheen to his black jeans.

"It hurts! I don't know what happened to no bald-headed woman!"

"She got shot. Like you. Only she was shot dead by my momma."

Clarence wet his lips, trying to figure it all out.

"Shot dead?"

"You heard right."

The .22 kicked and the second round went right where Bobby aimed. Clarence flopped and twitched as the team in the blue helmets recovered a fumble on their own twenty-six yard line. The crowd roared.

Clarence was heavy, and at first Bobby was not sure that he could get him onto the couch. After about fifteen minutes of tugging and yanking, however, Clarence was in an upright position. Bobby returned the cowboy hat to Clarence's head and put the sunglasses back in place. From the front, Clarence looked fine, except for the black hole in his forehead. The back of his head was another matter. Bobby opened *The Late, Great Planet Earth* to the part about the battle of Armageddon and placed it on Clarence's lap, fixing the book open with one of Clarence's large, pale hands.

"We're even now, old buddy," he said. Then, for old time's sake, he shot Mona's T.V. set as a marching band played "God Bless America" and thousands of balloons ascended to the ceiling of the Hoosier Dome. The shattering glass and blue smoke gave Bobby a momentary twinge of nostalgia.

He had not counted on Clarence to give him a sign, but that

was the way it worked out. He washed the blood from his hands, then drank a beer and ate a can of Vienna sausages. Yessir—Alpha Omega has to get going.

He loaded his guitar and clothes into the pink Cadillac. As he backed out of the driveway, he tried to imagine Mona and Colonel Earle arriving for their Christmas celebration. The car radio played a recording of a pack of dogs barking "Jingle Bells". It sure will be a sight, he thought. I wish I could be there. But I got to get moving, heading out in this fine, fine car.

19

The searchlights combed the clear, starlit sky above Graceland-by-the-Sea, as the bold, triumphant music poured into the night. Bobby crouched beside the Cadillac and shivered; glad, finally, that he and Beverly had traversed all those back roads. It had been easy to find his way to the fence that marked the rear boundary of the park, almost as if he had been guided to the exact, perfect spot. They had often parked there and watched the lights from the mansion, the ferris wheels, and the water slide. He had contemplated the happy pilgrims while Beverly went on and on about illusion and reality.

She's out there now, he thought. Right in the middle of it. He had killed the Cadillac's lights as soon as he passed through the back gate and on to the paved road that ended not far from the mansion. Around him, the ground was skinned and raw—cleared by Short Enterprises for its version of a Las Vegas style hotel, the grand, future venue of Alpha Omega. The earth was dry and cold as he fumbled beside him in the dark for the .22 and the mask. He had been lucky to find the mask: the Dead Elvis, complete with synthetic hair. It had cost him a good bit of his remaining money, but when he saw it in the novelty store on Ocean Boulevard he took it as a true, final sign. He had not even known why he stopped at the store, until he saw the smiling rubber face that beckoned to him from the wall display.

He was also lucky that the security guards did not patrol the back fence, although he could make out a single, uniformed figure lounging under the floodlights at the rear of the mansion. Bobby guessed that the rest of the security force was out front, by the main gate, or at the music hall. The wedding reception would follow in the mansion. According to a spokeswoman for Short Enterprises, the demand had been so great that the wedding had been opened to the public, which meant that Beverly had decided to sell tickets.

He fit the mask over his head, stuck the .22 into the back waistband of his jeans and started toward the mansion. He jogged slowly, acutely aware of the bare featureless ground that lay between him and his destination. The searchlights still poked into the heavens, and prolonged cheers rose from the music hall. They musta said "I do", he thought. Soon Beverly and Johnny Love and Mr. Short and all the celebrity guests would be busy congratulating themselves.

He reached the edge of the parking lot and took cover among the cars, crouching low, ducking and sliding from point to point. At the edge of the driveway, he halted behind a Rolls Royce. There he lay on his stomach near the front of the huge, silvery car. Something's changed, he thought. He lay still, trying to figure out what it was.

The mansion was much larger than he remembered it—like it had grown since he was expelled. He had never seen it that way, and his new perspective was, he realized, not simply due to his angle of vision. The structure itself had also taken on an awful brightness. It was as if the lights behind the windows were unquenchable, never-ending fires. The longer he watched the mansion, the more it seemed to grow, like a living, breathing thing. If I get any closer, he thought, it might suck me right in. The first time he had seen the mansion, he had taken it for his rightful home. I don't know it now, he thought.

He hefted the pistol, and startled himself by wondering why he was there. He had started with a plan of sorts, stewing within him as he drove around after he killed Clarence. Somehow, he would get rid of all the falseness by going to the mansion, to the wedding. That was as far as he had gotten. But what can I do, he thought. The mansion, like Short Enterprises, like Beverly, was too much for him. They were too much for anyone. If I did all of them like I did Clarence, if I even burned this place up, it would be back in a week, he thought. Maybe it would be here again, maybe it would be someplace else—with people just like the ones that thought it up to begin with. And other people would come to get told lies. They loved lies, he thought, and I loved them too.

He considered returning to the Cadillac and fleeing. He saw, though, that flight, however doomed, would come, no matter what. There was Clarence and the trail would be clear enough. He could, when he was caught, tell the police all that he knew of Graceland-by-the-Sea. But the police were owned by the same people that owned the mansion. They own the lies, and they own the truth, he thought, as he looked at the glowing structure once more. It pulsated under the lights, mocking him. It was then that he saw that he could not flee without making some gesture of necessary, selfish purification. The world was beyond purification or salvation.

"It's time," he whispered to the scarred ground. "It's time."

The mask had twisted a little and he carefully adjusted the eye slits until they were properly aligned. He inched his head above the hood of the Rolls until he could see the guard—his old friend Howard Dunn—very clearly. The music became more distinct; Mr. Short's favorite, "How Great Thou Art". Howard Dunn sipped his coffee, unaware of the masked figure moving among the cars.

Bobby could not take his eyes from the mansion. I never had a real plan, he thought. Except I know now that this is the worst place that ever was. He raised himself up and casually strolled into the open. In the space of a few steps, he was beyond the cars and illuminated by the stark brightness of the floodlights. From the corner of his eye he saw Howard Dunn drop his coffee and reach for his pistol. Bobby kept moving, ignoring the guard, not fully sure of what he would do next.

"Hold it there," Dunn cried, as Bobby ambled toward the corner of the mansion that held the sacred chamber; Alpha Omega's bedroom, the bridal chamber-to-be.

"Nobody's allowed back here!" the guard quavered, as he advanced on Bobby. His pistol was in his hand, awkwardly at his side. Bobby stopped and turned. Dunn halted a good fifty feet away, obviously afraid to come any closer. He gasped as he got a good look at Bobby. The pistol stayed at his side, however, even as Bobby jerked the .22 from his waistband and leveled it.

"Throw it over this way, Howard."

"I'll shoot, I swear I will."

"No, you won't. Toss it to me. I gotta do one, maybe two things, then you can go on your way."

Dunn hesitated, glancing down at his gun as if he were seeing it for the first time.

"Come on," Bobby said. "Take my word for it. This won't even take long."

The gun landed with a soft thud at his feet.

"Thank you, Howard," Bobby said genially. "Now I've gotta be taking care of some business."

"How do you know my name?"

"I know all sorts of names."

Without thinking then, and without aiming, he fired all six rounds from the .22 in the direction of the mansion. To Bobby's satisfaction, one round blew out a floodlight. When the .22 was empty, he carefully laid it down and picked up Howard Dunn's .38. The reports of the bigger, heavier gun echoed against the side of the mansion, competing with the Muzak Christmas carols that now bleated forth. There was more shattering glass. Chips of brick and mortar arched through the glow of the surviving floodlights.

By the time he had emptied the .38, shouts could be heard from the mansion. Faces appeared and vanished in the fire-bright windows. Let's see if the son-of-a-bitch keeps growing, Bobby thought. He placed the .38 beside the .22 and removed the mask. He carefully arranged the mask face up, so that the limp, smiling face of the dead Elvis was turned toward the sky. When he was satisfied, he nodded to Howard Dunn.

"I told you it would be fine, didn't I?"

"Damn," Howard Dunn said. "Oh, damn."

Bobby ran, not stopping to see if the mansion was the breathing thing that had confronted him earlier. He heard more shouts. They were after him now. He made straight for the Cadillac.

The beer joint was painted a faded red, and it had a rusted Budweiser sign out front. It was called Tip's Place, and was a few miles beyond the last, nameless, little crossroads town that he had passed through. Bobby had driven there through the dusk, past the flat, yellow-brown winter fields—miles from Graceland-by-the-Sea.

He did not know why they couldn't find him, but they had failed so far. He had spent all of Christmas Day hiding by a slow, black-water river, the car backed among a stand of oaks. Once, he watched as a helicopter circled low enough for him to make out the pilot and observer. They had flown on, bobbing back and forth along the river's course. He had slept, waking in the cold night and driving on. He was not sure where he was, and no longer had a destination. All that mattered was to keep moving for a while longer.

He was nearly out of gas, and had given up the .22. He did not want to think of what would come. It would come, he knew. While driving, he had, in the beginning, scanned the radio for news. He had found it: Gunman assaults Graceland-by-the-Sea; no injuries reported; wedding celebration of Alpha Omega goes on as scheduled; gunman with smashed face suspected in Myrtle Beach slaying. He had been news for a day or so, until he was replaced by other stories. Still, the power of the world bore down on him. It was insistent, oppressive—possessed of its own truth. They, those who ran the world, knew his name and understood that all roads lead back to them.

The parking lot in front of Tip's Place was empty, but there was a pickup truck in the driveway beside the small, frame house that stood nearby, a short way back from the road. Bobby watched as a man walked over from the house and unlocked the door. A red neon sign blinked on in the single window. OPEN, Bobby read. That's good.

Tip's Place reminded him of the Burning Love Temple, and that reminded him of other things. He had spent the last two days remembering—retrieving what he had lost. There was Hootchie-Cootchie and his scrapbooks. Hootchie had hoarded all those memories, trying to keep them from getting away. Then there was Beverly; she could remember each time she used somebody or something up. She seemed to think that there was no end of people and things at her disposal. He had to admit that the supply might be limitless. There was nothing to stop her, and those like her, from getting all they wanted. He couldn't figure why it was so important to her though. Maybe because she never forgets anything, he thought.

He was sorry that he had forgotten about the music, just as he was sorry that he had killed Clarence, who after all was only doing what Beverly expected him to do. The music, he thought. Now, at the last, he saw that it was the only thing of any worth. Hootchie-Cootchie had taught him that, and Tommy Aycock had tried to remind him of what he should have held fast to. Bobby shook his head, regarding his monster's face in the rearview mirror, its lines softened and blurred in the dying dusk.

"I see it now," he said aloud, as he climbed from the car and lifted the red Harmony Rocket and amplifier from the back seat.

Tip's Place smelled of stale beer, but it was modest and clean: a halting point for the worn out. Inside, Bobby found a bar, three booths, a pinball machine, and a television set. An angular, beaten-looking man in a white shirt was watching the evening news. He smiled when the door opened. Then he got a good look at Bobby's face.

"You Tip?"

"Yeah, that's right," the man replied tentatively. "What can I do for you?"

"You ever have live music in here?"

"No . . . just people playing the juke. I mean, I don't pay nobody to sing, if that's what you're asking."

Tip reached over and turned off the television. As he pulled his cigarettes from his shirt pocket his hand shook. The pack fell onto the bar and a couple of Pall Malls rolled against a jar of pickled eggs. Tip scooped up the pack, shook out a cigarette, and lit it unsteadily.

"Something bothering you?" Bobby asked.

"No, sir. Like I was saying, I don't have live music. You might try over to Florence. They got some big clubs down that way . . ."

"Listen a minute, I don't want money. I only want to play. What do you say?"

"I don't know . . ."

Bobby pulled out the last of his money, thirty or forty dollars, and tossed it on the bar.

"Take it. Hell, I'll pay you."

ALPHA OMEGA

"I can't do that." Tip's eyes fell on the money as he spoke.

"Go on, take it. Best deal you'll ever get."

Tip put the money under the bar. "You want a beer?"

"Naw. I don't need a thing. What you think of this face I got?"

"I don't think anything about it. A man can't help what kinda face he's got."

"You're wrong there; I coulda helped this one, but I didn't. That's the way it is."

"Maybe I will have a beer," Bobby said. "You got Old Milwaukee? I used to drink Old Milwaukee all the time. That was back in other days."

Without a word, Tip opened an Old Milwaukee and handed it to Bobby.

"It tastes damn good, right?" Bobby asked.

"Oh, I've always liked my beer." Tip had backed away from the bar, placing himself in front of the portrait of a Jackalope. From the photograph, a horned rabbit peered around his shoulder.

"I don't know the last time I've really tasted anything. You've heard of me before, haven't you?"

"No," Tip said weakly. "I don't believe you've told me your name."

"I used to be Alpha Omega. You gotta heard of him. I bet you watch television a lot in here while you're getting beer for your customers. Learn about almost everything that's going on, too. Shootings and all that. And I bet you've seen me before—one of those artist's conceptions the cops come up with. Man, if you've seen one of those conceptions of this face, you wouldn't forget it."

"I . . . I don't pay no attention to that stuff—no more than anybody else would. You say Alpha Omega, from over at Myrtle Beach? I thought . . ."

"I said I *used* to be him. That's changed. Took me a while to figure it out, but I did."

317

The door opened and a girl about sixteen or seventeen entered. She stopped by the bar, her eyes widening as she took in Bobby, Tip, and the guitar. Then she smiled, slow and shy. She's got a good smile, Bobby thought. Tip cleared his throat.

"This is Kimberly, my daughter. She helps out around here sometimes . . ."

"Hello, Kimberly," Bobby said.

She nodded to him. She's seen one of those conceptions too, he thought, and now she's got the real thing right in front of her.

"Is that your guitar?"

"Your daddy said I could play."

The girl sat at the bar, down at the end near where Bobby had pulled up a stool. Her father handed her a Coke. She watched Bobby set up the amp, plug in the guitar and begin to tune up.

"Is it OK if I ask what you're going to play?"

"Some by the Dead Elvis, and some I learned from Arthur 'Hootchie-Cootchie' Magee—the greatest guitar player who ever lived."

"I've never heard of him, but I'll take your word for it," she said. "Did you know . . . what was his name?"

"Hootchie-Cootchie? Yeah, he was my best friend. He's dead now. Been dead. Died and kept right on going like he was alive. He could make the music come through, even after he died. That's surely the truth. Did you know that I'm dead too?"

Tip lit another Pall Mall and glanced down the bar toward the telephone that sat beside the cash register.

"Don't touch that phone, Tip." Bobby said. "I'm gonna play, remember."

"I wasn't thinking of it," Tip said. "Not at all. You want another beer?"

"Not now. I'll tell you when. Kimberly, do you know that I gave your daddy all my money just for the chance to play here? All he's gotta do is give me a beer every now and then and let me entertain him. Gave him all I own except for the Cadillac out front.''

"Pink, just like they said on TV. I've never seen one that old, either," she said.

Tip groaned as she spoke, swallowing smoke, coughing a little.

"On TV, huh. So you heard, like your daddy over there."

"Oh, yeah," she said calmly. "A day or two ago. Not that I pay much attention to the news. Are you as bad as the TV guys say you are?"

Bobby laughed. He was glad he had a chance to meet her.

"You'll have to judge that for yourself. I'm not out to hurt nobody. And all I'm really gonna do is show you how the music oughta be. Does that sound bad?"

"No. Only I think Daddy's a little bit worried. Is that right, Daddy?"

Tip continued to cough. He did not answer. His eyes were watering and Bobby could not tell if it came from the coughing or if he was crying.

"Wait now," Bobby said. "Nobody's got to worry. I don't even have a gun on me. You hear that, Tip?"

"He hears. Don't you Daddy?"

"Yes, honey. I hear."

"I just need me a place to stop for a while," Bobby said. "That's all. Anyhow, I was telling you about that car of mine. It's just like the one the Dead Elvis gave Gladys, his momma. That's one of the many facts I know about him. A gift for his momma. How about that? Where's your momma, Kimberly?"

"She died November before last. It's been pretty hard on me and Daddy."

"We're all right," Tip said, recovering a bit of his voice.

"Hard," Bobby said. "Yeah, I expect so. That would be hard. My momma's . . . somewhere. And I'm sorry about yours."

"Thanks," she said.

"You drive yet?" Bobby asked.

"I got my license last August."

"That Caddy is yours then. Take it." He handed her the keys and she giggled as she stuck them into her jeans pocket.

"I'll hold on to them," she said. "Until you change your mind."

"I'm not changing my mind on that. No way. I don't need it now anyhow."

"She can't take your car, Mr. . . . what did you say your name was?"

"I didn't. But it's Bobby. Bobby Snipes." He paused, surprised that the old name had come out. "Bobby Snipes," he continued. "And the car's hers. I don't want to hear you say no. And she's the only one that gets to drive it. She might let you ride in it though."

"I will," Kimberly said quickly.

"I didn't come here to cause problems, Tip," Bobby said again.

"I hope . . . I hope not," Tip said.

"You're not going to do like you did at Myrtle Beach are you?" Kimberly asked. "I sure hope you aren't."

"I give you my word of honor," Bobby said, running his fingers down the strings of the red Harmony Rocket. "I'm not going to hurt a living soul. That part's over with. And the dead can't hurt you if you know they're dead. Not like Elvis and Alpha Omega."

Tip lit another cigarette and coughed again. Kimberly sipped her Coke and Bobby smiled at her with his monster's face. She smiled back like she encountered such faces every day. He hit a couple of practice chords, and was gratified at how easily the sounds came back to him. It was almost as if he had never betrayed the music. It was as if Hootchie-Cootchie was right there beside him, serious, living and whole.

Bobby played some of the old blues runs, reveling in the spaces between the notes. Then he did three of Hootchie-Cootchie's originals without pausing between the songs.

"What do you think?" he asked Kimberly when he finished.

"You're kinda great," she smiled again. "I wish I could do something like that."

"You've gotta pay attention to the music. You listen much?"

"Only when I'm around the house. And when I'm with Brandon in his truck. Brandon's my boyfriend. He's got a great sound system. He loves Guns 'N Roses."

"Find you some music you can live with. That's what matters. Tip, I'm gonna play a few for you."

Bobby went through "Hound Dog", "All Shook Up", and "Mystery Train", dipping and rolling with the melody line, giving it the full Dead Elvis effect on the lyrics.

"You like that Tip?" he asked as the last notes faded.

"That . . . that was just fine. You're exactly like Elvis. I mean that."

"I used to sound *better* than Elvis. I'd say we are about even now, though, because we are both dead."

"Don't talk that way," Kimberly said. "About being dead."

"I am, though. Saying different won't change it."

Tip's face had begun to twitch, and, while Bobby was playing, he had edged closer to the phone.

"What you doing, Tip? You tired of the music?" Bobby asked.

Before Tip could answer, two young men a few years older than Kimberly came in. They wore jeans, work boots, plaid shirts and baseball caps. Except for a difference in height, they might have been twins. They halted when they saw Bobby.

"What the hell," the taller one said.

"He's sure got a *face*," said the other.

"What're you drinking, boys?" Tip asked, obviously trying, and failing, to sound nonchalant.

"Who are they?" Bobby asked Kimberly, as Tip passed two long-necked bottles across the bar.

"Just boys that live around here. I don't know their names. I think they work in the mill in Cheraw. They stop in here a couple of times a week."

"They like music?"

"Why don't you play something and find out."

"Talking to you sort of makes me wish I wasn't dead after all."

"I told you to stop saying that stuff."

The boys sat down at the far end of the bar, talking quietly between themselves. Twice, the shorter one twisted around for a look at Bobby. Bobby had seen their kind before, and he had nearly been one of them. He would have been, he knew, if only a few things had been different. He might have worked in the mill every day and stopped off for a few beers in the evening.

"Hey," Bobby called to them. They turned toward him slowly.

"You wanta hear anything special?"

"Whatever," the shorter one said. "You the man with the guitar."

"That I am," Bobby smiled. I feel good, too, he thought with puzzled astonishment. Like I wasn't even dead. Slowly, tentatively, he began to play "Isolation", one of his own songs—one he used to play with Tommy. Soon, the words and the chords came easily, and he did two more of his own. The music carried him up to a place he wished he had never forgotten.

"Damn," the tall boy said when Bobby stopped. "That's real good. Let me buy you a beer."

"I'd appreciate that," Bobby said. The boy put his money on the bar, but Tip was nowhere to be seen.

"Now where did he get to?"

"He was here a minute ago," the short boy said, "But he left without saying a word."

Kimberly went behind the bar and got a fresh Old Milwaukee for Bobby and two more for the boys. "These are on the house," she said.

"Where do you think your daddy went?" Bobby asked, as she returned to her seat.

"Next door, probably. To call the law. I guess he figured you didn't want him to make the call from in here."

"That's right. But he's a good man. His kind usually call the law." He plucked slowly at the guitar strings.

"You aren't going to do anything crazy are you?" Kimberly asked.

Bobby looked up slowly from the guitar.

"Girl, I think you know the answer to that."

"Sorry. I guess it's just what we heard on the news."

She's pretty, Bobby thought. I can't remember the last time anyone seemed pretty. "It's funny to be dead and lucky at once."

"I don't know what that means," she replied.

"I hope you never do."

"How about another song," the tall boy called from the far end of the bar.

"I probably got time for one more," Bobby said. But as he picked out the opening bars from "The Plague", the first of the state troopers, faces smooth and indifferent, came through the door.

Tip came in behind the last one. His face was still tense and still twitched periodically. Despite the December chill, he had sweated through his shirt. The two boys dropped their beers, stood up, and backed away from the bar. Kimberly remained on the barstool beside Bobby.

"You Bobby Snipes?" one of the troopers asked.

"That's right. And I'll be coming with you just as soon as I get through with this song."

Another trooper—they were all large and possessed of a slow, cumbersome power—stepped toward Bobby with his hand on the gun at his belt.

The trooper who had spoken, his eyes on Bobby's face, held out his hand to halt his eager buddy.

"You got a gun on you, Bobby?" he asked.

"You know, I left my gun back up the road."

"Back in Myrtle Beach. I suppose you realize we've been looking right hard for you."

Bobby nodded, his hands poised above the guitar strings. More than anything he had ever desired, he wanted to play this song. The troopers, or at least one who seemed to be in charge, spent a long moment considering Bobby's request.

"All right," he said finally. "Don't you be dumb, now. There's innocent people in here."

"Thanks," Bobby said. He concentrated hard and the music flowed out of him and filled Tip's place.

". . . the Plague whispered and cried
It preached and lied
And the people ran out to meet it . . . "

He closed his eyes as the music came back to him for the last time. Somehow, it seemed like a beginning, a birth of some kind. He played on, his fingers moving so fast it was impossible to catch their motion.